Praise for Samantha Wilde's
THIS LITTLE MOMMY STAYED HOME

"Joy is an amusing character. . . . [Wilde] writes with an authenticity that will . . . entertain."

—*Publishers Weekly*

" 'I was cracking up from page one,' says writer Jessica Brody. . . . 'I couldn't turn the page fast enough.' "

—*Woman's World*

"Witty, frank and sometimes bawdy look at the stresses and strains of new motherhood . . . This is familiar territory, but worth revisiting for the smiles it brings."

—*Hartford Courant*

"Mothers will laugh as they nod along. . . . The quick hits of lean, raunchy comedy tantalize readers like bites of spicy chocolate. . . . Joy charms the reader with her wit. . . . Could serve as a ministry to mothers."

—*Nantucket Today*

"Wilde gives us insight into a new mother's world. She deftly tackles this experience with raw humor as she expresses the psyche of the new mom accurately. This is an amusing tale that will resonate with women, especially new mommies, everywhere."

—*Romantic Times*

"Think of the funniest person you know, give her a baby and a month without sleep, multiply by ten, and you've got the incomparable Samantha Wilde rocking the hilariously appalling realities of motherhood and the modern marriage. This book belongs on the bedside table of everyone who's ever been a mother, or had one."

—KAREN KARBO, author of *The Stuff of Life* and *How to Hepburn*

"Here's a talent test: when a narrator's doldrums make a reader laugh out loud. Samantha Wilde's inkwell must be filled with truth serum because this brave and funny book gets the postpartum peaks and valleys so very, winningly, right."

—ELINOR LIPMAN, author of *The Pursuit of Alice Thrift*

"[This] is the funniest novel I've read in a long, long time. What a treat! Mothers everywhere deserve this book."

—ELLEN MEISTER, author of *The Smart One*

"Samantha Wilde is the irreverent, knowing, laugh-out-loud, brutally honest but most treasured best friend that every new mommy craves and every reader relishes. They should issue this smart, hilarious novel along with newborn onesies and nursing pads."

—PAMELA REDMOND SATRAN, author of *Babes in Captivity*

"Riotously hilarious, unabashedly honest, and positively impossible to put down. Samantha Wilde's debut is a must-read for all moms and non-moms alike."

—JESSICA BRODY, author of *The Fidelity Files*

"*This Little Mommy Stayed Home* had me laughing out loud before I finished the first paragraph. . . . Beyond the clever title and absolutely adorable cover lies an all-too-real story about the ways in which life can take some unforeseen twists and turns once two become three."

—5 Minutes for Mom

"This novel was well written and Wilde's descriptive flair was vivid throughout with descriptions and comparisons I found unusual, but accurate. . . . If you want a laugh-out-loud, interesting and absorbing read on new motherhood, check out *This Little Mommy Stayed Home*."

—Novel Escapes

I'll Take
What She Has

ALSO BY SAMANTHA WILDE

This Little Mommy Stayed Home

I'll Take
What She Has

a novel

Samantha Wilde

Bantam Books Trade Paperbacks 🐓 New York

A Bantam Books Trade Paperback Original

Copyright © 2012 by Jessica Sam Wilde

All rights reserved.

Published in the United States by Bantam Books,
an imprint of The Random House Publishing Group,
a division of Random House, Inc., New York.

BANTAM BOOKS and the rooster colophon
are registered trademarks of Random House, Inc.

ISBN 978-0-385-34267-4
eBook ISBN 978-0-345-53576-4

Printed in the United States of America

www.bantamdell.com

2 4 6 8 9 7 5 3 1

Book design by Liz Cosgrove

This book is for friends of a lifetime:
Sara Prentice Manela, 31 years
Sarah Thompson Evans, 22 years
Kathleen Scott, 16 years
Katherine Gray Silvan, 13 years
All of whom I have long ~~envied~~ admired!
And treasure beyond measure.

And for every person who has longed
for greener grass.
May you come to find that no one's grass
is as green as yours.

Acknowledgments

Frankly, it took a village to write this book. I am truly grateful for all the inspiration, support, feedback, and assistance I have received in various forms, beginning with my agent, Christina Hogrebe, who, at each bend in the road (and there were many!), offered an optimistic, expansive outlook on the process. Meg Ruley helped bring this book into final form, buoyed my spirits, and lifted my failing confidence. For a writer, having others who believe in your work cannot be underestimated. Actually, that goes for all of us, regardless of what we do.

Many editors formed this novel. Danielle Perez, who edited the first draft, expertly brought it out of idea form. Kerri Buckley read the next drafts and encouraged it on with clear, direct suggestions. Marisa Vigilante took over and in an astute, powerful letter reshaped the entire novel to make a cohesive whole; thank you! And lastly, Kelli Fillingim, who adopted it as her own and shepherded the book to publication.

I am thankful for all the gifted staff at Bantam—editors, publicists, marketing, and administrative staff—for their care, enthusiasm, and expertise.

A number of individuals allowed me to interview them and offered useful insights and context: Jacquelyn Au, my dear, good friend; Leanna Calkins, another lifetime friend; and Peter Laipson, the dean of faculty at Concord Academy, who gave me valuable input for an early draft of the novel. I am also in great debt to Leslie Huber and Brian Leaf for countless animated book talks and reassurance and to all the women from the Girlfriends Book Club (girlfriendbooks. blogspot.com) who gave expert advice during a hard time. Also to Nancy Thayer, my mother, who undoubtedly read every draft and continuously, patiently, tirelessly, and generously gave me time, advice, praise, and constructive criticism.

Given the setting for this novel, I would like to acknowledge the staff, faculty, and experience of Concord Academy, the high school I attended. Dixbie is nothing like CA, CA being entirely more hip, progressive, and world-class than the fictitious. Dixbie School, however my own experiences at a boarding school did help with the imaginative setting; any errors in proper school policies and operations are entirely mine. I am especially thankful for my mentor there, Clare Nunes, whose encouragement was so empowering, I continue to draw upon it all these many years later.

Karina Cupp, who sometimes watched the children as I hammered out the versions of this novel, never faltered in cheerfulness, helpfulness, kindness, and gentleness. She brought harmony and beauty into our home with each visit, enriching our lives, and loving us all; I am so grateful for her!

Alicia Beaupre, our best neighbor, also spent time with the children, playing with and loving them. Alicia and her entire family have consistently given to me and my family over the years in ways we can't ever repay. Their neighborly love, help, and kindness have been a tremendous blessing.

I have many wonderful friends, some of whom directly helped with this book. My thanks and admiration go to Michelle Hammer, Jen Skags, Gwen Leaf, and Christyna Capalongo. A special shout-out for Rebecca Lizak, who on a number of occasions, through a few encouraging words, picked me up by my bootstraps and gave me the strength to carry on.

I am always indebted to: my oldest, dearest tribe of friends—Sara Manela, Sarah Evans, Kate Scott, and Katherine Silvan—my yoga students who incalculably enrich my life; those I work with in ministry; my Goddess study group; and my church family at Hope United Methodist of Belchertown.

As always, I am thankful for the love and care of Jan and St. John Forbes and my own parents Nancy and Charley Walters, as well as for my brother, Josh Thayer's, support and presence in my life.

My husband, Neil Forbes, in the midst of his own worthy, consuming work, took time to talk to me about the book from inception to completion. His influence and ideas made innumerable differences for both the book and the writing of the book. And, needless to say, for my life, which he has helped to make very rich indeed.

My beloved children, Ellias, Adeline, and Emmett, holders of my heart, bring me more joy, satisfaction, understanding, learning, and delight than a thousand novels. I thank them for forgiving me for my distracted moments as I worked on the novel, and for loving me in spite of my various imperfections. With them, the grass is always greenest.

And to the God of Love who sustains my very existence, I owe everything, all the time, and gratefully so as I wouldn't want it any other way, my heart is full of thankfulness.

I apologize if you helped in any capacity and have not been mentioned here. Please consider yourself thanked and remember that I haven't slept much during the past five years!

I'll Take
What She Has

1

Nora

Late August

"I don't want to be at the funeral for a cat. It's ridiculous. And depressing."

"She was a Himalayan," I protested.

"Nora." Annie shook her unruly brown curls at me, which only aimed them higher to the sky. "She was only a cat."

"She was *Tabitha's* cat. That is entirely different from being *only* a cat."

"And look at the crowd." Annie shook her head again, this time in disbelief. What appeared to be the vast majority of the faculty milled about outside the pristine white Colonial-style chapel on the campus of the Dixbie School, a suburban Boston co-ed boarding school for the moderately inept. We had all received Tabitha Hunter's email detailing her plan for a full service with eulogy for Evangeline the cat and in loyalty to Tabitha, one of the most eccentric of our teaching staff, who also had deep ties both familial and financial to Dixbie, given up a gorgeous August afternoon to come together. Dixbie has many distinguishing features, among them the fact that the median age of teachers hovers near seventy. Tabitha Hunter, at eighty, though professing to be fifty, tips the scales in the geriatric direction, and on not a few occasions, parents on tours will ask if we don't share our grounds with a retirement home. Tabitha is not our oldest teacher, but she is the most important. Her parents helped to found the school, and for lack of a better one, she serves as our mascot.

"Shall we go in?" Tabitha pronounced with her sumptuously articulated vowels. Unlike Annie, I *liked* Tabitha. "And darling," Tabitha took my arm and pulled me to the side, allowing the rest of my colleagues to enter the chapel, "would you hold this for me?" She pressed a large silk bag with gorgeous red lions embroidered on a tapestry of orange, maroon, and deep purple into my arms. "I will be right back." Then she hobbled down the narrow, tree-lined path in the direction of the main campus.

Annie, who'd already gone into the chapel, poked her head around the door and gave me a devastating look. "You're the one who dragged me here and you're not coming in? I don't think so."

I gestured to the bag in my arms. "Tabitha's orders. I'm holding this for her."

Annie stepped out of the chapel and came over to me. "Beautiful bag." She lifted a hand and stroked it. "What's it for?"

"I don't—"

Annie drew in a sharp breath, stopping me mid-thought. "You don't think? . . . Oh, my God. It's the cat!" she squealed, and then covered her mouth. "She put the cat in there! That is so Tabitha."

"Um." I swallowed, feeling the bile rise in my throat. I'm

not one to be squeamish under normal circumstances, but holding a dead cat, even in a lovely tapestry bag, was too much for me.

"I so wish I still smoked," Annie said.

"It's totally bad for you. And you're breastfeeding. And you haven't smoked for a decade."

"All good points. Still, wouldn't this be the perfect moment to light up? If we were in a movie, I'd be smoking now."

"If we were in a movie, I wouldn't actually be holding a dead cat. I'd be holding a bag made to look like it had a dead cat in it. Which would be much better. This is awful. Where did she go?" I looked along the pathway for Tabitha. A lone figure in black was walking in our direction but it wasn't Tabitha. "Annie," I whispered under my breath. "*Look.*" I pointed up the path.

The woman clad in black, with a sheer red shawl casually slung around her shoulders, strode toward us. In direct contrast to Annie's wild, untamed do, her thick mane of gently waving blond hair rippled out behind her *á la* shampoo commercial. The kind where they succeed in making women look like their hair is rushing behind them in undulating tides, usually with the use of fans, lots of product, and airbrushing. Seeing a real, living breathing human being with that sort of style stoked the flames of my already raging inferiority complex.

"It's her," Annie said.

I'd like to say we didn't stand there staring with our jaws brushing the ground, but we probably did. Cynthia Cypress had come.

"I hope I'm not late," she said, stopping in front of us.

"No. We're waiting for Tabitha."

"Oh, how darling! I adore it." She reached over and gave the bag an admiring pat.

"Evangeline's in there," Annie stated smugly, gratified to be the bearer of disgusting news.

"Well, we don't actually *know* that. I mean, Tabitha only gave it to me to hold. She didn't tell me what was inside. I guess it kind of does feel like a stiff cat body, if I really thought about it, but it could be any number of things. It could be—" Annie gave me her standard shut-up look, and a well-practiced one as she's known me since my fifth birthday, twenty-eight years ago. Over those nearly three decades I have availed myself of every opportunity to say stupid things. At that moment, instead of acting properly mortified for blathering on about feline rigor mortis, I started to think about my hair. Have I mentioned my hair—my limp, thin, mousy brown hair?

Cynthia shook her windswept tendrils in a graceful gesture of sympathy. "Well, it's nice of you to help out." Then she opened the chapel door and walked inside.

Being so caught up in the moment of deep hair analysis, wondering, truly wondering, how I could acquire the same buoyancy Cynthia sported, I didn't notice Tabitha return.

"Bastards," she said, taking the bag out of my hands. "They won't loan me a shovel, won't let me bury Evangeline on the school grounds. Not behind my house. Not next to the chapel. Not in the playing fields. Not even in the backwoods! I've lived and taught here for five decades! I essentially own half of this place. Absolutely unacceptable. I will bury her right here in front of the chapel and put in a grave marker of exceptional size. Who do they think they are?"

"Do you still smoke?" Annie asked, in her classically non-sequiturian way.

"I stopped when it was fashionable," Tabitha responded without skipping a beat. She smacked her lips together and asked, "Why?" And then, as she didn't care about the answer, she ambled away from us to go inside, turning only once to say, "Hurry up. I've got a cat to eulogize."

Once inside and seated snugly up against Annie in a packed fourth-row pew, I employed great effort to keep my eyes on Tabitha, not looking once to find Cynthia Cypress.

Cynthia, the newest hire in the history department, would start teaching when the semester began in September. No one knew her, not properly anyway. As she had no teaching experience, rumor had it she'd been hired on looks alone (probably her Pamela Anderson rack and Grace Kelly face). I think she got hired because she married the head of the history department, and the only attractive man at Dixbie without a prescription for Viagra, David Hayworth. To me, he's *the* David Hayworth. There is only one of him, and he married Cynthia Cypress and not, for example, me.

"No one knew Evangeline like I did," Tabitha was saying from her spot up in the simple wooden pulpit, waving her arms gracefully in the air as though she were molding a statue. She had black hair—well, she didn't *have* black hair, she probably had white hair or gray hair or no hair, but she wore her hair dyed black as a crow's feathers and swept up in a French twist. She'd put sparkly combs on either side of her head, and not a hair shifted as she spoke. She looked the quintessential art teacher. "She had an extraordinary temperament, as far as cats go, but even among my many friends, she held a unique place. Why, she was practically a person. She had a habit of using the toilet. No litter boxes for a creature as elegant as she. And, as all know who visited us, she was especially delicate when it came to eating . . ." Tabitha carried on for what seemed like hours, holding forth on every singular virtue her cat had possessed until it seemed likely that Evangeline was the greatest being ever to have lived, Mother Teresa reincarnated into a shedding, twenty-pound ball of fur.

Meanwhile, I *still* hadn't looked over my shoulder for Cynthia.

I could feel Annie rolling her green eyes next to me and sighing at Tabitha's every other word.

"Don't I have something better to be doing?" Annie whispered.

"Don't be rude."

Annie cocked her head sharply to the right. "Every time I see Cynthia Cypress I feel fatter." I looked in the direction her head was pointing. Cynthia sat in the row across the aisle with the kind of posture you see only in yoga magazines.

I looked away and shushed Annie, irritated to have my focus shifted onto the one person I was attempting *not* to think about. Since I couldn't bear to listen to Tabitha's wandering cat monologue any longer, I decided to think about my friendship with Annie. It began during a time when Annie could have modeled for fat-camp pamphlets. As a kid she sported the sort of tumbling jelly-roll belly you usually admire on a porky baby. I knew her through the usual social ostracism that gets visited on all fat people, knew her through her struggles with the StairMaster (when she first got on, she couldn't believe it didn't move your feet *for* you), through the all-yogurt diet (and accompanying intestinal pains), and the special weight-loss-enhancing vitamins that resulted in a strange rash on her nose. I never did care, not then or now, how much she weighed. I am in no position to judge: Annie is robust and healthy, while I've got the figure of an asparagus stalk. And while she was emphatically an overweight kid, she's a perfectly reasonable-sized adult. As a matter of fact, she's a great deal prettier than I am, with the flattering curves I'd acquire only if I stuffed my bra and got myself one of those rent-a-bums that you add to your nonexistent backside so you look like you actually have an ass.

I was thinking all this, what seemed to me to be an entirely appropriate inner discourse during a dull cat funeral, when I was startled out of my reverie by the sight of Cynthia Cypress climbing the two steps by the pulpit onto the platform. For a moment she stood in such stillness, she looked like a mannequin. Then she opened her mouth.

Considering that I'd already spent time with a dead Himalayan in my arms, the wave of heat, nausea, and dizziness that came over me had a perfectly logical origin. Still, I couldn't help thinking of an earlier conversation with Annie.

"Please come to the service," I'd entreated. "It will mean so much to Tabitha."

"Tabitha has ten other cats. What's the big deal?"

"Five," I said. "But that's not the point. She's an old lady without any family. Dixbie is her family."

"You know I've never got along with her."

"That's because you're both stubborn and outspoken. Besides, Cynthia might show up. Don't you want a chance to talk to her?"

"You're the one who loves Cynthia."

"I don't *love* her! I don't even like her. I don't even *know* her!"

"You love her."

"You make it sound like a crush."

"It *is* like a crush. Like the kind you used to get in junior high."

"I didn't have crushes on girls in junior high."

"Yes, you did. Remember how much you idolized Tina Rupert?"

"Tina Rupert was popular! Everyone idolized her."

"You made a special thing of it," Annie said. And fine, maybe I had, but I hate the way Annie gets to point things out to me from my past like she knows me better than I do. We went to school together in Iowa from kindergarten through eighth grade, until her parents divorced and her mother moved her to Chicago. We had the friendship that only girls parted against their wills can have, writing hysterical, hyperbolic letters detailing how the world had ended with her move. I never found another friend like Annie, not in high school, not in college. All those years, I missed her. I pined for her. She was my original BFF, and being pathologically shy, I never did make another one. When she called to tell me about the opening in the English department at the Dixbie School, where her partner, Ted, had been teaching for three years, I salivated. After that, I applied for the job; salivating doesn't get you very far (especially on paper). Once hired, I moved across the country, from rural Iowa to suburban Boston. Out of Iowa for the first time in my life at thirty-one, a fact I routinely try to hide as I'm well aware how *small* it makes me sound. By the way, I am not small, despite being narrow. I'm nearly five feet ten if I stand up properly, which I never do. Except in basketball, tall girls always finish last. Or maybe it's just me.

"Anyhow, you don't need to defend yourself to me," Annie went on. "I know this is really about David."

"How can you say that?"

"Because I know you." And she did. She knew me, sometimes, better than I knew myself. I'd never had a sister or a brother to love and hate me all at the same time; I had Annie.

Cynthia, now standing in front of us, illumined by the strong afternoon light flooding in through the giant arched chapel windows, sang with such sweetness and soul, I decided if I were David Hayworth I would have married her, too. Her song ended and Tabitha's loud, tremulous voice commanded us all to pray.

I took a deep breath and said a prayer for Evangeline. That she would have a good life in kitty heaven replete with catnip, lazy mice, and humans to scorn (no cat fantasy being complete without them). I prayed for Tabitha to quickly recover from her loss, that despite Evangeline's irreplaceable, almost supernatural cat abilities, she might find a way to go on living happily with her remaining tribe of felines. Then I said the same prayer I'd been praying insistently since my thirtieth birthday, which, at thirty-three, meant I'd said this one a literal million times so that it no longer resembled a humble plea, but came out in my head like a demanding toddler having a temper tantrum because she couldn't get what she wanted.

And in the middle of this petulant prayer, Cynthia started to sing again, a crushingly emotional version of "Morning Has Broken." I ought to have cried. Tabitha Hunter did. Instead, I couldn't stop wondering how Cynthia, who no one knew, got connected with Tabitha. Then finally, as she held the last note, and her creamy, bisque skin and pink cheeks glowed cherubic, I thought, *shit, shit, shit*—and really I never swear but it couldn't be helped—*she is beautiful and she can sing like an angel, too.*

2

Annie

The night of Tabitha's tedious, melodramatic cat memorial, in desperate need of recovery after having expended so much energy feigning sympathy (pretending to be kind always taxes me), I wrapped myself in my favorite purple bathrobe, put *Lost* on the DVD player, and ate a pint of Ben & Jerry's chocolate ice cream for dinner. This is how my partner, Ted, found me. But first, Hannah, nearly two and a half years old and already showing signs of being gifted at the kinds of moves practiced on the World Wrestling Entertainment channel, ran into the living room, dove violently into my lap, and immediately began begging for a taste of my ice cream. Toddler begging is defined by these important qualities:

1. It's constant.
2. It's a crescendo.
3. It knows no end.

Which reminded me of why I have a time-tested rule: don't eat anything you like in front of small people. I have heard and even seen other folk under thirty-six inches behave themselves around sweets and treats; not my Hannah. Even though she is my child, and I love her, she is the most demanding, Mussolini-esque child I have ever come across.

"It smells in here," Ted said, a few steps behind Hannah.

"That's the first thing you have to say to me?"

"That's the first thing I noticed."

"I've got terrible gas."

"Excellent news." Ted threw himself down on the couch. He scratched his caveman/Paul Bunyan beard, which I do occasionally pick food out of, and moved his glasses up to rub his tired hazel eyes.

"Where's the baby, honey? As far as I remember, I sent you off with two kids this afternoon."

"Asleep."

"And you left her in the car?"

"No. She's in her car thingy. In the kitchen." Lily, at five months and in stark contrast to Hannah, is something like a docile, aging dog. She sleeps and eats and coos, and in general makes her sister look like a wild maniac. When I first had Hannah, I didn't believe the mothers who said it got harder as the babies grew. What's harder than not sleeping through the night? Now that I know better, I don't take any delight in telling other mothers the truth: newborns are the easy phase.

Ted hadn't taken his eyes off the television since he'd come in the room. "How can you watch this garbage?"

"You'd love *Lost* if you ever gave it a chance. It's like a soap opera for men."

"I try not to watch anything the students watch. That is how I remind myself that I'm an adult." Ted teaches math.

This year he's got the freshmen for Algebra 1 and the seniors for Calculus. He also coaches and mentors and runs a few clubs.

"Oh, right, because nothing else would remind you of that? Like having children, maybe?"

"Children? What children?" he said jokingly.

"By the way," I spooned another mouthful of ice cream into Hannah's very happy and very quiet mouth, "I love you for taking them today. I had a fantastic evening of pure self-indulgence. The perfect antidote to the high drama of a house-pet eulogy."

"I do what I can," he said, eyes still fixed on the screen. When I looked at him a minute later, his eyes were shut and he'd begun a low, heavy snore.

"You wore your daddy out, didn't you, Hannah?"

"I went on the big slide!" she said in response, her brown eyes widening with the memory. Her enthusiasm melted my heart. Among child-rearing professionals, children like Hannah are euphemistically dubbed "spirited," code for "challenging," "difficult," and "good birth control." In the first place, this is wrong; Lily's birth came like a runner-up prize some twenty-one months after Hannah's and in spite of my concerted efforts not to reproduce again anytime soon. In the second place, I *like* spirited children, or anyway, I desperately want to since she is *my* kid. Hannah has vibrancy and buzz, albeit sometimes in a piercing, fingernails-down-the-chalkboard way. She has more *joie de vivre* than all of Paris in spring. I remind myself of this fact when her dictatorial, demanding, insistent nature fools me into thinking I don't want anything to do with her.

"What a lucky girl you are." I kissed the top of her head.

There wasn't any ice cream left. Alas. I'd have to find some appropriate kind of dinner for her. "Let's heat up some frozen pizza, okay? But try not to wake up Lily. We don't want her to eat up all our pizza, do we?"

"Mommy, she doesn't have no teeth!" Hannah said quite seriously.

"Oh, that's true. I forgot. Well, then I guess we can eat our pizza in front of her."

"She's a baby, Mommy." She shook her exasperated little head at me.

"That's right," I said, putting her down on the floor and pushing myself up from the chair. "And you're my big, bossy girl."

Later, I had to rouse Ted off the couch and get him to bed, a practice I loathe because if I leave him there to sleep, he gets mad at me later for not waking him up, and if I wake him up, well, naturally, he gets mad at me for waking him up.

"I was having the best dream," he said, yawning so widely I could see all five of his fillings.

"So was I. In my dream I was asleep *in bed*. I'm going to go make my dream come true. Are you coming?"

He reached up and took my hand, using it to pull himself upright.

"You want to tell me about the memorial service?"

"For the *cat*."

"Annie, we have a cat. You love cats."

"You know Tabitha and I don't get along."

"That's because in her you've met your match."

"What an insult! She's like a geriatric Shirley Temple who never got her moment on the stage. I thought she was going to break out into a tap dance today. She shouldn't teach fine arts, she should direct the theater program." We were holding hands now, walking up the stairs, and I felt happy, for maybe the second or third time that day (*really* happy), because I love talking to Ted—it has an infinite comfort to it, as though the world isn't real and we can, with words, rearrange it to our liking. Or maybe it was simply the act of holding hands with him, the man I feel knit to, as close as I feel to my children. No, closer.

"But it went okay?"

"Fine, I suppose. It dragged on forever. Nora couldn't peel her eyes off of Miss Cypress."

"How is she?"

"As thin as ever."

"I don't mean how she looks. Did you talk to her? What's she like?"

"No, we didn't talk to her. Not much anyway. She slipped in late and headed out early. She did sing during the service, although how she and Tabitha hooked up I have no idea. Ted, she had on high heels! High heels for a cat funeral at a stodgy prep school—"

"Where everyone else wears ballet flats." Ted finished my sentence, laughed at me, and playfully patted my head.

"Or maybe she wasn't wearing high heels. Maybe her feet are permanently slanted like Barbie's!"

"One can only hope," Ted said with a grin.

In the bedroom, I started to undress. De-robing is the wrong moment to think about a woman with Barbie-doll looks. My own naked thighs do not bring to mind the narrow, tawny legs of Barbie herself. They bring to mind instead small-curd cottage cheese, not a bad thing when you're feeling hungry for a nutritious snack, but not when you're contemplating your own anatomy.

I pulled on my flowered pajamas, grabbed my copies of the *The Economist* and *The New York Times* off the dresser, and slipped into bed. I'm a news junkie and a political wannabe. My first passion—albeit uncovered through unexpected accidents—child-rearing, has led me to amass three whole bookshelves of manuals, as if children could function like cars and behave properly once you have read and applied the wisdom of the directions. My second passion, hating politicians, gives me a break from the narrow confines of my first passion. As you can imagine, given the hopelessness of changing government and children, I am left with little free time and an extremely bad attitude. I have always been a pessimist; it seems to me the only reasonable position.

"You know how I've always detested Barbie." I smacked the newspaper open. Ted was pulling off his boxers, revealing a bottom much shapelier than mine. "In fact, if I even see one, I get queasy. Literally. Seasick. Vertigo. Nausea. The whole business. Barbie is feminism's worst nightmare. She represents all that I hate about the way our culture thinks of women."

"I thought you hated Barbie because your cousin used to cut off your Barbie dolls' heads and put them in your mashed potatoes, then laugh at you when you spat them out."

"Maybe on the surface." I brushed the idea away with a hand. "But really it's a much more profound issue. And thanks for the memory, *sweetheart*."

"Just saying, you used to play with them," he mumbled under his breath as he climbed into bed next to me. He pulled off his thin-framed glasses, scratched his beard, and closed his eyes. "You want to know what I think?"

"I doubt where a woman as good-looking as Cynthia is concerned that you *can* think."

"I think money has something to do with it."

"Money always does," I sighed. I did not want to talk about money again. As it was something I never had enough of, none of our conversations on the topic did anything to improve my mood.

"I'm trying to say something nice, if you'll let me. I'm trying to say that because she has wealth—"

"She's well-kept." Ted and I have a habit of knowing exactly what the other one will say.

"Money to join the gym, get a trainer, facials, that kind of thing."

"Yes, good point. So maybe she did pay to have her cosmetic surgeon permanently alter her feet." Ted gave me a good laugh for this one. Then he leaned in and kissed me in that I-want-some kind of way.

But don't get excited: I don't do hot sex scenes. Being rabid with the kind of exhaustion mothers of infants know all too intimately, even the thought of sex exceeds my capacity. Not to mention the fact that Ted and I managed to produce one child while using birth control and the other while still ignorant of the imperfection of birth control; we have finally discovered the best way to ensure it doesn't happen again. After our loving kiss, I told Ted that if he dared get his penis within five inches of any part of my body, I would leave him in short order—with the children—and go to law school. Either that or become a plus-sized escort for corrupt, wealthy, dysfunctional politicians. It's debatable where I'd have a greater influence on the government.

"Do you really think there's a demand for high-class plus-sized prostitutes?"

"Everyone has their fetish," I pointed out.

"Did you catch up with Nora? She called earlier, before the funeral, to see if you wanted to walk down with her."

"I met her on the way. She honestly cannot stop talking about how hard she and Alfie are trying," I said.

"You make it sound as though they're applying for college."

"Hey, I didn't make up the pregnancy lingo. People who have reproductive sex are *trying* because baby-making is an activity without a guaranteed outcome."

"Not in our case," he said lightly.

"We have nothing to complain about," I stated with an equal amount of levity. After all, I don't. I've delivered two healthy children—with the accompanying forty hours of labor, four bouts of crippling hemorrhoids, and sixty-two small stretch marks. Among my other noncomplaints you can include sleep deprivation, daily run-ins with all variety of feces, and conversations that need to be repeated twenty-five times that go something like this: "Red bird, Mommy." "Yes, that's a red bird." "Look, Mommy, red bird." "That's right, sweetie, a red bird." "Red bird, Mommy." "Yes." "See the red bird." "Right. You can see the red bird." "Red bird flying, Mommy." "That's right. Birdies fly." "Red birdie flying." "YES! I SEE THE RED BIRD FLYING!"

"Don't forget the preparatory house meeting tomorrow night with Celeste and Eric," Ted said sleepily, turning off his bedside light. Celeste and Eric Hooper live in the same dorm.

And forgetting would be impossible. Nine months of the year I live with thirty adolescent girls. The Dixbie School, where the main ingredient of every cafeteria meal happens to be mayonnaise, houses all faculty on campus—an exquisite, if run-down, campus, too, with majestic brick buildings, some in need of repair; enormous playing fields; a river and a forest; enormous, historic (read: in need of updating) Colonial, Victorian, and Greek Revival houses for dorms (I live in an apartment in one of them); and easy access to Boston.

If you teach at Dixbie, you live at Dixbie. If you live at Dixbie, you live with students and receive the endearing title of "houseparent." Ted and I share the responsibilities with the Hoopers. Given his already overloaded teaching schedule— Dixbie downsized a year ago and graciously allowed the remaining teaching staff to work more for the same amount of pay—and his commitments as the track and lacrosse coach, as well as sitting on a number of school committees, as well as the Hoopers' age (they have to be past retirement age), the majority of houseparenting tasks fall on my shoulders. In Zucker House, our home, I make sure the kids have their lights out by eleven, run a monthly dorm meeting, and issue permission slips for weekend trips into the city. Additionally, I act as the great mother to my flock in times of adolescent woe; I have been cried upon by no small number of hormonal girls. I can certainly appreciate the acutely, uniquely traumatic years of high school. This is one time in my own life I wouldn't relive even for the promise of thin thighs, civilized toddlers, and a swimming pool full of ice cream. Once in a life span is enough for public humiliation at the all-school dance. You're thinking, big deal, everyone's humiliated by high school. Or maybe you guess I got my period in the middle of the dance floor while wearing a white skirt (too cliché for the likes of me). Or my crush turned me down for a dance, you wonder? Not even close. I sat down on a chair and it broke. A metal chair *can't* break, of course, unless someone's rigged it in your honor. And that honor would be mine.

There is one exception to Dixbie's houseparent policy and it comes in the form of a breathtaking, fully remodeled Victorian house, the only one with a paint job from this decade, on the edge of campus. It's too small to be a dorm, though far too large to be deemed a typical house. As a rule, the largest family on campus gets first rights. Lily's birth in April elevated us to that much-sought-after status, and I consider my future life in Meadow House to be no small compensation for the cruelties that accompany bringing a new human into the world via a channel so small some people carp about tampons. I have yet to see a newborn with a tampon-size head.

After Lily's labor and delivery, a period of twenty hours resembling a grueling marathon of stoic endurance on my part (or foolishness in refusing drugs, depending on how you see it), the nurse checked my postpartum diaper and said, "You've lost an unusual amount of blood." There wasn't a muscle in my body that didn't ache. I'd thrown up twelve times. Blood loss seemed a trivial concern. At that moment, I closed my eyes and pictured my new life in my new house without the pitter-patter of thirty pair of adolescent sneakers. Call me superficial. A bleeding woman deserves at least one selfish, shallow indulgence, and getting the best house on campus and a much-needed dose of privacy—not to mention *three* bathrooms compared to our current 1.5—was mine. Ted and I were still waiting on the go-ahead to move from Sally Whetstone, the head of Campus Affairs. As a matter of fact, she was a bit tardy in contacting us. I put it on my mental to-do list to phone her before the week ended, hoping I wouldn't do what I often do when it comes to this list of things stored in my head: forget.

I call the cause of this forgetfulness my partial metaphoric lobotomy, a condition more commonly referred to as motherhood. The very condition my dear friend Nora currently pines away for as if it were the air itself. I looked at her that day after the cat funeral while we chatted on the chapel lawn about her abysmal failures in the baby-making department. I look at her decked out in khaki shorts and a pink shirt with a kitten on it, her brown hair tucked behind slightly oversized ears, her brown eyes full of the pure kindness she brings with her everywhere she goes like an adoring puppy, and said, "I remember how it is." I'm fairly good at this form of bald-faced lying. Luckily, Nora didn't correct me. She knows as well as I do that I never enjoyed the luxury of *trying*. Or for that matter the extravagance of planning. Two babies in less than two years? I am more than a triumph by Nora's standards.

I might have told her how lucky she was to sleep soundly at night, how lucky she was to go to the bathroom without a little person on her lap, how lucky she was to—well, to get to have *sex*. But hey, I understand. Sleep doesn't seem that important when you've been getting a lot of it. Sleep, however, is underrated. If everyone in the world got enough sleep, all wars would cease; we'd all be creative enough to come up with some ideas to end famine, disease, and bad television. I'm absolutely convinced of this. In fact, it's my platform if I ever run for office. It has also never been much use telling Nora how lucky she is. She simply cannot see it. When I was fat, she got to be skinny. When I had screaming parents, hers insisted on family meals every night and dinner games afterward, as though they dwelt in some 1950s television sitcom. For the greater part of my thirty-three years, Nora has been a lovely counterbalance to the messiness of my life, with the simple, clear lines of her world drawn with fluid precision.

Not for the first time she asked for advice that day, my advice, my coveted mother-of-babies advice, on how to conceive. Against my natural instincts to lecture and complain, I simply pulled her in for a hug. I knew how much she wanted a baby; she'd always wanted children much more than I had. We rarely spoke of this injustice—that I, who hadn't really wanted them so much, should have two, and she, who wanted them more than life itself, could not manage to make any.

"Give it time," I quipped like a regular Carol Brady, to pick one TV character that I adamantly am not. And why *aren't* I a regular Carol Brady? You know, more cheerful, upbeat, *perky*?

Let me put it this way. Fat childhood; bitter, battling parents; gruesome divorce between my parents at the critical identity-forming age of thirteen, followed by a lifetime of paternal absence. I did briefly believe that my period was brought on as a direct punishment for being the child of divorced parents until my mother clarified the matter by assuring me that all women suffer equally in this one area—very democratic of Mother Nature, I'd say. No hopes for Olympic glory and no interest in academic excellence, I found salvation doing what I loved, painting. The visual arts happen to be a great haven for cranky souls. I went to art school. I taught art. When I met Ted, we made a baby the first time I used a diaphragm. Which, now that I think of it, ought to have been shared with Nora as a little tidbit of inspiration. ("Have you tried a diaphragm?")

Ted started snoring again. I nudged him with my elbow.

"I wasn't done talking," I said.

"In the morning," he grumbled.

"Did the papers come yet?"

"What?"

"The *papers*. How can you say 'what'? Did the papers come?" He snored again, loudly. "Ted." I shook his arm.

"No," he said, rolling over. And then, more gently, "I'm sorry."

3

Nora

"You're kidding! Annie, you must have misheard."

"Why would I kid?" Annie shouted into the phone. "Where my life is concerned, I have no sense of humor."

"But I don't understand."

"*You* don't understand! What about me? She doesn't have any children. In fact, there aren't any other children on this mayonnaise-infested campus. And I have TWO. When, all of a sudden, did this rule-abiding, stubborn institution decide to break with hundred-year-old protocol?"

"I really can't believe it. Are you sure it's not a mistake—"

"Nora, for heaven's sake, stop believing that bad things don't happen to good people. Life isn't a *Mister Rogers* episode. I absolutely heard right. I heard it from the horse's mouth. Sally Whetstone told me over the phone after I dialed her directly."

"But—" I struggled to come up with another scenario. I had no reason to think poorly of Cynthia Cypress. There had to be a logical reason that she and David ended up in Meadow House, the classical Victorian reserved for Annie's family. An allergy to mold in the only available apartment? What I knew about Cynthia could have fit on one of those three-by-five cards I hand out to my students for final exams, and none of it pointed to mixed motives.

"Have you talked to anyone else about this?"

"Nora, you are *always* the first person I call."

"Right." That didn't leave us much to go on. At least another person's perspective could add some sense to the situation. I barely knew Cynthia.

I thought back to the first time I met her. It happened to be the initial day of my pre-wedding makeover. Last October I went to Brownston's best spa for a practice updo and a manicure. I couldn't say no to the receptionist who wanted to sell me eight hundred dollars worth of products. I am one of those people incapable of saying no, a condition brought on by neurotically nice parents. Besides, she promised me this particular line of organic cosmetics would transform me into a swan, and being an ugly duckling, I couldn't resist. Along with this extravagant and unnecessary splurge on makeup—before that, I'd owned exactly one lipstick—I decided I needed new clothes. I would be married soon to a man I wished I was just a little bit more excited to marry, so I did everything in my power to ramp up the occasion in hopes of inspiring myself.

This meant parting with some of my more beloved sweatshirts, sweatpants, and pink socks. My hairdresser, Dani, advised me to purchase some high heels in order to give my hair more bounce. Up until that magic moment in my life I had not realized this powerful connection. It gave me the perfect excuse for my lame mane; for many months after, I blamed its lack of body on my sneakers.

I purchased a pair of shiny black, sling-back three-inch heels along with a variety of shirts and skirts to match my rouge, a trick that apparently takes a decade off your face. When I mentioned my new shoes to my mother, she said, "But why? You can't walk in the mud." Mud walking is a prized virtue in my family.

I blame the shoes. The day I put them on for classes, I was running late. I'd spent too much time trying to figure out how to use the new eyelash curler. If you think it's so easy, you ought to read the page-long articles the beauty magazines publish on just this topic. It is NOT a normal, native ability. I don't care what anyone says. If you're curious about why I hadn't learned this skill earlier in my life, consider my mother's opinion on the topic: "You're too pretty for makeup. Makeup is for girls with no natural beauty." Not to be outdone by my Aunt Bertie: "Makeup comes from Satan." You get the picture. As a direct result of my shoes and eyelash incompetence, I ended up tumbling down the three cement steps that lead to the main academic building, shiny, pointy new shoe over shiny, pointy new shoe.

When I finally landed, I found myself flat on my back at the bottom of the stairs. One shoe had flown off into the bushes; my bag hit the ground five feet away. At that moment, like a phantom in a dream, Cynthia Cypress appeared.

She ran toward me with all the grace of a prima ballerina *en pointe*. Her head did not move, but that hair flew out behind her as if *Vogue* had set a fan directly on it. More significantly, she ran in heels. Not unlike the ones I had managed to prove myself incapable of merely walking in. She wore a bright red coat tied at her small waist with the collar up. Me: one shoe on and one shoe off, lying prone on the ground in the pouring rain. Cynthia: perfect.

I didn't know who she was. I'd never seen her before. Even without knowing that this woman, this *vision* coming toward me, would marry (*The*) David Hayworth, I could feel the weight of her importance.

Apparently she could too, because while it appeared this lady in red meant to rescue me, she actually ran straight past me and up the stairs into Lyle Hall, as if she were late and hadn't seen me at all.

And maybe she hadn't.

Maybe. If she were blind, that is.

I did not see her again, or for that matter give her any thought, until three weeks later when, while walking down the aisle on my father's arm at my wedding, I spotted her sitting next to David Hayworth. I hadn't seen much of her face that rainy day, but I knew the hair. It was unmistakable, shiny as a crown on her head. I held tighter to my father's arm so I wouldn't reel and fall over. Right then, walking down that aisle, I realized that the same woman, the vision who had left me collapsed on the stairs during a downpour with one shoe missing and a broken umbrella, was David Hayworth's date to my wedding. And David Hayworth? He was the man who *might* have been at the end of the aisle that day, standing by the altar to meet me, had I only been less determined to have what I wanted.

"Nora, did you fall asleep?" Annie demanded from the other end of the line.

"Oh, sorry." I pried myself back from those dreadful

memories. "I was thinking about Cynthia, hoping to come up with an answer."

"I'm going to talk to her in person," Annie said.

"You are?"

"You bet I am. No one takes my house that easily."

"Do you think that's a good idea?" The mere thought of confrontation brought a film of sweat to my palms. Among my many unfavorable personal characteristics, the most prominent has to be my well-earned reputation as a do-gooder. I have always been thought of as a "nice" person—to the exclusion of any other more interesting qualities. Cringe all you like; I certainly do. To have that as the defining quality of my personality makes me feel like someone's idea of a new puppy—"Aw, what a nice little doggie!"—when, in reality, that puppy is chewing through shoes and peeing all over the rugs.

For the record, I neither chew leather nor lift my leg in public.

But Fruity, my husky with the confusing palate of a rabbit (she loves carrots) and a human (she adores sushi), *has* started to pee on everything. She's fifteen. I'm trying to act cool, like *incontinence? What's so bad about that?* Or maybe I'm just being myself about it, scrubbing the rugs, throwing them out when needed, and loving her up despite it. Maybe it's just another way of being professionally nice.

Fruity, however, has nothing to do with any of this.

"Wish me luck," Annie said.

"Good luck," I managed. "But do you think—" The line went dead. I don't blame her for hanging up. I would have hung up on me. Still, I wished there were an alternative to a personal conversation with Cynthia. Maybe calling up Dean

Friedman? He serves as our dean of faculty. The man sports a Charlie Chaplin mustache and the general campus consensus is that he has no life outside the school—no wife, no children, no family, no friends, though he has been seen walking around the playing fields with his metal detector—and maybe because of all that, I truly like him. He's also gentle, soft-spoken, and in that Dixbie way, has become a bit like family.

When I arrived at Dixbie three years ago, the brisk New England brassiness and the trendy maturity of the students shocked me to my Iowan, Lutheran roots. Probably this seems like an insult to all sophisticated Lutherans and Iowans. Not everything can be blamed on my rural, Midwestern childhood. Most of my weirdness came direct from my family. As far as the Helpsom-Fulchs were concerned, you got new clothes in the fall and shopped exclusively at the bargain rack. We were firmly middle class, but I am the child of a woman who considers frugality the ultimate virtue. If she calls you thrifty, she has paid you her highest compliment. Her knack for conserving funds led to curtains made from tablecloths, tablecloths made from curtains, napkins made from curtains, and handkerchiefs—oh, yes! it's true, and she *made* me carry them to school—made from, you guessed it, napkins. All this came years before reduce, reuse, recycle became hip. Worst of all, she never did have good taste in tablecloths.

Meanwhile the Dixbie School, a fading beauty with opulent though slightly neglected historic buildings, situated in affluent Brownston, Massachusetts, started as a girls' private high school in 1930; it's now co-ed. Since the school prides itself on faculty retention, you can't imagine how lucky I felt

to get a position here. Annie called me and in total excitement and honorable seriousness shouted: "It's so awesome!
Dr. Rachel Brownisweather just died of a stroke."

"Can you tell me why that's awesome?"

"Where have you been? It opens up a position in the English department with your name on it! The dream job, the
perfect timing, and I can get you in! It's really incredible. Do
you know the last time they had an opening in the English
department? Nineteen ninety-three! Best of all, we'll be together again!"

When she called I'd been subbing for a year at Tarryville
High School, a job that, though intermittent, still gave me
horrific, regular nightmares in the form of flashbacks in
which I appeared all of fifteen, with overgrown bangs,
permed hair, in rolled-up hot-pink sweatpants, dancing un-
forgivably to Mariah Carey while the entire school laughed
mercilessly, something that obviously never happened. I may
have owned hot-pink sweats and, okay, I had several perms,
but I surely never danced in public.

When I wasn't subbing or having nightmares about my
awkward past, I moped around my parents' house acting as
lost as I felt. My mother insisted I drive around the elderly
members of her church to doctor's appointments, eye exams,
and the grocery store. Idleness is her favorite sin. And by favorite, I mean she talks about it all the time and makes sure
no one in her immediate vicinity falls victim to its evil ways.
I remember once, as a little girl, the way most little girls do,
telling my mother I felt bored. She immediately put me to
work cleaning around the bathroom faucets with a toothbrush. Quite honestly, I never got bored again.

Given the state of my life, I leaped at the chance to come

east. The fact that I had to move clear across the country and that I didn't know my way around a boarding school meant nothing. If I stayed in Tarryville, I would have started wearing synthetic cardigans like all the old ladies I hung out with—and that would have been the best of it.

Luckily for me and my students, I'm not a bad teacher. I even got nominated last year for the Sylvia Sternberg Excellence in Teaching Award. At the last minute, they awarded it to Tabitha Hunter (for the fourth time) with the hopes that it would propel her into retirement; though she undoubtedly ran Dixbie behind the scenes due to some money her parents gave to the school back before cars were in fashion, the administration longed for a new era. Unfortunately, it had the opposite effect, reinspiring her commitment and reinvigorating her teaching.

I attribute my success in the classroom to the fact that I'm more like a ninth grader than a thirty-year-old. Adulthood isn't my forte. I look better in pink than black, better in sparkly sneakers than high heels, better with pigtails than a bob. I don't like anything new on TV. I never understood the adult world, and I've been reluctant to completely join it—hence the post-college years spent living under my parents' roof.

After Annie abruptly hung up, I put the phone down and went in search of Fruity. I wanted to give her an afternoon walk. It was Monday. Classes would begin in a week. I stopped in the hallway and stared at my wall calendar. One more week of vacation. I looked sadly at the letter "P" written boldly on today's date, my way of keeping track of all things reproductive. I closed my eyes and prayed for a baby. Then the phone rang.

"Hello?"

"Nora? This is Dick." Dick Friedman, Dean Friedman, the Charlie Chaplin stunt double. "How are you? Enjoying the last dog days of summer?"

"Oh, yes. Alfie and I have one more trip to Vermont planned before classes resume."

"Wonderful. Look," he paused to swallow noisily. "I was wondering if you could do me a favor, take Cynthia around a bit, show her the campus, that kind of thing."

"Cynthia? Doesn't she have David?"

"Technically, of course, but I always pair new faculty with a buddy. Don't you remember how Becky showed you the ropes when you first arrived? So I thought, who's better and nicer than Nora Galusha? No one!"

"Okay."

"Give her a call. She's had the professional tour. You can give her the personal one."

"Right," I said, leaning against the wall and trying hard not to sigh into the phone. And when should I call her, I wondered. Before or after my best friend, Annie, personally confronted her to test the Meadow House assignment?

4

Annie

I headed out, as I always do on Wednesdays, to the Brownston Family Center, where I wouldn't go, wouldn't even be paid to go, if it weren't for one beautiful equation: Hannah + three hours at the family center = one very, very long nap. The place teems with toys of every stripe. They have more building blocks than I have hairs on my legs. I didn't just give up leg shaving in some kind of wild, feminist protest; it's simply a matter of priorities. On any given day I have enough time to either shower or get laundry done. On the days I opt to shower, I have enough time in the shower to either wash my hair or wash my body, generally not both. That pretty much leaves out any opportunity for body hair removal. I wear a lot of long skirts.

Hairy legs, however, are not welcome at the Brownston Family Center, affectionately known as BFC for those in the know. It's a bit like middle school, only much, much worse. I'm happy to say that no one there has rigged a chair to break the instant my fanny hits it, but that doesn't mean the women are any warmer to me than my pubescent classmates were.

"Hi, Ann," Julia Tucker said to me as Hannah raced over and ripped a toy out of her daughter's hands. Julia is the volunteer head of the center, heroin-addict skinny, and chronically busy, despite the fact that she is, like the rest of us, *merely* a stay-at-home mother. I think she has OCCD—obsessive, compulsive committee disorder.

"It's Annie," I corrected her.

"Annie?" She looked genuinely stunned, though we've known one another for years. "Are you sure? I always thought you went by Ann."

See what I mean? Are these people from another planet? "I've been called Annie since birth, if that helps at all."

"Lily's grown so much," she cooed, desperate to move on from our awkward conversation. Lily hung over my arm like a handbag. The BFC mothers are such inspiration for accessories.

"They do that."

"Oh, Margie, there you are!" Julia exclaimed, seeing her best buddy walk in the door, her designer toddler following just one step behind. She always did have this way of recoiling from me like a finger off a hot stove. Margie Hoover, her closest friend and the social director of the center (how could it possibly need one?), blazed in wearing a tight-fighting T-shirt and glued-on jeans. Her outfit couldn't offset her blotchy skin, however. Everyone knew—everyone at the BFC, anyway—that Margie's husband had an affair with the elementary school principal. Devastated, she lost fifty pounds. I could almost muster the compassion to feel badly for her if she didn't own a horse farm, an apartment in Boston, and a house on Martha's Vineyard. If she wanted to, she could *buy* herself a new husband.

"We can catch up later," I said under my breath and to Julia's backside.

"Catch up later," Hannah began to chant in a delighted song. If I cared, I would have been mortified.

Here's part of the problem. Technically, I don't *own* in Brownston. In other words, I don't *live* in Brownston. Living on the campus of Dixbie puts me in an altogether different category. It's sort of like I've been shipped in from the ghetto to improve their national standing in the diversity competition. If Ted and I wanted to buy in Brownston, we would need a million dollars—for a shack. Then I'd have to get a job so together we could make enough money to afford Velveeta for dinner. If that were the case, I wouldn't ever come to the BFC because the BFC is the congregating place of stay-at-home mothers. I am the variety of SAHM who sacrifices to spend all her time with her children; i.e., I clip coupons, buy used, and drive a minivan from the disco era, although to be fair to myself, our slim family wallet isn't entirely *my* fault.

I turned away from Hannah's play—she'd climbed onto a rocking horse and proceeded to gleefully scream "Giddy-up!" a thousand times—at the sound of Suze's voice.

"Thank God," I said, taking a good, long look at the woman in front of me. Yes, she did appear designer, like all proper Brownston moms, her jeans eased on with the help of a shoehorn. Still, Suze Bard had something the other mothers didn't: a sense of humor. Oh, and an interest in other people. I'd discovered, in my attempts to make small talk with other BFC moms, that narcissism is rocky ground for friendships. Two years ago Suze miraculously walked up to me and started talking about the Senate race. I would have loved her for this act of intelligence alone, but that she turned out to be kind and lively and funny bound me to her in complete devotion. I adored the woman. If she said run—despite the fact that under normal circumstances I would run only if something very scary, say Julia Tucker, were chasing me—I would run.

"My partner in crime," she said.

"You look well rested." In Suze's case, it wasn't the sleep. It was the Botox. And you're right, no thirty-three-year-old needs Botox. It's just all the rage. She can afford an expensive, whimsical hobby, if plastic surgery can be called a hobby, which I'd venture to guess it can considering how many women with no other interests beyond their own faces engage in it. Andy, Suze's extremely successful obstetrician husband, is heir to the First Steps baby food industry, and, no surprise, wealthy beyond one's wildest dreams. He's not gorgeous to look at—a little short, a little balding, a little arrogant—but he does have a charm about him. He's powerful and chivalrous, which might make up for his general absenteeism as a husband and father. *Might* being the operative word. Personally, I'd rather skip the Botox and hang out with my partner.

Suze came over and hugged me hugely, wrapping Lily up also.

"Finnegan, be gentle," she called out to her son, a small boy with a generous nose (I'm being kind here), busy slamming a plastic fire truck into the wall. Then she turned to me. "What's the word, hummingbird?"

"I've been kicked out of my own house."

"What?!"

"You know how I'd been promised Meadow House, how Whetstone told me once the baby came we'd be the biggest family on campus? And that's the campus rule. That's been the rule forever. Apparently, the rule has been broken. They gave it to Cynthia and David."

"The new woman who makes you feel fat?" Suze weeded through her enormous leather diaper bag and withdrew a tissue for Finnegan. "Colds can't be starting already, can they? It's barely September."

"Children drip. It's part of what they do."

Next, Suze pulled out an enormous hand sanitizer, gave her hands a good going over, then reached out for Lily. "Come here, you little peanut. I want to feel a baby again. Oh, how I miss my baby being a baby. He's all grown up." We both looked at Finnegan. At that exact moment he had his finger locked into a nostril.

"You're not focusing," I complained.

"I'm sorry," she said with a playful smile. "I haven't been able to concentrate since Finn's birth."

"Well, please try."

"Okay, so that style-slut stole Meadow House out from underneath you?"

"And quickly. She's already moved in." I tried not to hyperventilate saying the words. On Monday, I'd walked over to David's apartment in search of her, only to find the place completely empty. Then I headed over to Meadow House, where I found the two of them sitting in rocking chairs on the front porch.

"She has kids?"

"No, she does *not* have kids. David does not have kids. In fact, I happen to know secondhand from Nora that David's future does not include children."

"It must be some kind of mistake. Everyone at Dixbie does bleeding heart so well. Bunch of grandmas."

"It is not a mistake. I have stepped inside their extravagantly decorated home. I have been given the grand tour." Right at that moment Hannah and Finnegan began to tussle over a red puppet, forcing Suze and me to intervene. We earned much wailing from the two angry little faces. When Hannah threw herself on the floor and began screaming, "I WANT puppet," Suze turned to me and said, "She's so cute."

"Very funny. She's a sumo wrestler."

"Just what you'd want in a girl. A hot temper will serve her well."

"You know she's a serious problem," I said, not at all reassured by the thought of her future hot-temperedness.

Once I'd comforted Hannah with a cracker and nursed Lily, and once Finnegan and Suze had come back from the bathroom and found us at the art table, I finally had a chance to get in another word to Suze. "You up for a mom's night out? I'd like to speak to you in something other than haiku."

"You have to ask?" She threw me a look, raising just one eyebrow, a skill of hers I couldn't help but admire.

"How about lunch?" I looked around. Meghan Handle and her daughter Chessy had just arrived, and that meant it was time for me to make my exit. I'd had a run-in with Meghan recently I didn't want to relive.

"Any special reason you don't want to finish telling me the story here?" Suze asked.

I nodded toward Meghan. "That woman gives me hives. I don't want to hang out with her. She's so *Nanny Diaries*."

"You may be in luck. I heard through the grapevine she's been offered her old position as a litigator."

"Why does everyone need to pretend motherhood isn't a real job?"

"Chessy will be better off without her."

"Still, I hate the defection from the cause." For a moment Suze looked bewildered.

"The cause?"

"Motherhood."

She gestured toward Hannah and squeezed Lily in close. "Ah, right. The *cause*. Motherhood: more than a job. A *life-style*." She laughed.

"Thank God someone understands me," I said, loud enough for others to hear.

After spending the usual thirty minutes loading my human cargo into the car—Lily first, amidst much protest, followed by Hannah pleading to go back in and play—I drove all of us straight out of Brownston and into Acton to get a coffee from Dunkin' Donuts. Was it just for the scenery, you ask? Absolutely not. They don't have Dunkin' Donuts in Brownston. That's the way Brownston is. They wouldn't muddy their downtown aesthetics with something so working-class.

The drive gave me plenty of opportunity to contemplate. In fact, said contemplation trumped *NewsTime,* which I normally listen to obsessively because it makes me feel certain that the world will definitely end by the time the program's finished. It's like crack for cynics. Great stuff, really.

Every time I go to the BFC, I end up wanting to procure some gainful employment. No, that's not accurate. I don't want to work—I want the funds it could provide. I want to show up driving a vehicle that saw the assembly line in this century. I want Hannah to sport the seventy-five-dollar rain boots all the other girls tromp around in. Truly, I believe that the hand that rocks the cradle rules the world. Unfortunately, that hand doesn't make a dime on all that rocking, and in this cash universe, money makes for legitimacy. You can lullaby your little heart away, but no one's going to give you a new wardrobe for it. You can birth and breastfeed a hundred children, but no one's going to give you a paycheck at the end of the week. You can't trade in your eighteen sippy cups for a Florida time-share or send in your child's happy smile with your L.L. Bean order in place of a check.

As miserable as it is to be the poor relation at the BFC, I don't want to go back to work. I'd always planned on staying home with my children. Before I had the girls, when I taught art part-time at a local community college and spent the rest of my days painting, I had a few gallery showings. Now, I devote myself to my girls, and as much of a non-job house mothering appears to be from the outside, I'm quite busy. Just last night while reading emails from members of the Young Feminists Club, the campus group I founded and run, I learned that the girls want to hold some sort of enormous, educational event on feminism this year. It will require hours of oversight and management on my part. Of course I agreed; their passion inspires me. All this was generated by one innocuous comment from Amanda Braden, a senior who said mournfully, "No one knows who we are at this school." And Pepper Heid, a precocious sophomore with one hell of an attitude, said, "Yeah. Who *are* we? Do we even know who we are?"

All of this tumbled around my sleep-deprived head as a result of the conversation I made the grave mistake of having with Meghan a week ago. While watching our daughters finger-paint their hands, I made a few comments on the adorableness of their art projects and then said, "I would rather be here watching this than anywhere else in the world."

Let's be honest, this is not a new nor a radical thought, yet Meghan looked at me as though I'd confessed to child molestation. "For one thing," she said. "I'd rather be getting a massage. For another, enjoying a real cup of coffee. Why can't we get good, organic Nigerian beans here?"

"Let me clarify: half of what I do all day consists of mindless drudgery, like reading the back of the macaroni and cheese box, the other half of futile repetition, like cleaning my house. Watching Hannah make art is the highlight. It's a pleasure."

"I'll tell you about pleasure. I gave myself a spa day last week. Thank God I go to Kripalu next week. Have you been there? Wholesome food, lots of yoga classes, beautiful views. You should think about it."

I thought about it for the thirty seconds it took me to do the math. We couldn't afford name-brand toothpaste, let alone a vacation where I pay to eat bean curd and get instructions on how to chant *om*. And if I got a job, something I didn't want to do, then I certainly wouldn't have the time for recreational eyebrow waxes or whatever the hell they do to you at a spa.

At last, I pulled up into our driveway at Zucker House. Nora sat on the stoop. She didn't look happy.

"What's up?" I asked, hopping out of the car, and then added, "Don't just sit there. Grab a kid."

She came over to the van and helped unbuckle Lily.

"Right," I muttered, "take the easy one."

"Hello, Lily love," she said, smiling and cooing at Lily, who was only just beginning to wind down from a hysterical crying fit. Normally, crying bothers me, but Lily cries every time we ride in the car, so I've effectively learned to tune her out. The first few months it nearly drove me to a nervous breakdown, handily held off by pumping up the volume on the local news. Now that I think of it, it's probably the news that makes her cry.

"I just got back from the BFC," I told her.

"Any kids named Pear yet?"

"Very funny." Nora knew how much I hated the BFC. In fact, she was one of the few people in my world who understood the origin of my relative poverty. I'd also bored her for hours with stories of the other mothers. Here's one perfect example: After I'd been going for about a year with Hannah and had just got pregnant with Lily, I attended the BFC on a particularly slow day. There were only three other mothers and myself. During that time they all exchanged cell phone numbers with one another while I stood right next to them being wholly ignored. Why? Because I don't get a weekly mani-pedi? Because my clothes drape and don't suction in my body parts? Because we don't have a four thousand-square-foot house? Who knows? Who cares? When I think about them, the end of the world doesn't seem so bad.

I pulled Hannah out of her seat and set her on the ground. "You have ten minutes to play outside," I told her firmly. "Then it's lunch."

"Okay, Mommy," she said pleasantly. She doesn't know what ten minutes means any more than I do. It's a phenomenon called Mommy-Time. In other words, Mommy makes up time because for children it doesn't exist. Frankly, it feels damn good to be in control of something.

"Did you work things out with Cynthia? You never called again."

"Not much to work out considering they'd already moved into Meadow House. Seems Whetstone took her time breaking the news to me."

"You mean David and Cynthia have already moved in? How?"

"By hiring someone to haul their furniture, I'd imagine."

"That's not what I meant and you know it," Nora said with as much frustration as a peaceable person like Nora can muster.

"I know what you mean. They promised her the house." I turned to look at Hannah; she stood pounding the pavement with a large branch. "They wrote it into her contract."

5

Nora

I squinted to read the time on the wall clock in the kitchen. "Wow, it's so late. I really should get home."

"Have another one first." Annie held up a wine spritzer.

"These define gross. I feel like I'm getting drunk on lemonade."

"I couldn't agree more." She giggled, an uncharacteristically silly giggle. "I think I've had them in the cupboard for years. At least we're thrifty drunks; your mom would be so pleased."

"Unlikely! I doubt my mother has ever been drunk."

"Everyone's been drunk once," Annie stated, taking another hearty swig of our revolting libation.

It was nearly midnight. We'd been sitting in her living room since the girls fell asleep. Ted left us in peace to go read in the bedroom after Annie assured him that there was non-alcoholic breast milk in the fridge should Lily wake up hungry.

"I feel better already," Annie said, leaning back into the fat, brown recliner.

"I feel worse." We'd spent most of the evening trying to come to a conclusion on how Cynthia managed to get Meadow House written into her school contract. With help from the wine spritzers, we decided she must have given someone along the line a very good blow job. This was amateurish and immature and we both knew it, or anyway we'd know it the next morning when we woke up with headaches, but it did ease the tension somewhat. Despite the liberating qualities of our drink, I had yet to confess to Annie that I was Cynthia's official school tour guide.

"Does the whole David thing get to you?" Annie asked.

"You're talking too loudly."

"We're alone in my living room. Who's going to hear us?" I shrugged. "Anyhow, I don't have volume control," she practically screamed at me. "Answer the question."

"No," I said, much more quietly. "I'm over it."

"Good. Alfie's much better for you."

"You think?"

"Of course! Don't be silly."

I sighed, a nicely inebriated kind of sigh.

"What's the matter? Something wrong with Alfie?"

"Nothing's wrong."

"Nora, you're pouting. I've known you since you wore training pants to bed. What's up?"

I put my spritzer down on the coffee table and covered my eyes. I would never be drunk enough to talk about my problems with Alfie even to the one person who could comprehend them.

"Is it the pregnancy stuff?"

"Yes and no."

"Come on, Socrates. Don't make this a riddle."

"I don't want to talk about it."

"Right. Then it must be your sex life." Annie leaned forward in the recliner to look me in the eye. "Don't tell me you *still* haven't had an orgasm with Alfie."

"Did you hear me say that I don't want to talk about it?"

Alfie and I had been trying to get pregnant since our wedding back in November, or, more accurately, *I'd* been trying. Alfie didn't care when the baby came, whereas I was staring my thirty-fourth birthday in the eyes, and it scared me so much my ovaries got goose bumps. I attribute my lack of success in the bedroom to this sense of failure that permeates our sex. When I ought to be in the throes of passion, I see us as two people running a marathon. We start to lose ground, slipping away from the crowd at the front. Quickly we wind up at the end of the line, only to be handed the "honorable mention" ribbon. We couldn't make it; we miss having what everyone else got. Or at least *I* miss it. I miss getting the most basic life accomplishment, the one that comes so easily to so many that babies show up in trash cans and in junior high bathrooms, and live in foster homes for years for want of a good mother. And I miss getting the one thing I have longed for my whole life, a blood relative.

"That's enough feeling sorry for yourself!" Annie got up out of the chair and walked into the kitchen. "I've been listening to you for years bemoan the fact that you cannot climax." She came back in with a pad and paper and stood over me for a minute like a Mafia mom giving a threatening lecture. "As your friend, I can't let this go on any longer. You're thirty-three years old. No more excuses." She began to scribble madly on the pad.

"What are you doing?"

"I am drawing you a picture of the clitoris."

"What?!" I pulled the pad out of her hands. "Annie! It looks like a demented nose!"

"What do you expect? I'm not doing a live drawing."

"Oh, man." I felt a laugh bubbling up, which I tried to suppress. It wasn't funny.

"Now I want you to remember the times in your life when you *did* have an orgasm. Let's try to re-create the movement."

"Annie, you're crazy." She was furiously drawing again. She passed the pad to me and I lost it in a fit of hysterics. She'd drawn a set of hands, hairy man hands, fondling the enormous nose. "Is this someone picking their nose?" I asked as tears streamed down my face.

"You've had too much to drink," Annie said, all schoolteacher. "I'm trying to help you."

We both got quiet at the sound of Lily's crying. When it continued, Annie cursed.

"Ted must have fallen asleep. Oh, Nora, can you go rock her? If I go in there she'll just want to nurse and I've had too much to drink. She'll probably fall asleep without a bottle if you just sing to her."

"What about Ted?"

"He sleeps like an obese cat. He can't hear her."

"Okay," I said, hiccupping my way into the nursery.

I picked little Lily up out of her crib. She fit in my arms like a wriggly sausage. Annie long ago told me not to hold her against my chest, "unless you intend to breastfeed," so I pressed her against my shoulder. I would have started to sing, too, as I normally did, if I hadn't started to cry. I'm sure it was because of the wine spritzer overdose and not all the orgasm talk or the feeling of Lily in my arms.

She settled down and began to purr against me, growing heavy, then finally deeply asleep. Her head smelled like Grandma Lucy's sourdough bread—something real and tangible, a pleasure enjoyed, not a fanciful expectation, not a hopeful, hypothetical future child. How insignificant everything else seemed in that moment compared to her—a living, breathing being, happy in my arms.

I don't want to give the wrong impression. Alfie, my husband, *is* my knight in shining armor; I just haven't realized it yet. I'm sure one day I'll look at him and see his white horse and his manly coat of armor. One day, I'll look at him and get the love shivers. One day, he'll give me orgasms. But then let's not be picky; only one man has ever given me orgasms. For the life of me, I haven't been able to figure it out. And no, thanks, I don't want any illustrated how-to books on the topic, even if they come from a legitimate mainstream publisher and not my best friend. Alfie may not be David Hayworth I-stepped-out-of-the-L.L.-Bean-catalog good-looking (flannel shirts, blond hair that falls over one eye, broad chest and barrel voice, skis in winter and sails in summer), but he has perfectly straight teeth, an endearing lopsided grin, and a head of thick semi-long brown hair that I love to run my hands through. He's a consummate cook, unflappable in times of stress, and well thought of at the law firm of Ollure, Munson and Mins, where he is one of five attorneys exclusively practicing divorce law.

I don't take my marriage to Alfie lightly. Where I come

from, staying married constitutes a prime, inimitable asset, considered much more important than what you do for work, what you believe, or *who* you marry. In my family, you get married to stay married. And you stayed married *not* because of love—"too frivolous," my mother always says—but on *principle*. My Grandma Lucy, of the sourdough bread, takes a more realistic view: "We don't divorce. If you're unhappy with each other, someone's got to die." Then she laughs. It's a running joke in the family on account of how many male ancestors kicked the bucket before their time, including Grandma Lucy's first husband, who keeled over one day into his dry, butterless mashed potatoes. Grandma Lucy had been working very hard to keep him alive (so she says) by feeding him heart-healthy food. On the other hand, her high school sweetheart had just moved back to town. After my grandfather Fred died, she married Frank, that same high school sweetheart, and the word is, she'd never been happier (sorry, Grandpa Fred). She fed Grandpa Frank potatoes *with* butter. You tell me: did Grandpa Fred die for lack of butter or lack of love?

"You have ten aunts and uncles," Grandma Lucy always says when she begins the story of her ten pregnancies. This included six births and four miscarriages. Despite the fact that a few of my so-called aunts and uncles were essentially tadpoles during life and death, they were all children to her. "You ought to love them all as I do," she often said. By way of explanation, when I, as a young child, pressed my mother about my mysteriously absent relatives, the phrase "died in utero" got tossed about. I spent a good portion of my childhood trying to figure out where in Iowa "utero" was.

Grandma Lucy claims fifty years of marriage to Fred—

and ten to Frank. Her mother, Great-Grandma Edwina, amassed sixty years between *her* two husbands before she died of a stroke, hanging clothes on the line, at eighty. My Great-Aunt Lilabeth was married sixty-five years, shared amongst her three husbands. Since I am newly married, I haven't had the chance to distinguish myself yet with the phenomenal feat of enduring marital contentment. On the upside, I've yet to kill Alfie.

After Grandma Lucy, Aunt Bertie is the next most formative influence in my life. Since my sixth birthday, she has lived with my family. One of her favorite pastimes is blacking out anatomical words in the dictionary—imagine my surprise when I found out my nether region was *not,* in fact, a petunia, but a VAGINA; no wait, imagine instead the surprise of my health class teacher who for the life of her couldn't keep a straight face when I confessed my shock at learning the word for the first time. Aunt Bertie changed, and directed, my life with her formidable dysfunctional presence; Lois Green with her inexplicable and dysfunctional absence. Lois Green, my biological mother. The woman who handed me over to my adoptive mother at three weeks old. Given the peculiarities of my adoptive family, I have spent my lifetime wondering if I might have been better, or at least different, had my birth mother raised me.

Thinking on my slightly deranged family while rocking lovely Lily tightened the knot of longing in my belly for a *true* family. I gently delivered Lily back into her crib. She murmured, pressed her lips rhythmically together as if dreaming of nursing, then rolled to her side, fast asleep.

"I'm going," I told Annie when I came out of the nursery. "I'm wasted."

"Thanks for staying. You made a rotten day better."

"Look on the bright side. We're closer to one another. If you moved to Meadow House, I'd have to walk for seven minutes to see you instead of five."

"Ever the optimist," Annie said, hugging me in closely.

6

Annie

September

That Saturday, I walked a screaming Hannah down the hallway from the cafeteria, where we'd feasted on breakfast Dixie style (three kinds of yogurt, seven choices for cold cereal, three for hot cereal, and fruit salad). But the fun was officially over. Lily had a diaper that needed changing; its odor wafted up in rhythmic waves timed perfectly with my stride. Meanwhile, Hannah, whose cheeks burned an enraged red, wanted candy "NOW!" which is exactly what she was screaming at the top of her lungs. Beads of sweat began to form on my upper lip from the effort of holding Lily and pulling Hannah along.

"Hannah, you must stop it. Right now!" She threw the full force of her weight at my legs, an unexpected maneuver even given her history of wrestling feats, and I slammed backward, saved from falling by the wall behind me. I grabbed her by her fat little fist and started pulling. "We will talk about that when we get home," I managed between clenched teeth. She wasn't having any of it. She catapulted her tiny body onto the floor and began to perform her best *Exorcist* imitation.

I stopped, paralyzed by my own anger and overcome with a sense of futility. Hannah's fury confounded me. Like a broken-down car, I stood in the middle of the hallway unable to move. Thankfully, this being the Saturday before classes, students were only just beginning to arrive. I had the hallway to myself, which meant, at the very least, that no one was observing my impossible child and my own incompetent parenting.

"Get up off the floor. We're going home right now to tell Daddy about this." She paused briefly. She never acts so poorly in front of Ted; I hoped the mere mention of his name would bring out her better side.

"CANDY!" Alas.

"Hannah," I knelt down beside her, trying to look her in the eye as all the experts recommend, but she'd begun to flail again. Then Lily started in. I could feel her wet backside. I didn't want to look. An exploding poopy diaper on top of a tempter tantrum seemed more than I could bear. "Hannah, look at me." She started to kick my shins. As I reached down to furiously swat her feet away with all the energy of a mother pushed over the edge, I felt the presence of another person in the hallway.

I looked up to see Cynthia Cypress in a red sundress walking toward us. She had her luxurious, thick hair pinned on the top of her head.

"Is everything okay?"

I began to answer honestly, planning to say something along the lines of "Do I LOOK okay?" when I heard something incredible. Silence. Hannah had her gaze set on Cynthia's head. Her pretty little hair clips were actually butterflies, as I could see now that she had come closer.

"I want," Hannah said, pointing to Cynthia's head.

"Do you like my butterflies?" Cynthia touched the clips. "Here," she said, taking out one at a time. "Let's see how they look on you." Hannah bolted upright at perfect attention. She made not a sound until both clips were in place.

"Thank you," I said. "I'll return them—"

"Keep them. Please," Cynthia answered, smiling first at me and then more generously at Hannah. "They do look *so* pretty on you!"

And then she walked on, leaving me, still like a broken-down car, in the middle of the hallway, unsure of what to do next, until the pungent scent of baby diaper assaulted my nose.

"Let's go home," I commanded. Hannah was already ten skips ahead of me.

"Show Daddy," said my own personal manic-depressive, now restored to her senses. "Come on, Mama," she said with a bounce and flip of her head, as if *I* had been the problem all along.

When I recounted this sordid toddler drama for Suze, I could feel my blood pressure rising.

"Honey, you're only thirty-three years old," Suze said on Sunday over lunch. Ted had gallantly offered to put the girls down to nap so I could have a much-needed mom's time-out with Suze. "You're not a broken anything."

"Motherhood is so failure-oriented, or maybe it's just Hannah. I find her verging on the impossible. I could probably handle one of those rages a month, but she loses it *every day*. I have tried everything—the calm voice, the time-out, ignoring her, sitting on her, yelling at her. She makes me crazy." I took a sip of my white wine knowing Ted would give Lily a bottle of pumped breast milk. "I can have a few good days, and then, bam! I'm back to battling my inner Mommie Dearest. As if having a physical fight with my intractable toddler weren't horrible enough, I had to do it with an *audience*. I am thoroughly mortified that Cynthia saw me hitting Hannah's feet."

"In self-defense," Suze pointed out.

"Ha! It was terrible. *I* was terrible. When Hannah acts like that, you've seen them, the tantrums can go on for upward of an hour—every time that happens, I feel completely helpless. I feel incompetent. I feel ruined. And worse, I feel like smacking her. It makes me ripping with anger." I took another sip of wine. This was not hyperbole; it was all true. Since birth, Hannah has had a special way of bringing out the worst in me. She'd been a colicky baby, the kind who screams for three hours straight while you pace the house debating whether or not to call the parental stress hotline to warn them to watch for any babies flying out of second-story windows. *Look out below!*

"You're incredible with Hannah. I've seen you with her when she gets like that. You're calm and patient and compassionate. I don't know how you do it."

"I don't do it!"

"Correction: you don't do it *all* the time. Let's be honest, Annie—most mothers have their ugly moments, some a lot worse than what you describe. You've got to forgive yourself."

"I've got to do better," I said, more to myself than to her. After Hannah's fit in the hallway, I'd spent the rest of the day, in the small increments of peace and quiet I got, looking through my burgeoning parenting library at discipline books. I took a bite of bruschetta. "I think I've figured it out."

"Figured what out?" Suze whipped out her BlackBerry and gave it a peek. "Figured out why she has these fits?"

"No. I've figured out what to do about my own inability to parent."

"Annie—"

"I have to heal my inner child."

"Okay. Where's the waitress? I need another drink."

"Seriously. I found this book on my shelf that I bought but never read: *Parenting from the Inside Out*. It's all about getting in touch with your own experience as a child and making peace with your parents and parenting your child into wholeness—" I stopped to watch Suze typing a text message. I'd completely lost her attention.

"Annie, you so have it together. I only have one parenting book and I don't think it even counts, because it focuses on childbirth." This didn't surprise me. As much as Suze loves Finnegan, she spends more time at the gym than with him, an indulgence made possible via her nanny and her disposable income. I can't tell whom this is worse for—Suze or Finny.

I flicked a crumb off my bosom. "If having a parenting library is a reflection of 'having it together,' then you're right, but I wasn't talking about that. I'd moved on. To my inner child."

"Sorry." Suze put the phone back in her Gucci bag. "I promise you have my full attention now."

"Never mind. It's not even interesting. I just want to be a better mom. I want to be patient and peaceful and gentle and calm, regardless of the volcanic toddler eruptions. And I want to be fun. I want to be the mom Hannah brings her teenage friends home to meet. When she's a teenager, of course. Also, I don't want to feel so mad at her all the time; I want to like her. And this book suggests that if you can get in touch with your own little child, your relationship with your kid will change."

Suze finished up her salad while I talked. I looked out the window at a couple of Dixbie kids walking down the street, their parents strolling beside them. The campus is a short walk from downtown Brownston; they were probably coming in for lunch after moving into their dorm rooms. A few of them lived in my dorm—Miriam Sternberg, a sophomore; Ginger Lorry, a puny, chicken-legged freshman whose face I recognized from the school directory they issue in June; and Isabella Duckley, another sophomore who, conveniently enough, did not walk but waddled. I waved.

"Annie, now you're not listening to *me*."

I turned back to Suze. "I'm sorry. What did you say?"

"I said you're the single best mother I've ever known. You're always doing interesting, creative things with Hannah. You're devoted to Lily. You're like the mother archetype."

I laughed again. "You only say that because I'm fat."

"Correction: you're voluptuous, like one of those ancient mother goddess sculptures, but that is *not* why I'm going out of my way to compliment you. It's your attitude I'm talking about. Your natural disposition with the kids. You're good at it, just good at it, the way some people are naturally good doctors, or naturally good cooks. Sometimes it feels so hard to me." And then she started to cry big, blubbering, blathering, snotty tears.

"What? Suze? What are you crying about?" I watched a tear slide down her face and drop onto her empty salad plate.

"How do you think I feel? I don't have *any* books. I don't know what I'm doing. You may not like your kid, but at least she loves *you*. Finn doesn't even like me. And sometimes," she started to choke-cry, "sometimes, when I'm playing with him, I get so bored I can't stand it, I just have to check my email. It's like an obsession. I can't think of anything else even though I know I won't have any important emails. I'm the worst mother ever!" she wailed. "I'm so bored when we're together, and you . . . at least you want to be better at it. I just want a full-time nanny."

I looked at Suze, crumpled over the table like a used-up tissue. My heart broke for her. "It's not any easier for me," I said.

"But it is!" she cried some more into her salad plate, which she was in close danger of falling completely into. "You're a natural mother. And me? I'm like a Stepford mom, I'm like one of those awful moms you read about in books who cares more about her manicure than her son."

"Suze." I reached out and put my hand on her arm. "That isn't true."

She looked up at me sharply. "Which part? Which part isn't true?"

"All of it. Any of it."

"Come on." she blew her nose into her cloth napkin. "Don't feed me lines. You and I are different. We just are.

You're good at all this stuff. You know what to do with macaroni and leftover toilet-paper tubes. You think it's fun to spend an afternoon teaching Hannah to make cookies. You can nurse Lily while cooking dinner. I ran out of breast milk for Finn on the third day! And you like talking child development. You know all the stages and the diseases and the words. When I look at you with Hannah and Lily, it looks so normal and natural and right and it makes me think Andy and I ought to have stayed DINKs."

"Suze—"

"Don't contradict me! It's all true." She set into wailing again.

"Let it all out," I finally said, looking over her shoulder at the waitress backing away from us. "You'll feel better if you let it all out." This seemed like the right thing to say; as for me, I hadn't cried in years.

That night I found myself preoccupied to the point of clumsiness at dinner, dropping not just one, but two plates of carrots, which thankfully were only carrots and so could be washed. I had to make a special effort with the bread, as I knew no one in my family, including my easygoing partner, would have anything to do with freshly rinsed bread.

Hannah, who possesses an uncanny ability to tap into my moods, especially if she senses that I am not fully present, terrorized me mercilessly.

"MY CARROTS!" she yelped during dinner when I attempted to put them back in the refrigerator. She didn't want to eat them. Of course she didn't want to eat them. Toddlers don't use things in the standard way that adults do. They don't see things as we see them. Carrots are not food. They are design implements. They are fairy wands. They are pieces of a house made for an imaginary mouse named Ubu, or whatever unusual name she can dream up.

"Hannah, I can't understand you when you scream and cry. Could you please use your big-girl words?"

"UBU'S HOUSE GONE!"

"Carrots are for eating, honey. Not for playing with."

"NOOOOO!!!!" Pan to the wide-open mouth scream. This stuff is better than Hitchcock. If you want scary, live at the will of a two-year-old.

"What's going on?" Ted came in from the bathroom.

"Mama needs a time-out, that's all. My turn in the bathroom."

"NOOOOO!!!" Thrashing. Writhing. I pictured myself turning around and going all-out Joan Crawford on her. "No carrot houses! No carrot houses!" I would scream at her, beating her with one of the baby carrots. This image gave me enough comic relief to turn my mood around.

"Do you think Ubu would like some cottage cheese to go swimming in?" I asked when I returned to the kitchen a few minutes later. Peace reigned for all of three minutes. Then Hannah threw a spoon in the air and it landed on Lily's vulnerable baby head, at which point Lily, sitting in her Bumbo seat and busy chewing on a plastic spoon, let out a maddening cry.

"Can you believe," I said, picking Lily up and jiggling her while I kissed her head, "that Suze thinks *I'm* good at this?"

"You *are* good at it."

"I'm raising a future Ted Bundy. How can you say that?"

"Ann, she's only a kid. This is the way all kids act."

"I don't think so." I sat back down, pulled my shirt up, and proceeded to nurse Lily back to comfort.

"Well, let's not talk about it right now." He looked at Hannah, who was busily giving her carrots a dunking in the cottage cheese. "After they're asleep."

"Ugh. I'm always too tired then."

We chewed in silence for a few minutes. "You are a wonderful mother," Ted said through a mouthful of food. "Just look at you."

"Never had much of a choice, did I?"

"Unexpected blessings," Ted said, gesturing toward the girls.

"I'm not complaining." I gave him a look. "Am I?"

I was sitting in the rocking chair in the nursery later that night with my feet on the ottoman, Lily and Hannah both fast asleep in my arms, when Ted came in.

"Foot rub, please," I whispered.

"What kind of greeting is that?"

"I wish I could say it was the standard one."

"Which one do you want me to take?" he asked.

"Your favorite one."

"Very funny." He picked up Hannah and gingerly placed her in her crib. I buried my head in Lily's soft, curly hair.

"Don't take this one. I like holding her."

"How else can I give you a foot rub?"

"Twist my arm, then." He picked up Lily, who whimpered, and brought her to her crib in the other nursery.

I crept out and joined Ted in the living room.

"Sit down. I'll do you," he commanded.

"You'll 'do me,' will you? Sounds good."

"I'll do your feet."

"You're a good man." He picked up a foot and started to knead it with his knuckles. "I've decided I don't like Cynthia."

"I never imagined you did."

"Oh, not just because she managed to connive her way into the house that is rightly ours, but because yesterday, when she gave Hannah those clips? I think she knew what she was doing. She meant to outshine me, to out-nice me, to show me up as an awful mother."

"Feeling a little sensitive, sweetheart?" He picked up my other foot and rubbed.

"Don't you remember I sat next to her at Nora's wedding?"

"I'd forgotten that."

"Remember how she wore a purple dress that tightened around her bottom like shrink-wrap around a hot dog? You can't have forgotten that. She might as well have worn a sign: 'Look at my perfect ass.'"

"I have no recollection of her derrière."

"Did I already call you a good man tonight?" I wiggled a big toe into his belly. "You are a good man."

I learned from Cynthia, during Nora's reception dinner last October, that she had moved from New York City. When I mentioned to her that I'd gone to the Rhode Island School of Design, she told me she'd had an ongoing relationship with the famous painter and professor Leonard Maroutte. I once took a class with Maroutte, a special workshop so expensive I had to put it on my credit card and didn't pay it off for a year. The fact that Cynthia, who I couldn't imagine had any artistic ability whatsoever (I had nothing to base this on, I just literally could *not* imagine it—maybe I didn't want to), had landed in the sack with the prestigious, aging painter boiled my blood. I agree it doesn't take that much. I've got my blood on simmer most of the time. Don't misunderstand. I didn't want to sleep with him. That whole geriatric thing turns me off. But knowing *she* had riled me all the same. When I told her about my semester abroad in Paris, she told me about her year off traveling around Europe with only a backpack. When I told her I'd once received an invitation to do a series of paintings for *Town & Country* magazine, she told me she'd dated one of the mag's editors. When I told her I became a feminist at thirteen, the same time as my mother and under strict orders, she told me she'd been one since birth.

Or something like that.

I could have enjoyed several more hours of this competitive conversation if I had not been four months pregnant and green with nausea, as well as the mother of one sleepy toddler. With the perfect reasons to excuse myself, I did.

"I can take Hannah," Ted began when I stood up to leave. I could tell he intended to be gracious, having no idea of the kind of suffering I'd endured at the hands of She Who Had Done It All Better Than Me.

"I'm tired," I said, shooting a meaningful look his way.

"Oh, you're having another baby!" Cynthia said joyfully with a long look at my belly. "Any day now! That must be so exciting. Do you feel ready?"

I looked at her—her hair, her smooth creamy skin, her nails manicured to perfection. "I imagine," I told her evenly, "that in five months, when the baby is due, I will feel ready."

She didn't even have the good graces to look ashamed, though she made a profuse apology.

"She's been out to get me from the beginning," I told Ted now, as he pulled gently on my toes.

"You are a woman who needs a hobby," he said playfully.

"Speaking of money to afford hobbies, anything come in the mail?" Ted shook his head. "What's the holdup this time?"

Ted laughed rather unhappily. "After all these years, you don't understand? She's mad at me. Besides, even when the divorce is final and we aren't paying lawyer fees, we'll have the alimony."

"*You'll* have the alimony," I clarified. "I never married that woman."

"Consider yourself lucky."

"I'm having a hard time with that right about now."

"I'm sorry." He squeezed both of my feet. "Worst mistake of my life."

"I know, I know. I'm not mad at you. I just wish I could buy the girls some clothes from somewhere that doesn't smell like mothballs. Never mind keeping up with the Brownies, I'd like to keep up with fashion trends from this decade."

"I thought you believed in buying used. I thought it was politics to you, environmentalism, the right thing to do."

"Sure it is, Ted," I said, closing my aching eyes. "Sure it is. When you have a *choice*."

7

Nora

One day in early September, Alfie and I lay side by side on the bed in a postcoital slump, the kind that ought to be blissful and sleepy but instead smacked of disappointment on both sides.

"Maybe we need to stop trying," Alfie announced into the cool air between us. I could feel him up against my arm, the big bear of his body, a comfortable, warm, embracing bear that's eaten too much honey.

"I don't want to stop trying. I want to have a baby."

"I think the pressure is getting to me." Alfie rolled over and looked at me, his thick, straight brown hair, which he wears hippie long so it slides across his face when he turns, obscuring one of his brown eyes. "You know what I mean?"

I did know what he meant, I just didn't want to talk about it. He meant our sex had lost its fun, that orgasms were harder for him, that it felt like a chore.

"You don't want a baby as much as I do."

"That's true," he said. "That's always been true. I'm happy to wait."

"Do you know how long I've waited? I've been hoping for kids since I found out about Lois."

"But together we haven't been waiting that long." He reached out and gently stroked his index finger down the top of my nose. "We haven't even been married a year."

"I'm old," I said, turning away from him, frustrated by his lack of understanding. "I don't have many chances left."

"How can you believe that?"

There were a lot of reasons to believe it, chief among them the media. In April, I would turn thirty-four, which is one year away from thirty-five, which is when you cross over that scary line into geriatric-pregnant-lady territory and your chances of giving birth to a turtle dramatically increase.

For another thing, I got married in hopes of making a baby, a *family*. Why couldn't Alfie get it?

Maybe he couldn't get it because I couldn't exactly say it. And I couldn't exactly say it because it didn't sound so good the way I thought it in my mind. I ended up saying nothing. His question lingered in the air around us like a bad smell. Enough of a stink, in fact, that it led me to Annie the next day and her packed feminist bookshelves. It was time to take action.

"What are you looking for?"

I didn't want to admit. "That book you told me about. The one that can help you get pregnant."

"Oh." She smiled, or maybe smirked, as she withdrew a large, heavy paperback from the bottom shelf. "This would be the one." She dropped it into my hands.

And that is how I found myself that afternoon giving my

cervix a feel. This, according to *Taking Control of Your Fertility*, can alert you to the signs of ovulation. I also read about studying my cervical fluid, and if this idea bothers you in any way, then think what it did to me! I'd prefer to do completely without a body, let alone having to inspect the stuff that comes out of my petunia (fluid, which up until that day I did not realize had a point). Desperation will bring you to crazy places, places you never thought you would go, places you would not dare to go, places like the interior of your vagina.

While I was trying to assess the height, shape, and level of softness of my cervix, the phone rang. Nothing like a conference call from my mother and Aunt Bertie to bring me back to reality. When they asked what I was doing, being unflappingly honest, I said: "Learning how to get pregnant. Annie loaned me a book."

"What's the big deal about getting pregnant? *I* never got pregnant." Aunt Bertie also never got married and most likely never had sex. I wasn't about to point this out. It so clearly offended her that I wanted something she'd never been lucky enough to entertain. "There's a lot more to life than children."

"I know, Be-Be." This was my childhood name for her. It generally has a softening effect.

"Why waste your breath talking to her?" my mother chided. "If you want to talk to someone who *knows*, talk to me. Bertie doesn't even like children." The truth about Aunt Bertie is that she likes children well enough. What she doesn't like is sex. She's the original, dyed-in-the-wool prude, more repressed than the Virgin Queen Elizabeth.

"Okay, then. What should I do, Mom?"

"You know what to do," came the reply, followed by one of her infamous sighs. My mother has an infinite variety of sighs—small, big, thick, thin, sweet, angry, hopeful, resigned, tired, and, the best of all, *done*. She can cover whole paragraphs with a single sigh. Never mind that she'd missed my meaning completely. I would never willingly discuss sex with my mother. I'd rather eat Styrofoam peanuts every day for the rest of my life. Whatever else my mother did during the decade that she and my father tried to have a baby, I am confident enough to bet my life that it did not include charting the consistency of her vaginal discharge.

"What you need is a doctor," Bertie said.

"Yes, that could help, I suppose. If anything can help." My mother refuses to release her own bitterness about failing in the reproductive department. She won't talk to me about Lois Green. "You're ours, and we wanted you," she's keen on saying, "So don't think another thing about it." Who couldn't think about it again? That's like putting a meal in front of someone and asking her not to eat. Given the fact that my adopted family exists in such an idiosyncratic world—if I have not made this abundantly clear, perhaps I ought to share my father's favorite pastime: taxidermy—I've always wanted to know if my birth family was more normal. Even slightly more normal would be a good thing.

"We wanted to find out if you've talked to Elle recently?" my mother said, briskly changing the topic.

"Maybe a month ago." My cousin Elle is the black sheep of our family; she became a sex therapist, and a famous one at that. "She called to talk about some work problem. Why?"

"You ought to call her," my mother said elusively. "You *know* how she's always felt so close to you." Elle claimed me for a best friend, a closeness I didn't reciprocate. Elle is the kind of person one gently refers to as "over the top."

"Okay," I said. "When I get a chance." After hanging up the phone, I headed back to the bathroom to retrieve my copy of the fertility book that I'd left splayed open on the floor so I could refer to it for guidance, although no matter how hard I tried, or how many ways I managed to squat, once even throwing my leg up on the edge of the sink in a largely ungraceful maneuver, I could not discern the productiveness of my cervix. Having always been an A student, flunking out of my own reproductive and sexual class seemed painful, ironic, and inevitable—the sure sign that no matter whose child I actually was, I belonged to the inhibited Helpsom-Fulchs.

When the phone rang some ten minutes later, I knew immediately it had to be Grandma Lucy. Her call meant, with all certainty, that, in addition to my mother, grandmother, and Aunt Bertie, Aunt Lucy (yes that's Aunt Lucy and Grandma Lucy. Grandma Lucy likes *herself* just fine), Aunt Shelley, Mrs. Marshall (my third-grade teacher and my mother's best friend, who I still, after all these years, have to call Mrs. Marshall), and Aunt Rose, Elle's mother, who, though she lives in Florida, stays in close gossiping distance through her handy iPhone, were all privy to the content of my most recent conversation with my mother, including my fertility woes.

"Sweet thing," she said when I answered the phone.

"Hi, Grandma. If you're calling to ask me to phone Elle, I promise I will."

"I'm calling about *you!*" she said with some consternation. Her six children have produced only four grandchildren; Elle and I are the only girls and have long been the recipients of my grandmother's devoted, annoying attention.

"Your mother says you've got some book about how to make a baby? No book can teach you that!"

"Actually—"

"You're not eating enough butter."

"Grandma!"

"What? You think I don't know anything? Keep in mind *I* got pregnant ten times. I did it with butter. Every time, it was butter. You're too skinny; the baby won't stick." I rolled my eyes at Fruity, who flapped her tail on the wood floor.

"Okay. I'll try butter."

"Don't be so glum. There's nothing to be glum about."

"It's just—"

"You're wibble-wobbling," she proclaimed. This is the way she describes anybody who isn't perfectly direct.

"I'm sorry."

"Say it, child!"

"Do you think some people are just luckier than others?" It felt good to blurt it out. This thought, this hidden thought that threads its way through every other thought I have about myself, began at age five when I realized I didn't come from my own parents. It cemented in my brain at sixteen when I was voted "Most Likely to Stay at Home" in the school yearbook. They made this category up especially for me. "How sweet," my oblivious mother had remarked.

"Just because I believe in lucky stars, kitten, doesn't mean I make a habit of believing in luck." Try that for a Zen koan. "But some people are *stupider* than others, and you're not one of them. You eat your butter and then get back to me. And another thing: babies don't come with a return envelope, so don't be in such a hurry to get one."

Then I spent a few minutes listening to Grandma Lucy describe the church auction. "Imagine bidding so *enthusiastically*," she said with disgust. "Like you must have it! And in the house of the Lord, no less."

After that uplifting chat, I went to the grocery store. When I came back to find Alfie reading the newspaper in the living room, I kissed him and offered to cook dinner, a chore he normally does. I put butter in the rice, butter on the fish, butter on the broccoli, and butter on the bread.

"You're trying to kill me," Alfie said pleasantly as we ate, well aware of the great Helpsom-Fulch family tradition of marriage unto death.

I woke up the next morning, checked my panties for signs of useful viscosity, then headed to the cafeteria to meet Cynthia Cypress for breakfast. I'd promised to eat with her whenever I could, my way of being hospitable and satisfying Dean Friedman's request. I'd already given her a grand tour of the grounds and she'd invited me to town one afternoon for a coffee. I'd carried out all my relations with her in stealth mode. Since I knew Annie rarely made it to the cafeteria for breakfast during the week, I didn't have to constantly look around for her like a spy from a poorly acted action movie. I didn't want Annie to see me consorting with the enemy. Although she'd done an admirable job of refraining from violence where Cynthia and Meadow House were concerned, she had no affection for the woman who'd stolen her home and made a point, every time we got together, to lambaste Cynthia.

While walking down the path toward the cafeteria, I ran

into David Hayworth, the man who didn't marry me. He let me know that Cynthia requested I meet her at Meadow House for breakfast instead.

"She's made a frittata," he said. "And baked oatmeal and fruit salad."

"Oh." I marched onward. I had nothing else to say to David. Nothing.

Indeed, Cynthia *had* made a four-course breakfast.

"Do you ever get a bug to cook?" she asked, laying out colorful woven placemats on the large butcher-block table in her kitchen. I might have answered if I hadn't been so busy looking around at her *stuff*.

"I love to collect," she said, seeing my gaze roam around the room. "And to travel." Her house made *Better Homes & Gardens* look like a dump site. Everything was beautiful to look at; everything had a place, a way of sitting or hanging, an arrangement. Rugs from India lined the floor, Moroccan bowls sat on a coffee table, above the mantelpiece a watercolor hung—not a picture of anything, but colors, pastels and a bright spark of maroon, pretty enough to wear.

I dug into the extravagant breakfast acutely aware of a running mental list of all of my inadequacies. I found myself, as now seemed to be my habit when around Cynthia, a woman of few words.

"Good," I said through a mouthful of baked oatmeal.

"I learned to make this when I lived with the Amish."

"You lived with the Amish?"

She smiled. "They're such beautiful people. I learned so much about simplicity, you know?"

I didn't know. And I didn't see anything all that simple about Cynthia's home. It's fine, of course, for people to have gorgeous houses and disposable incomes equal to my yearly salary that they use for acquiring hand-stitched throw pillows from Nepal. But Amish it is not.

"Social anthropology is a bit of a hobby," she said.

"I like dogs," I replied. Yes, moronic, yes, inarticulate, and yes, I really said it. "You know, for a hobby."

"You breed them?"

"I just like playing with them. Fruity's my dog now. Living with her is like living with a comedian. She eats sushi!"

Cynthia cocked her head, not unlike Fruity does when confused. "Is it okay for dogs to eat raw fish?"

"She's a dog," I answered, and Cynthia nodded, with what seemed to me to be the slightest touch of distaste. Perhaps Cynthia did not like dogs. And then I thought, of course she doesn't like dogs! Her house is perfect. Dogs can't live in perfect houses. Dogs have muddy feet and shed all the time and pass gas during dinner parties and you have to collect their poop in little plastic bags and carry it while you walk. Could I picture Cynthia with a poop bag? Not a chance.

I checked my watch. "I have a morning class to get to soon. You should come to our place for breakfast sometime."

"I would love that. It can get lonely being the new kid on campus." I looked at her face for signs of sincerity. I doubted her loneliness. For one thing she had David. For another thing, she had David.

"Thank you for the meal. It was incredible."

"Cooking at home relaxes me," she said. "So much better than having a restaurant."

"You had a restaurant?" I asked, incredulous *again*.

"For a while," she answered vaguely.

I helped put the dishes in the sink and then she walked

me to the door. Once I left her house, a troubling thought plagued me: I would have to return the favor. I would have to invite Cynthia to my apartment with its stacks of books and legal papers that Alfie leaves around, and not simply because I was raised to do the proper, polite thing and return an invitation, but because I had said it. I'd made the invite. I would have to make good on it. What had I been thinking?

During the following week I found multiple reasons to put off the breakfast while I furiously worked to make our apartment more attractive. I spent a good deal of time down on the bathroom floor with a toothbrush, an activity I am at least competent at, whereas I know nothing about accessorizing my couch, something I'd never thought I would even *want* to do. But there I was, a woman in search of the perfect throw for the back of our sofa and some truly viscous bodily fluid. I barely recognized myself.

One evening, during the third week of classes, Fruity whined incessantly at the door, despite the fact that I'd taken her out ten minutes earlier. As I wasn't in the mood to scrub one of my rugs another time (Cynthia collects rugs, I collect urine *on* rugs), I hooked her up to her leash and brought her outside yet again. "You're a good dog," I said, giving her a pat on the head as we walked down the stairs.

When I first found Fruity, wandering the streets of Brownston, she smelled like a compost pile. She was blind in one eye, collarless, and nothing but skeleton under her furry, matted coat. Being the ultimate softy for abandoned creatures, on account of my affinity with all orphans, I had to save her, and lucky for me dogs are allowed in dorm housing. The first time I saw her, she had a banana in her mouth, which is why I named her Fruity. If there's fruit, she'll eat it. I keep my apples on top of the refrigerator.

Fruity introduced me to Alfie—if running in front of a stranger's car and almost getting killed counts as an introduction. I don't mean Fruity almost got killed; I did. I was at the wrong end of the leash, being dragged across the street after a tossed apple core. Of course it was winter and icy, and I've never been very good on my feet.

Alfie started to cry the first time we met—on account of almost killing me, probably, but I still fancy that love at first sight choked him up. I'll never forget his words. "If I didn't have such good brakes," he said, shaking his head, while I dusted the snow, sand, and salt off the brown down coat I'd inherited from my Aunt Lucy. Alfie says he can't remember my first words to him, but he *does* remember first setting eyes on that massive, neck-to-ankle, brown coat of Aunt Lucy's. He told me on our fifth date that he thought it had the shine of a 1970s relic someone had saved in a cupboard for twenty years. "The way it looked new, pristine, and yet old and outdated at the same time," he said, clinching the deal for me. I'd already decided Alfie was the one, partly for some dishonorable reasons that had nothing to do with him, like timing, impatience, and the ticking of my biological clock. However, as it happened, Aunt Lucy *had* saved the coat in a cupboard for twenty years—although she did confess to wearing it on cold nights as a robe to save on heating costs. I took Alfie's uncanny understanding of that coat as a sign. Alfie was *it*.

I remembered all this as I walked Fruity to the backwoods, letting her sniff here and there for clues from the wild world. She stopped by a large oak tree. I stood beneath it thinking about my first meeting with Alfie, thinking about how we couldn't make a baby, wondering if I'd made a mistake, if you can really base a marriage on an ugly down coat and a starving ache to make a family, when Tabitha Hunter crept by.

"Lovely night," she said. "Feels rather magical, don't you think?" I'd always thought of Tabitha as rather magical herself, with her jet-black hair and layers of batiked, flowing shawls and dresses.

"I do love fall."

"I've just come from Cynthia and David's." Tabitha, as our honorary Queen of the School, made a point to know everyone. "Wonderful news, isn't it?"

I frowned. "News?"

"About the baby! Haven't you heard about the baby?"

I felt a pang, a deep green-eyed-evil-monster-with-a-foul-mouth-roaring-in-my-belly kind of pang. I expected to grow fangs and sprout thick hair on my arms and howl at the moon. "A baby?"

"And a springtime baby, no less. May first seems quite an auspicious day, don't you think?" I nodded. "May Day." She gave Fruity a pat on the head. "I'm off to my kitties," she said, whether to Fruity or me I couldn't tell. Blurry with envy and despair, I did not care.

8

Annie

"David isn't worth crying over," I said to Nora, who had buried her head in the corner of our sofa. Despite the dire situation, I couldn't help but ponder what sort of interesting tidbits—soggy Cheerios? broken macaroni necklaces? aging popcorn?—she was currently pressing her nose against.

"Not David," she whimpered. "Baby."

"Baby?" Hannah asked, looking up from her puzzle-making endeavor. "I'm not baby!" I could see the beginnings of a fit.

"Not you, sweetheart." I patted the soft curls on her head. "You are a big girl. Big and strong." This seemed to satisfy her. It did nothing for Nora, who continued to quietly suffocate herself on the seam of our floral couch.

Over the course of our friendship, I have witnessed many a tear from Nora.

Back in Iowa, when we were kids and bound to each other by our shared social awkwardness, me for being the fat kid, Nora for being shy and pathologically unfashionable, you can imagine the kind of popularity the two of us enjoyed; at least chubby and tablecloth-pants had each other. Crying took up a good portion of her free time, and she always used to ask why I didn't cry. Her peer worship inspired a regular bawling session. While she idolized the popular kids, I simply hated them. Cry because they ignored me? Never. I didn't want to be them. I didn't want to be friends with them. I wanted to kill them.

Now I'm not the fat kid, I'm the pleasantly plump mother. And Nora doesn't live under her mother's roof. This hasn't changed our reaction to events, however. I still get angry and never cry. Nora still weeps like a fountain.

"This *is* about David and he *is* a supreme—" I looked at Hannah, not engrossed enough in her play for me to swear in front of—"expletive." Nora answered with a whimper. Not that I needed her response to confirm the obvious.

Nora and David Hayworth dated, three years back, when she first arrived at Dixbie. Nora fell head over heels in love, the kind of swooning you see in romantic comedies, and given her rather overzealous pursuit, David responded reasonably well. He never felt quite the same, and really, who can? A woman madly in love has no equal.

Things went along for many months, Nora in a fog of bliss, David a satisfied happy, until they had been dating nearly half the year when Nora brought up the BIG issues. Every woman knows the two biggies: marriage and children. I can still remember the conversation we had, after the fact; it included the typical weeping and wailing.

"He told me if I hadn't brought up marriage, he would have. He wants to marry me!"

"That's wonderful," I'd said, perplexed. "Are you crying out of happiness?"

"No! I'm crying because he doesn't want children."

"Well, no one really *wants* children," I said. "They just seem to happen."

"Don't be funny. I don't want you to be funny right now. I feel like a gutted fish."

"Actually, I wasn't being funny. I meant what I said. He'll come around."

"He won't come around. He doesn't want them, not now, not ever. He never has. He thinks it's wrong to bring more people onto the planet. Because of the uncertain economy, or maybe he said it was bad government or the global starvation? Oh, I can't even remember!" she cried. "Don't badger me."

"Nora, I'm sorry. I'm only asking."

"I'm trying to tell you, he absolutely, positively, will not put children into his life plan."

"Adoption?"

"What?" She'd looked at me then with red-rimmed eyes and a hint of hatred, an emotion rarely seen from the Nora of my childhood, the girl who wore braids until age twenty and keeps a copy of Beatrix Potter stories on her nightstand. "Don't you know me at all?"

Ah, it was a regrettable question, though a logical one. Some people who don't want to birth children don't mind giving orphans a home. Not so for little orphan Nora, who has vowed to make it her life mission to acquire some blood kin, primarily by making babies. When we played house as children, she would steal all the dolls. "I'm going to have ten children," she once told me. "No one has ten children," I replied. And later, when we were old enough to understand our craziness, she said: "I'm so hungry for family, family I'm connected to with my *body*, I sometimes imagine giving up birth control even with the guys I don't like, just to see, just to get pregnant. You know?"

I didn't know. As an adult, I didn't want children, not right away. Famous artist came first on my to-do list; only later could I imagine knitting booties. But I did know that nothing could have made more sense coming out of Nora's mouth. She always believed non-adopted folk were luckier, that blood relatives counted in a way adopted ones don't, and that once she had babies of her own, life would miraculously change—like Sleeping Beauty waking from a dream, all her problems would disappear.

This is so far from my experience of the reality of motherhood I can't even begin to educate Nora on her misconceptions. Not that I don't think having kids is worth it. Of course it's worth it. Once you've had a baby you realize there's nothing else really worth doing. Everything else is simply filler. I believe this down to the nail of my little toe. Yet I couldn't understand Nora's *hurry* for kids. I'd salivate just thinking of her quiet house, her free time, her ability to go out with Alfie on a whim. She still enjoyed the kind of spontaneity I'd never have again. Motherhood isn't only some kind of logistical hassle similar to pet ownership, it's a whole *emotional* entanglement. Did I want Hannah to eat ice cream for dinner the other night? No, of course not. I wanted her to eat a few carrots first. And a piece of turkey. Did I feel like the world's worst mother for shooing her out of the house with Ted on a regular basis? You better believe it. Is that even realistic? To judge myself for such a small infraction? Of course not. Hence, the emotional bondage I'm talking about. Janis Joplin didn't know what she was singing. Freedom's just another word for nothing's come out of your uterus.

Nora pulled herself out of my gross sofa cushions. "Why? Why would he have a baby with her and not with me?"

"It's been a few years. Maybe he came around, changed his mind, saw the beauty in family."

"They've only been married a few months! That means they started trying right away. He lied to me! He lied to me because he didn't want to be with me. I've never felt so horribly betrayed in my life. The *only* reason I broke things off was because of the baby issue. If I'd known, if I'd thought for one minute that he would relent, I never . . ." She sobbed again.

"Mama," Hannah interrupted brightly. "I peed on the floor."

"Oh, Hannie!" I stared down at the wet spot on the rug with a sinking heart. On Hannah's own request, I'd bought a potty from the consignment store and put it in the bathroom. I let her go around the house without diapers. "Let's get you cleaned up." I recovered my compassion, lifted her up into my arms, and stroked Nora's head on the way out of the living room. I stopped myself short of saying something trite and true like "life sucks" or "we all have it hard" because I knew it wouldn't help. On the other hand, life sucks and we all have it hard. When I came back to the living room all dolled up in rubber gloves with some paper towels and rug cleaner, Nora had left, and the empty room smelled like the toilet bowl in a fraternity house.

I scrubbed the rug while Hannah shouted to me from her potty seat, the place I'd left her. I'd cleaned up similar accidents four times that week.

"Hannah," I said, once back in the bathroom. "I think you need to use diapers again."

"No, Mama," came her firm reply. "I'm big girl."

"But sweetheart, you can't keep peeing on the rug."

"Lily wears diapers. Not Hannie."

"It's okay to wear diapers. You're not even three yet! Lots of kids your age wear diapers. I even know a four-year-old who wears them!"

"But I'm spe'cal, Mama," she said, standing up from the little potty and giving herself a wipe. "I'm spe'cal 'cause I'm yours."

I kneeled down beside her, pulling her soggy pants off her fat legs. "Now that, my dear, is the absolute truth."

"Nora wants a baby," she said next, hopping beside me like a bunny on speed. "Can you give her one?" she added before running bare-bottomed down the hallway.

Leave it to an impossible child to ask the poignant question. I *wished* I could give Nora a baby, rub up against her and pass on my exuberant fertility genes. Occasionally I even wished I could give her one of my two. Now that I have two children, I'm more able to accurately reflect on how much more logical it is to simply have one! But here again, I am the "luckier" one, so how can I complain?

I'll tell you how, as I sit stuffed into my tiny apartment while Cynthia enjoys her three thousand square feet, I can long for a clean slate. I had imagined Meadow House would be just that, a new beginning for Ted and me, a real home, a home that would come at the same time as his divorce pa-

pers. We would finally be a family. Nora may be busy aching
for a blood connection; all I want is a legal document.

That night I passed a peaceful hour with my *WSJ,* and then
Ted, fresh from a shower, snuggled in with me and destroyed
all the positive effects of the miserable news I'd read with a
single sentence:

"My family wants to do Thanksgiving at our place." He
said the words like a dying man.

If I'd known this was coming, I would have eaten the entire quart of Oreo-cookie ice cream for dinner.

"Only for one night." Ted doesn't like his family any more
than I do, not that there's anything unlikable about them. To
the contrary, they're exceedingly, excessively nice, like sales
clerks who really, really want you to buy something.

"All of them?" I asked, rhetorically, of course, because
Ted's family only visits en masse. In fact, they only do everything en masse. They take vacations together. They spend
every birthday together. They conveniently all went into the
same profession. Ted's father, George, is a doctor. His mother,
Betty, is a doctor. His brother, Stetson, is a doctor. Who married a doctor. Just gag me now. His sister, Lindy, is a doctor.
But wait! She married . . . a doctor!! And his youngest
brother, Laithe, is finishing up his residency. In pediatrics.

That would make seven adults traveling to visit us, and
three children: Hillary, Stetson's daughter, and Alison and
Aaron, Lindy's twins. None of them seem to have recovered
from the shock of Ted's defection. (A teacher is not a doctor.
A teacher is nowhere near as important as a doctor.) Nor can
they comprehend me. They're awfully nice to me; they just
don't understand anything but medicine. I, for example,

studied art. But we don't talk about art over the family dinner table. We talk about medicine and sickness and surgery and hospitals. They have the distinct ability to make me feel profoundly alone and completely foreign.

"I'm sorry," Ted said, still hiding behind the comfort of his arm.

"Why do they have to come here?"

"You know how they are. They like to travel to wherever the youngest grandchild is. They think they're doing us a favor, so we don't have to drive so far with Lily."

"If they spent Thanksgiving in the local sanitarium, *that* would be doing us a favor."

"You are a long-suffering wife. How about some nonfertilizing sex to improve your mood?"

"As long as I can go first." I looked at the clock. "And it has to take less than ten minutes. I need a minimum of six hours of sleep tonight."

"I can't properly perform cunnilingus in under ten minutes."

"I doubt that, soldier. You are the master." He looked at me sheepishly. God, I love him. He threw off the covers and nuzzled between my legs.

But instead of the usual ripples of pleasure and waves of ecstasy, I kept getting flashes of Cynthia and Meadow House, then Hannah throwing a tantrum, then our bank statement.

"You're not into it." Ted looked up at me.

"How can you tell?"

"First clue? You're silent. Second clue? You're stiff as a board."

"Sorry, honey. It's not you." I slid my hand through his hair. Ted rested his head on my thigh. "I think I'm not happy.

I think I'm going to try therapy. Did I tell you that yet? I need to get in touch with my inner child."

"You aren't happy? I don't get it." Then Lily cried out, her voice shrill over the monitor. We both held our breath, hoping she'd go back to sleep. We could only wait a minute; Hannah's such a light sleeper any noise can wake her.

I pulled on my pajama bottoms and stood up.

"Hey, honey," Ted said, flat on his back now, looking at the ceiling.

"What?"

"I got a call from the attorney. She's back in the hospital. We have to keep waiting on the papers."

"Wow." I stopped in the doorway. "You know how to make it pour when it's raining, don't you?"

I pondered this while I nursed Lily. I haven't gained much in the way of profound wisdom in my thirty-three years, but I can offer with absolute conviction one universally true piece of advice: don't be someone's second wife. My own mother was my father's third wife, a condition I avoided like a terminal disease, in part because my father went on to have a fourth wife, leaving my mother to drown herself in an ongoing parade of feminist revival meetings, women's groups, and male-bashing in the great tradition of Andrea Dworkin. But then, Ted is nothing like my father. His first marriage was a mistake, albeit a stupid one. Not that falling in love and getting married at twenty-two is so unreasonable; I can understand it completely. But this *woman*, his wife and someday-to-be ex-wife, makes me seem like the Dalai Lama. Instant refresher course on my personality: I am a curmudgeon, which, though I know little about religion, must be the antithesis of a Buddhist peace leader.

This woman, the source of our financial devastation, is Aileen Scrudger, pronounced Ah-leen, not to be confused with the more ordinary and useful name Eileen. Ah-leen is a pit bull among women. I've longed for years to send her a book called *Letting Go*. She has held onto her marriage to Ted like Norman Bates holds onto his mother in *Psycho*. Way. Too. Long. The years of attorneys' fees and legal charges and waiting have aged me more than Hannah. Every time she gets ready to sign the papers, she uncovers a new problem in the paperwork or acquires a new ailment that prevents her from signing them.

I carefully placed Lily back into her crib, made a pit stop in the bathroom, then curled back up in bed with Ted, who had turned off his light.

"I thought you would be happy to at least know not to wait on the papers right now."

"Should I be happy? I'll be happy when it's over. Besides, we won't have any more money when she signs the papers, will we?" Ah-leen was hell-bent on a monthly chunk of alimony that would decimate Ted's teaching salary.

After an oceanic pause, Ted said, "No."

"Then I won't be happy. I'm not happy being poor because Ah-leen thinks she deserves something for putting you through graduate school and because she's pretending to have chronic hypochondria syndrome."

"Chronic fatigue."

"That's what I said."

"At least we can get married once it's over. Unless you've changed your mind."

"Unlikely," I said, pressing up against him. "I've wanted to marry you since the day I saw you in the dentist's office asking for a floss recommendation."

"Romantic, Annie."

"So is alimony. And divorce and separation and court and crazy ex-wives."

"I only have one ex-wife," he pointed out.

"Thank goodness for that or we'd be living under the bridge!" A knock came, strong and insistent. I looked at the clock. "Eleven o'clock. Someone must be crying. I'll go. They always want me at this time of night. And to think we haven't even had time to talk about Nora yet. I wanted to fill you in."

"I know about David and Cynthia," he said, rolling over as I got out of bed and grabbed my bathrobe. "I imagine she's livid."

"More like limp with tears. Nora doesn't do anger." The knock came again, this time more hesitant. "Here I come," I said, opening the door.

Ginger, that new freshman from Connecticut with the bony legs and freckled face, stood on my doorstep looking all of ten years old, though she was fourteen. Eyes red and blotchy, she sniffed, "Can we talk?" before she burst into tears.

"That's what I'm here for," I said, leading her into the kitchen and putting on the kettle.

It didn't take much sobbing for me to figure out that Ginger feared she'd made a mistake coming to Dixbie. Over the years we'd had our fair share of homesick students. Being away from home at fourteen isn't easy for any of the kids, even the ones who eagerly left their oppressive parents in the dust kicked up from their designer shoes as they headed alone to the dorms. I wouldn't mind being oppressed by wealth. Anyhow, Ginger did not fall into this category; instead, she was making a home for herself in the "squeaky wheel" department by spending long hours on her cell phone in the hallway where everyone could hear and crying to her mother about the insufferable nature of communal life. "I don't even shower alone!" she wailed at one point, leaving Ted and me in stitches of hysteria imagining her mother's response. We expected the "what kind of place is this?" phone call to come next and were well prepared to show Mrs. Lorry that every shower is an individual unit but that the showers happen to be in the *bathroom,* which is used by other students. Mrs. Lorry never called—which might be the problem. Boarding school, with a disinterested parent, can seem like far too much neglect to be benign, no matter how many interesting classes you take.

I microwaved some popcorn for Ginger and let her watch some TV. She clung to me like a baby possum when she hugged me good-bye.

"You make me miss my mother," she said into my upper arm. Then she pulled away. "Which is funny because she isn't anything like you at all. She's not around much. She's a pediatric oncologist. Also, she's not so into hugs." And then she finally left, and for a moment I felt sorry for her, for all the girls like her, and grateful—big, fat, obesely grateful—that I had my girls with me day in and day out, that I had the job no one seemed to care about—that full-time mother gig—except the small people who find it so handy to have a mother around to torture.

9

Nora

October

As far as I can tell, nobody, not even the most hardened criminal—not that I've ever *met* a single criminal of any kind, hard or soft and no fair counting my grandma who may well have innocently used and misused butter—wants her dog to die.

On the other hand, I want to get pregnant.

I know the mere thought is unforgivable. I should be jailed by the ASPCA. I should be forced to do community service work cleaning out dog cages at area shelters for the rest of my life. They should have a picture of my face at every dog rescue organization, followed by a line of bold print: DO NOT LET THIS WOMAN ADOPT A DOG.

I took Fruity out for a walk after coming back from Annie's, where I'd wept my heart out over the treachery of David Hayworth. The air had finally begun to change. The extra wiggle in Fruity's backside personified the transition; the brisk air always perks her up. We stood there together, sniffing the cool evening breeze. To pass the time while she rooted for just the right place to do her business, I began to ponder big, existential life questions like why men are jerks, why I'm a fool, and why other people get children and I, for all my trying, don't. While I know it's true that many other people have kids and pregnancies, including Annie, who doesn't have the sense to be grateful for her unexpected good fortune, I kept thinking of Cynthia until it seemed likely that she was the only pregnant person to ever walk the face of the earth, the emblem of pregnancy, the reason for pregnancy, the symbol for all things big, round, and fertile.

This doesn't exactly help make obvious the connection between my failure and Fruity, but then, given the nature of my thoughts on the great mysteries of the world, logic has no place. One moment, I couldn't stop thinking about Cynthia and David, and really what I meant was Cynthia having the baby *I* ought to have had with David, or to be concise, *my baby*, and the next I looked at Fruity with a murderous gaze.

On the off-chance that I actually did kill my own dog, I'm sure I couldn't explain this in a court of law and be acquitted by a jury. Still, I want to defend my good, nice name by attempting to describe my train of thought.

First it requires knowing that Cynthia and David married in June in one of those glorious mountaintop ceremonies where the sun sets at the exact moment vows exchange. Or so I imagine. Unlike me, David didn't invite the entire Dixbie faculty. In fact, none of us were invited. They sent out an announcement card after the fact. I used the thick paper one day in July to kill a fly.

Then you have to know that I stared down at Fruity's thick brown fur back while she dropped a bomb, reaching into my bag for a plastic baggy to do the dirty work. And as I bent over and held my breath, knowing that picking up poop is just part of what you do when you have a dog, when you love and care for an animal, the way getting up in the night is simply what happens when you have an infant, it came to me, *wham,* like lightning straight to my brain. Fruity is my cosmic placeholder for a baby.

I tripped over myself running to the dorm to share my inspiration with Alfie.

"You're going to have to explain that one."

"Well, it goes like this. You have to let go of one thing before you get another. It's kind of like the law of life. I've already got a baby, a furry canine baby, but you know what I mean."

"Where do you get these theories?"

"Are you forgetting how I grew up? That Grandma Lucy once heard you could die if you wrote your name in red pen and hasn't touched a red pen since? That Aunt Bertie had one suitor, her only chance, and didn't marry him because he smelled like fish sticks and she only eats fish on Friday? And, if you recall, that she would only go out with him on Friday? Or that my Aunt Lucy really did make her son wear garlic cloves at night during the winter so he wouldn't get a cold?"

He laughed again. "Yeah, but I always thought you were the sane one."

"I am!"

"And what about Cynthia?" he asked.

"What about her?"

"Who died so she could get pregnant?"

"Oh." I hadn't stopped to consider this. "That's a really good question. I have no idea. I don't know anything about her, actually, now that you bring it up. I don't even know how

she met David or what her parents do or where she went to
college, which doesn't make sense. We've been spending so
much time together."

Alfie smiled indulgently at me. "What have you two
talked about?"

"I don't know. I guess about Dixbie. She told me a lot
about her furniture and where she traveled to buy it."

"You're in luck then," Alfie said, patting the sofa beside
him to urge me to sit down. "She invited you to a tea party."

"What?"

"While you were out, she stopped by and—"

"Who? Cynthia?"

"Yeah, and she gave me this." He held up a smooth creamy
envelope, but I didn't care. I looked around at the living room
in desperation, in despair, in horror. I hadn't done much in
my home renovating/reorganizing efforts and on that particular day, since Alfie had been working from home, our living room had the slovenly feel of a teenage boy's den. I froze
with mortification.

"Did you invite her in?"

"What? Sure. You think I made her stand in the doorway
like a Jehovah's Witness?"

"I always let the Jehovah's in," I said. And I do. It doesn't
seem very nice not to. "But that's not my point."

"What *is* your point?" Alfie asked, now very confused.

"Did she sit on the couch?"

Alfie cocked an eyebrow and turned his head slightly. "I
don't think so. She wasn't here for long. Are you worried
about something?"

"Not really," I said, not at all wanting to explain to Alfie
how embarrassed I was at the state of our apartment given

the immaculate, harmonious nature of Cynthia's decorating prowess. I stopped short of asking whether she'd seen the bathroom, the only room I'd finished beautifying. And even then, I doubt my efforts would have impressed her unless she tripped, fell on the floor, and found herself at eye level with the foundation of the toilet.

"Do you want the invitation? It's for a tea at her place."

"A tea?"

"Tea party. Same thing." He put his big feet up on the coffee table and reached for the remote. For a moment, I didn't like him. I knew with certainty that David Hayworth wouldn't put his feet up on an imported native wood table from Peru. Then I realized how ridiculous I'd become, with my idea of cosmic placeholders and dislike for my perfectly adequate husband and our comfortable home. Only simultaneously, I decided I *wasn't* ridiculous, that I was justified, that David had no right to have a baby with Cynthia, that Fruity had no place taking up my future baby's spot, and that my husband had no sense putting his feet on our coffee table, despite the fact that I picked it up at Ikea ten years ago.

I took the invite from Alfie and held it in my hand. A good half-hour later, during a commercial break, he asked, "Going to open it?"

"Not yet," I said, noncommittally. I wanted to open it alone.

After freshman English class the next day, I came across Annie, Lily, and Hannah in the cafeteria. Hannah consumed herself with begging for frozen yogurt from the school's brand-new machine, while Lily perched on Annie's hip sucking placidly on a pacifier.

I had made up my mind not to mention the tea party to Annie, given her low tolerance for Cynthia, when Annie startled me by announcing that she had received an invitation.

"I guess she fancies herself the queen of England."

"I'm invited also."

"Well, I hardly assumed she'd only invited me. I think she invited a number of people." Annie narrowed her eyes to slits. "Nora, you thought she'd only invited you, didn't you? Like a date."

"I did not."

"Some things never change."

"What are you saying?"

"I'm saying, you've always liked the popular kids, the beautiful ones, and fell all over yourself in front of them."

"I'm an adult now," I protested. "And Cynthia is new here. She doesn't know many people. Besides, she's a perfectly likable person. She's not snotty or stuck-up at all."

"I don't happen to hold the same opinion."

"But you are going to the tea, aren't you?"

"On the basis of curiosity alone."

Hannah, who up until this point had shrieked rather quietly, hauled off and smacked Annie in the shin, presumably a reprimand for failing to listen to her request. I watched Annie's face change. Confusion came first, then a pink of embarrassment—after all, we were in the middle of about fifty students all eating and milling about, as well as a dozen faculty members—then fury. She knelt down and whispered something in Hannah's ear.

"I've got to get her home," she said, straightening up. "I guess I will see you at the tea."

"Of course."

"David will be there," she said meaningfully.

"Of course!" I wasn't a fool. Or maybe I was a fool.

Since hearing of Cynthia's pregnancy, I periodically, if every ten minutes could fall under that heading, imagined some fated retribution for David. Nothing big. Maybe a tiny disaster that would throw him off balance. I didn't want him to head to the fiery pits of hell; I merely wanted a *little* suffering. A broken leg? A broken car? Cynthia leaving him for another man? I still had some work to do fine-tuning the details.

I felt tears prick my eyes, then begin to seep. The thought of crying in the cafeteria didn't appeal to me. "I'll walk with you," I said to Annie. "I can carry Lily."

"Oh, good friend!" She passed the baby over. "Now I can carry my little terrorist." She picked up a much subdued but still pouty Hannah.

"What did you say to her?" I asked.

"That if she hit me again she'd never eat anything sweet for the rest of her life." And then, once we were outside, she asked, "Are you crying?"

"Allergies."

"No point lying to me. I happen to know you don't have allergies."

"PMS. It always makes me weepy."

"For more reasons than one," she said.

"I'd prefer if you didn't rub it in."

"I'm just trying to be supportive."

"I don't want support," I said. "I want a baby."

We had talked this way our whole friendship, a pressing kind of banter, skirting the edges of friendliness. It was the hallmark of our friendship, but because of it I knew we didn't

lie to one another. In fact, in many respects, Annie's direct-
ness pushed me forward in good ways. I'd like to think I'd
done the same for her, though I was never as brazen and
caustic and sassy as she. However much we bickered, I cher-
ished her. She was my go-to person, the holder of my history,
my bestest friend.

"Then what?" Annie said, exasperated. At first I couldn't
tell if her exasperation was with me or with Hannah, who
was too heavy to be carried and wriggling in her arms. "What
will happen once you get this baby you want so much? Do
you think your life will all of a sudden get easier? Do you
think you'll magically begin to have orgasms and better taste
in clothes?"

"Annie," I began, ready to reel her in. Really, there was no
reason to be unkind.

"I'm serious! Is this what you want?" She stopped on the
path. "You want this life? Crabby kids and no time for yourself and no money to buy nice clothes? Is this what you've
been pining away for all these years? Some person not even
two feet tall making sure you realize on a regular basis that
you aren't half as good a person as you thought you were?"

"I don't—"

"And do you think it will magically change your marriage? If you think a baby will bring you and Alfie closer together, then you haven't been paying attention! You'll be
tired. Being tired will make you angry. Being angry will make
you tired. Being tired will make you hopeless. Being hopeless
will make you angry." We were still stalled on the path. Annie
let Hannah slide down her body onto her own feet. Hannah
stared up at her mother with a look of fascination. "And that's
your dream! Don't you have the imagination to dream of

something less provincial? Every woman in her almost mid-thirties wants a baby. It's so cliché. I expect more of you, Nora, and yet you are a broken record, lusting after a disaster." Annie ended on a high note, what sounded like a squelched sob. I could count on one hand the times I had seen her cry over the twenty-eight years of our friendship. Come to think of it, I could count on one finger.

"Annie." I reached over to her. Since she spent so much time being pissed off, I expected tirades from her, usually about politicians and other people. Rarely did she strike out at me.

"I'm sorry." She grabbed Hannah's hand and pried Lily out of my arms. "I didn't mean all that. This isn't about you. I think I need to get home."

"Annie," I called to her backside. "You don't have to go. I'll carry Lily." She neither looked back nor stopped. "You can talk to me," I said, loudly enough for her to hear, but she kept walking.

When I thought about it later, I decided it was rather selfish of Annie to have a breakdown when *I* had the real problems. Not that I don't get how hard motherhood can be. She's been telling me all about it since Hannah's birth. Even before her birth, Annie spouted off about the woes of pregnancy, particularly as hers was an unplanned one. And Hannah is a handful, but Lily is darling and low-maintenance. Besides, Annie has Ted, who, in addition to adoring her and making a regular habit of showing it, helps tremendously with the girls.

No, she stole my thunder. She should have known better. She was suffering a hard day, whereas I have substantial issues to contend with. Sure, it's hard to have a toddler yell at you; on the other hand, she *has* a toddler. And beloved mate. Not that I don't have one. Not that I don't love the one I have. But David. Having a baby.

David Hayworth looks like an underwear model. He can go three days without shaving. His skin, baby soft, tans to a cinnamon-roll brown in the summer, when he spends his days sailing and swimming. He tried to teach me to ski the winter we were together, a humiliating experience that involved my landing face-first on another skier's bottom. There's more, but I'd rather not talk about it.

I walked back to the cafeteria, checking my watch. I had ten minutes before my next class. I wanted a frozen yogurt. I took it and ate it outside by myself. Some of my students walked by and waved. I felt particularly obvious in my aloneness, almost spinsterly, almost like Aunt Bertie. I spooned it down quickly, savoring the sugary cold. When I finished, I dumped the cup in a garbage can on my way to class and thought: What if it doesn't happen? What if Annie is right? What *am* I waiting for? What if I never get my baby? Then what? Regrettable thoughts coupled with my massive, speed-eaten dessert. I felt sick throughout my second freshman English course of the day. I left in the middle of the class to use the restroom, not surprised to find my period had come, and that it didn't make me sad, as it usually does. It made me angry.

10

Annie

Meg Stauffer's office smelled of patchouli. The walls of the waiting room, royal purple, made a nice backdrop for a variety of black-and-white fine-art photographs of random body parts. So far, I liked her.

Of course, I'd yet to meet her. In three minutes—presumably she had me waiting until the exact moment the clock struck six—our session would begin. Despite my unwed status, Dixbie had been giving me partner benefits since Ted and I moved on campus. Through our insurance carrier, I got ten free therapy appointments a year. I figured this would be far more than I would need. Surely my inner child was not buried that deep; four or five ought to do.

I had called the insurance company and asked for a list of therapists in the greater Boston area. "Also," I told the chipper twenty-something on the phone, "I want only women on the list. And feminists."

"Excuse me?"

"I'm looking for a female, feminist therapist."

"Um."

I held back on saying, "Do you need me to spell that for you? F-e-m-i-n-i-s-t," as I heard her typing away in the background. "We don't have that specialty."

"There has to be one therapist in the greater Boston area with those credentials."

"I can search for 'women's issues,'" she replied.

"Can you define that for me?"

"Of course!" She seemed relieved to know something. "Anorexia, bulimia, compulsive overeating, anxiety, depression, divorce, insomnia, menopause, fertility complications, and separation."

"Right, then," I said, much more depressed than I had been when I phoned. "Why don't you simply give me the list of every female therapist within driving distance who accepts the insurance. I'll do the rest myself."

And so I did. I called two dozen different numbers and listened to two dozen different answering machines until I heard a voice that didn't make me want to run away screaming. Honestly, am I going to see a therapist who has a voicemail message that makes me feel worse after listening? Some of those women need to get in touch with their own inner child.

Meg Stauffer's message had a lightness to it, as though she'd recorded it while in a mild hurry before running off to take a hike, eat tofu, and spend the evening in quiet meditation. In addition, when I located her on the insurance's website, her brief listing contained a bio and a picture. Her bio included the words "specializing in women's empowerment." That was about as close as I was going to get to feminist.

I had yet to decide if the fact that she had an immediate opening boded well or ill. On the one hand, it could mean she was a very bad therapist and didn't have enough clients. On the other hand, she might simply have heard the desperation in my voice and, being supremely compassionate, taken pity on me.

I left a dubious Ted at home with two cranky children. "Do you really think this is what you need?" he'd asked, a question I'd already asked myself. Only coming from him, it hit me as arrogant. Not that I'm mad at Ted. Ted is the person I would have with me on a desert island. Ted is the man in my ship; we're floating in the same boat. He's my soul brother. He didn't like the idea of me pouring out my woes to someone other than him. He likes to solve my problems.

And I didn't entirely know what I was doing myself, sitting there, studying Meg's bookshelf, quite pleased to see a copy of *Our Bodies, Ourselves* proudly displayed. I took this as an omen that I had done the right thing.

At exactly six, she opened the door. I have never been keen on perfect punctuality, as it seems to go hand in hand with a rather boring and rule-abiding nature. However, she smiled at me warmly, her long gray hair pinned on the top of her head with several bobby pins, her purple sneakers peeking out from underneath an ankle-length black skirt.

"Come right in, Annie," she said, as though I'd come for dinner. "Make yourself at home." I loved her instantly. She sat down in a purple armchair and gestured toward an abundant blue couch with sinking cushions and far too many throw pillows, many clearly ancient. I sat across from her, deep in the sofa, and felt as though I'd been hugged. So there. Therapy had already done it to me and I had yet to open my mouth. Perhaps my inner child would require only one session.

Given my raging lunatic of a mother, and the *War of the Roses* divorce she and my father went through during my childhood, you might peg me for a perfect therapy candidate. My mother never impressed upon me the importance of talk therapy save in a group setting; she strongly believes in women's groups of all kinds. At any given time, she belongs to at least five different ones. "Women at Midlife," "Women Healing from Divorce," "Women Without Men," "Women Who Hate Men," and so on. Once, during college, I suggested she become a lesbian, as this seemed the most logical choice for a woman who had nothing positive to say about the opposite sex and spent all her time in the company of females.

"Don't think I haven't tried it," she replied. "I can't do with the sex. Muff-diving simply doesn't suit me. I like to think of myself as a nonpracticing lesbian."

Right, so, maybe I *should* have taken myself in for psychological help at that point, but nothing seemed to be the trouble. In fact, I don't feel I've had many troubles in my life that require professional attention. In that way, my mother's tirades on the hardships of life have served me well. I did not grow up imagining I ought to feel happy and sunny all the time or live a life where everything worked out. I feel bad for people who expect more; it must be so disappointing. Life with a rain cloud as a parent is excellent preparation for adulthood.

Not until Hannah did it even occur to me that I had anything to fix. Even with all the troubles Ah-leen brought to the table, I didn't feel a need for assistance. Ted has always been a love-doll, not to mention a loyal friend, a confidante, and the first person to hear any interesting story I possess; and Nora, my almost sister-friend, the second. Talking to them is free. But Hannah holds a mirror up; Hannah *is* a mirror, reflecting back all variety of unsavory personal characteristics I must have possessed all along but only now have become aware of.

I wanted to tell Meg all this, though I had no idea where to begin.

"Can I tell you a little bit about how I work?" she said, leaning forward slightly in her enormous armchair. She wore a large broach on her purple embroidered coat, an emerald turtle.

"Please," I said. "I've never done this before and I'm almost hoping to get out of here without having to talk at all." She didn't smile. She laughed.

Saturday afternoon when we walked to Meadow House together, neither Nora nor I brought up my outburst from the other day. I didn't know what to say, and she couldn't stop obsessing about her pants. She might as well have been on her way to the guillotine. I had to tell her in no uncertain terms, a dozen times, that not only were her dark, plaid wool pants *not* awful, I loved them, just absolutely loved them!

"I couldn't find anything else. But will they work for a tea?"

"Nora." I held up my hand like a stop sign. "Cynthia will not even notice your pants."

"Have you noticed *her* clothes? Her clothes are beautiful."

"Money."

"And taste."

"She's a show-off," I said.

"How can you say that?"

"Don't you remember that I sat next to her at your wedding, where she went on about all her accomplishments like we were dueling for the best-life award?"

"I don't remember that. She's actually quite reserved. Could you have confused her with someone else?"

"Nora, you've seen the woman. How would that be possible? Besides, I have a clear recollection of cursing you for seating me next to her. I yelled at you in the bathroom. You told me not to yell on your wedding day. You said 'even coming from a tired, sick pregnant woman' it was unacceptable."

Nora laughed. "I would *never* say anything like that."

"My dear friend, you don't speak like that to anyone but me, but if you think all I get from you is the nicey-nice stuff, you are sorely mistaken."

"At any rate, I hardly sat you two together on purpose. The invitation went out to David Hayworth *and guest.*" Nora swallowed nervously. "Have you seen her house?"

"You've got the memory of a new mother. Of course I've seen her house! I got the grand tour when I went to find out why she was in *my* house."

"Everything she has is beautiful."

"Would you stop going on about her? I'm getting sick to my stomach."

"I hope David's not there."

"Nora, he lives there. He's going to be there. You haven't had a problem with him for the past two years. Why start now?"

"I didn't have a problem with him before because *I* broke

off with him so I could find a man to marry who wanted kids. Now that's all changed. I feel belatedly humiliated."

"That seems like the world's worst waste of time and energy," I said as we approached Meadow House. "You must have better things to do than retroactively getting upset."

"Like fight with you?"

"I'm sorry about the other day. I didn't mean what I said. If it makes you feel any better, I talked about it in therapy."

"You've actually gone? You've gone already? Why didn't you tell me? Aren't I supposed to be the second one to know things, after Ted?"

"Yes," I said, taking her hand and giving it a squeeze. "And only you and Ted know about my psychologist. Okay?"

Before I could tell Nora more, Cynthia opened the door with a broad, animated smile. She'd swept her hair up on the top of her head and stood resplendent in her signature red, this time a bold flowing blouse over dark blue jeans. Red shoes, too, embroidered with yellow flowers. She towered above me in heels I wouldn't even wear if I took a night job as a hooker.

"Roger Vivier," she said, noticing me staring agape at her shoes. "I adore them. He's my favorite designer."

I was wearing Birkenstocks. And wool socks. Nora had on Keds.

I don't know Roger Vivier from Stephen King, though Suze kindly informed me later in the week that he's a famous shoe designer. Let's not even get into how many starving children could be fed by Cynthia's footwear. No, I changed my mind. Let's get into it. African continent, anybody?

Cynthia led us into the kitchen.

"I'm afraid no one else could come," she said rather quietly. "It must have been a bad time of day."

"David?" I asked, on Nora's behalf.

"He's got the boys' track team this afternoon." Then, more
happily, "We'll have fun anyway. I like an intimate gathering.
Come see my teas."

An array of teas lay artfully lined up on the counter. When
I say teas, I don't mean small boxes wrapped in cellophane
that she picked up at the local grocery store for three dollars
a pop. And I don't mean a choice of four flavors that any normal person might possess in her kitchen cupboard. I mean:
she grows herbs, harvests them, dries them, mixes them,
bags them, and *voilà!* Cynthia Cypress tea in a wealth of va-
rieties and preciously, delicately wrapped in clear baggies
with silky ties.

To be fair, a condition I have no interest in being, three of
the choices were in fact not homemade. Maybe to make up
for this horrific failure on her part—condescending to *buy*
such a thing as tea!—she'd baked several dozen types of cookies. But no, of course I don't hate the woman. That would be
so small of me.

"I love to collect," she told us. "I have a teacup collection."
She served us tea in two of her collected cups, both of which
she'd made herself during a pottery class.

"It's practically iridescent!" Nora cooed over her cup. "It
sparkles like a diamond." I made a face at her. She ignored me.

We spent a good deal of time talking about Cynthia's art,
her trip to Kenya where she worked in a slum, and how difficult it was going to be for me to wrench the halo off her
golden head (not really, but I thought of bringing it up).
Nora, as she sometimes does when she's anxious, talked far

too much and far too quickly about absolutely nothing. She has that Home Shopping Network gift for talking paragraphs about irrelevant topics; I think she spent a good five minutes remarking on the wood grain on the table. Finally, we branched out into new conversational venues when Cynthia asked, "How long have you been married?"

I waited for Nora to answer the question. "Annie?" Cynthia said.

"Oh! Ted and I? Well—"

"They aren't actually married," Nora said, taking over in the most unfortunate and insulting way. "They haven't been able to get married, not yet, though you plan to, don't you? And it's not her fault. See, Ted has another wife, or anyway, he has a first wife. Is that what you call her? And they haven't divorced yet. But they are separated. That doesn't sound very good. Maybe you should explain, Annie, I'm making it sound much too complicated when you two really love each other and so it doesn't even matter and marriage is merely a technicality, don't you think?"

I noticed that Cynthia's eyebrows lifted just the slightest.

"What Nora means to say is that our situation has some garden-variety snags." I kicked her under the table.

"Life is so messy," Cynthia said in a sympathetic way that made me feel like a toddler who peed in her bed.

"Ted and Annie are perfect together," Nora said, struggling to make things better. "They've been together for four years and they still act like newlyweds." She looked at me and bit her lip. "Or whatever the equivalent is when you haven't been married?"

I'm a lay-it-all-out-on-the-table kind of girl. I don't hide things. I'm not shy. I'm not embarrassed. This happens to be, however, one area of my life that I don't shout about. Not that there's anything wrong with being someone's second wife, or having to wait four years to do it. I don't happen to like the way it looks from the outside, that's all. And Nora knows this, which is why I couldn't grasp her uncontrollable glibness regarding my relationship, and I couldn't help feeling that she wanted to make herself look better than me in front of Cynthia.

Ted and I met soon after his separation from Ah-leen. They were college sweethearts. They married at twenty-two. They burned and crashed. Ted told me when I met him, and I believed him, that the love fizzled from their marriage years before I came along. Normally, there's no harm in dating a newly separated man, especially not one you instantly fall for, sink into, devour like thickly frosted chocolate cake. Had I known that eight months later I would be hurling into my city apartment's toilet due to a contraceptive malfunction, *perhaps* I would have waited a little bit longer.

At any rate, we were in love and a baby was coming and the divorce would get settled soon enough. Except poor Ah-leen has a hospital addiction. Seriously. Ted tells me she loves the food, adores being waited on hand and foot, and finds she can't get the kind of attention she needs without several twenty-four-hour staff members checking in on her day and night. "She has terrible insomnia," he once told me. "She confessed that she sleeps like a baby in the hospital." Apparently this is because, due to her crippling hypochondria, and despite the frequent checks from nurses, the hospital is the only place she feels safe enough to sleep. But enough about crazy people.

None of this can be shared with homemade-tea-and-pottery chick. I momentarily hated Nora for spilling a confidence. Then I forgave her, because she looked so hopeless in her plaid pants and blue velvet shirt. Also because she so clearly venerated all things Cynthia; I could see it in her face. You can see everything in Nora's face. Her transparency is her trademark.

"You'll have to hold another tea, when more faculty can come," Nora said as Cynthia refilled our teacups from an art-deco blue and white teapot.

"That's a great idea," Cynthia replied. "We could have weekly faculty teas, sort of like you and I have been getting together for breakfasts." Cynthia smiled at Nora. I frowned at her; how had she failed to inform me of these *breakfasts*? "It's a sweet thought," Cynthia said as though talking to herself. All of a sudden I became third-wheel girl, odd-one-out, which-of-these-three-is-not-like-the-others.

"How are you feeling?" Nora asked. "With the pregnancy?"

"So far I feel fantastic! No morning sickness at all. In fact, I'm full of energy. I've been working on a quilt. Would you like to see it?"

At this mention, because obviously it isn't enough to make all one's own dishes from clay and harvest and mix all one's own tea from herbs, one must also design and stitch all one's own bedclothes from scratch, I longed to make a face at Nora, but she eluded me. She stood and walked behind Cynthia like a woman in a trance. I got up and poured my tea down the drain.

At home, Hannah, inspired by my visit to Cynthia's, had arranged an elaborate picnic–tea party for us in the living room using a throw blanket to cover the floor, some old socks of mine for napkins, and plasticware from our kitchen junk drawer for utensils.

"What are you having at your picnic?" I asked.

"Tea," she replied.

"Anything to eat?" I sat down on the floor beside her. No sight of Ted; I assumed he'd put Lily down for a late-afternoon nap.

"Chocolate cake with tofu," she announced proudly. She served it up onto our socks. We play-ate in blissful silence for a few minutes.

"Thank you, Hannie. This is truly a lovely picnic."

"Oh, Mama. You're such a piece of work." I choked on my invisible cake. She must have overheard me the other day talking to Ted about his mother, a woman I frequently refer to as "a piece of work." "You must be done by now." She took my sock and rolled it up into a small ball. "Hug time," she announced, then she curled up in my lap for all of ten seconds. "I'm doctor, Mama," she said then, leaping out of my arms. "Lay down."

Obediently, I lay down on the floor. She poked me here and there, crawled around my body looking for something, then said, "Okay. Lay up now. You good."

Um, yes, if only I felt good. Instead, I felt pummeled and punched. By Cynthia Cypress, for one thing, and her better-than-thou ways, as well as by Nora, although I suppose my nonmarriage isn't her fault. I thought of my meeting with Meg. She'd nearly brought me to tears. As a rule, I refuse to cry; I don't like crying; it makes me sad.

"Sweet cheeks," Ted strode into the living room. "Lily's

out for the night, I think. Mind if I go for a jog? Did you have fun?"

"I wouldn't use that word. Go ahead. I'll make some dinner." He kissed the top of my head on his way to the door.

"Suze called," he shouted over his shoulder. "She wants you to call her back tonight."

"Suze isn't fun like you, Mama," Hannah said, returning to sit in my lap. Then, "Read me a book." I reached over and grabbed a board book from the coffee table.

"Why do you think Suze isn't fun? Mama has so much fun with her. She's my friend."

"She doesn't have a fun face," Hannah answered. I realized this was true. Between the Botox and her motherly discontent, she rarely smiles.

"What about my face? What does my face look like?" I dreaded the answer, knowing my tiredness showed, my perpetual grumpiness, my—what did Meg call it? My *internal conflict*. Can a child see something so complicated, even a smart child like Hannah?

She reached up and patted my cheek. "You have Mama face," she said, to my great relief. "I like it when it's quiet." Then she popped out of my lap once again. "Let's play baby. I'm the mommy. Lie down. I wrap you up."

This is how Ted found me, forty-five minutes later, ensconced in a blanket, faux-sucking my thumb, half on the floor and half on Hannah's tiny lap as she recounted a story she claimed Nora told her about an orphaned ogre. Given its fantastical nature, I was certain the colorful tale belonged to Hannah.

Ted's arrival broke our happy bubble, or maybe Hannah

got hungry. Either way, she geared up for a long shouting whine when I stood up to make dinner. She wanted me to keep being her baby. When I explained that babies can't make dinner and that daddies have to shower, she crawled up into my skirt and bit my belly.

11

Nora

Soon after Cynthia's tea party, I developed a strange tic: every time I spotted her, even from afar, I searched for signs of the pregnancy. I looked for the tiniest bump in her abdomen, a tendency to be clumsy, swollen ankles, blotchy cheeks, shortness of breath, unusual fatigue, weakness from vomiting, paleness from nausea, constant eating to ward off sickness. As I knew every symptom in the book for early, middle, and late pregnancy, having read a half-dozen pregnancy books cover to cover, I considered myself somewhat of an expert on the matter, or at least what it ought to look like from the outside.

I thought of her in particular at vitamin time, which is first thing in the morning when I swallow my oversized prenatal vitamin with a short prayer: "Let this have a purpose." Undoubtedly I have more folic acid built up in me than they keep at the vitamin factory. If I die and give my body to science, they can use me. When I down the vitamin, Cynthia's image pops into my brain. Not that I don't like her. I like her a lot. I just don't want to think of her when I'm face-to-face with my lack of pregnancy. Also, the only thing I've gathered from gawking at her whenever we spend time together is that she's happy. I can't say happier than me, because I don't know how happy I look from the outside, but I want to say happier than me, because, and let's be honest, how could she not be?

This is not fair to her, because she didn't even know I was trying, but I occasionally got a whiff of her smugness, as though she had her thumbs in her ears and her fingers waggling while she chorused, "I'm pregnant and you're not." As she had never been anything but kind to me, I'm not proud to report that I spent a good deal of time hoping she might encounter some of the more awful side effects of pregnancy. One day, sitting with Cynthia at lunch, I accidentally dropped my spoon. While hunting for it, I took that unique opportunity to scan her miniskirt-clad legs for spider veins. It took me an unreasonable amount of time to get back my utensil, but I did acquaint myself intimately with the shape of Cynthia's calves.

I am not normally jealous, but it is true that since birth I have had legs shaped like tree trunks. Have you ever noticed the shapeliness of a tree trunk? No, I'd imagine not. That's because they *have* no shape. "They're strong," my mother always pointed out. Aunt Bertie, whenever I complained about them, quipped, "You're lucky to have two." I can only imagine that if luck had anything at all to do with my body, I would *have* a shape.

Still, despite this small obsession, I enjoyed my time with Cynthia. She really had a gentle, sweet way about her. She never complained, and she often had little gifts for me, a chocolate bar she'd picked up or some exotic fresh fruit she found at the Asian grocer. I ignored David whenever I saw him. I simply refused to think about him. I was able to, at least mentally, disconnect the two of them, to cultivate my friendship with Cynthia and deny my past with David. I'm a capable woman, after all. I'm able to balance all sorts of contradictory forces, such as being friends with Annie and Cynthia at the same time or engaging in nonrecreational sex, or being a prude who keeps track of her fertility signs.

Aunt Rose, from Florida, called. She'd belatedly received the news of my academic attempts at baby-making with a number 2 pencil. She wasn't happy to be the last in line to hear the news, and she took out her righteous anger at being left out of the loop by pontificating for close to an hour on the wonders of fertility medication, insisting I immediately undergo hormone therapy. In her final act of family bullying, otherwise known as support, she'd put Elle on my case, and I guiltily admitted I'd forgotten to call my cousin.

"No need," Aunt Rose said. "She'll be coming for a visit."

"I'm sure they mean well," Alfie said after I told him that my cousin, Ellie Mae Ruthie Leigh Blenderhorn, who to everyone's great relief simply went by Elle, intended to visit. "Don't you like Elle? I thought she was your favorite cousin."

"She's my only female cousin, for one thing. And my other two cousins, James and Michael, are much older. Elle and I always played together as children. She still insists I'll be the maid of honor if she ever gets married."

"Isn't she a sex therapist?"

"Indeed. Aunt Rose reminded me of this about twenty times during our conversation. She thinks Elle could help me."

"That's nice." Alfie stood next to me at the kitchen sink chopping onions. He was making his famous spaghetti sauce from scratch.

"Actually, it's awful."

"What if she really *can* help?"

"The two things aren't related. Pregnancy has nothing to do with—" I shrugged my shoulders, not wanting to bring up orgasms in the kitchen. "You know. She helps couples with their pleasure problems; she doesn't know anything about fertility."

"Oh." Alfie dumped the onions into the sizzling oil. They crackled, and I jumped back to avoid a flying drop of hot oil. "I wish I could make *you* hop out of the pan," he added, though glumly. Neither of us laughed.

"For the record, when she comes, or *if* she comes, because she hasn't called me herself, I'd appreciate it if you wouldn't bring my problem up."

"Me?" Alfie blushed. "Unlikely. But if you are close to her, couldn't you say something? If she knows all about stuff like that, it might make a difference."

"What she knows about won't help in the conception department. A hundred, um, orgasms couldn't get me a baby."

"Aren't they good for their own sake?" Alfie asked.

"I suppose."

"You're so single-minded about the whole thing."

"And that's wrong?"

Neither of us spoke after this. The food sizzled and cooked. Alfie dropped noodles into boiling water. Fruity came hunting beneath our feet for scraps; I valiantly re-frained from wishing her ill. Then I started imaging a scenario where I would feel comfortable confiding anything to Elle. It involved a great deal of alcohol. She does *not* have a good bedside manner.

"Aunt Rose says she might get her own show on TLC. I think she said it's called *Sex Talk*. It will be a reality show where Elle visits couples who need sex therapy and helps them out. Kind of like *Supernanny* for the libido. Apparently her manager is in negotiations right now with the network."

"Nora." Alfie turned toward me, a broad wooden spoon in his hand. "I *want* you to be happy in the bedroom. If you would tell me what to do . . ."

"It's not you," I said, waving a hand at him, walking out of the room backward. "It's me. Come on, Fruity, let's go for a walk!" I hooked her up to her leash. "I'll be back for dinner."

Relieved to escape, I walked toward the river, deciding to focus on the beauty of the campus instead of my argument with Alfie. I appreciated all the October glory, rosy and golden and burnt. I love the Dixbie campus; it hums with life. Students crossed my path, some heading to the music studios to practice cello or violin or piano, others to the gym for a quick swim before dinner, others to the cafeteria for an early dinner before study hall. The energy and vitality of the kids lifted some of my irritation. The air of possibility and purpose, all the movement and desire teenagers express, especially at Dixbie, where some of the worst parts of high school, the cliques and the extreme social ostracism, matter less as so many of our students are the types who, in a public school, would be outsiders. I'd never felt more at home than I did in this place.

Then I tripped on a stick, toppled over Fruity, and narrowly escaped landing on my face. A hand reached out to save me.

I knew that hand.

"Steady there," David said.

"Thanks!" I ridiculously brushed my pants off as if I'd fallen into a pile of sand, though I hadn't so much as a speck of dirt on me.

"Off for a walk?"

"Yes," I said after a quick debate on the use of sarcasm with old lovers. It dawned on me to say: *why avoid the obvious.* But then avoiding the obvious was exactly what was called for. "We missed you at the tea party."

"Cynthia said it was fun. I figured it might be nice for her to get to know people without me present, find her own friends, that sort of thing."

"Oh." I stared down at my shoes. I wanted to say something; I didn't know how.

"Well, I'm off."

"David." He continued to back away from me on his way to somewhere. "Did you mention to Cynthia? Does she know about . . . us?"

"You know, I don't know that I did. Or maybe in passing? I guess I did mention it once, that we'd dated for a little while."

"Right," I said, suddenly feeling profoundly awkward. Darlene Muse, one of my freshman English students, walked by with a clarinet case. She gave me a shy wave. "Just so I don't speak out of place," I said quietly and quickly.

"I get it." He nodded. "I never worry about you speaking out of place." He half-smiled. "You're such a self-possessed person. I'll see you later. I've got an Environmental Club meeting."

"Bye." He turned and strode away, a long, level step that carried him quickly up the path and out of sight.

I walked on toward the river, mulling over his words. Had we "dated for a little while"? Was that all? The man had said he wanted to marry me; surely that earns a better summary than "dated for a little while."

As I reached the meadow behind the playing fields, I took Fruity off her leash and allowed her to run free. She scooped her hind legs tightly underneath her as she bolted to the river. I knew she would swim and that it was useless, but I called after her, "Stay out of the water." A moment later I heard the great splash.

What a miserable day, and now I would have to give Fruity a bath so she wouldn't stink up the house with eau d'murk. I would also have to face Alfie, who I knew would want to take me to bed and try out some new method that would fall terribly flat. Periodically, whenever the issue came up, he would endeavor to get more creative during sex, asking a hundred questions, touching me in sixteen different ways, and the more he tried, the more I felt like a floodlight was shining directly on my petunia, a situation that makes me distinctly unaroused. I've got an introverted anatomy. I refused to indulge in memories of sex with David.

Why? Life is about more than a few brief moments of ecstasy, at least for the normal person, perhaps excluding cousin Elle, who spends an extraordinary amount of time steeped in exploring fleeting moments of pleasure. She was always that way. Once, at the ripe age of fifteen, during a family visit in Florida, she broke out an anatomy book and gave me a lesson that blew my mind for a variety of reasons, not the least of which was how any one even remotely related to

Aunt Bertie could own such a book. Now Elle lives in Philadelphia because, as she says, "Cities need the most sexual
healing." She takes her profession very seriously.

She's a mutant, a mutant Helpsom-Fulch, a genetic mistake in the uptight gene pool. For a few years my family
stopped inviting her and Aunt Rose and Uncle Jim for holidays because no one could stand to hear her talk gonads over
the apple pie. And then she became so well known, so popular, so in demand with her phone-in show and syndicated
column, she didn't have time to come. This suited my Aunt
Bertie fine. Aunt Bertie has more than once declared Elle
mentally ill. Talk about the pot calling the kettle black.

I hollered for Fruity and started walking back toward the
dorm. I didn't want to keep Alfie waiting on me for dinner. I
wasn't mad at him, not truly. It simply wasn't his fault, not
any of it—the sex failures, the conception failures, my own
mixed motives as his wife. So what that he lacked David's
looks and sophistication? Or for that matter, David's skill in
bed? I knew the last time I'd had an orgasm, and David Hayworth had everything to do with it.

I put Fruity back on the leash and power-walked up the
path, not wanting to waste another second thinking about a
topic that unnerves me. I'd just as soon have been born without a body, for all the trouble it causes.

Beverly Slater, the housemother in Field House, the dorm
closest to the woods, came running down the walkway after
me, waving her hand and looking rotund in a flying, mauve
muumuu.

"Nora! I saw you walking by. I've got to talk to you! You
are just the person I was looking for. Oh, stop walking! I can't
catch up!"

I stopped. Dread crept up my neck like a spider. Beverly never has anything good to report. She keeps track of everyone on campus. I've even seen her with binoculars. She leads the chorus and teaches music classes. She's in her late sixties, unmarried, white-haired, terribly overweight, and slightly hard of hearing, a critical flaw in gossip as it ensures she never gets her stories correct, but is hell-bent on sharing them anyway.

"Hi, Beverly. Something going on?"

"Oh, goodness, isn't there always! You've got to be the first to know about this, my dear." She pulled me in close until we were more than hugging, her massive bosom bumping into my side. "I take it you haven't heard."

"I can't say that I have."

"Poor Annie, what a hassle this will be! Apparently she didn't make it to the most recent Social Committee meeting." Beverly spoke the words as though she'd eaten a sour grape.

"Probably because she was at home with her children."

"The Feminists Club earned a good deal of discussion."

I took the bait. "Why?"

"Being her best friend, I'm certain you know all about it. Cynthia, the new teacher, has volunteered to take over the responsibilities of the group. Given that Annie has so much going on at home, and since she isn't on the teaching staff, *some people* at the meeting thought it a very good idea." She whispered and looked around like an FBI informant. "Of course, *I* didn't say a word. I know how hard Annie has worked for those girls over the years. Why, she started the club!"

"I know." I shook my head, not sure whether to be amused or amazed. Considering how often Beverly misheard, it was possible things weren't quite as she imagined. On the other hand, if Cynthia really did want to chair Annie's club, Annie would not graciously step aside; I knew that as surely as I knew the sun would rise the next day.

"That Cynthia has a number of exciting, *new* ideas. Now, we all agreed it was only fair to talk to Annie. Maybe she would welcome the break from her duties."

"Actually," I said, "I think she's pretty attached to the group."

"Well, we are all collegial at Dixbie. Maybe the two of them can co-chair the group," she said brightly. I could smell her breath and it smelled like cat. "That was my idea!"

Considering Annie's views on all things Cynthia, I very much doubted she would want to collaborate with her anytime before pigs fly. "I'm not so sure," I told Beverly.

She frowned. I could tell this was not the answer she wanted to hear. "You ought to be the one to tell Annie," she said, with much less satisfaction. "Since you *are* so close to both of them."

"I hardly know Cynthia!"

"I see you girls together *all* the time."

"I'm showing her around campus," I said, now irritated by her pressure. "I've got to go home."

"What's that, dear? You've got a mole?" She looked expectantly at my face, hoping for a confession of skin cancer or something equally compelling.

"I have to go home," I said loudly into her good ear. I started to walk away and then paused. "Did you say Cynthia brought up the idea to take over the club?"

"And with a whole plan of action, too," she answered with a healthy dose of rubbernecking pleasure rounding out the smile on her face. I gathered she knew only too well what Annie would have to say about that.

"I'll put in my earplugs before I let Annie know," I said, continuing on my way.

"Can't hear you, dear," she answered, the October breeze slapping her billowing dress against her mountainous thighs.

When I got home, Alfie, looking sheepish and out of place, sat at the table in a dark kitchen, a small tea candle, not even in a holder, lit on the table, our plates heaped with food. I tried not to sigh like my mother. I tried in my heart to be grateful. I sat down and pulled one of the cloth napkins he had carefully folded beside my plate onto my lap.

"Annie called while you were out," he said, searching for neutral territory. "She wants you to write down the ogre story. Apparently, Hannah keeps asking for the *real* version. She said even a few lines would be enough. I told her I don't know about it. She also mentioned she's gone into therapy. I can't believe it. She's doesn't seem the type." Alfie rambled on, something he didn't often do. I could see how much he wanted to make things nice between us, right between us. But my mind wandered off, far from the table and his tasty Italian dinner. I was thinking about Olive the Ogre. What a good idea Annie had! Why hadn't I thought of it before?

"Nora?" Alfie finally asked.

"Oh, sorry. I'm drifting." I brought all my attention back to the table. "I want to tell you about Beverly. She accosted me on my way back. According to her, a feminist coup may be in the works."

12

Annie

"Perfect timing!" I jumped out of the car and waved at Suze. We both arrived at the family center at the exact same time.

"Why does it take me so long when I've only got one kid? You have two, and you can get out of the house just as quickly," she asked, pulling herself out of the car and bending into the backseat of her Mercedes to unhook Finn.

"Oh," I said, with a faux nonchalance. "I get so much *practice*." Suze tried for a laugh, but it came out sounding like a half-filled whoopee cushion getting squashed. This stopped me in my tracks. I turned away from the van, where I'd been ready to peel the girls out of their car seats, and went straight over to Suze's backside. She still had her head in the backseat.

"Suze, are you crying about the fact that it takes you a long time to get your toddler out of the house?"

Suze feigned ignorance. "I'm not crying!" she stammered, surreptitiously wiping away a tear.

"Suze, you are crying. And so is Lily." I could hear her

wailing from inside the minivan. Suze still hadn't pulled herself out of the car; she was fussing needlessly with Finn.

"Go on," she whimpered. "Get Lily out. Let's go in before we all freeze."

"No one's ever frozen in October," I stated. I opened the van door, stuck a pacifier in Lily's mouth; checked on Hannah, who was busy drawing with Magic Marker on her hand; then closed the door again. "This is important. Every time I see you lately, you're crying. Now fess up."

"I really don't want to talk about it right now."

"Right now is all we have. My children are quiet for thirteen seconds. Don't waste precious time."

"I'm afraid you'll be angry with me."

"My goodness! What did you do? Have you joined the NRA? I can't think of anything that would make me mad at you."

"I've been keeping something from you," she said, pulling out a wadded-up old tissue from her red DK jacket. "I called the other night to tell you; you didn't call back."

"What? What is it?" My internal OMG alarm began to ring. What had I missed? Someone dying? Finn getting ADD? A botched plastic surgery on her belly button?

"I got a job," she said, more to the pavement than to me. "I started last week."

"How did you feel when she said that?" Meg Stauffer asked gently, both of us firmly recessed into our respective sitting nooks in her sun-flooded office.

"I'm going to say a few things now I don't want repeated. I'm not sure they have anything to do with my inner child or why Hannah makes me insane, but the anger that came up when she told me had a lot in common with the kind Hannah arouses."

Meg laughed throatily. "I don't repeat anything I hear, how's that for a promise."

"What I mean is, I don't want you or anyone to hold these politically incorrect thoughts against me. And, if I ever run for office, which is unlikely but I wouldn't wholly rule it out, I don't want these ideas to be used against me."

"I'm paid to be neutral," she said with a mischievous wink. "I'm paid to keep out of your future political career."

"I'm serious, though. This is an unpopular, unfavorable idea among the thinking class. I talk about it with only a select few people. Here it is: women with young children should not work." I waited for a bolt of lightning to straighten my hair. Nothing. I looked carefully at Meg's face. Her expression hadn't changed.

"Go on," she said.

"Frankly, I have a whole host of frightening conservative beliefs, ideas that would give my mother—who spent a great deal of time hoping I would understand the plight of the woman incarcerated in her home by society's expectations that she care for her child—cardiac arrest. The first and worst I just admitted: I truly do not think women with young children who don't need the money should leave their children in day care. Even the idea of day care for my girls makes me itch, like hives-in-your-nose kind of itch. Imagine leaving your baby, a three-month-old baby, in the care of strangers?" Now I was off and running. "And another thing. Women should breastfeed. Really, they should. I know I'm supposed to be tolerant and accepting and open-minded, but for goodness' sake, why would you go out and buy something that Mother Nature gave you for free? It's pure stupidity. All the studies show how important it is, what a difference it makes, and you've got these hospitals giving women formula samples and sending them home with sore nipples! And these two might not be connected, but formula-fed babies are a hell of a lot easier to send to day care, aren't they? I would no sooner send my kids into full-time care at some germ-infested money-making establishment with strung-out twenty-somethings who watch babies because they have no college degree than I would let my milk dry up while I spent precious time washing bottles! Honestly, *washing bottles?!* Who has time for that? Get out your boob and use it as it was intended!" I found I'd broken out into a light sweat. "It's scary, isn't it?" I said. "I'm like Laura Schlessinger trapped in a feminist's body."

Meg laughed again. "So how did you feel when Suze told you she got a job?"

"Naturally, I kept my mouth shut. I'm a friend. I have to support her. She's doing what she thinks she needs to do in order to survive. Motherhood hasn't been easy for her—ha! Like it's easy for anyone. What I mean to say is that she hasn't taken to it, not any of the phases. I can't say I'm surprised, although I know for a fact that Suze feels the same way I do on the subject of working mothers. We've had more than one conversation on the topic. In fact, it's how we bonded. She *agreed* with me that caring for one's own child was significant and worth whatever suffering you might have to endure."

I *did* support Suze. After her declaration, I put my arm around her and hugged her. I asked about the details, how she ended up taking work at our local historical society, a good use of her skills as an archivist. I didn't mention our previous tête-à-têtes on the dreaded condition of working motherhood. I did not bring up our unspoken pact that as hassled, bedraggled stay-at-home mothers we belonged to a special group, one that women who worked outside the home—a ready, daily escape—would never understand. We were on the front lines, doing the tireless, tedious, exhausting labor that day to day seemed like nothing, but in the end would matter the most. We were the ones wiping our baby's noses, smoothing diaper ointment on their fat bottoms, jiggling them for hours, reading them wordless picture books, teaching them baby sign language. We had agreed that our work was invaluable, irreplaceable, and no woman, however nice, could, for ten dollars an hour, perform motherhood the way we could. I did not ask Suze what happened to her thoughts on this matter because, while in theory I am a jerk, in practice, I weaken. I didn't want to be mean to her.

"Mmm," Meg said thoughtfully. "So how did you *feel* when she said that?"

"How did I feel? Like I was saying, I understand where she's coming from. She's never been happy simply staying at home with Finn; although to be honest, with her part-time nanny, she's only done some of the mother grunt work anyway—"

"I said *feel*," Meg reiterated. "Not what you think, how it made you feel."

"Oh, you're looking for the touchy-feely stuff? Fine. I felt abandoned by my best friend. I felt deserted. And I felt worried. What will we even have in common any longer? It was one thing when she paid the nanny so she could get her hair done every week and go shopping. If I had any money, I imagine I would flee my kids for occasional short, self-indulgent outings. But this is entirely different. She's a woman who doesn't need the income who's accepted a forty-hour-a-week position. I'll tell you how I feel—I feel sorry for Finn. He's the same age as Hannah. He won't know why she's not around. He'll take it personally."

"I don't know," Meg offered delicately. "I don't know about Finn. I was curious about Annie, about what Suze's decision to work meant for *you*."

"I've told you, haven't I?" In fact, I'd done nothing but talk. My mouth felt dry. All the talking had made me tired. I'd essentially emptied out my soul to this woman, all the ugly ideas I possess that no self-respecting feminist would dare admit. After all, I believe in a woman's right to choose, from cloth diaper choice to pregnancy termination to employment. This standard, one my mother so vehemently expounded upon right before she left for another rally, raised me more than she did. My secret, traditional, backwoods views on the mother issue didn't come out too often; Suze had been one of the few people I shared them with.

"Why would anyone pay someone else to watch their kids? I can see paying someone to perform your open-heart surgery or teach your teenagers how to drive or even clean your toilet bowl. But to hire someone for the one job no other person can do—mother your children—" I started filling Meg in again. Hoping to draw my point home so that she could see the divide Suze had stretched open between us, but she interrupted me again, which, while I'm no expert, seemed like very bad therapist manners.

"Do you want to know what I think?"

"Of course!" I prepared myself for a logical lecture on the

rights of women, on the variations of women's needs, on the fact that women like herself had fought for years to be able to both work *and* have children. My mother had said it all before. I could repeat it. Intellectually I even agreed with it. Regardless, I could not imagine leaving my children for many more years. Did this make me a mutant liberal?

"I think you are *ambivalent*," she said, all too clearly and slowly, and with the glitter of a dare sparkling in her eyes.

I seethed the entire drive back. Ambivalent! I have never been ambivalent in my entire life about a single thing. Not even about the ketchup packages they give you at fast-food restaurants; I have an opinion about those, which I won't bore you with when there's so much else of importance going on, but I assure you, it *is* an opinion. (Okay, how about why are they too small to be useful?) I would even go so far as to state that I am constitutionally incapable of either neutrality or ambivalence. This is my signature, my passion. As awful as Hannah can be, I see very clearly that I have passed this trait on to her. For example, yesterday morning she "accidentally" dropped my hairbrush into the toilet after I'd demanded she dress herself in something other than a bathing suit. When I made it clear that her act of revenge was completely unacceptable, she puffed up her tiny chest and shouted, "I have right to dress myself howanyway I see good!" This, I know, she gets from me.

Meg's words opened my inner gates of Hate. Sure, it had occurred to me on the impossible days when Lily teethed by ceaseless crying and Hannah ruled me with an iron thumb that I missed painting, missed time to peruse art textbooks

or saunter through city galleries. I'm only human, after all.
But this is hardly a sign of ambivalence!

Long before Hannah came along—accidentally and pre-
maturely, to be sure, but it's not as though I didn't want children eventually even though I didn't want them right then,
and okay, maybe I have some residual feelings on that topic,
but *still*—I felt strongly about mothers taking care of their
own children. All it took was ten minutes in one of my wom-
en's studies classes in college and five seconds in my mother's
company to realize that women Off Saving the World do
more good for the imaginary future of their children than
they do for the actual ones wistfully sitting at home alone,
wishing for a mother. More than once growing up I fanta-
sized about being adopted by Nora's mother, Janet, a domes-
tic goddess to be sure, armed with a duster and an oven mitt.
And, yes, she was a bit of a downer, stuck back in a Puritan
Mayflower sort of religious and cultural landscape, but I
could overlook all that to have someone make me a dinner
that did not get served on a foil tray with a separate compart-
ment for veggies, meat, potatoes, and hot apples. I do not
need years of therapy to learn that my own mothering is entirely a reaction to my mother's way of doing it, and doing it
poorly. I *get it*.

Meg must have misunderstood something. This is the
only plausible explanation. I took a deep breath. I liked her. I
would clear up the confusion next time. In the meantime, I
would try not to hold her inaccurate assessment of my personality against her. I am definitive.

I stepped up onto the front porch when a voice called out
to me.

"I'd been hoping to catch you," Cynthia said, coming to stand beside me, a fluffy red shawl thrown over her shoulders, a black beret with a large red flower tilted on her head. I refused to look down at her shoes.

"And you have." I did not smile. I did not like the woman. Nora assumed she had good intentions with her tea party. I suspected she wanted to show off her opulent house with its myriad excesses. I even uncovered, in her bathroom, drawers of extras—extra soap, towels, toothbrushes, and toilet paper, as though in preparation for a world shortage of hygiene supplies. I cannot trust a woman who wears three-hundred-dollar shoes while teaching fifteen-year-olds, or is that just being picky?

"We missed you at the Social Committee meeting."

"Okay," I said. *And who made you empress of attendance?* "It hasn't become mandatory, has it?"

"Oh, no!" She gave a ladylike giggle. "We took up the topic of the Young Feminists Club."

"I had no idea it was a topic."

"I thought perhaps you might enjoy a bit of a break from your duties. The school hasn't passed on any club activities to me. I'd be perfect for the YFC."

Now I think, given such a statement, that something outrageous and dramatic was called for—spitting on her fancy shoes, passing out cold, or maybe simply slapping her porcelain cheeks.

"I founded that club three years ago. As you can imagine, I've become attached to it over the years." I tried to look relaxed, casually unconcerned, so she wouldn't gather how she'd activated my fire-breathing dragon.

"I thought you might feel that way." She pressed her hands

together like a child praying. "Wouldn't it be wonderful if we co-led the club? That would ease up some of the responsibilities you have, and we could work together in sisterhood." Did she just say *sisterhood*? "At Sarah Lawrence, I was the head of the women's organization."

I tried this one on for size. I doubted her *über*-feminine, fashion-saturated, makeup-heavy manners went that well with the butch style of radical feminists who sport oversized, shape-concealing clothing, armpit hair brushed and head hair unbrushed.

If Cynthia had wanted the Knitting Club or the Culture Club, I would have been sympathetic. Sharing the Environmental Club with David would have made practical sense. But this sort of robbery is what I've been up against my whole life. Cynthia had no idea, trapped as she was inside her Barbie-doll body, of the problems that affect the female race. I had created the women-centered/girl-power/liberation landscape on campus because I know a thing or two about oppression, and not merely from my mother's endless lectures.

"Annie, wouldn't that be fun?" She shone her dentist-brownnosing smile at me.

I thought of Professor Ingrid March at that moment, the RISD legend. Everyone hated her. She taught Early Feminist Art, and The Feminist Vision of Visual Language. She's the leading expert on historical feminist art. As obscure as that may be, in her field, she's nothing short of Madonna. She's always in the *New York Times*. Of course I took all her classes. Almost all the women in the program took all her classes, and we hated her. *Despised* her. Or most of us did, anyway. And why? This woman, she was all about empowering women, she'd devoted her whole life to creating a feminist theory of art. She was the woman symbol writ large. And guess what? She wore tiny little high-heeled shoes and fancy, girly clothes. She dyed and curled and coiffed her hair and wore eight layers of pancake makeup. As far as we could tell, she was nothing more than a hypocrite. And *that* is what I think of Cynthia. Either you're breaking the mold or you're still struggling inside of it. Either you're offering the next generation a freeing idea of womanhood or you're dishing up the same old corsets at the corner store.

I don't care if you don't agree with me; as I pointed out before, I don't do ambivalence. So let me be brief: Cynthia is oppressed by her designer shoes.

"I can't see that working," I said, giving her my ten-watt, I-forgot-to-floss-last-night-because-I-didn't-get-to-sleep-until-after-the-last-load-of-laundry-got-done-at-one-a.m. smile. Then I spun around on the heel of my simple, black sneaker and went inside.

"I quit," I said, walking into the living room, looking at my husband and daughters playing tent on the floor, a large orange sheet I'd kept since my own childhood hovering above their heads.

"I won't take that personally," Ted said. Lily tried to belly-slither her way over to me. She showed promising signs of crawling in the next several years, but being so plump and pleasant, she lacked the proper motivation. Hannah crawled at six months. Lily, already seven months, seemed to question its greater purpose. However, she *had* managed to untie my shoelace on a number of occasions, something I took memorable note of, as in, this child is a genius!

"Don in'rupt, Mama," Hannah said.

"We're flying to Mars," Ted explained. "On important business."

I scooped Lily up and sat down on the couch to nurse her. "Lily and I will stay on earth. Someone needs to look after it."

"Daddy, play!" Hannah demanded. Ted proceeded to make rocket-ship noises. Or maybe he passed a lot of gas.

"Cynthia stopped me outside. She'd like to take over the Young Feminists Club."

"Really? I guess that will free up some of your time."

"I don't *need* my time freed up. I enjoy leading the group I began. It's fun. And what's wrong with doing something other than caring for your children and matching your socks every now and then?"

"Simmer down, cowgirl," he said, followed by a dreadful imitation of a horse neighing.

"This is not an invitation on her part, Ted. She's *snatching* it from me."

"Snatching, naughty," Hannah contributed.

"Yes, snatching is very unkind."

"Well, maybe you two can do it together."

"I'm too disgusted with you right now to speak," I said, lifting Lily up and giving her a nice burp. Then she wiggled off my lap onto the floor and sat for a minute, sucking on the ugly orange sheet. "How have you failed to remember that I don't like this woman?"

"Then why did you go to her house for a tea party?"

"That was merely a sociological experiment."

"It seems to me," Ted went on, "that you and Cynthia have quite a bit in common, especially if she's interested in the club."

"I'd rather have something in common with a cockroach."

"Tickle me, Daddy!"

I kneeled down and peered under the sheet at the two of them. "Hannah, use your big-girl words, please. Say, 'I'd like some attention, please.' Also, it's okay for Mama and Daddy to talk to each other. We need time to talk."

"NO! Tickle ME!"

"Ted," I warned. "Don't do what she asks until she uses her big-girl voice." He rolled his eyes at me.

"Yes, master," he said playfully. Then he ignored me and tickled her energetically while I rolled onto my back and let Lily lie on my tummy and chew on my nose. After a while, Hannah grew quiet and tucked into my armpit.

"Missed you," she scolded. "Hannah go everywhere with Mama, 'kay?"

"Speaking of," said Ted. "How was therapy?"

"I'd almost forgotten! I was too busy being pissed off about Cynthia. Ted, answer this as honestly as you can given the present company. Do you think I'm ambivalent?"

"In general, or about something specific?"

"About work. Work and motherhood."

"Sure," he said.

"What do you mean? Is that your answer?"

"Why wouldn't you be? You had to give up your career, and we both know it isn't a bed of roses doing all the child-care."

I tried not to throw Lily in his direction, mostly because it didn't seem nice to involve an innocent bystander. Had I something inanimate in my arms, it would have been hurled in his direction.

"That doesn't make me ambivalent."

"I guess," he said, now busy getting tickled by Hannah,

who always does like to return a favor; she's got a superior sense of justice.

"I'll give you another chance. Do you think I'm ambivalent about staying home with the girls?"

"Nothing's changed in the past fifteen seconds," he said cheekily. "I don't see why you wouldn't be."

"But that doesn't mean I am!" I shouted.

"Aren't we all ambivalent?" he answered, followed by a loud plop and a hysterical Hannah giggle as he pretended to remove her nose. I reached a foot over and kicked his backside. "Ouch!" he cried. Then the baby bit my cheek and, as I had to choose between laughing or crying, I laughed. I certainly did not want to be forced by Hannah to wear a princess Band-Aid on my face for the rest of the night.

She rolled back into me and put her hand on my face. "Mommy, you my best mommy."

"I'm glad someone appreciates me," I said.

13

Nora

November

I did not, on purpose, become Cynthia's best friend. I had at least one good reason not to: David. And while I tried hard to ignore him and disregard his casual reference to our relationship as "dating," it didn't always work. I know I should have relied upon my good-girl roots and forgiven him, as in, "Hey, it's cool that you didn't marry me because I wanted kids and you didn't and then two years later you married another woman and she immediately got pregnant and, woops, you forgot to mention me to her! Those things happen!" Only, it was not cool. But Cynthia kept seeking me out. Over the first few months of school, she developed a cult following at Dixbie, and for some reason, she chose me as her comrade. Hanging around near David amounted to a small penalty for the rewards of Cynthia's company, although that makes it sound as if I'd thought about the situation and *decided* to become her friend, which isn't at all the case.

We didn't have much in common. She exuded coolness in the same way that I oozed gracelessness. And it's not as though I'd never known anyone like Cynthia—I had. It's just that no one like Cynthia had considered me friend material before. I'd like to pretend, for the sake of my ego and whenever Annie accuses me, that I'd developed immunity to the kind of local celebrity status Cynthia held. Through sheer presence and beauty, she'd solidified a reputation in short order as the person of the moment. One night after my Creative Writing Club meeting, I went to the girls' bathroom. While in the stall, a few students came in and "like," "um," and "you know'd" their way through quite a conversation. "Did you see her wearing *this*?" "Did you know that she did *that*?" "Did you hear she invited her entire World History class back to her house to look at her *artifacts*?" Being privy to such intimate worship, I didn't feel comfortable exiting the stall until they left. I sat on the toilet for twenty-seven minutes; I timed it with my stopwatch.

My friendly tours of the campus and invitations to breakfast rolled into daily contact, phone calls, and exclusive weekly teas as the semester progressed. She never invited Annie again to a tea, but I attributed this to her endearing dislike of crowds. She said once, in passing, that she did best one-on-one. And somehow, as I saw more of Cynthia, I saw less of Annie.

"Are you trying to spend time with David?" Annie asked me once in October.

"That's mean. Cynthia and I have a good time together. He has nothing to do with it. In fact, I'm mad at him."

"Well, it doesn't show. You practically live at their house." I did not explain that part of the reason for this had to do with the fact that I didn't want Cynthia to spend any time in my shabby apartment. "I feel like we're back in high school."

"That's not fair," I countered, although, frankly, Cynthia's affection toward me did remind me a bit of being a teenager. For example, during our faculty meeting in October, she passed me a note.

"Is there anything missing from the agenda?" Friedman had asked, as I slunk in a few minutes late. I slipped into the only open seat, right beside David Hayworth. Since our breakup, I'd drawn the line at sitting beside him during school functions; it always seemed a reasonable way of separating my personal and work lives. Given my stimulating hatred for him, I would rather have skinned a rabbit with my teeth than take the spot where we'd have to brush elbows. I had no other choice.

I noticed Cynthia sitting on his other side. She smiled at me. I furtively scanned her body for pregnancy signs. Her shirt wasn't tight enough to reveal any belly. Her face looked as thin and high cheekboned as always, no signs of unusual swelling. And she *still* didn't look green with nausea. I kept expecting to find her bent over a stack of crackers. I smiled back, pushing away my snoopy thoughts; she was my new friend, after all. I had no reason to be petty.

I studiously followed Friedman's words, paying no mind to the smell of David's aftershave or the rhythm of his breath, or his long, strong fingers that periodically tapped the table out of boredom. Friedman's voice droned on about classroom policies, a topic I certainly felt challenged to lose myself in, but I tried. Then a hand slipped inside my hand. It couldn't be that David Hayworth was attempting to hold my hand during a faculty meeting with his wife sitting beside him—a wild, inappropriate rekindling of our love as if to say, "I made a mistake, Nora. It's you I should have married!"

He removed his hand and I looked down to find a small piece of paper curled up in my palm. I imagined, briefly, foolishly, that David Hayworth passed me a belated love note, an apology with an acknowledgment of his error.

Cynthia, from the other side of David, gave me a meaningful look.

I kept my eyes on Friedman's face as I opened the crumpled paper, then glanced down at it as quickly as possible. Scrawled in flowery cursive was a single word: *Tea?*

That afternoon we had tea together on the large, screened-in porch at the back of Meadow House, and when I left, she said, "Thanks for being a friend, Nora." And so our weekly tea began.

I made a valiant effort to prepare my house for her eventual visit. This generally concluded with my giving up hopelessly. I found some new curtains on sale and hung them in the living room, thinking they looked rather archeological and sophisticated, until Alfie asked, "Did your mother send those along?" The next day, I dropped them off at Goodwill.

Though Cynthia didn't talk much about her personal life, the more time I spent with her, the more comfortable I felt. She was easy to talk to, an eager listener, and she never barked advice or insulted me. Not that I could ever have told Annie, but being with Cynthia was more cheerful. Soon enough, I began to confide in her. I confessed my pregnancy complications one afternoon over a cup of her mint tea.

"You *must* see my OB/GYN," she said enthusiastically without a single question as to the details of my failed attempts. (Truthfully, I appreciate this quality in her, the way she never interrogated or inquired too deeply.) She floated up out of her chair and headed into the house to get me one of his cards. Once I had the thing in my hand, I could literally feel Cynthia's good luck emanating from it. I didn't dare look at it until I left, afraid to jinx the spell. When I finally pulled it out of my pocket later that evening, I got goose bumps: *Dr. Davis Mercy.* Could a name like that be more fateful? Cue the Enya, it was a mystical moment. Fruity would be able to live after all. I had a new superstition and it involved salvation through Cynthia's gynecologist.

I called the office the next day and the receptionist told me I couldn't see Dr. Mercy until February. Then a week later she called to let me know of an immediate cancellation. I grabbed this neon sign courtesy of the universe and ran with it. I canceled my student midterm meetings scheduled for that afternoon, took Fruity out for an energetic ball-playing session, fed her homemade oatmeal with flaxseed for dinner, and patted her warm head as I skipped out the door. *Hey, Fruity, live as long as you want!* Who needed a doggie-baby recycling plan in order to get pregnant? Not me.

I felt like I was going to see Dr. Oz. What I knew of Cynthia added up to a paltry nothing. She often discussed her clothing, her rugs, and world travel, but she didn't tell me how she got pregnant or why she got married or how long she had wanted children. By offering me Dr. Mercy, who I knew would be the absolute best gynecologist money and influence could buy, given Cynthia's enormous clout, I felt she'd shared something precious with me. Not anything confidential and personal, but a treasure just the same.

"I'm here for an introductory meeting," I told the bubble-gum-chewing twenty-year-old receptionist, noting that the front desk looked alarmingly like real marble.

"Name."

"Nora Galusha."

"Okay. You're aware he's not taking on new patients?"

"What?" My knees went weak. "I thought I had a new-patient appointment. Someone called me today to let me know of the cancellation."

"I have you down for a 'meet and greet,'" she said blithely, as though the doctor would also be serving cocktails and canapés. "Meet him today and we'll keep your file. We'll call you when he has an official opening." She popped a bubble.

"But, I thought . . ." I didn't know what to say. I wanted to take her wad of pink gum and stuff it up her nose; animosity toward random people was new for me. I wondered if my David hatred was overflowing or if my pregnancy lust was beginning to take its toll. I certainly didn't used to have thoughts like that. I wanted to go postal on the receptionist and stick the gooey wad in her hair.

"Here you go. Fill these out." She passed me a novel's worth of papers.

I took the clipboard. "Cynthia Cypress referred me," I said in desperation as I fingered the magical Dr. Mercy business card in my coat pocket.

"Excuse me?" The girl looked up at me—for the first time meeting my gaze directly.

"Cynthia Cypress sent me."

The girl nodded enthusiastically as if, all of a sudden, we were speaking the same language. "I just love Cynthia," she said, clicking away on her computer, happily animated. I held my breath. "We totally have the same shoe size, and she brought me the hottest heels the other day in, like, perfect condition! Oh, look." She pointed at the screen as if I could see it. "I forgot!" She laughed. "I made a note here that you're

Cynthia's friend. She told me you'd be coming in. I just didn't recognize the name. She calls you Norie. You're all set. I'll put you in the system. Cynthia and Dr. Mercy are this close!" She held up two fingers smashed into one another.

I paused. I no longer hated the receptionist. Or I did on account of all she'd put me through emotionally in the previous three minutes, but I also loved her, though clearly not as much as I loved Cynthia. "You can call me Norie, too," I said, feeling chummy, my heart restored to beating. She gave me a friendly smile before returning to her computer and her gum.

Within minutes, a sprightly RN in blindingly white scrubs escorted me into the inner sanctum. I sat in the small office nervously jiggling my knee, perversely worried that somehow Dr. Mercy wouldn't like me and would expel me from his practice once he uncovered my social insignificance and inability to bribe people with gifts. I wished I'd known to bring a gift—but what? A houseplant? High-heeled shoes for a male doctor wouldn't cut it. While I was pondering my future doctor, some glamorous young hunk of manliness equal to a name like Mercy and worthy of Cynthia's adoration, a distinguished, well-built, salt-and-pepper-haired doctor entered the room.

It was Davis Mercy, and indeed, he was handsome. It had not dawned on me before to consider what it might be like to have a sexy man ask me to spread my legs and put them in stirrups. As he talked easily and asked a series of questions, I felt the perspiration forming on various and sundry parts of my body in anticipation of the exam. I began to feel acutely self-conscious. I wished he were old; although he had to be fifty, I wanted him older, with a red nose and an ugly bald spot he combed over, as well as long, thick nose and ear hair and tuna-fish breath.

Worries, irrational and ridiculous, popped up one after the other. I'd showered that morning, but maybe I ought to have showered right before I came. When was the last time I shaved my legs? Had I remembered deodorant? Would he compare my anatomy to Cynthia's? I had no doubt in my mind that Cynthia Cypress must have the world's most flawless petunia, although I truly didn't want to think about it, not while talking to her obstetrician. Not ever.

"Okay," I heard him say through the fog of my anxiety. "Why don't you change into the gown. I'll be right back."

After he left, I carefully and slowly peeled my clothes off. I cursed myself for not being more flexible as I attempted to ensure I didn't smell too *female*. Oh, man, what had I come to? I wished for the zillionth time that it could have been easy for me to conceive. I found the whole process of nonconception humiliating.

When the doctor walked back in, I noticed his thick, tan hands. He smiled at me. "Now lie down and put your feet in the stirrups."

Oh. I lay down, little by little, urgently searching for something that would improve the situation. If Dr. Mercy put his hand where I knew he would, it would feel like adultery. It had to. I'd known him for five minutes and I already had a crush on him.

"Dr. Mercy?" I asked, with my knees locked tightly together.

"Go ahead and relax your legs."

"Can I ask you a question?"

"By all means."

"Are you married?"

I thought he chuckled. Maybe he simply cleared his throat. "Twenty-five years. To the same woman, no less."

"And she knows you do this for a living?"

He laughed throatily. I wished he hadn't. It was a sexy laugh. "I delivered all three of our children."

"Right."

"Just take a deep breath. This won't take any time."

I took a few deep breaths, slightly more at ease knowing he was a married man.

"Ah," he said, feeling around. "You've got a ruby pelvis."

"I do?" What was a ruby pelvis? He said it without explanation, as though I ought to know. Undoubtedly he employed the secret language used among wealthy women and their charmed OB/GYNs. I didn't want to give away my ignorance. Ruby seemed pretty good, I guessed. How did the hierarchy work? If I had a ruby pelvis, that would mean Cynthia must have a diamond pelvis. And was there also gold, or did they merely rate pelvises by gemstones?

After I dressed, Dr. Mercy came back in for a final talk. He recommended I continue to try the old-fashioned way, at least a little longer, though he did order some blood tests.

"It's only been a year. You're healthy and young. Give it a few more months. I don't see any reason to get excited about intervention at this point. Any final questions?"

I hesitated before I spoke, afraid to reveal the truth. "Well, actually, during the exam? You mentioned something. You said I have a ruby pelvis?"

"I did?" He looked confused. Cute and confused.

"Like the gemstone?" For a moment he sat still, thinking, his eyes crinkling up endearingly in concentration. "I just don't know what you meant by a ruby pelvis. Are there other kinds? Pearl or jade?"

Then he began to laugh again, hoarse and low. When he finished, and wiped the tears out of his eyes, he looked at me with genuine kindness and possibly a touch of curiosity and said, "Roomy. I said you have a *roomy* pelvis."

I can't overestimate the relief I felt leaving Dr. Mercy's office, not simply because no pecking order among pelvises existed, but because the best gynecologist in the area deemed I could have a baby the old-fashioned way. Once alone in the car, I let myself laugh. Leave it to me with my cavernous persecution complex to fear I had a lesser vagina. Inevitably, my laughter led to crying. I often have thought Faucet would have been a lovely middle name. Having failed terribly at femininity over the course of my life, I could not stand to fail at reproducing. I'd always feared a future like my past, one of non-belonging to the world, to the world of family. My tears dissipated quickly, though. With my roomy pelvis, I had hope. Surely with Davis Mercy, I had hope. I called Cynthia when I got back on campus. I wanted to thank her. I wanted her to be the first person to hear the good news that I had been found normal.

A week later, when Thanksgiving recess began, Cynthia called me up and said, "I have a present for you. Meet me in ten minutes in the main parking lot." She did not ask if I had other plans, which thankfully I did not. I took her invitation as a command and made it to the meeting spot in under seven minutes.

She hopped into her steel-gray BMW and opened the door for me. "Come on! We don't want to be late."

"Where are we going?"

"Someplace you will love."

Three hours later, I emerged from Salon LeTrulle, mani-pedi'd straight to heaven. I tried to pay for the services, but Cynthia wouldn't let me.

"It's for your birthday," she said.

"My birthday isn't until the end of April."

"Half-birthday, then."

When we got back to Dixbie, I tumbled out of the car giddy with the kind of girlfriend joy you feel when you finally find your BFF in sixth grade and she spends the entire weekend at your house, where you both eat raw cookie dough and watch eighteen movies.

I didn't see Annie when I got out of the car, or notice her when I hugged Cynthia good-bye, or even hear her when she first called my name. I headed home through the windy, woodsy path where I usually walk Fruity.

"I SAID, 'What makes you tiptoe through the tulips?'"

I turned around to see Annie, dressed in a thick black coat and an ancient red wool hat with a black stain on the top. She was smoking a cigarette.

"Annie? What are you *doing*?"

"Rebelling."

"You gave up smoking. What about Lily?"

"I already pumped. Ted's going to give her a bottle. Besides, she's eight months old."

"But . . ." I was at a loss for words. The sight of Annie with a cigarette totally popped my happy balloon. "But, it's *bad* for you." Never mind that Dixbie has a no-tolerance policy when it comes to tobacco; no one can smoke anywhere on the campus, including in the backwoods behind the parking lot where the kids go to smoke—and often get caught.

"I'm not inhaling." She laughed. "Seriously. I'm not."

"Then why are you doing it?"

"To figure things out. Whenever I used to smoke, it helped my brain function."

"Ten years ago, before you had children and a job and mature means of solving your problems."

"That's where you're wrong. I *don't* have mature means of solving my problems. The way you say it, I'm not even sure I'd want any."

"Is this about Aileen?"

"Only peripherally. Mostly it's about therapy, my in-laws arriving tomorrow to ruin my holiday, the divine hardships of motherhood, and a few other things like ambivalence, empty bank accounts, and club takeovers." She threw the cigarette on the ground and stamped on it with her Birkenstock. "Anyway, what were you and Cynthia up to?" She stamped on the butt some more. "Since you two have become inseparable, you must know she infiltrated the YFC. She's started coming to meetings. She wants to make us *letterhead*." She said this with a molasses thickness of disdain as she continued to obliterate the cigarette. "I can't see you two have anything in common." At this point, the remains of the cigarette must have been firmly established in the tread of her sandal. No cigarette could endure such a beating.

We stood together for a moment in the quiet, eyes down, contemplating the ground where once the cigarette butt lay.

"Rest in peace?" I offered.

"Yeah. Amen."

"Are you going to leave it there?"

"I don't think it's identifiable anymore."

"Where did you get them?" I asked.

"At the gas station, like everybody else. I did have to sell the van to afford them, though." She did her snorting, lion roar. "Since you and Cynthia are so close, maybe you can help me understand her motivation. Is she a Republican? Is she trying to use the YFC to convert the girls to reading fashion mags?" She stared me down, full on, her curly hair rising up behind her in the dusky November light like a dreadlocked Rastafarian do.

"Um."

"She's come to the wrong place. There are fifty other private schools in New England full of posturing, wealthy girls. My young feminists are nerds who wear hair bands when they dress up. What's she after?"

"I don't think she's after anything. I don't think you need to make so much out of it. Maybe she really does want to help with the club. She's a very kind, thoughtful person, you know."

"Is she?"

I wanted to defend Cynthia. I thought of mentioning her gift of the spa day as proof of her generosity, but it seemed rude, somehow, given Annie's limited funds. I also knew what she thought of frivolities like manicures. Instead, I said, "You had tea with her. You know what she's like." Annie rolled her eyes. "And she set me up with her OB. He's extremely sought after; it's difficult to get an appointment and she got me in."

"How lucky." The acid in her voice could have eaten through metal.

"Annie, what's going on? You can't honestly be so upset with Cynthia. Has something happened with the divorce?"

"Nora, 'Marriage is a tool of the patriarchy meant to enslave women' functioned as the rallying cry of my adolescence. Do you truly think not being married is such a problem for me?"

I did. I did because she often spoke frustratedly about the divorce process dragging on, about how much she wanted to be "free of the first-wife oversize baggage," as she called it. I shuffled my feet and kept my mouth closed. I was glad my fancy, Berry-Swirl toes were well hidden in my sneakers. "It's a rough time of year," I said, as if we were two strangers talking about the weather, talking about nothing.

"I suppose you're right," she responded before walking away.

That night, after an optimistic romp with Alfie during which I reached over and tapped Dr. Mercy's business card on the bedside table for good luck, I thought about Annie.

Growing up, Annie was the smarter one, or at the very least, the more capable one. I admired her candor and sassiness and worldliness. When I shrunk away from the bullies on the playground, she stood up to them, tossing out a few insults she'd learned watching television my mother wouldn't let me see. One of her greatest protests against the status quo of elementary school cruelty came by way of her Twinkie-eating. Every day at lunch, despite comments on her girth, she proudly unwrapped and devoured a Twinkie. In sixth grade, she took a dance class with me and six other girls. When she came into the studio with her black leotard and pink tights on, the other students barely suppressed a laugh.

"Dancers used to be fat, didn't they?" she said loudly to Madame Violana, our teacher. "In the early 1900s, right?" Madame Violana opened her mouth but nothing came out. "Didn't they?" Annie demanded, still standing boldly at the front of the room, one hand on a roll-y hip. Violana, who pulled her hair back so sternly she'd given herself a receding hairline through repetitive bun-wearing, wasn't accustomed to confrontation from tweens. Finally, in her thick European accent (I think she may have been Italian, but no one talked about difference in Tarryville), she said, "You are right. Go to the barre." Then she clapped her hands. "Robust! They were robust! No one says 'fat' in my classroom." I should mention that Madame Violana weighed in at just ninety boney pounds.

Annie had courage, perhaps from living through her parents' embattled marriage and acrimonious divorce. I'd admired and longed for the air of maturity she carried even at ten. "It will pass," she'd said to me whenever her parents fought while I was at their house. "It always does." Then she'd close the door to dampen the sound and start playing again. I doubt I would have been able to maintain such indifference in the face of a crumbling family structure.

By the time she got around to dating during her college years, she had more skill at rejecting men than anyone I know. She also had more dates than I did. Whenever we talked on the phone, I'd hear about a new lover already come and gone. It wasn't indifference, after all. It was something else I couldn't name.

Still, I admired her as her hard edges got sharper. She was so concrete in my mind, the opposite of my own imprecision. Her solidity had always drawn me to her, since I clearly lacked my own. In my mind, I was one of the pine trees with shallow roots that goes down in a windstorm, and Annie was a three-hundred-year-old oak that won't budge. Whatever else may be true from her childhood, it gave her character, strength, and endurance. In that way, she was very easy to love and respect. Though in so many other ways, she was inflexible, caustic, and lately, far away. I missed the ease of our earlier friendship when we were more equal in our lives. I missed enjoying her company, but the truth was, I preferred my time with Cynthia. Who wouldn't favor her golden touch?

I fell asleep realizing I had forgotten Annie's early-November birthday. It came like the answer to a riddle. It explained her distance when we met on the path. I *always* remembered my oldest friend's birthday. After all, that's what nice people do.

I fully intended to rectify this situation the next day, possibly after my trip to the grocery store for Thanksgiving turkey or possibly before Alfie and I caught a movie in town at the new art cinema. There would be plenty of time to patch things up, and if an enduring friendship offers nothing else, it offers easy forgiveness—no relationship can last so long without it.

There was one problem with my plan. It didn't take into account an unannounced, though not entirely unexpected, visit from my cousin Ellie Mae Ruthie Leigh Blenderhorn, Ph.D.

After a series of fervent knocks, I opened the door early in the morning with a towel still wrapped around my head to find her standing in the dorm hallway, a bulging electric-pink suitcase by her side that said one thing: *long visit*.

"Elle!" I cried.

14

Annie

I roasted a turkey.

Not any turkey, the biggest, most ridiculous turkey ever cooked. I needed enough meat for nine adults and five children. I also needed a commercial kitchen. Even though I'd prepared as much as I possibly could in advance, I still had every burner firing.

George and Betty, Ted's parents, were in the living room watching the children, who had turned the couch into a boat and the coffee table into a dock. Stetson, Ted's brother, and his wife, Lucinda, had gone to the bathroom to clean up, though the length of their stay made me wonder if they weren't up to more than that. I have not personally found lengthy car rides to have any erotically stimulating qualities, so found this possibility rather unlikely, but thirty minutes' washing up led me to no other conclusion. I did feel some sympathy; as a mother of young children, I know you have to take your moments as a couple whenever you get them.

Laithe, the youngest sibling, took his cell phone outside

to talk to a mysterious new girlfriend no one had yet met. And Lindy and her husband, John, were in the kitchen chopping vegetables for me and boring me to tears with the minutiae of their medical practices.

"I said to Mrs. Hanson, no matter how many times you come here to get checked out, I will tell you the same thing. You do not have a heart condition. I've run every test possible. You're suffering from a severe case of generalized anxiety," Lindy droned on as she rhythmically cut carrots.

Give the poor woman some medication, I wanted to say. Or maybe with luck she'd find herself a more compassionate doctor.

"The last thing I did was remove a possible skin cancer. First time I've taken one from the interior of the belly button," Lindy went on.

But it would get worse. Bunions and boils and cancers and tumors and prostates and infections and surgeries and rashes, until your eyes water from the sheer misery of it. The buzzer for the turkey rang out.

Ted came in with Hannah on his shoulders to see if he could do anything to help.

"We've got it covered," Lindy said. "Many hands make light work."

Ted smiled at me in sympathy.

By the time we'd all crowded around our dining room table, the four little kids sitting together at Hannah's art table, sweat dripped down my back. I held Lily, the little furnace, in my arms. She'd taken to howling whenever I put her down, a condition I do not remember Hannah ever suffering. I attributed this to her rather stubborn refusal to master crawling, a skill she was more than prepared for. I would lay her down on her belly on the floor, and she'd pull up her knees and consider. Then she'd look at me and drop back onto the floor. The child is sharper than a knife's blade; she knew it was far better to be carried than to crawl across a dirty floor. As a result, I'd developed a truly unathletic version of tennis elbow; after hours each day of holding her eighteen-pound weight, I could no longer fully extend my arm, a topic I assiduously refrained from mentioning in front of my in-laws for fear of an impromptu exam.

"You certainly have missed out," George was saying, a continuation of some conversation they'd been having in the living room.

"Not everybody can work for the common good," Betty said. She works in a women's health clinic. "Do you know the other day I performed an aspiration for a seventeen-year-old girl who'd been raped by her brother? You'd be surprised how much of that I see."

"Mom," Ted said. "The children."

"They hear it all the time," George said. "I grew up listening to my father talk about his practice. That's what inspired me to go into medicine."

"But Dad, I really don't think we should talk about abortion at the dinner table." Ted spoke in the quiet, retreating way he did whenever his parents were around.

"Fact of life, son," George said.

"And thank God for the modern methods," Betty went on. "I'm *saving* lives every day—not losing them. I could tell you about it, how things were, even fifteen years ago. You wouldn't eat if I told you about thirty years ago."

"Should we go around the table and say something we're

grateful for?" I suggested, hoping that the conversation wouldn't fall apart the same way it did when the topic of breast implants hit the table last Easter. For a full meal, the ethical implications of stacked racks filled my ears. After that, I would have *killed* to talk Easter bunnies with Hannah.

No one heard me, or no one listened. Alison and Aaron, Lindy's five-year-old twins, began screaming at the sight of the Brussels sprouts on their plates, their mere presence contaminating the nearby and more desirable food. Laithe got another phone call on his cell and left the room to take it.

"We think he's in love," Betty offered, proudly. "Fellow pediatric resident."

Ugh. It was going to be another marriage between doctors. Couldn't these people branch out?

"Annie, you're still not working?" Betty asked without waiting for an answer. "How are your little projects going? Don't you volunteer with the schoolkids?"

By this I assumed she meant the Young Feminists Club. "Lily's only eight months," I said in explanation.

"I went back after three," Lindy commented.

"Now, I *did* stay home with Laithe until his six-month birthday," Betty said, tapping George on the arm as if to remind him. "Six months is all a baby needs developmentally. Surely you can't find the necessary fulfillment doing the," she paused, searching for the right words, "the *things* you do with the dorm kids."

"Mom, Annie's main work consists of taking care of our children. On top of that she's a housemother and runs one of the largest clubs on campus," Ted protested.

"Well?" Betty smiled rather insincerely.

"It's important to have meaningful employment," George said, a huge piece of turkey on his fork. "How goes it with your club?"

How it went with my club could not be discussed in mixed company; no one under twenty, preferably, considering the host of insults that accompanied my feelings on the matter of Cynthia's intrusion.

I thought back to the most recent meeting before Thanksgiving recess, during which the girls carried on about getting more feminist tracts on the freshman required reading list while I dutifully took notes. We'd spent so much time discussing the major educational event they wanted to hold in the spring, and debating the methods of enlightening the campus on all things feminist, that we all could not bear another moment of it. Reading lists, at least, involved fewer disputes.

"I am *so* sorry to be late," Cynthia proclaimed, throwing the door open wide and prancing in. She was wrapped in a long, heavy red shawl that sported a black fur collar. A little murmur of pleasure rose up from the group. "No need to review for me. I'll catch up later." She sat down next to me. I controlled the urge to stand up and move to another seat, mostly because I'd like to pretend I no longer act like a twelve-year-old in public.

"Thank goodness you're here," Sarah Muskurt said swoonily as though her teen idol had arrived.

"We're working on changing the reading list," Ginger added. I had persuaded her to join the Young Feminists Club, certain it would fill the empty hole in her life. I'm happy to say I couldn't have been more correct. She'd blossomed in the group and no longer wailed on the phone in the dorm for hours. However, the smile of admiration she gave Cynthia did nothing to endear her to me. I had hoped *one* of the girls would see through Cynthia's finery to the emptiness within. Alas.

"What about Camille Paglia?" Cynthia said.

"Genius," Pepper practically shouted. I wrote "Paglia" down in my worst penmanship.

Mayonnaise aside, I liked Dixbie. It was home, and these girls were my people. When Ginger's mother fetched her the other day to take her home for Thanksgiving, Ginger brought her specifically to meet me. She said to her mother, "*This* is the woman I've been telling you about."

"You're the first person I wanted her to meet," Ginger told me then, quietly and aside, with that freshman mix of pride and shyness. How could I not be touched? Whatever else may be true, I *like* being liked, even by anxious fourteen-year-olds. And yet, despite her attachment to me, during the meeting, every query went in Cynthia's direction, every worry got addressed to her. I sat there in a bleary haze of frustration, feeling something all too familiar. The fat kid sitting alone in the cafeteria with only Nora by my side lives in me somewhere, and since Cynthia's takeover of my club, I felt she was the only person the girls could see when they looked at me. Lorilee Albright, the club's senior chair, tugged me out of my pity party when she closed the meeting by saying, "Are the rumors true?"

"What rumors?" Cynthia and I said simultaneously.

Now, Dixbie continuously churns its rumor wheel. Gossip constitutes an important part of the social education of all teenagers. Ted and I were fond of following the mini-dramas, love affairs, shocking secrets (such as someone coming out of the closet, or a previously good girl getting caught smoking). But it had been a relatively quiet fall for scandal, save for a collective campus Cynthia voyeurism. I heard at least one conversation a day in the dorm speculating on Cynthia's pre-Dixbie life. (Was she an heiress? Had she been a model?) If I had to hear the word "enigma" thrown around one more time, I figured a lesson in synonyms would be in order.

"The school isn't in trouble, right? That's what Cooper Litence told us, and he said he heard it from his dad, who is one of the trustees, that we put all our money in the wrong place, and we may not be able to open again next year. Cooper usually checks his sources," Lorilee continued. "But I guess even he can make a mistake, if, um, you know, neither of you know anything about it."

"I haven't heard anything," I said. "I can promise you that won't happen. Institutions like this one don't just close." I was going to say more, but all eyes were on Cynthia. Clearly, my opinion didn't count.

"Aren't you a trustee?" Lorilee asked, something I'd never heard before.

Cynthia smiled pleasantly. Without answering the question, she said: "I will absolutely look into it." Then she flashed her snow-white smile.

"It's fine," I said to Ted's family over the Thanksgiving dinner, relinquishing these bad memories. "The club is great." I passed the turkey.

"Still, a club isn't enough for a smart woman like you. This is the perfect time, Annie, to take on some work. Best to get on it before you lose your ambition. I'm sure you can agree how useful it would be for you to take on a job." Betty looked over at me. I registered the cautious disapproval on her face, hoping she registered the thinly guarded disgust on mine. In the first place, I resented the public reference to our financial situation. Ted and I had both decided we would make do with less in order for me to stay home; neither of us felt it was fair to force me into work simply because he'd married a lunatic who wanted all his money. In the second place, I knew staying home *was* the useful thing to do.

"Don't be sour, dear. There are many reasons to get out and work. Think of the women of my generation. We fought to overcome multiple barriers so that our daughters would have the chance to have children *and* work. In my day, no one wanted to stay home. We wanted to get out and make a difference in the world and help people and lead active lives. We battled like hell so that you could have everything that a whole person needs. It's such a shame when you don't take it. Surely you know all this. Your mother has done so much in her lifetime."

I looked at Ted to see if he shared my homicidal thoughts. Despite her superficial sweetness, Betty had a clever way of offending. I didn't doubt that she believed what she said. That she had no idea how rude she was. That she'd look good with a pitchfork in her heart.

"Excuse me," I said, standing up. "I've got to go check on the dessert."

"I'll hold the baby," Betty offered.

"You do have to consider the standard you set for your girls," Lindy said as I left the room.

I wanted to scream. I stood in the kitchen for a few minutes staring out the window at the dark night. What I really wanted to do was go in there and tell Lindy and Betty that I'd been around to see my girls do every first, from rolling over and crawling and walking (in Hannah's case), to the littlest accomplishments like clapping for the first time, cooing for the first time, eating their first Cheerio. Betty didn't work so hard for all women to end up corporate with unsuspecting infants stuck in day cares; she fought for women to get a choice. And I was perfectly sure I'd made the better one.

"Don't let them get to you," Ted said, all of a sudden behind me, with a hand on my shoulder. "You know how they are. They don't mean anything by it. I got a ten-minute lecture on how I could still get into a decent medical school and go into general practice. Can you believe it? After teaching for seven years, they're still on me to go into medicine."

"I'm so mad I could spit."

"Just don't spit on me."

"What's wrong with these people? It's one thing for women of your mother's generation who feel like they've done us a favor, but what about younger women like Lindy? For that matter, what about Suze?"

"At least we live in a town with lots of other stay-at-home mothers."

"Brownston? You're kidding, right? Most of the mothers in town work. The Brownies, the ones that don't? They don't spend time with their children. If you're not home with your kids, it doesn't count. If you have a full-time nanny, you are *not* a stay-at-home mom, I don't care what anyone says. It may suck for us not to have any money, but if money makes you walk away from your kids, I'm *glad* not to have it."

"I know. I agree with you. Remember, we made this decision together." He crept over and stood by the door to the dining room for a second. "You can go back in. It's safe. They've moved on to vaccines."

"I hate my life right now," I said.

"Honey, they'll go soon. You only have to survive until tomorrow."

"It's not just them. It's everything and everybody—your mom, Nora, Cynthia, you thinking I'm ambivalent, Suze off working all the time. I feel like the only fish swimming up-stream. Not just because I'm home with kids. I don't have any friends."

"I'm your friend," Ted said.

"I ought to have more than one."

"Seriously, Annie? I think this therapy thing might be hurting more than helping; since you started you've been more agitated than usual. If it isn't making you happier, do you really want to continue?"

"You want to make me happy? Call up Ah-leen and get her to sign those papers. And then make her get a job so I don't have to go to three different grocery stores to get the best sale on chicken thighs, or be the only one at the BFC who hasn't bought a new pair of pants in this millennium. Or get reamed out by your mother at the dinner table because she thinks I ought to be working." Ted's shoulders slumped.

"You want a doctor for a husband? Join the club. I would make more money, at least, and then no one could get mad at you for not working."

I shook my head. "It's not the money. It's the fact that the whole world is against me. For once, I'd like to have some-thing of my own. I'm okay if we can't have our own house, our own savings account, our own family holiday without a bunch of maniac relatives, or even my own club full of progressive young girls. But maybe I could have one person, just *one*, who knows how I feel, why I'm doing what I'm doing in the world, one friend."

"I'm that person."

"I'm sorry, honey." I shook my head apologetically. "You don't really count. You're my *husband*."

"What about Suze and Nora. You've known Nora forever and you're always with Suze."

"Update time, my love. I haven't seen Nora for more than five minutes in about four weeks. She's having a virtual love affair with Cynthia. She forgot my birthday for the first time in twenty-eight years. And Suze doesn't have time for me. Not even for a quick phone call. Gone are our weekly BFC play dates, our weekend mom's lunches. With work taking up all her day time, she needs every spare minute to pretend to mother Finn. She actually hasn't called me since she first told me about the job." I was prepared to carry on like this for a while when Betty called from the dining room. "Annie! Do you have any more mashed potatoes?"

Oh, the world felt against me. I put both girls to bed in our room for the night. Lindy and John and Alison and Aaron were in Lily's room with an air mattress on the floor. Stetson and Lucinda and their daughter, Hillary, were in Hannah's room. Betty and George had one of the dorm rooms we'd cleared out. I got some satisfaction thinking about them sleeping on hard, uneven twin beds. Laithe got his own dorm room, a narrow single with a slit of a window, not that he would notice. He'd probably lie in bed and text all night.

I hated everyone. I couldn't sleep I hated everyone so

much. I spent a little time hating Ted's family—with good reason, clearly. Then I spent some time hating Nora for deserting. How was it possible that she couldn't see Cynthia's self-absorption? Then I spent some time hating Cynthia and wishing her bad hemorrhoids and a sixty-hour labor. From there I spent some time angry at Suze for decamping. All of this loathing built into a general hatred toward all people everywhere, with a particular emphasis on doctors, people who can afford/who wear designer shoes, and mothers who work.

I finished up my anger-fest with a heaping dose of self-loathing. Being with Ted's family reminds me of the children's game "Which of These Things Is Not Like the Others." Being different has its upsides, like when you're the only fat kid in school and so you develop fortitude and some really cool imaginary friends. A part of me, however, hated the different in me and ached to be part of the group. Did this mean that on some deep, dark hidden level, Meg was right and I was ambivalent?

It's not as though I'd never *thought* about working since the girls had been born. Days happened, long days, hard days, boring days, tedious days, when I hungered for an adult outlet. I assumed most people, even working-outside-the-home people, experienced long, hard, tedious days.

Ted rolled over with a grumble, pulling the sheets higher on his shoulder.

"You're not sleeping."

"I'm too pissed off."

"Take some deep breaths."

"I hate everyone."

"At least you're not leaving anyone out. That's very democratic of you," Ted whispered.

I pulled the comforter up tightly under my chin and started to count down from one hundred in the hopes that it would calm my mind. I'd learned this little trick from Meg. Could Ted be right? Had my sessions with her wreaked havoc? I liked having an hour to talk about myself without interruption, without having to jump and fetch somebody something or listen to anyone (except myself) whine or complain. It did seem, though, that I was in a worse mood than before I began the therapy. Had Meg made me angrier, or was I simply being more honest?

When I got to fifty, a flash of memory hit me from the YFC meeting. I opened my eyes. "Hey, Ted? Did you hear anything about the school being out of money?"

"What?" he mumbled, half-awake.

"Did you hear the rumor about the school having to close? My little feministas were asking about it."

"Only from Beverly," he said. "And she rarely gets her facts straight. Let's go to sleep, huh? We've got to take my parents to Walden Pond tomorrow. We need all our strength."

"Right." I closed my eyes. I returned to one hundred and began again.

15

Nora

The four of us sat around the table observing a moment of silence. "For the sacrifice of the turkey," Elle said, nudging me with her elbow. "Out of respect."

"What a lovely idea." Cynthia, who sat to my right, folded her hands together. Only minutes before, I'd removed David's place setting. Alfie and I had invited both of them for the Thanksgiving meal, but David was home sick, some gruesome stomach thing that I could only feel was a direct intervention from the powers that be on my behalf. I did not want to look across the candlelit table at his face. Not now, not ever.

I hadn't meant to invite either of them over. My apartment still resembled itself; it would not have dawned on me to host the holiday meal if it weren't for Elle, who stated, "Thanksgiving for only three! I won't have it! Don't you have any friends we can invite?" When she met Cynthia the next day in the parking lot, she took it upon herself to invite her and her "significant other" over for the dinner, despite the fact that I do not own matching china for five. After Cynthia enthusiastically accepted, I spent five hundred dollars at the mall. Alfie came home that day from the grocery store and said, "Who lives here?" When he sat on the couch, he picked up a throw pillow and said, "What *is* this?"

"A-men!" Elle hollered, to close out our turkey-moment-of-silence.

"Are you religious?" Cynthia asked Elle, placing the twenty-dollar napkin I'd bought the day before neatly into her lap.

"Not strictly speaking," she answered. "Although it seems like such a good idea during the holidays, doesn't it?" I bit my lip, horrified that Cynthia would now be witness to the institutional zaniness of the Helpsom-Fulch family. "Although," and she reached out and tapped the thigh of the cooked bird on our table, "I doubt this one's a believer."

"I was vegetarian for a few years," Cynthia said. I didn't know this about her. I watched Alfie carve the turkey, mortified that I might be serving up a bird she wouldn't eat.

"But now you're pregnant," Elle said, giving us all the opportunity to be completely confused by her train of thought. "How do you feel? I puked all day long."

"You have children, then?" Cynthia asked, holding up her plate as I dished out the green beans.

"Not anymore." She smiled rather freakishly. Elle had never been pregnant. I had to assume she was being perverse. Her dyed electric-red hair looked nearly purple in the low light. "So, are you able to keep things down? Dealing okay with the deathlike exhaustion?"

"I feel fantastic."

"Now what about the sex? Patients have told me it only

gets better." At this point, one might expect her voice to drop, a whisper to emerge. Not so. She began to speak louder. "Nipple sensitivity, in particular, comes up a lot in my practice. And with all that extra blood pooling in your clitoris, it's no wonder so many women become multi-orgasmic during the second trimester."

Alfie dropped his fork. I think he was shaking from the urge to laugh, not, as I was, from pure and unadulterated humiliation.

"Have you listened to my radio program before? *Sex Is Sex*? I *was* going to be on TV. But why talk about me? Nora mentioned that you've been to India. I've heard excellent things about the Tantric practices and breathing techniques to raise your kundalini energy. I, myself, learned Tantra from a beautiful Indian man."

Alfie and I looked at one another, appalled by Elle, but Cynthia didn't seem bothered in the slightest.

"Let's dig in," Alfie said, having served the turkey to all but Elle.

"They're really quite simple." She closed her eyes, as if to demonstrate right there, beside our table, her uncanny knack for cosmic orgasms. "Begin by feeling your belly, and deep in your belly, your root chakra connecting you to the primal energies of the earth."

"You know what," I said, putting a halt to the horror, "dinner probably isn't the best time to learn those techniques. Seeing as we still have to," I wavered over the word, "*digest* our food." I attempted a friendly smile when what I really wanted to do was send Elle straight back to Philadelphia—in a rocket ship.

"Well, anytime you want to learn, Cyn," she said, reaching

across the table to tap Cynthia on the arm, "I'm here for you. Raj taught me everything he knew. He passed on all of his best tips, and I've retained them."

"What a kind offer."

Really, it would hurt to go on detailing the events of the evening, as they didn't get any better. By the time we were eating dessert in the living room, Elle had worked herself into a frenzy of sexual education excitement, thinking she had a real follower in Cynthia, who simply nodded, smiled, and affirmed her the entire evening.

"We have to reclaim the sacred feminine power," Elle preached, a bite of pumpkin pie perched on her fork. "It's my personal calling to restore the right image for women everywhere. We must create a revolution based on the power of the yoni. Our sacred cave! The blossom of womanhood! The feminine principle!" I must have looked bewildered, when I meant to convey an expression of horror, because Elle took a good look at me, then said, "The vagina, Nora! I'm talking about the vagina!"

"I'm familiar with that body part," I replied, feeling helpless. Alfie reached for the TV remote.

"Men should worship women as goddesses." I couldn't muster a response. Luckily, Alfie interjected.

"Anyone mind if I turn on the football?"

"I need to go to the bathroom, anyway," Elle said, getting up.

Once she'd left the room, I immediately apologized to Cynthia.

"No need to be sorry. She's quite entertaining and completely uncensored. I can see how she's become so successful in her field."

"Still, I never intended for Thanksgiving to turn into *The Vagina Monologues*."

"I have nothing against the vagina," Cynthia graciously replied. "Although I probably ought to go home and check on David. Hopefully, he feels better."

"Of course!" I stood up and my dessert plate plummeted to the floor. I'd forgotten it was on my lap. Cynthia knelt down and picked it up before I could even bend over.

"It was so nice of you to include me," she said, walking to the door.

"Thanks for coming over!" Alfie called from the couch.

"I'm sorry it was so—unusual."

Cynthia put on a zebra-striped wool coat. "I had a lovely time. You're very lucky to have such an animated relative. I don't have any cousins." She placed a velvety hat on her head. "Come for tea soon?"

I accepted with a nod, grateful, and not for the first time, for Cynthia's consistent charm. She even made it seem like a good thing to have a cousin like Elle. Although I imagined she must have sympathy for me, it was kind of her to say something uplifting about Elle's regrettable company. Not that I didn't love Elle in the way you dutifully love your family members. In fact, there had been a time, when Elle first became a licensed sex therapist and took great joy in pushing Aunt Bertie's buttons, that I admired her candor and provocative nature. But up against Cynthia's subdued good manners, Elle looked practically barbaric, like one of those monkeys with the raw, pink protruding buttocks running around beside the other cute, hairy monks; you feel you need to look away.

I closed the door behind Cynthia with relief. Altogether,

it had been the most embarrassing night of my life, if you exclude my adolescence in its totality. I leaned against the closed door, exhausted. Since I'd spent the majority of the past two days shopping, cleaning, and rearranging the furniture in my apartment, every bone in my body ached, and I *still* thought the place looked lousy.

It was a moment when I would have loved to call Annie, only I realized I had never made good on my promise to make a belated birthday phone call, and now the oversight seemed intentional, though it wasn't. I could hardly admit to myself that while Annie knew everything about me and shared everything about herself, being with Cynthia felt like a night at Cinderella's ball. After Elle first met Cynthia in the parking lot, she'd said, "It must be hard to be so good-looking. Personally, I prefer a little ugliness here and there, say in the nose, or around the eyes. It's far more interesting. But I suppose someone has to be made by the angels."

I debated asking whether Elle truly believed in angels, ultimately deciding against it on the strong suspicion that she did and probably had a few to invite over for Thanksgiving dinner.

For a few minutes after I closed the door behind Cynthia, I stared blankly at the wall calendar, zoning out. Then I went over and looked more carefully at the month of November. There was no *P* anywhere to be found.

Wouldn't it have to be late on Thanksgiving, so not a single pharmacy within a thirty-minute drive or grocery store still held its doors open for the urgent needs of a possibly pregnant woman? I spent a good ten minutes calling around before considering asking Elle, on the off-chance that in her enormous suitcase, and with her prolific sexual expertise, she might happen to carry around pregnancy tests the way some people carry around spare tissues.

Only I couldn't bear to hear another word come out of her mouth that evening. I stared at Alfie and her watching the football game with a great deal of gratitude that, despite her narrow focus, she did have interests outside of her profession. It didn't surprise me that she would follow football. Almost all the men in the Helpsom-Fulch tribe enjoy things that bounce—any kind of ball will do. The exception to this would be my father, who golfed only out of family obligation whenever Uncle Roy, Aunt Lucy's husband, invited him. As I mentioned before, stuffing animals made up his pastime.

"Come sit with us, Nora," Elle said from her nest on the couch. "We can talk about the cutest players, like old times."

"I don't remember doing that."

"We always did! Whenever we were together for Thanksgiving. Don't you remember Aunt Bertie scolding us for being so 'carnal'?" Elle laughed. "Boy, does that woman need some of my advice!" Alfie laughed now too. "Poor Aunt Bertie," she said. "It's not easy being ugly."

"Elle! That's not fair," I said, although I could feel a laugh beginning. No one had ever said the truth about Bertie, not out loud.

"I've always liked her," Alfie said. "She's so consistent."

"That's sweet." Elle reached over and put a hand on his shoulder. "You've got a good man, Nora," she said, looking over at me. "Don't know what I've done wrong to miss out on that."

I had a few ideas, such as the perpetual sex talk. No man wants to go out on a first date with a woman who asks him if he's circumcised (she once recounted this actual date to me), but I kept my mouth shut and joined them on the sofa.

I tossed and turned in bed that night, unable to fall asleep without knowing whether or not I was pregnant, and equally afraid of finding out. I alternated between hopefulness and hopelessness; I did not want to be disappointed. The awful dinner with Elle and Cynthia faded straight into the background.

Frustrated, I finally crept out of bed. Without waking Alfie, I tiptoed into the office. Fruity, who sleeps with us sometimes and sometimes sleeps in her dog bed on the floor, followed me. When I sat down at my desk, she curled up right on top of my feet, not a bad way to keep your toes warm.

How to distract my mind? Write my final exam for freshman English? Design a new class? I had been asked to teach the junior honors course in the spring, currently entitled "Shakespeare and His Sisters." Instead, I mindlessly took out a scrap of paper and began to draw. Before I knew it, I'd drawn a whole landscape filled with animals and, in the center, one funny-looking creature with a large bow in her hair. I pulled myself away from the desk and looked at her. Instantly, I knew her; she was Olive, Olive the Ogre. That's when I remembered Annie's request to write down the Olive story I'd been telling Hannah. I got out a whole sheaf of paper and began.

Almost two hours later, Alfie found me this way, crouched over the papers, intensely sketching and occasionally writing a few words.

"Can't sleep?" he said, putting his big hands on my shoulders and giving them a squeeze.

I pushed the papers underneath a file folder. "I'm late," I told him. "I think I'm a few days late for my period." I could almost feel his smile in his hands, in the way his breath changed.

"Really?"

"I haven't been doing such a good job charting since Elle arrived. She keeps getting me up early for coffee and I'm out of bed before I remember I need to take my temperature." Actually, I'd had a hard time staying consistent even before Elle arrived. The method only works with perfect accuracy. If you get up and pee before you take your temperature, all bets are off. "I'm perfect at recording things on the calendar, though, and according to the calendar, I'm late." I decided not to turn around and look at him. "I'm afraid to be wrong. I'm afraid to look at my chart, in case it does say something one way or the other."

"I'll look for you," Alfie said. "Tell me where it is. Oh, and what to look for."

Then I turned around to face him. Fruity moved off my feet and tiredly got up to rub against Alfie. I noticed she looked stiff, pressing up to stand with her hind legs trembling.

"Actually, if we look together, that will be good enough. If you don't mind getting it, it's in the drawer of my bedside table."

"Okay," he said, and then he shuffled out of the room. I listened to the sounds of his slippers on the wood floor.

"This it?" He came in with a pile of charts.

"That's it." He passed them to me and I stared down, looking first at the current month, then the two prior months. "Last month was twenty-nine days," I said. "This is the thirty-second day."

"That means something?" Alfie asked hopefully. I shrugged my shoulders. "Want me to get a test? I'll go first thing in the morning." He smiled at me, tentatively, and my heart clenched. His tenderness hurt to observe; I could feel how much more I wanted a baby than I wanted him, how much more he wanted me than a baby. I pushed the thought away.

"Yes. Please."

"Great!" He clapped his hands together like a little child.

"Don't say anything to Elle. She'll want to perform the test herself."

"I promise," he said, taking my hand to pull me out of the chair. "This will be our secret."

16

Annie

December

I brought a list with me to my meeting with Meg. A *List of Issues to Discuss:*

1. Why has talking with Meg amped up my ire?
2. What motivates Cynthia Cypress to mess with my life?
3. Why don't I have anyone to talk to about my issues except Meg?

This last weighed heavily on my mind. I didn't want to make Meg feel bad, but I shouldn't have to use good insurance money to get someone to listen to me. I've always considered myself a little prickly; on the other hand, plenty of people like cactus plants and they aren't warm and fuzzy. Plenty of people, for that matter, had liked *me* over the years. Now, I entered the desert of friendship.

For one thing, Nora and Cynthia running off together like the Bobbsey twins left an enormous gap in my social life.

I am not exaggerating when I say that every time I saw Nora in the month of November, she was with Cynthia. Funny thing, as I always gave Nora credit for being deep, and here she'd become as shallow as a puddle. I had yet to discover a single cell of substance to Cynthia.

Suze had a far better excuse. At least she'd left me for a job instead of a more attractive friend.

The odd thing about therapy, as I discovered, is that you can arrive certain you will talk about the troubles you have taken the time to carefully write down so you won't forget them, only to open your mouth and find yourself talking about Thanksgiving dinner, an event of so little consequence it didn't make it to the list.

I rattled off the story of my (almost) in-laws like an auctioneer. Meg listened attentively. When I finished, feeling as though I'd lost a few pounds of the weight of the world on my shoulders, she folded her bejeweled fingers in her lap and said, "Annie, have you thought any more about the topic of ambivalence?"

"Where in the story that I just told you can you see any uncertainty on my part, any confusion, any doubt?"

"In your reaction."

"That doesn't make any sense."

"Of course it doesn't! From the inside, things rarely make sense. What strikes me, as an observer, is the strength of your anger and opposition toward Betty's suggestion. Why it brings to mind Lady Macbeth."

"You think I 'doth protest too much'?"

"What I think," she said, "is probably not useful. But what I have observed and heard from you so far is this: You came to therapy wanting help with your daughter and her Amazonian will as well as her rage. Without taking up that issue in depth, you've shared with me the loss of your friend, Suze, and the force of your convictions concerning mothers who work without financial necessity. In what you share today, about Ted's family and their views on employment, I hear a sense of the pressure you are under, real and perceived, from all sides."

"Exactly!" I said. "I'm being pressured."

"In my experience," she replied, "pressure is most difficult when it pushes up *not* against something we do not want—in which case disinterest is usually the response—but when it pushes up against something we are afraid to want, or perhaps, on some level, truly do desire."

"Why would I want to work? That's ridiculous! We *need* the money far more than Suze does, and I still won't do it. I want to be with my girls. I've always believed this was the right way to do things—and I've told you why."

"Perhaps you can pay attention to how angry this makes you."

"I am!" I said, with no small amount of frustration.

"Annie," came her gentle response. "Tell me more about deciding to have children. How did Hannah and Lily come into the world?"

"The old-fashioned way."

She laughed merrily. "That's not quite what I had in mind. You mentioned when you first came in that you had two 'accidental daughters.'"

"Oh, right. I only meant they weren't planned. Or, they were planned for several years down the road. Ted and I always assumed we would have children *after* the divorce finalized."

"You're still young," she said. "Were there any other reasons for delaying having children?"

"Other reasons?" I looked up at the smooth white ceiling. "Well, I suppose, I planned to get a little further in my painting. See if I had enough talent to build a career. I'd just begun having gallery shows before Hannah's birth."

"Painting and showing work seem quite compatible with motherhood. After all, you can paint in off-hours; you can show your work periodically without taking away too much time from family."

"But I didn't want to paint! After Hannah was born, I wanted to be with her. I didn't want to feel divided in my affections. Painting isn't like, oh, I don't know, filing or answering phones. It requires dedication, uninterrupted hours, the leisure of letting your mind wander." I thought of the last time I painted seriously, a series of abstracts I made a month before Hannah's birth. I'd thought, a few times, about taking them up again. Meg had a point that I could use my evening hours, or even nap times. It wasn't truly the time that stopped me. "It isn't the time issue. I wanted to be the mother I planned to become when I was younger."

"And are you that mother?"

Oh, the pointed questions! Meg had a delicate way of peeling apart the noise and finding the silent places inside me, away from the flurry of my own arguments and objections. I sat there for what could have been five minutes, probably the longest time I've been quiet and still since I had kids, trying to find an honest answer to her question. I decided, given how intensely I longed to make peace with my own child by finding peace with my inner child, that I had to be ruthlessly frank with her and with myself. After all, I didn't want to spend a whole year searching out this great inner child, this happy person within. I wanted to get it done and move on.

"No," I said. And then I felt tears threatening. I pressed my thumbnail into the palm of my hand to stop them. "I don't really like this," I told Meg. "Couldn't you be a little *less* observant?" If I'd known how hard this would be, I would have searched out a bad therapist, someone who pretended to take notes but really doodled irreverent cartoons, someone who pretended to listen but really thought about her favorite episode of *Extreme Couponing* while I chatted on hopelessly.

"You know what it is," I said, the urge to cry subsiding. "My mother spent the first half of my childhood consumed with her dysfunctional, miserable marriage, and the second half fighting for causes. She wasn't ever around, even when she *was* around."

"Are you like her?"

"Not at all. For one thing, we love each other. Ted and I, the whole Aileen disaster aside, have a wonderful partnership. He's my dearest friend. I feel utterly at home in his company. Anyhow, it's unlikely we'll ever divorce since it's beginning to seem unlikely that we'll ever get married!" I laughed ruefully, but Meg looked serious.

"Are you like your mother in the way you express anger and discontentment?"

I took a tissue and blew my nose. Then I chucked it across the room, aiming for the trash basket fifteen feet away like a pissed-off rebellious teen. We both watched it land in the middle of the room, where it looked both forlorn and surprisingly innocent. "Maybe."

"Annie, if you'll allow me to make a personal comment. *All* mothers, at least at one time, feel ambivalent, not in their love for their children, but over the sacrifices that come quite inevitably when your life changes so dramatically."

"I thought I was talking about the awful things Betty said and how ridiculous it is to expect me to go back to work if I don't want to."

"No." She smiled at me, her eyes crinkling deeply. In that moment, she struck me as very kind. "We are talking about your anger and inconsistency about your role as a full-time mother and how it is affecting your relationship with your children—and your friends."

For a moment I couldn't look at her. It seemed that she had said something horrible and true. "This isn't what I had in mind for my life back when I had the luxury to plan it."

"Speaking from the point of view of seven decades, I suggest you make peace with that fact; life is largely made of the unexpected."

A few moments later, while walking to the car, I listened to a message from Suze on my cell phone. This allowed me a short reprieve from the intensity of the therapy, which I briefly considered resigning from until it struck me that the only thing worse than delving even further into the dark corners of my life was quitting halfway done. Still, after hearing Suze's bright familiar voice drawing me back into my comfortable, if imperfect, life, I decided to take a few weeks off from the therapy. When Suze mentioned she had Wednesday off and wanted to meet me at the family center, I exhaled with relief. A morning with Suze could repair much of what ailed me. I could see Meg again in a few weeks if things didn't improve on their own.

I pulled up to the dorm feeling slightly more like myself when I spotted Nora in my rearview mirror walking along the sidewalk with her cousin Elle, who I remembered clearly from a number of visits during my childhood, although now her brown hair flamed magenta and her fitted wool coat revealed a sizable bosom. I didn't want to say hello to either of them. But then I did. Probably because I felt lonely, although I hoped it wouldn't show, that I wouldn't wear my loneliness like some poorly applied electric-blue eye shadow that no one would mention to me but everyone would talk about later, with alarm, among themselves.

"Hey, stranger," I called to Nora, remembering how hearing Suze's voice cheered me up. I aimed for a jovial tone.

"Oh, Annie!" She looked worried. "I've been meaning to call you."

"Have you?"

She and her cousin walked toward me. "You remember my cousin Elle," she said. "She came for Thanksgiving. From Philadelphia."

"Didn't you used to be heavy?" Elle asked as she shook my hand.

"Aren't I still?" I said tartly.

"Please! I remember you as a kid. You look fantastic. You've grown into your body."

I didn't thank her for the compliment.

"I'm sorry we haven't come around. It's been pretty crazy, with the holiday and midterms." I put up a hand to stop her apology. While I knew I needed it, I didn't want to hear it. It would only make me feel worse by exposing the all too evident. "And I missed your birthday," she said. "I don't think I've ever done that in almost thirty years!"

"You have a lot going on." She'd omitted her blooming friendship-romance with Cynthia and how it clearly ate up all her free time. And, graciously, I thought, so did I.

"Actually," she said, and a smile drew up her face. I looked at her, noticing that in another of her fits of fashion indecency, she wore black pants and a navy-blue sweater with a large white cat on it. And when I say "large white cat," think taxidermist. Her white socks poked out from between the hem of her pants and her black sneakers, very Michael Jackson. Yet she pulled it off, because she's slim and sweetly, tenderly pretty without knowing it. I'd always envied her narrow frame; even ugly clothes fall well on her. "I wanted to tell you some news. Will you be around later?"

"Sure," I said, though I couldn't read her face well enough to know what she was referring to, or whether she meant to keep it secret from Elle. "I'm always around."

"Annie has two beautiful daughters," Nora said to Elle.

"Future anarchists," I said with a laugh.

"I'm glad we ran into you. Cynthia asked me to pass along an invitation. She's having a little dinner party at her house on Sunday night. Beverly will be there, and Tabitha Hunter, Friedman, some of the young faculty. Seven o'clock."

"I'll check my calendar," I said, irritated that Cynthia wouldn't go to the trouble of asking me in person and that Nora wouldn't have a more personal invitation for me. When had we last hung out?

"We're off to the gym," Nora chirped.

"Desperate for a workout, I am," Elle chimed in, whether

oblivious or to save us from a tension-filled moment, I don't know. "I need to get my endorphins racing again, release some of those in-love hormones and charge up my system. You know exercise releases the same hormones as sex. If you aren't getting one, you'd better make room for the other."

"Huh," I said, and I waved as they walked away, feeling more alone than I had before, and also more encumbered. I could not go to the gym. Ted was waiting for me to come take the girls. Lily would want to nurse. My hour and a half away for therapy constituted all my free time for the day. If I wanted happy hormones, I'd need to get them the quick and easy way: by eating chocolate.

Once inside, I found Hannah working at our mini art table and Lily napping. I released Ted from his duties.

"I'm going to hit the gym on my way to the office," he announced before he kissed me good-bye.

"Oh, the irony," I said, more to myself than to him. "I'm going to find our winter hats." It had become so cold, I could no longer keep pulling hooded sweatshirts over the children's heads and hoping it would suffice. It had been a happy fall for Hannah, who frequently put her bathing suit on her head as a hat and told me firmly, as if I were the unfashionable fool, "This will keep me warm." However, even I have a line, and 32 degrees is it. I needed to face the dreaded, overfilled, much neglected closet.

What I did find while looking in the coat closet for a proper winter hat was some unopened mail from a few days earlier. The envelopes were tucked inside one of my snow boots. Hannah has a thing for paper. Undoubtedly, she'd been pretending to be the mailman, and my boot had become the mailbox. I could see the toddler logic in this even while it didn't amuse me.

I opened a few bills and then recognized the address on the outside of a large, thick envelope. My breath caught in my throat. "This," I said, placing the mail on the living room table, "Daddy can open."

"Who you talk to, Mama?" Hannah asked.

"I don't know."

"Do you have a 'magnary friend?"

"I probably should," I told her, coming to kneel beside the little table where she was rolling a crayon across a piece of construction paper. I forced myself not to make too much of the envelope, staring into Hannah's brown eyes with great focus. "Can I help you with your art?"

"Can you show me how to drawer the faces 'gain?"

"Sure, honey." I grabbed a crayon and drew a face for her. Hannah had been going through a human-features fascination phase. She loved for me to draw her wild faces with big eyes and noses; then she would try to imitate them on her own. Nothing she drew ever remotely looked like a face, but then, when it comes to children, realism has nothing to do with it otherwise bunnies wouldn't walk and mice wouldn't wear clothes, as they do in every children's book.

When does that change, I wondered as I scribbled in the details of my face. I added some hair and began to fill in the background, worried and excited as my brain kept pulling me back to the envelope. Had it finally happened?

"Mama, *help*, not do," Hannah requested, attempting to pull the crayon out of my hand.

"Sorry, sweetie. I'll get you a new piece of paper."

As I walked over to the bookshelf where I keep the art supplies, I heard her say, "Mama, that's pretty. It looks like me. You a good drawer, Mama."

I came back and looked at my scribbles. I hadn't intended to draw Hannah, and yet somehow I had. "I used to be good," I said, laying down a new sheet of paper. Hannah looked up at me, as though she couldn't understand.

"What's 'used to be'? Is it like the olden days with horses?"

I chuckled, bent down, and squeezed her into me; how could I possibly be ambivalent about this? And I heard Meg's voice, the words she said just before I left: "I don't mean to say you are ambivalent about your *love* for your children. I mean to offer that you may be ambivalent about your *life*, a condition, you should know, most of us suffer from when we have gathered enough age to finally realize we are living the time we always referred to as 'what will you be when you grow up?'"

"I like it, Mama. I know it good." She picked up the paper with her likeness and smiled at it. "This a fridge piture."

In our family, only the best and favorite works of art make it to the front of the refrigerator. I watched Hannah happily amble to the kitchen, leaving me in a wash of envy. What did I envy? I certainly didn't long to be a toddler again. Diapers and potty training hold no appeal, nor do temper tantrums and strictly enforced bedtimes. Seeing as I can eat ice cream for dinner without getting in trouble, I clearly have the better end of the stick.

So what? Ah, so what. I got up from kneeling and plopped down on the couch. To be so easily pleased by something so small? To be fulfilled by what I could do, however minute? To be charmed by the world around me? To still be able to wonder, as though looking at an absolutely blank canvas, "what will I be when I grow up?"

I wasn't old. I'd just celebrated my thirty-fourth birthday, yet as I watched Hannah gallop back to me, the truth stung me like a paper cut, quick and acute. Hannah simply did not expect more from me; she may even have lacked expectations altogether. Where art was concerned, she wasn't searching for Picasso; my sketch was beautiful because she had no points of comparison. And that was the whole trouble, wasn't it? My own expectations. And yes, as Meg suggested, my life. Nothing was wrong with my life. Hannah leaped up onto the sofa to suffocate me with kisses and hugs. No, nothing was wrong with my life at all. It simply did not live up to my expectations.

17

Nora

I found it difficult to focus on anything outside of the pregnancy. I was glad for the vacation week, since I knew I wouldn't be able to teach a class without slipping up and saying "baby bootie," "When is my first ultrasound?" and "Yippeee!" Alfie and I literally jumped up and down in circles after I took the test, which drew Elle's attention, and she came running from the kitchen to see if something was wrong.

"See, I told you I could help you get pregnant," she said, more despondently than seemed right for the joyous occasion. "I show up and wham! baby Galusha."

My interfering family is notorious for taking credit where it isn't due. Elle had nothing to do with it and Dr. Mercy and Cynthia had everything to do with it, which wasn't any more logical a theory but to my mind made all the sense in the world. Cynthia led me to Dr. Mercy, and Dr. Mercy renewed my flagging hope, and hope made me more receptive to Alfie, and Alfie and I finally made a baby.

"You have to call your mom and Gram right away!" Elle commanded. "They're getting chapped knees from praying so hard for you."

"Oh." I didn't want to call either of them, not until the truth settled in. I knew my mother—however happy she would be inside, she would say something dour and grim, remind me of how many women miscarry. Then I'd have to take on Aunt Bertie, who would have her own preferences— perhaps for an immaculate conception. I did want to call Gram, though, who at least would have some basis for taking credit for the triumph on account of the butter advice. "Maybe later."

"Well, don't you want to call someone?" I thought instantly of Annie. I wanted very much to tell her. We had gone through so much together. And of course I planned to, when I had a chance.

"Not really," I replied. She stood before me, my cousin, in disbelief, her short red spiky hair motionless and shiny from excessive product use. I was beginning to wonder what she was doing visiting me. We weren't that close, I really *didn't* need her help conceiving (a point I could now make more strongly), and didn't she have a job, a significant job full of radio broadcasts and TV appearances? She hadn't even opened her laptop since arriving.

"If I was pregnant right now, I would call people. I wouldn't wait. Waiting is stupid." I tried to smile at her. She was spoiling my perfect moment. Elle and I may be the same age and have countless mutual holiday suppers in our past, and once, at age four, I idolized her for possessing eight Cabbage Patch Kids, but she did not make the top-five list of people I would want to share my most sought-after life-changing moment with.

Alfie and I were still holding hands. I could almost feel the awkward, uncomfortable tension the infertility had created over the past year falling away from us. I wanted to be with him and no one else. Elle, however, had other ideas.

"I would be on the phone first thing telling everyone I knew. That's *when* and *if* I have a baby. Clearly I do not have room for that nonsense in my extremely full life . . ." Why was she being so rude? I leaned into Alfie and kissed him. He nuzzled me, and I curled into his neck. It must be bliss, I thought to myself; only bliss could allow me to feel such happiness despite Elle's selfish, droning monologue.

"This dinner party we're going to would be the time to make an announcement. You'd save yourself some time on the telephone, and everyone could clap for you . . ."

I tried to imagine myself delivering a public announcement at Cynthia's dinner party and it was so completely out of character I laughed, which got Alfie laughing in that contagious way that comes over you when relief and joy and delight mingle together because you've finally got the one thing you want. Elle started laughing too, or something like laughing. It occurred to me only later that the honking noise she made may have come from tears.

Nothing could have been better. The thought of going to Cynthia's dinner party, facing David across the table, with the lovely secret of my future child, satisfied me to no end. I spent a lot of time on this daydream. I wouldn't say anything, as Elle imagined. Knowing for myself would be enough. No longer would I have to search Cynthia for new signs of her pregnancy. No longer would I have to look at David with that sense of bubbling anger that he would lie to me, choose someone other than me, betray me so obviously.

I didn't have a chance to deal with the other pressing issues, like Elle, like Annie. I wanted to wallow in my good fortune. I wanted it to saturate me the way the sorrow had. I practiced smiling at myself in the mirror. I practiced saying, "I'm pregnant." I started to visualize Cynthia passing all her maternity clothes in my direction. I stopped feeling so inadequate next to her.

Elle and Alfie and I walked together to the dinner party on Sunday night. I did think about phoning Annie to see if she wanted to walk with us, but then Elle took so long choosing an outfit that we were late and there wasn't time to call; I didn't really want to, anyway. I didn't want to hear her complain all the way to Cynthia's house.

When we arrived, a crowd had already gathered.

Abby Humur, the French teacher, waved at us. She couldn't be a day over twenty-five. She grew up in Paris, although her parents are Americans who went there for the politics, at least I think it was for the politics. She told me once during a noisy holiday faculty party, and it's possible she said her parents went there for the antics. She keeps to herself for the most part; we rarely talk. Once in the kitchen, I spotted Tyler, who's married to Jennifer; they are the only other young couple on campus. He teaches chemistry. She teaches dance. She weighs ten pounds. I am just sure of it. Once I saw her, on a very windy day, get blown straight off the ground. They also run the campus Republican Club and the Guerrillas for Christ Organization, both of which strike me as out of place and slightly embarrassing at our progressive, secular school.

I still hadn't set eyes on either David or Cynthia when we made it to the living room, where we found Beverly sprawled out on the couch with a bowl of peanuts in her lap as though she had volunteered her belly to serve as the coffee table. Annie and Ted were standing by the window talking to Dean Friedman in low, serious voices. I decided not to interrupt.

I'd deposited Elle in the kitchen so she could admire the many handmade pots Cynthia left out with hors d'oeuvres.

"Are you bisexual?" I heard her say as I wandered back in, Alfie holding my hand. The crimson wave of horror washed over my face. Elle was facing Abby, she of Parisian sophistication. I couldn't help imagining that being bisexual in Paris is very much in. I've never been to France myself, but I do know they go topless on the beach, which struck me as a happy situation for bisexuals.

Ridiculous thought processes about sexual preference and swimwear, however, are not the correct response when your cousin is interrogating someone about her bedroom behavior. I debated who to save—myself, by leaving the room, or Abby, who did not deserve to have Elle unleashed on her.

"Personally, I don't label myself. Labels are too small for a person to fit inside. I wouldn't say I'm one thing or another. I believe in sex—"

"Is there anyone who doesn't?" Alfie said in his booming voice. I loved him dearly in the moment. Even Abby laughed. Elle took a long drink of her champagne.

Just then I felt an arm around my shoulder on the opposite side to Alfie.

"Yay, you're here!" Cynthia said warmly.

"I'm going to get a drink," Alfie said. "What would you like?" He turned and looked at me, a wave of reciprocal pleasure passing between us. "Water?"

"Perfect," I said, thrilled not to be able to drink the wine.

"Are they real?" I heard Annie say, coming up to us. She was talking to Elle and gesturing at her substantial cleavage. I nearly choked on a piece of shrimp.

"Man-made. Alas," Elle said, much to my surprise. I didn't know she'd had a breast job. Not for the first time, I wondered what else I didn't know about my cousin. As if this were the exact invitation she awaited, Elle began a discourse on breast reconstruction surgery. Annie admirably listened for a solid five minutes until Elle excused herself to the bathroom.

"Your cousin could be used as an implement of torture," she said to me.

I wanted to laugh, but felt a tug of familial loyalty. "She's not so bad."

"Exactly my point. You are a nice person and she's a self-obsessed sex maniac."

"Why am I always the nice person?" I asked.

"I'd venture to guess, having known you for so long, that you were born that way."

"Nice is boring. I am among people what Saltines are among crackers."

"For the record, I like Saltines. And so do my girls." I started to thank her, but a clear bell rang out.

"I've always wanted to do this," Cynthia said, holding up a shimmery, silver hand bell. "Dinner is served!" Her cheeks were flushed from the warmth of the house and her voice sung out with ebullience.

"Do I look like that yet?" I asked Alfie. "With that amaz-

ing pregnant glow?" He stood away from me for a moment.
Then he nodded. It looked as though his eyes were tearing. I
didn't want to embarrass him by bringing it up.

"I am so thrilled you all could be here!" Cynthia said once
we had all sat down. The table, beautifully laid with calligra-
phied name cards and sterling-silver napkin rings, blazed
with the light of four multicolored candles in sculpted holders. "I've wanted to get to know everyone better." She raised
her glass. For a moment the sound of clinking glasses filled
the room.

As we began our soup, Tyler looked up from his bowl and
over at the opposite wall.

"That's an amazing painting." He pointed at an oil painting of a sunset. I hadn't noticed it before.

"It's a Maroute."

"A real Maroute?" asked Tyler, impressed.

"Annie studied with him too," Cynthia said, causing
Annie to look up in amazement. I was amazed too; the only
time I'd seen them talk was during our tea back in October.

"I didn't know you painted," Abby said.

"I don't. Not anymore anyway. It was a college thing."

"Annie went to art school, at RISD. She showed at a few
galleries," Ted said proudly.

"Ages ago. And they were group shows," Annie protested.

"Why did you stop?" Beverly asked.

"I'm so busy with my girls. They take up all my time."

"Ah, motherhood taking a woman's soul. Happens all the
time." I nearly put my napkin over my head in shame at Elle's
remark. What was she thinking? "What a tragedy that so
many women give up what matters most when they have
children. They lose themselves completely, and when they

reemerge decades later, they don't know who they are anymore. I just finished a novel all about it." For a heavy minute, we all sat in silence.

"Actually," Annie said, undaunted, as was her way, "mothering my girls is the best work I've ever done, markedly more important than swirling colors on paper."

"You of all people must know how unfulfilling it can be," Elle pressed the issue. I thanked God it was Annie she was talking to. Annie could hold her own. Annie wouldn't be bothered in the least by the rudeness. Over the years, I'd seen her shoulder much worse with aplomb. At least she wasn't directing her rants at Cynthia.

"I like being with my children," Annie said in a measured voice. "Babies are nicer than most people I know." A classy last word from the queen of digs. Still, I felt obliged to step in, not just to defend Annie, who was the single best mother I had ever known, but out of responsibility for Elle.

"I hope to stay home when I have children. I can't imagine anything better for them or for me." Annie shot me a look of sisterly solidarity, familiar from our school-ground days. I swelled with love for her, and memory, and immediately wanted to share the good news with her. In fact, I couldn't believe that I hadn't told her yet. She used to be the first person to hear all my news.

"Biology is *not* destiny. For the first time in the history of humanity, we can choose when to have children, how many to have, and how much to keep working in the world. This may be the true mark of our advancement as a species," Elle continued. She took the wine bottle off the table and filled her glass to the brim. "*Not* having children is the next trend."

"I love being pregnant," Cynthia said dreamily, her skin smooth and creamy in the candlelight.

"I always wished for children," Beverly said.

"It can be very lonely without them," Dick Friedman said in his unhurried, preachy voice. It was amazing to hear something so emotional spoken with so little feeling, and not for the first time, I felt sorry for the man.

We may have continued down this gloomy conversational road if the phone hadn't rung at that moment. David popped up from his seat. "I'll get that. I'm waiting for a call."

"I'll gather up the soup bowls," Cynthia said.

"I'll help," I said.

"Is there any more wine?" Jennifer asked. "This bottle is empty already."

"I'll bring some back," Cynthia answered. I followed her graceful strides into the kitchen, where David stood by the counter looking somber. Instead of looking away and ignoring him, I thought again of the baby, *my* baby, and leveled my gaze in his direction.

"Any news?" Cynthia asked.

"Bad news. She's going into hospice."

I gently placed the bowls into the sink, hoping to slink away into the other room and give them some time together. Instead, though, they followed me back to the dining room where David stood at the head of the table as Cynthia sank down into her seat.

"You all may have noticed that Tabitha couldn't make it tonight," David began. "She has been quietly undergoing treatment for cancer." I heard Beverly gasp, and not out of empathy. She can't bear to be out of the loop, but this was no loop. None of us knew. "Tonight, they moved her into hospice care. She won't be able to come back home, to Dixbie, to teach." Cynthia looked especially saddened. Had she grown so fond of the old woman in so short a time? "I'm sorry to have to deliver the news," David went on. He squeezed Cynthia's shoulder in his hand and she began to cry in an astonishingly delicate way, without a heave or a snort or a wail.

"Tabitha is her aunt," David supplied, sitting down.

"What?" said Beverly, now clearly traumatized by her complete lack of gossip. "How can that be?"

"My mother's sister-in-law," Cynthia said, dabbing her face with a silky green napkin.

"Oh," Annie said, and I could almost hear the wheels of connection clicking into place in her brain. Tabitha had deep roots at the school and a great deal of clout. The Meadow House takeover now made sense.

"My adopted mother," Cynthia added, in far too rational and normal a way for the astonishing news she delivered. "Tabitha's sister-in-law, Adelle Hunter, adopted me at five and took care of me until she passed away."

"What?" I heard myself say, more loudly than I would have wanted to, and Alfie put his hand over the top of mine. A good thing, too, because it occurred to me that I might have fainted, if only I'd been the sort of person to do that kind of thing, but in my family, fainting, puking, and naps were not allowed. The Helpsom-Fulchs considered such things an unnecessary indulgence.

The dinner party carried on in a much subdued manner. Even Elle seemed affected by the news despite the fact that she didn't know Tabitha. Either that, or she'd become too sleepy to talk much. Every time I looked her way she appeared two blinks away from slumber. Once I saw her close her eyes completely and sway in her seat. Alfie and I exchanged whispers during dessert and agreed to leave as soon as possible.

Once we'd excused ourselves and gathered up Elle, I noticed she wasn't walking very well. "She drank too much," Alfie said, putting an arm around her.

"Oh." I hadn't noticed, truly I hadn't, because so many other incredible things demanded my attention. I wanted to process what it meant that Cynthia, glamorous, perfect, gorgeous Cynthia, was, *like me*, adopted. I wanted to process that more than I wanted or needed to think about poor Tabitha Hunter, the flagship teacher of our school, who Dixbie would now lose.

"We'll walk with you," I heard Annie say. She and Ted stepped out the door moments after us.

"Oh, good," Alfie replied as the wind slapped around us. "I could use your help, Ted." He gestured wordlessly to Elle, who'd almost sunk entirely into his side. This seemed a little worrying, but Annie grabbed my hand and pulled me ahead of Elle and the men.

"Did your cousin *mean* what she said or does she hate me?"

"Elle suffers from a terrible case of verbal diarrhea."

"Clearly."

"I'm sorry about what she said."

"Never mind. She's clearly boozed out of her head."

"Really?"

"That's what I love about you, Nora. Your innocence."

"Truthfully, I didn't notice."

"You've been preoccupied lately."

"I'm sorry."

"Don't be," Annie said, pulling her scarf up around her face. "You're providing me with a great opportunity to get in better touch with my anger." I looked to see if she was kidding. Her eyes were serious.

"I have some wonderful news," I said, wanting to steer the conversation clear away from our dissolving friendship.

"You're pregnant," she said.

"How did you know?"

"Cynthia told me at the party. I'm happy for you. Really I am." She began to stride away from me. In a few paces, the path would divide into two, one leading up toward Zucker House, one toward my dorm. "You deserve it. You certainly waited long enough."

"Hold on!" I ran several steps to catch up with her. "You don't sound happy. Why aren't you happy for me?"

"Did I mention *Cynthia* told me about my own best friend's pregnancy, when for years I've been listening to you wail helplessly in longing for just this day?" Her voice was icy now.

"I'm sorry. I meant to. We haven't talked much. And Elle came. I've been busy."

"Forget it. I don't want to rain on your parade. Congrats."

"Annie." I searched for what I wanted to say, how I wanted to reach out and grab hold of that moment we'd shared during the dinner, that commonality that bound us to one another. "You've been in such a bad mood lately," I said and instantly regretted it. It wasn't right, I knew it wasn't right, and I couldn't withdraw it.

She stopped on the dirt path and turned to look at me. I

could see she was tired, and her scarf had small holes in it. She looked smaller than she was inside her enormous blue down coat, the one she'd been wearing for years, maybe even a decade. "You're right," she said. "It's a good thing you have a new, happy best friend so you don't need to spend time with Annie the Grouch." Then she walked away.

18

Annie

Let me be the first to tell you that getting what you want isn't all it's cracked up to be. For example, it may turn your husband into a groomzilla, and while I like the man in a tux, the prospect of wedding planning, not to mention marriage, suddenly terrified me.

Ever since the finalized divorce papers arrived in the mail, the very ones Hannah stuffed into a boot, and I bid Ah-leen a long-overdue permanent farewell from my life, Ted couldn't stop hearing wedding bells.

"We need to have a serious conversation," he said pretty much every time I walked into the room.

Usually I replied with something like, "I won't stand for such a thing."

And he would joke, "Then sit down." He would ask, "Would you like to marry me?" And I would answer, "Yes. Do I have any other options?"

Not to be confusing, or, God forbid, ambivalent, wanting to marry Ted, the very thing I'd longed for to make our family whole, took on the danger of a skydive. I began to worry, as I never had before, what it would *mean* to be married. Ideas I'd never entertained before, perhaps on account of the unreality of our marriage given Ah-leen's perpetual, chronic, self-inflicted diseases, flew to my mind, chief among them: what if *we* got divorced?

I worried over the fact that my mother hated my father and Ted hated Aileen and something that happens once can happen again. Ted and I discussed these issues ad nauseum until our time together resembled a *Dr. Phil* program.

Amid all this, I endured Cynthia's dinner-party, during which three notable dramas occurred:

1. Elle inflicted her views on me.
2. I discovered my oldest, best friend had told Cynthia about her pregnancy before me.
3. We learned that Tabitha Hunter was not long for this world.

I had never liked Tabitha very much, but I certainly never wished a terminal illness on her, and I felt sorry, in a private way, for her loss. Dixbie has a feel to it, a way of being, and Tabitha, for all those decades of teaching and serving the school, had a mighty influence. I wondered what it would be like without her and who would take her place.

One night not long after that dinner, Ted and I put the girls down. Ted squeezed my fanny as we walked together to the living room holding hands. "Hey, love cheeks."

"Hands off, hot stuff. I could be fertile."

"I come prepared. I am Trojan man."

"Honestly? I'm not up to it."

"Something on your mind?"

"The usual litany. I won't bore you."

"It seems like things are going better with Hannah lately. The therapy must be working."

"You being serious?" I groaned. The other day Ted had found me all but sitting on top of Hannah's legs in an attempt to give her a time-out. In my own defense, the child will not go to her room, or sit on the sofa, or leave my side, if she's done something wrong. I wanted her to sit for two minutes—this was after she'd put Lily on the toilet and pressed her down until her fully clothed rump hit the water line. (I should add that it took nothing less than full bicep strength to wrestle her out of the toilet seat.) Given the crime, a tiny time-out seemed reasonable. But not for Hannah. She took great offense and would not sit. Which is when Ted arrived to hear wet-bottomed Lily crying and Hannah, squished like a grape beneath my legs, screaming. "I admire your endurance," he'd said, coming onto the scene.

Now he said: "You don't seem so angry about Hannah."

"I'm not as angry about Hannah. I suppose that's true. Now I'm angry about other things."

We sat down on the couch side by side. Ted kissed me, wrapped an arm around my belly, and squeezed. "We still need to set a wedding date."

"Ten points for persistence," I told him before taking a deep breath. It was the unfortunate moment when I would have to bare my soul. I'm not big on emotional confessions that don't include some element of rage. "Call me the reluctant bride. I've been waiting for four years, and now I have cold feet. It feels like you're asking me to jump out of an airplane."

"Annie, you're the original daredevil."

I scoffed. "Can we make it small? Do it in the courthouse?"

Ted looked disappointed. "I married Aileen in a courthouse."

"Right." I pressed myself away from him and sat up on the sofa to think.

"We could hold it on campus in the chapel."

"Oh." The idea startled me. It had never dawned on me, yet it hit me as exactly right. "You are a romantic."

"And you aren't?"

"I'm a realist," I told him, leaning my head back against the cushions and closing my eyes against a threatening cry. "It's a sweet idea, like buttercream frosting, but it would mean a bigger wedding and invitations and inviting family and some guy in a white robe and vows and a dress. I do not want to be stuffed into a white tube of tulle." I sighed. "Anyway, we can't do a real wedding. I don't have a maid of honor and we don't have any money."

"I'm sure Dixbie will give us the chapel for a few hours. And what about Nora for your maid of honor?" I shook my head. "Suze?" I shook it again.

"They have better things to do."

"It's a wedding. I'm sure they can make time for a wedding."

I wasn't. I wasn't sure of anything anymore, a fact I partly blamed on Meg and her witchy ways of turning the way I saw myself upside down. Here I'd lived an entire life without needing therapy and suddenly, by pursuing my inner child, my neuroses had multiplied like gremlins. I got tired just thinking about all my problems, large and small, and how

impossible becoming a sweet, skipping mother to my three—
including the younger version of myself—demanding children now seemed. In fact, I doubted it could happen.

My dread list included not only a wedding, but my Young
Feminists Club, where I would be forced to face Cynthia Cypress in close proximity. The December twelfth meeting
came before I had a chance to fake my own death in order to
get out of it, so I headed over to Lyle Hall with a heavy heart,
hoping that Cynthia would sign up for a Thursday-night
birthing class and bow out of all the meetings until the end of
the year. If I had a fairy godmother, this might have been the
case. Instead, I arrived to find her already in the room, having arranged the chairs in a circle.

"Hi, Annie," she said brightly. Her nails were scarlet. She
had a little bump for a belly. Her hair was pinned to her head
with a silver clip in the shape of a dragonfly and her winter
boots were slender, chocolatey brown, and unblemished by
the snow.

"Cold out," I said.

"I love winter. It's so cozy."

I stopped short of saying, "You would," and simply fake-
smiled. I sat down at a desk on the opposite side of the circle
and spent the time until the girls arrived pretending to write
notes on my yellow pad.

The meeting carried on forever, as they often did, with the
great debate over the exact day for our feminist education
event and heated, flaming conversation relating to the topic
of the title of said event in which, in response to suggested
titles, such things were said as "too boring," "too common,"
"too yesterday," "too long," "too meaningless," and, my favor-

ite, "too linear." When Cynthia offered the title "Feminists: The Who and the Do," the girls nearly catapulted over themselves to praise her genius. I might have liked the title if someone else thought of it. It was voted in by a near majority; I abstained.

"They are such an inspiration," Cynthia commented as we packed up to leave.

"Yes."

"I so wish I'd been a part of a group like this as a girl."

"Mmm," I said. I hadn't needed such a club. My mother supplied all the necessary components of female solidarity in one complete package. I could have shared this, if I had any intention of becoming friends with Cynthia. Her thievery of my friendship with Nora aside, I still didn't like her. She came across as too inhumanly perfect. Her complexion alone gave me pause to doubt her sincerity, although I know such things can't be helped, but, let's be honest, a pimple here and there, maybe a mole, a shiny forehead, a long hair threading from her chin, at least one of these might have allowed me to accept her as one of us.

"Have you seen Nora today?" she asked.

"No." I hadn't seen Nora in days.

"I'm going to stop in and check on her. I feel awful. Elle is still camped out with them."

"Right." I knew this, and I knew it must be awful for Nora to have a belligerent relative stuck in her guest bedroom. The mere thought of five minutes in Elle's company gave me a queasy stomach.

"I saw your girls with Ted the other day for the Sunday brunch in the cafeteria." I nodded, picked up my bag, and headed to the door. "They really are charming children."

"Too true." I flipped off the lights, eager to be out of her company.

"They seem to get along so well with their father," she said, as we both walked into the hall to head out of the building. I nearly tripped over my own feet at the implication of her words: *they don't get along with you.*

Outside of the direct ways Cynthia screwed up my life, I had always believed she thought poorly of me. Here was proof. She was mean to me. I no longer had to hate her simply for being rich, thin, and weasely.

"How is Tabitha?" I asked, because I did not trust myself to say anything else.

She shook her head. "Not very well, I'm afraid. She did such a beautiful job of working with the illness for so long. No one even knew about it. Now, she's faltering." Cynthia did look genuinely sad, I'll give her that.

"I'm sorry." We both walked through the exit door together and into the bracing December night air. I gave her a quick, cursory wave and stepped up my speed to get safely away from her before doing something lamentable like ripping off one of her fancy boots and hitting her over the head with it. I did not want my children to spend the rest of their lives driving up to visit me in the women's penitentiary for attempted murder-with-shoe.

Oh, I so did not want Cynthia to be a part of the YFC. Although it became apparent during that night's meeting that her help would make my life extremely easy. Anything she so much as mentioned, the girls took as law.

Which led me to wonder about her charisma. I can see how a beautiful and rather inscrutable—for Cynthia rarely spoke about herself—character can appeal to gaggles of sixteen-year-olds. If it were only the schoolkids who admired her, perhaps I could understand. But the faculty also held her in high esteem. During the dinner party, I'd heard Beverly talking to Friedman about the possibility of Cynthia winning the Sylvia Steinberg Excellence in Teaching Award. Of course, she wouldn't be able to win the award; historically it must go to a faculty member with a teaching record at the school, and this year no one doubted that Nora, who ought to have won last year, would be chosen. Still, it gave me pause hearing the two of them talk. Certainly, Cynthia couldn't be so incredible a pedagogue as to warrant deserving the award in three months' time teaching. It aroused my suspicions, and not for the first time. When it came to Cynthia, something was not quite right.

Ted met me at the door, took off my coat, and kissed me. The house was blessedly quiet, but I found I missed the girls, and before making my hot chocolate, snuck into their rooms to gaze at them sleeping. Hannah lay sprawled across the width and length of her crib like a gymnast in flight. She was gorgeous, eyelashes as long as broom whiskers. Her mouth was slack, her breathing a satisfying swoosh. I thought of dolphins. She's my kid; I can rhapsodize.

"Why do you think Cynthia and David ended up in Meadow House?" I asked when I came into the kitchen. Ted was at the stove whipping something up.

"Because Sally Whetstone lacks backbone. She asked for it and she got it."

"Ted, you're a smart man. Consider the facts. She's Tabitha's niece and Tabitha practically runs the school. Tabitha did her a favor."

"I suppose."

"I question her motives."

"For wanting Meadow House? Who wouldn't prefer it over a crowded, noisy dorm apartment?"

"Exhibit A: Meadow House—snatched out from underneath my children's bottoms—delivered to her in *a contract*. Exhibit B: YFC takeover, which she prepped the Social Committee for before her infiltration. Exhibit C: Friedman and Slater discuss her for the Excellence in Teaching Award."

"Exhibit D: Banana bread. We had a few bananas on their way to banana heaven. I figured I could use them up." He held the pan up for me to admire.

"Yum." I put on a kettle to boil. "I'm having hot cocoa. Do you want some?"

"Love some."

"Really, Ted, consider the evidence."

"You're getting carried away," he said with a wink. "That's what I love about you."

"I wish you would take me seriously. Something isn't right."

"Just because you two don't get along doesn't make her suspect."

"Actually," I thought about it for a moment, "in this case, it does. She doesn't know me well enough to dislike me. And that's not even my point, Ted. I want you to think about the larger picture."

"Right after we eat the banana bread," he said with a grin.

"No, *while* we eat the banana bread. How about Exhibit D: stealing my best friend. Since you are so neutral and generous in your assessment of this woman, tell me what's going on between the two of them. Tell me what they have in common. I *know* why Nora spends every waking minute trailing around Cynthia like a thirsty puppy. But why is Cynthia so enamored with Nora? Doesn't that strike you as odd?"

"I hadn't given it any thought," he said honestly.

"Well, please do." I took a bite of banana bread. "And get back to me."

The following Wednesday marked my long-overdue meeting with Suze at the BFC. I spent far too much time finding something to wear—not that I intended to wow anyone with my designer duds; I simply wanted a shirt without a stain on it.

I managed to get Lily to nap before we left. When I casually say "Lily" and "nap" in the same sentence, I mean: Lily screamed for twenty minutes, at which point I got her out of her crib only to find that she'd soaked through her diaper and her pants and onto her sheet. I gave her new clothes and sheets. Five minutes later, she wouldn't stop hollering. I went in to give her a piece of my mind, but the foul odor stopped me in my tracks. She had a poopy diaper. After I cleaned her again, she finally slept. For thirty minutes. Welcome to nine-month-hood, I thought to myself when I went to grab her out of the crib. Hannah tugged on my pants, pleading with me to put the baby down and finish our mermaid game, in which I pretend to swim on the rug with my legs wrapped together in a baby blanket and she pretends to capture me with an imaginary net. I tried not to dread the possibility that Lily's easygoing disposition belonged exclusively to her early babyhood, and that she would end up as strong-willed as Hannah. It just couldn't be true.

When we found Suze at the BFC, I hugged her to save my life, then I looked around. "I hope this place doesn't make me feel more alone than I do at home," I said, something it often accomplished.

"Not with me here."

"I miss you. Can you quit?"

"Annie." She looked offended, which surprised me. I'd meant it as a joke. "I *love* working. I feel fulfilled for the first time in years. Be happy for me, okay?"

"I am happy for you, I'm just unhappy for *me*."

"Well, I miss you too." She warmed slightly. We both looked down to watch Lily expertly crawling across the room. In the past week, she'd mastered the crawl at last and it made me feel suddenly anxious, because time was moving so quickly. My little baby was only getting bigger—which meant what? That there would be less and less for me to do at home, more and more reason to go out and work?

"I requested one Wednesday off a month. That can be our play date."

I wanted to say: *once a month!* We used to get together once a week, if not more often. We talked several times a week, and now I heard from her only when she could get around to it. Sure, I got how hard it must be to balance her workload with her family life, and balancing her nanny and her housekeeper's schedules—backbreaking, to be certain. But couldn't she be a little bit more sensitive to my plight? Did she have no idea what it was like to be abandoned?

"You want to hear the best part of working?" she asked, turning to me and grabbing both of my hands for a quick squeeze. "I finally enjoy my time with Finn. I can't believe it! Even though I'm so busy and stressed when I get home with all there is to do, I really like being with him. I actually miss him during the day. Once or twice I've even thought to myself, *so this is what it feels like to Annie,* to want to hang out with my own children." I knew she meant this as a compliment so I smiled. "I can't tell you how relieved I am to realize I'm not the world's worst mother. It's a better reward than my paycheck."

"Suze, you're an awesome mother."

"Not really." Finn came over and served her a plastic piece of pizza in a mini plastic pan. She pretended to gobble it up hungrily. "But it makes me feel so much better to know I like my own child."

"Good." I didn't know what else to say. I felt forlorn. She knew about my troubles liking Hannah. Couldn't she see *me?* I wanted to talk to Meg.

"Anyhow, I've been meaning to tell you about this meeting we had for the BFC the other night. Even though I can't be here as often, I intend to stay on the parent board. Julia Tucker brought up the best idea. She wants to hold classes for the kids—yoga, art, puppetry, dance, that kind of thing. I know you're going to cut my head off, but I volunteered you."

"To teach the yoga?" I said with a snicker.

"I suggested you teach an art class."

Hannah came running out of the playhouse in the middle of the room and threw herself against my legs. "Can we play trains?" she asked.

"Don't be mad," Suze continued. "We started talking about how much the kids love art, and the center has a ton of supplies, and before I knew it, I'd mentioned that you studied art. Julia loved the idea. She wants you to teach the pilot class. It will be great press for the center."

"I can't believe Julia would want me to teach her child anything."

"Trust me, they hate you a lot less than you think. Most of the time, they're only thinking of themselves."

"Small consolation," I said.

"Trains!" came a high-pitched little voice.

"One minute, Hannie. Mama's talking."

"Won't you at least consider it? Think how much fun it would be. You'd have five or six kids Hannah's age, and every supply you could possibly need. The commitment's only for one forty-five-minute session a week. It won't begin until the spring. Wouldn't you like to get back into your art?"

"I doubt giving instructions in finger painting would get me back into my art."

"You know what I mean."

I did and I didn't know what she meant. On the one hand, drawing with Hannah the other day awakened something inside me, something very small and not terribly ambitious, but something nonetheless. On the other hand, doing anything in service to the BFC appealed to me as much as going on a diet.

"I'll think about it."

Suze looked visibly relieved. Too relieved in fact. "Suze? The look on your face tells me I've got no way out. You signed me up for the class, didn't you?"

"Well . . ." She held her hands out, an open, innocent gesture. "They needed a definitive answer. How could I know you wouldn't go for it?"

"*Of course* you knew I wouldn't want to do it! You know me too well. You little mastermind. You've made it impossible for me to say no."

"You can say no, but—"

"Yes, and make all the Brownies who already can't stand me mad."

"If you won't get play trains, Hannah will pee on the floor!" Hannah announced proudly as though she had discovered the secret of the universe.

"Honestly," Suze said, ignoring her. "It would be really good for you."

"You think?" I said, as I allowed Hannah to pull me away into the other room with the train set.

It occurred to me only later, once we'd left, after Suze issued another plea for me to consider the class, that I had completely forgotten to mention my big news, the finalized divorce papers and my upcoming nuptials and the small matter of my bridal party. Either there wasn't time, or it wasn't important. Or maybe we weren't the friends we once were.

19

Nora

Even while it became increasingly clear that Elle had out-stayed her welcome and that there was something very wrong in her life, the three of us, Alfie, Elle, and myself, fell into a routine, a spin-off of *Three's Company* that felt, for the most part, almost normal.

I usually spent the first minutes of the morning cocooned with Alfie in a ball of sleepy bliss as we discussed the pregnancy and our future. "I'm so happy you are yourself again," he said one morning. "I've missed you." His own happiness touched me. Since I knew he didn't share the same urgent desire for a baby that I had, it reflected on his wish to make me happy, and in that I felt truly lucky.

Once he got up to shave and shower, I spent some time in the office getting ready for the school day, though more and more I put off my class preparation until the last minute and sketched my Olive the Ogre story, adding a few words to each page, or sometimes reading Beatrix Potter for inspiration.

Elle didn't wake up until well after I left for classes. What she
did with herself all morning was a mystery. Some days she
meandered down to the cafeteria to eat lunch with Cynthia
and me, who had a standing lunch date on Monday, Wednesday, and Friday when we shared the same open lunch period.
Instead of talking about how weird it was that she seemed to
have permanently moved in, Elle helped out by grocery
shopping and tidying up the house. She often cooked dinner.
By seven, she took up residence on the couch with a glass of
wine and watched TV with Alfie. Her conversation made me
crazy, but her company was amiable for the most part, though
I worried about her.

Cynthia and I spent a good deal of time trying to figure
Elle out. At least once a week during our tea party at Meadow
House, we gleefully discussed our pregnancies and drank her
uterine-toning raspberry tea, which she claimed would pro-
tect against miscarriage. Since her adoption bombshell, I felt
kindred to her. She never brought up her adoption, and I'd
yet to discuss mine, but privately I felt we shared a deep inner
bond. In a way, knowing about her adoption helped to make
sense of my attraction to her. I decided I must have sensed it
all along.

The only downside of our teas consisted of David's presence. He joined us sometimes. I didn't want to, but in his
presence I found myself flaunting my growing pregnancy,
making a great big deal of how wonderful it was.

One day he met me at the door and reached to help with
my coat.

"You don't have to do that."

"Do what?"

"Take my coat."

"You mean you want to keep wearing it?" He snickered slightly.

"I mean . . . okay." I let him tug it gently off my shoulders. With the small exception of the hand-to-hand contact earlier that one time during a faculty meeting, David and I hadn't touched since we dated. His hands on my shoulders gave me goose bumps.

"Are you cold?" he asked. "You're shivering."

"Am I shivering? I should probably get a better coat." I tried to laugh, but it came out sounding more like a prolonged and amateur belch.

Cynthia walked into the foyer. "Norie, you're here," she said. Instantly, I felt guilty, though without reason. I felt no affection for David.

That day, we all sat down together in the kitchen to drink tea. I wished David away to a meeting or a sports practice. He ruined everything for me; like a poison, he turned the perfectly sweet tea time bitter. And that had to be the day, with David present, that Cynthia would initiate a big conversation.

"I feel like I don't know you, Norie. Even though I know little things. What about the important stuff?" I feared she would ask for a confession about my love life, and I began to blush at the thought of having to bring up David in the anonymous third person while he sat listening. "Tell me what you love most in all the world," she said instead.

I can do profound questions. I can answer them honestly. I ventured to guess that even in front of Cynthia, who out-cooled me in every area of life, I could present a reasonably interesting version of my life and loves. But with David there, who knew so much about me, I didn't want to act like a fool. And since I act like a fool about 80 percent of my waking life, the outcome rose inevitably in front of me. For one thing, David knew the answer to Cynthia's question, if he remembered any of our deep-into-the-night conversations. It had become clear to me over my many visits that David really hadn't said anything to Cynthia about our relationship. I resented him for lying, for fudging the truth. On the other hand, I worried that if Cynthia found out, she would withdraw her friendship. I didn't want that. So I put up with David's irritating silence and the way he sat with us drinking tea like he belonged, like all was forgiven, like all had never happened, like he did not know the answer to the question.

"Um, most in the entire world?" I asked.

"Yes. Most in the entire world." Cynthia smiled dreamily at me while I thought hurriedly of an adequate response.

"Oh, let's see." I could feel myself turning red and squirmed in my seat. Never mind my boiling cup of tea; I was breaking out into a cold sweat of shame.

"Stream of consciousness," Cynthia demanded. "Say the first thing that comes to your mind. Or here's a better one: If you could do anything in the entire world," she paused for emphasis, "what would it be?"

Growing up, I had two answers to this question: have a baby and a real family, and write a book. As to the first goal, baby-making, given Cynthia's extensive travels and ability to conceive a baby at the drop of a hat, and my newly accomplished status as one who *could* make babies, this answer I immediately wrote off. And anyway, I wanted a baby, a family, as a way of giving myself real, blood relatives, a tribe of my own on this planet, a concept I always fumbled over in the telling. As for the second goal, the writing, I didn't simply want to write any old book, I wanted to leave behind a legacy. I fancied myself a modern-day Beatrix Potter. Just as children today read her words and fall asleep at night dreaming of her characters and their world—holes in trees and under hedges decorated with fine, tiny furniture and colorful art framed on the walls—a hundred years from now I wanted my tales to make it into the dreams of my grandchildren's friends. But as worthwhile as this ambition was, I realized the only person who knew of it was Annie.

Before I had a second thought, I said, "I'd write children's books."

"Really?" They both looked at me. If I'd said "pig farming," David couldn't have looked more surprised. It gave me a small wave of pleasure to see his expression. So he *didn't* know everything about me.

"Actually," I said, gaining steam with my confessional, "I'm about finished with my first book, *Olive the Ogre Finds a Home.*"

"Good for you," David said with a certain amount of doubtful amazement. I'm sure he wanted to say, "You never told me," but couldn't in Cynthia's company.

"Really!" Cynthia said again. She looked ready to hop straight out of her seat with excitement.

"It's only a rough draft." I'd finished the last page a few days before, though I wanted to go back and work on Olive's expression. She sat in a field of poppies surrounded by the new ogre family that adopted her. I didn't think I'd captured her happiness quite right. I needed to work on the look in her eyes. I chose not to mention that I never would have written the book if Hannah hadn't requested the story from Annie. I worried it would make me look like an amateur. A silly fear—I'm expert in silly fears—since I really was an amateur and I really wouldn't have gotten around to writing the book without Annie's entreaty.

"This is incredible! We were meant to have this tea." Cynthia always glowed rosy. At that moment she nearly shined. "You will simply not believe who I talked to just before you got here."

"Who?"

"My brother."

"Cynthia's brother is an agent with Holfer and Newton in the city," David supplied. They both stared at me, waiting for a response as if the name should mean something, and it did, in that kind-of, sort-of way. I didn't want to confess my own illiteracy on the topic. While I'd always *wanted* to write for children, I didn't imagine it actually happening. And since I'd only recently sat down to write my first book to please the demand of a toddler, I had yet to do a second's worth of research on publication because, and all of a sudden I was ashamed to admit this, I never took my own dream seriously. "They only handle children's books," he added.

"Only the premier agency for children's literature on the East Coast," Cynthia added with satisfaction. "My brother will look at it. He owes six of his eight cat lives to me."

"Really?" My head spun. I began to regret saying anything.

"I'll call and confirm, but I can guarantee it's a formality. If I say jump, he jumps. Do you want me to call right now?"

"Um," I hesitated. This wasn't the first time I'd been witness to Cynthia's powerful connections. Dr. Mercy came to mind, and the way the receptionist admitted me on the basis of my friendship with Cynthia. To have a book published based on our friendship? I had to do some lightning-fast mental calculations as Cynthia and David stared at me with expectation. I didn't want my book printed as a favor to Cynthia; it would always feel illegitimate. I wanted it to be good in its own right. "It needs more work," I said.

"What's it called again?" she asked.

"*Olive the Ogre Finds a Home*," I said.

"Ogres are very now," David said.

Cynthia pulled out her cell phone. "I would love to help you, Norie. Just knowing you makes me confident that it must be a brilliant book. I don't get enough chances to do things like this. Can I call him?" When she put it that way, it seemed as though I'd be doing *her* a favor.

"It truly needs a revision . . ." I held my hands up in the air and shrugged my shoulders in the universal gesture of helplessness.

"That's what a good editor is for," she said, gently pressing the button on her cell phone. "Let's see what my brother says."

I walked home that day as giddy as a teenager in love. Alfie and Elle were both out when I arrived, so I grabbed Fruity's leash and took her for a long walk on the trails at the back of the campus, bursting with happiness over my luck. I tried to take a measured view of the situation. Even if Cynthia's brother agreed to represent the book out of some eternal debt toward her, there were no guarantees that he could get a publishing house to buy it. When she called, he'd been out to lunch. She left a brief message on his work phone. I didn't ask if this was a birth brother or one through adoption; it seemed like a rude question, particularly as Cynthia didn't supply the information.

What felt most unusual that day as I walked along savoring my good fortune wasn't the slightly odd way I might end up getting a book published or the serendipity of the conversation during tea, but the sense of being lucky. I could not remember a time in the history of my thirty-three years when I believed myself to be a lucky person. To the contrary, I felt fundamentally unlucky. Cynthia embodied the charmed life. Her golden touch and her wand of providence were changing not just the details of my life but how I felt about myself.

I walked along wondering if I might have been wrong about myself all along. After all, Cynthia was adopted and she didn't walk around like an unwanted, unloved lame duck. Maybe accidentally meeting Alfie that day *was* lucky. His not running me over could definitely fall into that category. Maybe my geeky childhood was lucky, blessed instead of cursed, since it ensured I never dealt with drugs or unplanned pregnancies or dangerous boys. And maybe even the adoption was lucky. After all, it gave me the Olive story, and the Olive story now had the potential to help me realize my oldest dream. I had a clear memory of my mother saying to me once, at seven, when I told her how they made fun of me at school for not having a real mom and dad, "Believe me, if I'd given birth to you myself, you'd have more troubles." Could that be true?

For the first time in weeks, I longed to talk to Annie. She knew me so well. She would hear all my thoughts and ideas and cut through them to the truth. She dealt with bullshit and personal delusions like she was pulling weeds out of the garden. If I told her my ideas, she wouldn't allow me to go on believing something ridiculous. That's what I needed, in that moment, a way to trust my own feelings.

Without making the conscious decision to talk to her, I began to walk toward her dorm. As I'd never made a conscious decision to avoid her, this made sense to me.

Anticipating our time together, I walked more quickly. She was like a sister to me, after all, and our distance this fall would instantly become water under the bridge. She would get how strange life seemed with Elle in my house, and how consumed I'd become with getting pregnant. I decided to apologize first thing. Then she would forgive me, and I would hold Lily and hug Hannah, both of whom I realized, as I got closer to Zucker House, I missed.

When I got to the second floor of the dorm house, I pounded on the door, eager to see my friend's face and make peace. I could hear Hannah screaming and Lily's low wail, so I turned the knob and walked in, ready to help out. Annie always needed an extra hand.

She looked surprised when I walked into the living room. "I didn't hear you."

"I heard the children, so I thought I should just come in."

"Make yourself at home," she said, though without much enthusiasm. Lily was in her arms, fretting and biting her fist. Hannah lay on the rug near the coffee table, threatening to kick it with her feet.

"Can I help?"

"Do you know an orphanage?" Annie laughed, her lioness laugh, which made me feel better, like I was welcome, and

I only had to deal with the old, grumpy Annie I knew so well. "It's the witching hour, you know that," she said. "From now until bedtime everyone has no patience. Standard operating procedure."

"You look so calm." She did.

"Trying to get somewhere with flattery?"

"No." I laughed, or tried to laugh. She didn't seem so happy to see me.

Hannah finally gave up on her tantrum and ran over to give me an enormous leg hug. I picked her up and swung her around the room. "Tell me 'bout Olive," she said.

"I wrote the story down for you," I told Annie. "Actually, I have some exciting news about it."

"Good for you," Annie said, getting up and walking into the kitchen, where she plopped Lily into her high chair. She buckled her in quickly, then rummaged around in the refrigerator looking for something.

"Cynthia's brother—"

"I'm not interested in hearing about Cynthia."

"Oh."

Annie, having found the little pot of baby food she was looking for, grabbed a spoon and sat down at the kitchen table opposite Lily, who hungrily opened her mouth.

"You must have something else to talk about."

I still had Hannah in my arms and still stood in the living room, looking through the wide passageway to the kitchen. I didn't know what to say, so I said the obvious: "You're still mad at me."

"You aren't an honors teacher for nothing," she retorted, all sarcasm, and without looking at me.

"Tell the story!" pleaded Hannah.

"Did I do something?" I asked. Then I leaned into Hannah and whispered that I would tell her in a minute.

"You're too nice to do anything."

"I came over to talk to you," I protested. "I have so much going on in my life right now. You're the first person I wanted to tell about the book—"

"Second," she cut in sharply. "I'm the second person. Or maybe the fifth or tenth. Cynthia heard about the pregnancy first, didn't she? And whatever book you're talking about now, does she know already?" Now she looked up at me and I could feel myself blush crimson with shame, because of course Cynthia knew about the book. "Why do you like that woman? Are you so obtuse that you can't see the truth about her? She's bought her way into this school, and guess what? She's going to buy her way to your prize."

"What do you mean?"

"I overheard something the other day. They might give her the Excellence in Teaching Award."

"You could have heard wrong. The award always goes to a more senior faculty member; you know that. Besides, even if they gave it to her, that doesn't mean she *bought* her way to the prize."

"You're missing the point. It isn't about following the rules. Cynthia Cypress doesn't follow the rules, or haven't you noticed that? Will you still be her best friend when they hand her the award and a check for two thousand dollars?"

"Why are you being so spiteful? Cynthia's a good person. She's done a lot for me."

"Has she? I'd venture to guess this is all about David, anyway, Nora. No matter how close you get to Cynthia, it won't get you married to David. I feel badly for Alfie."

"That's not true!" I cried. "And it's not fair."

Hannah, oblivious, or maybe used to her mother's out-bursts, wriggled out of my arms and went to go play with a ride-on train.

"Are you sure?" She looked at me sharply. "You've always wanted to be with the pretty girls, but did you ever stop to consider why Cynthia wants to be friends with *you*?"

I knew, having seen her verbally pummel kids on the playground, old boyfriends, and politicians, how unforgiv-ingly she could fight. Though I always felt our friendship courted a kind of sisterly war, this was the first time I'd felt the full force of Annie's unkindness. Because she knew me so well, it hurt doubly.

"Really, Nora, did you stop to consider that she might have an ulterior motive? Or do you think she likes you be-cause you two have so much in common? Maybe you go shopping together? Paint your toenails with each other?"

I almost didn't have breath to respond. I'd walked in on a beam of sunshine, certain of her understanding. This was not what I expected. "Maybe I want to spend time with her be-cause she isn't such a constant energy-draining downer."

"Is that what I am?"

"Yes, actually, it is. Lately anyway. Have you stopped to consider that Cynthia and I might enjoy each other's com-pany? We have fun together. She doesn't constantly push my buttons. In fact, she doesn't push them at all. She's *always* doing things for me. She took me to the spa again last week—"

"Excuse me for not having the money to ply you with gifts. I had not realized that requirement for your friendship."

"Come on, Annie," I said. "What's really wrong?"

"This *is* what's really wrong." She got up from feeding Lily.

She tossed the little food cup into the sink. "The amazing thing is that you don't even see it!" She didn't elaborate, instead taking Lily out of her seat rather roughly and passing me on her way to the nursery.

I knew I had only that moment to say something, maybe an apology? Maybe an explanation? I called after her and thankfully she stopped, but then my mind went blank. I didn't feel like apologizing to her after her unnecessary rudeness. In fact, I wanted her to apologize to *me*. The insinuation that Cynthia was friends with me only in order to get something offended me deeply. It touched my weakest spot, that sense of being unlovable, unwanted, my inner orphan who could not inspire the love of her mother let alone attract the attentions of a beautiful friend. Annie knew this about me; I couldn't fathom why she wanted to be mean for its own sake, but she did. Or maybe I *could* fathom it. I opened my mouth and said, "You're jealous. You're jealous of my friendship with Cynthia."

She didn't reply right away, though for a split second the look in her eyes changed. No one else would have seen or understood. But I had memorized her expressions years ago, and I knew the fleeting look that passed through eyes, a look of recognition. I was right, and she knew it.

"I'm not jealous of her—*you* are. You want what she has, and it's pathetic," she said with a flourish that meant she had finished with me. I could feel my armpits sweating with anxiety. I didn't want to fight anymore. As gracefully as one can with a squirming baby in one's arms, she spun around on her heel and left the room, calling coarsely over her shoulder for Hannah to come. Instantly, Hannah bawled to hear the Olive story. "Now!" directed Annie in a ferocious tone. It was unlike Hannah to be so obedient, but perhaps she sensed what I did in Annie, an absolute unwaveringness, and she ran out of the living room without saying good-bye, leaving me standing alone with no one to hear my reply.

20

Annie

For several weeks, I refused to see Meg for fear she'd made my life worse. During those weeks, nothing got better and everything got worse. I expected to be *skipping* around the house with a feather duster in my hand after three sessions with her, mothering Hannah like Supernanny on Prozac. Then, as that didn't happen, and I continued to resemble myself, I thought pausing my therapy would restore the pieces of my life that had fallen apart. In lieu of this outcome, I had now managed to alienate myself from everyone in my life.

"And you're no better," I told Ted. "You think I'm ambivalent, Cynthia's honorable, and weddings are fun."

"Can't a groom enjoy this special time in his life?"

"Fine. Enjoy away. Meanwhile, your bride has been abandoned by her maids-in-waiting. I don't know how to wedding plan, I don't *want* to wedding plan, and I had *planned* to rely upon the help of Nora and Suze since I clearly cannot call upon my mother."

"Ann, call your friends and ask them to be part of the

wedding," he pressed. "A wedding constitutes A Big Deal. They will come for it. I promise you. Little fights don't matter compared to weddings."

I assumed Suze would come, provided I didn't hold the great event on a weekday, which I had no intention of doing, but I ruled out Nora. "Our friendship is over," I told Ted.

"You're being petty."

"To the contrary, my dear fiancé. I am right and you are wrong, about a few things. Did you hear they finalized the selection of Cynthia for the Sylvia Sternberg Award?"

"We've been over this. It's not certain."

"They made the decision on Tuesday. She'll receive it at the February ceremony."

"What does that have to do with Nora not coming to our wedding?"

"Everything. You'll see."

On the last day of classes in December, Dean Friedman called me into his office after seeing me alone in the cafeteria, a rare occurrence owing to Lily and Hannah's extravagant bouts with the flu. Ted volunteered to stay with them in the apartment while I scavenged the lunch line for foods they might eat.

"My kids are sick," I told him.

"It will only take a minute."

I entered Friedman's stinky office. For a few minutes, I listened to him go on and on about his trip to Rhode Island for Christmas and the new metal detector he planned to break out on the deserted beach. The image of his lonely figure making its way down an abandoned beach pulled at my heart like an undertow; I did not want to identify with the man, yet in that moment I did. I felt like him, solitary in the world. I so lost myself in this maudlin line of thought, imagining my wedding with no attendants, my children growing up thinking I had no friends, that I almost missed Friedman's change of topic.

"You can't be serious!" I said, whiplashing myself right out of pity land and back into his office.

"You would only be required to teach the one semester. Naturally, we'll hire a new art teacher for the fall—if it comes to that." He wavered for a moment, cleared his throat, and began again. "Considering how many of the students you already know and your prestigious art education at RISD, we feel Dixbie couldn't hope for a better replacement for Tabitha."

Stunned wouldn't accurately describe my reaction. "Sure you could. You could hope for someone who's taught at the high school level. And who doesn't have two little children at home."

"I'm sure you could arrange some excellent childcare or trade times with Ted."

"I'm not so sure about that. 'Excellent childcare' doesn't actually exist. Unless I'm taking care of my own children."

"You'd be helping the school out tremendously. We don't have the resources currently to begin another faculty search. Also," and here he leaned into his desk as though to come closer to me, "Tabitha herself recommended you."

"I find that laughable. Tabitha and I never got along."

"I am only reporting the truth. When I went to visit, she directly requested you take over the position."

"Trying to make me feel guilty? I have a hard time believing asking me to teach her classes would make Tabitha's death wish list." Friedman held up his hands as if this was none of his concern. "Dick, seriously, I want to stay home with my girls."

"The school needs you," he said, opening his frog eyes wide with the plea.

"I'll talk to Ted," I answered. "But please don't count on it. It's very unlikely."

I didn't anticipate Ted's wild enthusiasm. When I told him, he raced around like a little dog desperate to take a leak.

"This is so awesome! You'd be perfect. What an opportunity. "

I gave him a look. "What about our children? Where will Hannah and Lily go while I teach?"

"Maybe we could arrange alternating teaching schedules. Maybe Nora could help a little?"

"For the zillionth time, Ted, Nora won't speak to me."

"What about asking Suze? Where does she leave Finn while she works? Maybe the girls could go there?"

"Honey, you're dangerously close to sounding like your mother." I valiantly refrained from screaming at him. Truthfully, I couldn't believe his response. I'd assumed he would have said no, it didn't make sense.

"Annie." He put his hands on my shoulders. "In the first place, you're an incredible artist. In the second place, she only taught two classes, so the time commitment would be minimal. In the third place, you have to read between the lines. Dixbie is struggling. I overheard Beverly going on about the budget and faculty layoffs. I think they really do need you; they can't afford to bring in someone new."

"In the fourth place, we don't have any money because

Ah-leen gets an alimony check for a salary. I see you're defecting from the cause too. What about our decision, our mutual choice, to have me stay with the children until Lily's at least three?"

"It *could* help our bottom line, I won't deny that," he said softly. "But that's not what I'm excited about."

"I will not subsidize your mistake."

"You don't need to get mean."

"Fine. I'll fight fair. What if I don't want to teach?" What was it worth—all my time with the girls—if I could be replaced so easily by some childcare provider? "Can't you hear your words? I might as well be hanging out with your mother and Elle and Suze, for that matter. You think what I do is so easy to give up that I can casually accept a job and stop being with the girls full-time? You think it's an easy decision, worth making a little extra cash, because all along I haven't been doing much anyway by taking care of my own children?"

Ted wouldn't fight. "What if you *do* want to teach? Isn't this what you've been talking about in therapy?"

"If I were a llama, I'd spit on you now," I said, walking away. I didn't want to hear another word come out of his mouth, no matter how true it was.

Both girls had fallen asleep during my trip to the cafeteria. I peeked in on Hannah, who breathed like a steam engine through her stuffed nose. Despite the December cold, she looked sweaty. In the nursery, Lily lay sound asleep on her belly, motionless. I touched her back to feel her breathe, to make sure. I loved them; it was a certainty I did not think, but felt, the way one feels a bone in one's body—not consciously, but continuously, its presence reliable and constant.

I thought, while I stood by Lily's crib, feeling her forehead for a fever, of Nora's desperate drive toward motherhood and where it comes from, that acute longing not only for children, but to become a mother. I always imagined her pregnancy, when it finally happened, would unite us, the way my having children first divided us. We had both been vaguely aware since Hannah's birth of the injustice of the situation, that I didn't particularly want children right away and ended up with two of them in short order, while she yearned and worked for them and none came. It may also have surprised her, though she was too polite to say so to me, that I turned out so enamored of them and committed to my mothering. Once I had Hannah, I found I'd really been made for motherhood, though as a girl Nora was the one with the dolls and the play baby carriages and the dreams. Becoming engrossed in mothering is an embarrassing and irrelevant accomplishment for a modern woman. No one will write an article about you for having given birth and loved your kids, while one major review of an art gallery show could catapult you into fame. As children, I wanted the fame, Nora the family. I felt glad for her that at last she would get what she wanted. I even hoped that it would satisfy her. I could at least be that mentally altruistic.

And why was I standing over my little one with my mind on Nora? I sighed, a big, heavy, woe-is-me sigh, as I closed the door to Lily's bedroom. I wanted to talk to my friend. I wanted to know what she would say about this "opportunity." Yet she was gone to me.

I could hear Ted flossing in the bathroom. I kept track of his flossing. Considering that we met in the dentist's office while he rifled through an enormous free giveaway bowl of floss, it seemed the touchstone of our relationship. He even flossed my teeth once, on a date. It wasn't terribly romantic to have his finger deep in my mouth, but he did an excellent job, even found a small string of spinach, and it sealed the deal for me; I could love a man who did not worry about vanity, who did not rely on external perfection, who could remove a green slippery smudge from my mouth without embarrassment or concern and say, simply, "You ate spinach today."

"I hear you," he called to me from the bathroom. "I hear you moping about."

"I can't help it."

"How can you not be excited!"

"How *can* I be excited?"

He opened the door. He is the same height as me, maybe a half-inch taller. I love this about him. Real equality. Nobody can be your equal who isn't in the same wrestling class. It should be a requirement in marriage: height assignments, weight assignments.

He leaned into me. He had to know what I meant. He had to know me. He had to know the price I would pay to go, to know what I'd give up, either way.

"Sweetie." He kissed me again. "You will only teach part-time."

Then it occurred to me, maybe he really *didn't* know. Maybe, being the man, being the father, having worked full-time the whole of both girls' lives, he really couldn't understand that for all my complaints about the challenges of motherhood, for all my grievances and protests issued periodically (and daily) on the trials of caring for small children, I *loved* being with them. I even loved being able to gripe about it; it never meant I wanted out.

I went to do laundry with an ache in my belly that I felt

certain Meg would call ambivalence. Maybe I needed to call her.

Still, it was only a gnawing little ache, not some tornado of feeling. I tried to reason the emotions out logically, like an adult. On the one hand, motherhood hadn't turned out to be as thoroughly fulfilling as I'd imagined it would be. In addition, I hadn't turned out to be the mother I dreamed I would be, the woman who radiates peace and never raises her voice. Fulfilled came maybe 80 percent of the time, with moments reaching 100 and moments reaching 20 or 30. I don't need to consult an expert to know that no one gets to expect better job satisfaction than that.

I rationally laid out my options. I could experiment with the possibility of my own ambivalence over work by taking on the preschool class at the BFC. Though I truly did not want to become involved in the organization, it would serve as a good trial ground with far less commitment required than taking over Tabitha's classes. Or I could become a blogger or an Avon lady or deliver newspapers early in the morning while chugging an enormous coffee, if money was what Ted felt we needed. We did need money, we always seemed to need money, so this choice meant little to me. I'd adjusted my life to account for our meager income. I didn't need the expensive cosmetics of the Brownies or the twice-weekly takeout. Clearly, money alone couldn't motivate me.

It's not gut-wrenching. It's not tear-jerking. It's not catastrophic. It's simply life. It's not a Wonderland Oz World all-your-dreams-coming-true. No bullshit propaganda that women can have it all. Because nobody gets it all, does she? Not all at once. It's impossible. I'm not volunteering for super-personhood. I'm not interested. Life's no buffet. Little of this, little of that. Take Cynthia's hair and money and Nora's stability and kindness and Ted's humor and Tabitha Hunter's talent and put them on me. Then I would be what? What I've always wanted? Solvent, gentle, mother, artist, skinny person?

"Annie. I can hear you thinking," Ted said, coming to find me in the utility room.

"It's not possible to hear someone else's thoughts. Unless you can read minds."

"I can read your mind."

"Well, then stop. It's private."

"You wish Friedman had never said anything."

"Yeah."

"Because it would be easier *not to know* that there's a position for you right here at Dixbie that would use all your native gifts."

"Yeah."

"Why don't you keep thinking about it? See how you feel tomorrow. And quit farting," he said. "It stinks."

"It's not me!" I protested honestly. "It's the cat." Ted stared incredulously at our cat, Moo (named by Hannah).

"Wow," he said. "I'm impressed. I'm off to write a final exam. Call me on the cell phone if you need me. I think the girls are on the upswing."

"Okay." I closed the dryer door and gave him a quick hug. "And while I'm thinking this job offer over, why don't you brainstorm what would happen to the girls if they were sick on the days I taught." He paused to consider. "You can get back to me on that."

21

Nora

The minute exams ended, I put the final touches on Olive's lonely life in the forest. I gave her a happy ending, an ogre family of her very own. I photocopied the originals in the school office and mailed the copy to Cynthia's brother the day before our All School Holiday Party.

Cynthia insisted on having me over for a pregnancy-friendly nonalcoholic celebratory drink that night. I didn't want to make too big of a deal, worried that my taking anything for granted could jinx my chances of publication. Cynthia reassured me over and over again. "I promise he owes me some favors," she said. I didn't know how to explain to her that I didn't want an agent to represent my book because of some familial account balancing. I wanted it to stand out on its own. But as Cynthia wasn't forthcoming in explaining why her brother owed her something, I refrained from objecting.

Luckily, she wanted to talk about colors for her nursery. She'd found out the other day during an ultrasound that she was expecting a girl. An unbidden wave of jealousy rose inside me at the thought. I wanted a girl, and her having one seemed to mean I would have a boy, no doubt another outdated, old-fashioned Helpsom-Fulch superstition. Even the thought felt disloyal. Cynthia personified kindness; she showed me nothing save helpfulness. That night she plied me with bags of maternity clothes.

"We're almost the same size," she said, a kind if untruthful statement. She possessed a much curvier figure. I worried I would resemble a sack in her dresses, though I didn't refuse them. Truthfully, I couldn't wait to try them on.

Before I turned off the light for bed that night, the phone rang.

"You've been out of touch."

"I'm sorry." It was my mother.

"We're all worried about you."

"Don't be worried!"

"You haven't called." I hadn't called. I had a good reason not to call: I am a lousy liar. Alfie and I decided we wanted to wait out the first trimester before sharing the good news with our families. Given my family's zealous emotional complications, Elle's mysterious prolonged visit a perfect example of this, I felt it better to keep my treasure to myself. Who knew what would happen if I didn't?

My mother sighed, a grave sigh, a grievous sigh. "I'm concerned about your future."

"What?" What could she mean?

After a rustling and a shuffling, I heard my grandmother's voice, strong and insistent, come over the line. "Your mother has a terrible bedside manner." I heard my mother protesting in the background. "What she means to say is that she doesn't want you to end up like her, spending a life savings and all your time trying to have a baby."

I knew little about this time in my mother's life. Apparently, she and my father tried for children for almost a decade before they gave up and adopted. It was one thing to allow my mother to worry over my chances at conception, another to worry my ninety-three-year-old grandmother.

I took a deep breath and said, "I followed your instructions, Gram. I ate a lot of butter."

"And?"

"And, I'm expecting!" She whooped enthusiastically.

I could hear my mother fussing in the background. "What? What is it?" she said.

"Good for you! You getting the runs yet? Throwing up?"

I laughed. "Not so far."

"Keep on with the butter. The fat makes for smart babies. I tried to diet when I was pregnant with your mother. You can see how that turned out!" We laughed together. My grandmother always enjoyed a joke at my mother's expense—especially in my company. She used it as a way to make up for the uncomfortable silence surrounding the adoption. With Grandma Lucy, I never felt like an outsider.

"Thank goodness you won't have to do what your mother did. She nearly went crazy trying to have a baby. For three years before she adopted you she didn't work, she hardly left the house. Depression. Nowadays some doctor would give her six different pills and stick her in counseling. Back then, if women like your mother didn't have kids, they were considered incompetent." I wondered what she meant, *women like your mother*. She didn't elaborate. "No worries now, anyhow. You're baking a tidy loaf."

I heard a loud rustling, then my mother reprimanding my grandmother for disclosing so much. A moment later, my mother's weary voice came on the line. "Nora," she said sternly. "Would it have killed you to tell your own mother first?"

"I'm sorry. We weren't going to tell anyone. That's why I haven't called. I find it hard to keep a secret from you."

"Well, you should find it hard. I didn't raise a daughter to keep secrets. Now, Aunt Rose, on the other hand, she seems mighty fine with hiding family troubles."

"What do you mean?" I asked, genuinely curious.

"What do you mean, 'what do I mean?' Elle's right there with you, isn't she?"

"Yes. For weeks, Mom," I said in a whisper.

"Have you asked her why?"

"No, I—well, she hasn't said anything. Is something wrong?"

My mother clucked. "You dear girl," she said, with a mix of tenderness and amazement. "You have always been so unfailingly good-hearted, giving everyone the benefit of the doubt. I bet you haven't even asked her."

I hadn't, of course. "Is it very bad?" I asked, intrigued and scared at the same time. The Helpsom-Fulchs don't go in for scandal, unless you count the benign variety carried out in mild family feuds and repressed emotional lives.

"Why don't you ask your cousin? She came to *you* for a reason."

. . .

I had no intention of talking to Elle before the holiday party. Every second of my day was accounted for. I had to grade final exams, finish a few college letters of recommendation, meet with two students, take Fruity to the vet, help decorate the cafeteria with Cynthia for the festivities, and find something to wear. I hoped we might have a few minutes during the party, as Elle had taken to coming with me for many of the school events. She availed herself of every opportunity to have a free drink.

If I had to use only one word to describe what she wore for the holiday party, it would be cleavage. I know cleavage doesn't qualify as clothing, and it isn't really an accessory, but it's undoubtedly what Elle wore. It wasn't simply a feature of her outfit, either. It *was* the outfit, and I nearly asked her to change before we left the house. Alfie, to his credit, did not stare.

The holiday party, being the last hurrah of the first semester, buzzes with the thrill of relief. Exams are over; students head home the following day. Cynthia and I had dolled up the cafeteria with the use of many of her personal decorations, and when we entered the large room, it looked nothing like its perfunctory self. It held an air of magic. It made me love Dixbie all over again.

"There's your friend Annie," Elle said, pointing to her and Ted. "She's built like Humpty Dumpty, isn't she?" I looked around, hoping no one would overhear. "And Cynthia," she carried on, looking over at my friend who shimmered in an iridescent pink maternity gown that showcased her growing bump. "Her girls will sag in a few years. I'm so glad I was smart enough to get my done young." She walked away from us toward the drink table.

"My mother says something is wrong with her," I whispered to Alfie.

"Obviously," he stated, unexpectedly. I figured he hadn't noticed; Alfie never seems to take note of things like that. He also never brought it up. I assumed because it didn't occur to him to wonder.

Cynthia came up to us a few minutes later. She hugged me and Alfie. "Doesn't it look magical? Who knew this stodgy place could transform so well? Your wife did a good job decorating, didn't she?" Cynthia asked Alfie. He looked sweetly vacant, as he generally does in relation to beautifications of any kind.

"Can I get you two something to drink?" Alfie asked, for a moment my knight.

"Seltzer," I said, and Cynthia and I looked at each other conspiratorially.

"I'll have what she's having," she said, hooking an arm through mine. Alfie went off and Cynthia steered me toward two chairs pressed up against the wall. "I'm so happy you're here." She had a special way of making me feel wanted. That same sense of belonging that had always eluded me, she gave away freely and easily. I wished I could relive my argument with Annie and tell her this. It seemed important, like the missing link. If she knew, maybe she wouldn't be so angry.

"This is my first Dixbie holiday party."

"What do you think?"

"I thought people would dress up. Tabitha always made out that Dixbie prided itself on formality."

I chuckled, looking around the room. "Formality in everything but attire."

"I expected *glam*, Norie."

"Not at Dixbie. We do understatement. Anyway, the parties here are more like family gatherings."

"You look pretty," she said. I self-consciously smoothed down the silver, paneled maternity skirt I'd found in her bag of clothes. And then, unpredictably, "Speaking of people who are like family, what's the deal with Annie?"

"Why do you ask?"

"Her sourness." I'd never heard Cynthia remark on Annie before, on anyone at Dixbie for that matter.

"It's just her personality." I wasn't sure if I needed to defend Annie or not; I wasn't sure if I *wanted* to defend her.

"I feel badly for her kids. The other day in the cafeteria the older girl dropped an egg, poor thing. Annie was furious."

"Oh, no," I told her, quickly coming to Annie's rescue. I could agree with almost any criticism thrown at her, but not when it came to her mothering. "Annie's the best mother I know. I've never met anyone more dedicated, more proficient, more magnanimous in her mothering. Annie might have a bit of a temper, but her devotion is contagious; she adores her kids."

"You know her much better than I do," Cynthia said. Elle jogged up to us at that moment, some of her wine splashing onto her long, black tank dress.

"Ladies! What a party. Aren't you two lucky to live at such a cozy little place?" She sat down on a folding chair beside me. "You know what I've been meaning to ask you since I got here, only I've been so selfishly stuck in my own head? Well, the very reason I came to see you? To find out about your sex life with Alfie!" She tapped her head with a slender, nail-bitten finger. "It slipped my mind. Isn't that silly! Here I am, the country's sex expert, and I forgot to ask you how it goes with the orgasm debacle. Until a minute ago, I'm standing next to Alfie getting wine, and I think, you two have taken me in, taking care of me, and I'm useless. What have I done for you? Not much I can do, these days. But there isn't a person better equipped to deal with your sexual issues than I am. So spill it."

"Uh—" Waves of humiliation tidaled through me. Elle knew that my mother's birds-and-bees talk went like this, word for word: "Sex is something one *does*. It is not something one talks about." I also know she heard Aunt Bertie say, on more than one occasion, "*Most* sex is a crime." Her wild rebellion as a sex therapist certainly had its roots in our overdone suppression. Still, I do have to draw the line. My orgasms, or lack thereof, did not belong in a conversation during the holiday party, not to mention one with Cynthia present.

Cynthia stood up, clearly possessed of the good manners to know when to step away. David and Melanie Jones, the physics teacher, walked by at that moment, both waving good-naturedly at us while they carried on an engrossing conversation. They didn't stop on their way to the food table.

"Speak of the devil!" Elle exclaimed, finishing her glass of wine. "Didn't you tell me a few years ago that you had the best orgasms of your life with David? Oh, I'm sure you didn't say those exact words." She tittered lightly. "And I probably had to get you to drink during Christmas to loosen up enough to talk to me." She waved spastically at David. "David Hayworth, yes indeed. The man who gave my cousin an orgasm. I can't see why you ever left him, considering he holds such a place of honor. No offense to you, of course, Cynthia."

Desperate to stop Elle, I put a hand on my belly. "I think I feel a kick." Cynthia looked at me strangely, her brow furrowed, while Elle talked right over me.

"It's not the only reason to stay with a man, of course, but you can't underestimate the importance of climax for women. Research shows how important it is for a woman to have regular orgasms. It affects everything from complexion to blood pressure. What a shame, coz," she said, shaking her head. "Maybe Alfie can get some pointers from David. Do they ever talk? I guess I ought to be asking about *you*?" She faced Cynthia now.

I stood up and grabbed Elle's elbow. "I think you've had too much to drink." I started to pull her away. Cynthia continued to look at me with an expression I couldn't read. I only hoped that David really had told her about our relationship, while certain, from the disconcerted look on her face, that I hoped in vain.

"Have you ever had a ménage à trois?" she asked me, as I towed her toward the hallway. "You need sufficient multitasking skills to truly enjoy them, sort of like rubbing your belly and tapping your head at the same time. Some people can do it, and some people can't. Personally, I started training for them long before I even knew what they were. As a child, I could hula-hoop and juggle at the same time."

"Please be quiet, Elle."

"Why? Because the kids will hear? Sex education is part of adolescence. No one should have to end up, God forbid, getting to twenty without having had some experiences. I knew a virgin once, at thirty." Her blue eyes widened. "No, I swear, this is a true story. I was the first woman he ever slept with. All I have to say is that no one should have to go through that experience of, what do they call it? 'Saving yourself for marriage.' My God, he was like a psychiatric patient. Men *need* to release their sperm. If they don't, they get a backlog. It goes straight to the brain."

"TMI," I muttered, getting her safely out of the dining room.

"Honestly, it's a potential mental health crisis, all these aging virgins running around misunderstanding the world. Sex is natural, for heaven's sake. It's healthy! Each of us is living proof of that."

"Elle, enough!" I finally shouted. She looked at me askance. "Could you go home, maybe? I think you're intoxicated. A walk in the fresh air would be good for you."

"Fine," she said, handing me her empty wineglass. "If you don't like having your own flesh and blood around, I'll go." I couldn't help laughing, though it was a sad little laugh. "What's so funny?" she asked angrily.

"You're not my flesh and blood. Remember, I'm *adopted*."

"Ridiculous!" She started walking unevenly away from me. "You're the only one who cares about that. Flesh and blood doesn't make a bit of difference to anyone but you. As a matter of fact, my mother never stops talking about how perfect Nora acts. What a good job you've done becoming a teacher. How she wishes I'd gone into a reputable field. You have always been the favorite because you were *chosen*." The force of her words nearly knocked her down. She righted herself against the wall. "I wish you'd just get over yourself!"

It occurred to me, as I watched her stagger out the door, that I ought to accompany her. At that point, though, I didn't want to. I didn't want to help Elle home because I wanted to repair the damage she'd caused with Cynthia. I didn't want to wait another minute. I almost ran back into the dining hall, collecting my composure at the last minute. I scanned the crowded room for Cynthia, and when I couldn't see her, I searched for Alfie. As I walked quickly over to his side, a hush fell over the room, which, so bent on my destination, I didn't register at first.

I looked up to see Dean Friedman standing on a chair. For a second I worried he had lost his mind or drunk too much and would start dancing on the chair and throwing his clothes, one piece at a time, into the horrified crowd. I would have laughed at this image at some other time, some less anxious time. When Friedman began to speak in his regular, measured, heavy tone, I knew it was simply business as usual and felt annoyed that he would interrupt my quest to reconcile with Cynthia. It felt more and more dire by the moment. What did she think? What did she know? What would she forgive?

Only it wasn't business as usual. Alfie held my hand as we listened together to Friedman's prepared speech. As he talked, he pulled a small folded piece of paper out of his coat pocket and referred to it a number of times, as if he couldn't remember what he'd come to say. Considering the weight of his announcement, it seemed unlikely he would have forgotten a single bit of what he needed to convey.

"The administration felt it imperative that the entire school know now, so that you might all have the chance, over the holiday break, to consider your options. Nothing brings me more sadness," he said, choking up visibly. That's when it dawned on me that he wasn't using the note because he couldn't remember his message, he was using it as a foil, a way to step outside of the emotion. "Dixbie has been my home for two decades. It is a very special place. Unfortunately, as I said just minutes ago, our investments of recent years have been disastrous. There is no way to keep the school open after the end of this school year."

Hands were raised and voices called out. Friedman held up a thick, hairy hand to stop the onslaught. "I'm sure this seems like a terrible time to break the news. But I must emphasize that timing is essential. We want everyone to have sufficient time to prepare for next year."

"Why can't you sell off a few buildings?" Tyler shouted in what sounded like exasperation.

"This is a joke," I heard Beverly Slater announce with disgust. I looked over at her. Annie, standing beside Beverly, gazed at me. I held her gaze. An ocean of disappointment washed between us. When she looked away first, I knew she was still mad at me, that not even this would bring us back together.

"There will be a way to stay open," Alfie said to me, squeezing my hand tightly.

"The financial situation, due to many years of declining enrollment, has become calamitous," Friedman continued. I could see his hands shaking. My heart broke for him. He had no family but Dixbie.

"Save our school!" a student shouted. This was matched with a hundred more voices in rhythmic echoes.

I found the response moving, though the situation stunningly awful. Maybe it was the emotion, or the warm, crowded room, or the sense of the rug being pulled out from underneath me, and certainly it was the pregnancy, but at that moment, I threw up, a gregarious puke, too, for it made its way onto several of the people around me, effectively pausing the evening's unfolding drama, as students scurried to help clean me up. For years after, the smell of vomit brought to mind that terrible night, and funnily enough, because of Elle's outrageous behavior, from then on, I always thought of Cynthia when I puked.

22

Annie

Suze called the day the news hit the papers. "What will you do?" she asked.

"It's a media stunt," I told her. "A way to inspire some major donors to cough up major funds."

"Oh." She sounded confused. "The article makes it sound like a real financial crisis. They predict an unavoidable shutdown."

"I'm not worried," I said curtly, annoyed by her sudden interest in my life. She hadn't asked about the divorce papers or any other aspect of my life in weeks.

"You okay?"

"You don't even know the half of it. This full-time motherhood gig is hard. It's the real, thankless work that makes this world a place people can even live in, but you don't get any recognition for it. You don't ever get written up in the newspaper. How about this for a headline: 'Mother of Two Manages Nap Time Smoothly . . . In dramatic achievement, a Brownston mother of two kept temper tantrums and hysterical infant crying at bay, changed two diapers with one hand, and sang the entire Muppet album successfully. The result: two sleeping children.' But no, we don't get media attention. We don't get Excellence in Mothering awards."

"I know how stressful—"

"So what that I couldn't take it today and sent my red-eyed toddler away with her father? Is that so bad? I didn't kill her, did I? I didn't flush her baby sister down the toilet. I didn't call her unforgivable names or eat an entire box of snickerdoodles. I mean, I did pretty well, I'd say, for an average day." An uncomfortable silence followed. "Thanks for listening. I feel much better now."

"Of course, Annie. You can always talk to me."

I did not pause to point out the error in her statement. I could not *always* talk to her. In fact, I could rarely talk to her. Either she was busy working or busy trying to spend time with her family. That she graciously listened to me for all of three minutes so I could rant about a minor problem as a way of disguising my real anger at her hardly qualified her for the friendship award.

"You'll attend the Save Our School meeting next week, I imagine."

"Only because I look forward to adult venues where I can engage some of the vocabulary I acquired after kindergarten. As much as I appreciate the identity-forming and culturally enriching qualities of repetitive household tasks like washing sippy cups and folding laundry, a little time to talk in paragraphs, albeit about unnecessary strategic planning, could really improve my mood."

"I'm sensing a theme here. A motherhood theme. A stay-at-home motherhood theme. Are you mad at me?" This seemed like the perfect opportunity to agree and move on. Only I felt intractable that morning and petulant. I felt like Hannah when she doesn't get what she wants.

"Speaking of working mothers, did I mention my job offer?" I said instead.

"What? You don't want to work! You didn't even want to take on that little kids' class at the BFC."

I wasn't flattered by her response. If anything, it propelled me to act more attracted by the offer than I actually felt. As I told her about the position Friedman had offered me, I withheld the details of my reaction. I did not speak of that dreaded ambivalence. I wanted her to think I was as busy as she was, as important a person in the world.

"I can see you teaching," she said. "What a shame that the school will close. Maybe after this semester, you could get a position teaching at another private high school?"

Clearly, I had been too convincing, and her lack of intuition about my predicament irked me to no end. I hung up the phone feeling forlorn, a stranger in a strange land. She hadn't made a single mention of how difficult a decision it would be, how challenging it might be to leave the girls, even for only part of every day. Sure, I'd led her to believe I found the position desirable, but that didn't excuse her ignorance as to my character, my nature. After talking to her, I felt as though I didn't even exist, and just to prove it to myself, I went into my bedroom and stared at myself in the mirror for a while. Not surprisingly, this only made me feel worse.

Having tossed my children and husband out the door

earlier (I had not made up my bad day on Suze's behalf), I had some time all to myself. For ten seconds I flipped through a magazine on the coffee table, noticing its slightly tattered corners. Lily had ripped out more than a few pages, making it hard to read. Hannah had taken her crayons to some of the remaining pages with Van Goghian exuberance.

"Hey, sweet cheeks." Ted and the girls ploughed through the door with bursts of sound, making the previous moments of quiet seem like something I'd fancifully hallucinated. Given the years of ongoing sleep deprivation, hallucination felt as likely as anything else.

"Ted, what are you doing home? I thought you were all going to the grocery store."

"We're back! It *has* been an hour and a half." He pointed at his watch, then he pointed at the magazine. "I see you have succumbed."

"I got it for the girls. Looking at a bridal magazine does not mean anything."

"Not true." He grinned broadly. "In this case it means you're getting married."

"I'm wearing black," I informed him. "According to the experts," I tapped the cover of the mag, "black is entirely appropriate for a ceremony."

"The romance will kill me."

"Not if the wedding planning kills me first."

After taking off the girls' coats, he deposited Lily on the rug by my feet. Hannah went into the kitchen with him to unpack the groceries. For helping, she earned a dime to put in her piggy bank. This had been Ted's idea, a way to encourage her toward usefulness. Amazingly, it worked. She adored the coins. She took them out and put them back in the piggy bank (it had a large hole on the bottom with a removable plastic cap). Ted taught her how to count out the change. Her fascination with money inspired her to work, and I realized, with little satisfaction, that I had a capitalist on my hands.

"Play along," Ted called from the kitchen. "What does your dream wedding look like?"

I turned to stare at him, but he was too busy putting things into the cupboard to appreciate my glare. "I know you're kidding. I have never, and you well know this, *never* had a dream about a wedding."

"Every girl does. That's what little girls do. Just look at Hannah. She's always dressing up as a princess."

"I didn't say I never wanted to be a princess. I said I never wanted to be a bride."

"Moving right along. Should we invite families?" he asked.

"Too complicated to discuss right now."

"Okay. How about using the chapel? Did you decide about that? And a reception? Could we use the dining hall?"

"Ted." I picked Lily up and went into the kitchen, not wanting to yell my answers back to him, especially when I knew they would contain expletives. "Weddings, and all the beatific *bullshit*," I hissed the word above the baby's head, "that goes with them—the dress, the hair, the bridesmaids, the flowers, the food, the beachside location—*all* of that comes out of this ridiculous, damaging myth of beauty. Does a promise under a three-thousand-dollar tent mean anything more than one made on a linoleum floor in the courthouse? Does having a hundred guests impart some kind of loyalty, love, fidelity, or magic? You and I both know how marriages can and do end. I don't want to be one of those casualties. On the other hand, I don't want to lose myself in never-never land. I want our ceremony to be *real*.

"What we have right now is stronger and deeper than any marriage I know. If we have some elaborate wedding, how am I going to tell those little girls that love isn't stuff? That love isn't what money can buy? That love isn't matching accessories? I want them to know from the start that when the prince comes and takes the princess away on his white stallion, the story has only *begun*."

"Hey," he said, reaching over and stroking my arm. "I get it. No pressure. It can be low-key."

"And I can wear black?"

"Yes. You can wear black." He leaned in and kissed me sweetly.

"Why do you put up with me?" I asked.

"Because you're the best thing that ever happened to me. But can I ask a question without getting my head bit off?"

"Go ahead."

"What do you need with the glossy if you aren't going to have a proper wedding?"

What *did* I need with the bridal magazine? I looked down at the cover, a lovely woman smiling back at me, her face layered with makeup, her lips curling up in a carefully painted red smile. I haven't used lipstick since my mother forbid makeup in the house after her divorce. She liked to walk around our apartment in Chicago and spout catchy rhetoric. More than once she treated my friends and me to her favorite question: "Does a fish need a bicycle? Does it?" "Don't worry about her," I'd tell my friends. "She's a feminist."

"What I'm getting at is this: can I at least send you tuxedo links?"

"I bought it on a whim," I said about the magazine. "Since I don't have any girlfriends to talk to anymore, I thought it might give me some ideas."

"You're afraid, aren't you?" I didn't want to answer in front of the girls. Ted leaned in toward me and whispered in my ear. "I'm smarter than a man who hasn't gone through a divorce," he said. "I know more now. I made a mistake. I won't make another one. I want you for life. Our marriage will not be like your parents'. Promise."

I felt sentimental and close to tears, a condition I can't bear in myself, so I stumbled out without responding, escaping into my bedroom, where I put Lily on the floor next to the open bottom drawer of my dresser. She thinks pulling things out of the drawer and onto the floor is all the rage. I opened the closet to look for a bridal gown.

Please feel free to call me insane. Maybe my inner bride had indeed been unleashed and I *wanted* to plan my own wedding. Whatever the reason, I spent fifteen minutes looking through my closet for formal black things, or other possibilities that wouldn't make me look like the plastic chick on the top of the wedding cake.

Hannah found me this way with my head buried in our overstuffed closet.

"What you lookin' for, Mama?"

"I'm searching for my black funeral dress."

"What's funral dress?"

At last laying my hands on the subdued, ankle-length dress, I pulled it out of the closet and held it up for her to see. "Will I be a beautiful bride in this?"

"No," Hannah said, obviously displeased with my choice. She ran out of the room as quickly as her fat legs could carry her. When she came back in, she had the bridal magazine in her hands. "This," she stated, sternly pressing down one of the pages. I took the magazine out of her hands and scrutinized the gown. It was simple and flowing, cream-colored, with tiny pink flowers embroidered around the three-quarter-length sleeves. It looked like the dress of a classy princess. "You be most bootiful bride ever," Hannah announced with total conviction.

The next day, driving to Meg's office, I took a brief inventory of the state of my life. I prepared to paraphrase the events of the past few weeks for her. Taking into account my upcoming nuptials, my falling-out with Nora, the school's threatened closing, Suze's nonfriendship, and the Dixbie teaching offer, I felt confident I could not only fill my allotted hour with great heaves of emotion, I worried I might run over.

I gave Meg a truncated version of the events, then said, "Don't take this personally, but ever since I began therapy, my life has fallen apart."

A small smile crept around her mouth; I couldn't interpret it.

"You know," I went on, "I came here in search of my inner child. Instead of feeling more playful and loving and easygoing as a mother, accessing my little inner me, I'm more angry than ever. I've alienated my best friend, lost another friend to employment, and even finally getting Ted's divorce papers, the thing I've been waiting years for—years!—hasn't diminished my sense of irritation at the world. In fact, I feel more upset than I did when he wasn't officially divorced. Explain that."

She smiled again, this smile less mischievous and more

tender. "Annie, my dear," she began, lifting a hand to run it through her gray hair. As she did, her excess of bracelets sung out like wind chimes. "Did you ever consider the possibility that your inner child might not be easygoing, playful, and loving?" I hadn't. After all, this is a *child* we're talking about. "I think you found this little girl, the one you're so keen on reconnecting with. Only, it seems to me, she isn't at all what you imagined."

"She's all fight, like Hannah," I said.

"I wasn't thinking that. I was thinking this little girl is sad."

"My inner child is sad?" I asked, incredulous. I thought about how I wanted to cry the day before when I stood in front of Hannah and Lily, the black funeral dress in one hand, the wedding magazine with Hannah's pick for my wedding gown in the other.

"Just entertain that possibility," Meg said as I crossed my arms over my chest.

23

Nora

I wanted to think about Friedman's announcement, to focus my attention on my beloved Dixbie, but I had a more pressing problem: I had yet to talk to Cynthia about Elle's comments. Selfish as it may be, the personal needed to come first. Somewhere, Cynthia was thinking (or I thought she was thinking) about how I came to have such an extraordinary sex life with her husband. The fact that she didn't return my phone calls, or answer the door when I knocked on it, encouraged my belief that Elle's comments constituted a major, unwelcome news flash for Cynthia. Not for the first time, I cursed David, and not because he and Cynthia had plans to fly to Bermuda and go on a sailing excursion, although their holiday did cause me some trouble. In the first place, it left me only three days to contact Cynthia before they left. In the second, it gave me another reason to envy the woman I very much wanted to maintain my friendship with, despite the fact that her now husband was my once orgasm-producer. Ugh, how I wished Elle had kept her mouth closed!

Three different times I stopped by Meadow House and knocked. Three times, no answer. Each time I walked away through the empty campus, a sense of desertion swallowing me up. I refused to imagine a permanently altered campus. I would place my hands on my tummy and think about the baby. Then, nothing else mattered.

I burned in a soap-opera way for a chance to explain myself to Cynthia. I wanted her to know I hadn't purposely withheld the facts about my relationship with David. Then I worried this was a lie. I *had* withheld that information. Cynthia and I didn't talk about past lovers or our sex lives. Should I have brought it up? Did I seem to her, post Elle's drunken revelations, duplicitous? I wanted a chance to exonerate myself. I missed her. Without her, things seemed dreary. I hadn't realized how much time I spent with her until then. All the teas and breakfasts and little gifts and little trips—gone. I found thinking about the baby such a comfort and a surprise, as though the pregnancy belonged to Cynthia. I was so magical in my thinking in relation to her; I found without her, any good thing didn't fit. And then finally I felt grateful for the good things that belonged to me, that I had not merely borrowed from her.

I walked into the apartment after my last attempt to find Cynthia at home and was engulfed in a putrid smell that I knew didn't belong to me. Since the holiday party, I'd begun courting the toilet bowl on a regular basis and greeted each bout of puking with the happiness of a pregnant woman. Which is to say as much happiness as can possibly be mustered while ill. That day, the smell I came into was much worse than any I'd made of late and it nearly caused me to be sick again.

Elle stood in the living room looking vaguely apologetic. "What's that stink?"

"Fruity puked in the house. Ten different times I tried to coax her out; she wouldn't budge. I got out her leash, I got a treat, I opened the door. I tried explaining how nice the weather is for this time of year—not too cold, brisk, invigorating really. She won't get off the bed."

"Does that mean what I think it means?" I put the smell and the thought together. "Did she barf on my bed?"

"It's not that bad," Elle said. "First time, she did it in the corner of the room—"

"*First* time?" Things were sounding worse and worse.

"Second time, it was closer to the door. I did my best to get the floor clean, but I don't really *do* cleaning, at least not this variety. Also, I couldn't find any rubber gloves. Now the third time . . ." Elle carried on as I passed her and went into the bedroom to find Fruity curled up like a large, furry snake on my pillows. She picked up her head when she saw me, lifting her tail once and thwacking it against the headboard. "Fruity, what's going on?" I went to her and patted her gently, stroked her silky ears.

"Oooh, she's done it again," said Elle, who had followed me in. She backed up at the smell.

"Where?"

"Looks like behind the chair. I'll get the paper towels." Elle, for once short on words, headed out quickly.

I sat beside Fruity with only one thought in my mind: my own silly, superstitious idea that Fruity would have to die in order for me to have a baby. Now, I had my baby coming. What about Fruity? I touched her nose, which thankfully felt cold and wet as it should. Then I wrapped myself around her, sticking my face into her fur. I lay there mentally torturing myself with regret; why had I imagined Fruity's death would bring me a baby? What a stupid, useless, mean-spirited thought that was coming back now to haunt me.

Elle came in and stood beside the bed, holding the paper towels in my general direction. I didn't need a billboard to get the hint. "I'll do this one. You've done more than your share," I told her, reluctantly leaving Fruity. I was getting ready to indulge in a gruesome what-if fantasy that entailed a doggie cancer diagnosis and a bittersweet farewell to my beloved Fruity, when I discovered what appeared to be half of a regurgitated diaper on the floor behind the rocking chair.

Under normal circumstances, a half-digested diaper wouldn't fill me with gratitude, but this one did. As I'd walked Fruity off-leash in the woods the day before, she may well have uncovered this little treasure deep in the trees. She always had a weak spot for feces. She'd eaten all sorts of revolting items, including horse manure and tampons (yes this is true, and yes it was truly disgusting and she required a vet visit for dehydration), without getting seriously ill. I started to laugh with relief, glad that I hadn't mentally killed her with my irrational belief. Elle, perhaps mistaking me for a crazy person, shook her head and walked out of the room.

After de-stinking the room, I brought Fruity a bowl of water and a biscuit, both of which she greedily devoured. "Silly dog," I said, kissing the top of her head. She wagged her tail in agreement. The relief of her near-death experience turned diaper-vomit emboldened me. I left the room determined to finally talk to Elle.

Since my mother's phone call and the dreadful holiday party, I woke every day with a promise that I would confront

Elle, not only about her never-ending stay, but about her conspicuous alcohol consumption and its disastrous effects. Except every day I couldn't bring myself to say anything. Plagued as I am by my own niceness, I couldn't muster the strength for confrontation. I didn't want to hurt Elle's feelings. Alfie patiently stood by my hesitance, insisting I would "know when the time was right." Also, I'd lost Annie's friendship so recently. I really didn't want to rock the boat with Elle, but Cynthia's absence, her refusal to open the door for me, bolstered my limp interrogation skills.

Armed with a plastic bag full of dirty diaper, I left the bedroom in search of my cousin. I found her in the kitchen, pouring a glass of wine.

"I really did try to get her outside," she protested instantly.

"I'm not mad at you. She ate a diaper. It made her sick."

"Disgusting!" she wailed, then less dramatically, "Want a glass?" as she held up the bottle of wine.

"No, thanks."

"Right, the pregnancy. I keep forgetting."

"Elle, can we sit down for a minute?"

"Oh, no," she said. "You want to talk to me." I tried smiling. "You want to know when I'm going to leave."

"It *has* been more than a month," I said as gently as I could.

"Do you hate me?"

"Why would you say that? Of course I don't hate you. I don't understand, that's all. My mother mentioned that something happened. Did it?" She took a sip of her wine, and for once I couldn't wait for her to get tipsy. It loosened her lips. I certainly didn't want to pry the truth out of her. I don't do probing questions very well. I'm of the bury-under-the-rug school of emotional tactics, learned at the elbow of my own mother, who hardly clung to keeping her own counsel no matter the circumstance.

"I lost my job."

"Do you want to sit down?" I gestured toward the kitchen chairs.

"Not particularly."

We stood for a few minutes in silence as I deliberated on which question to ask first and ending up hopelessly saying, "I thought you came to help me with my sex life."

"Not that I did a good job at that. You haven't even let me show you my dildo collection."

"Is that a joke?"

"No," she said, chugging back the last of the wine. "It's quite extensive, including wooden, marble, plastic, and glass phalluses. You've probably heard of the rabbit. That's the one you should start with. It works both the cli—"

"Elle." I stopped her just as the rising creep of a blush overtook me. "Can we go back to the losing-your-job part?"

"My boss," she said, going to the refrigerator and pouring another glass. "My manager. My lover. He fired me. It's all too sordid for your innocent ears. I don't feel like picking your jaw up off of the floor. In your precious world, nothing ever goes wrong."

"That's not true."

"It's not? Tell me one thing wrong with your life."

"I couldn't get pregnant for a whole year!"

She laughed ruthlessly. And then she told me the whole story.

. . .

Late that night, once Elle had gone to the guest room to sleep, I cuddled up to Alfie on the couch. Since finding out about the baby, I felt closer to him than I ever had. The safety of our new intimacy allowed me to admit to myself some of the unforgivable thoughts I'd entertained over the past infertile year, chief among them the idea that I had only married Alfie for a baby—and that when no baby was forthcoming, I discovered I didn't want *him*. The worst thing about having such unseemly thoughts is feeling unable to confess them for fear of being judged. I never could confide this to Annie; she and Ted share an incredible closeness. She wouldn't have any idea of what it's like to be in an imperfect relationship. And I certainly wouldn't have said anything to Cynthia.

I didn't pride myself on self-awareness, no doubt an inheritance from my mother, who once when I mentioned that a friend had sought counseling, nearly keeled over in shock and stated, with distaste, "Counseling is for the mentally ill, not young adults who aren't getting what they want." I supposed she did have a point. My whole generation could do with a shot of stoicism. But even without possessing the skill of self-observation, I knew I'd narrowly avoided a disaster with Alfie by getting pregnant. I chose not to think what our marriage might have become in the absence of a baby. I chose to think of Elle instead.

"Can I tell you about Elle?" I said quietly to Alfie, not wanting Elle to overhear, though, given the magnum of wine she'd put down, I doubted anything could wake her.

"What about Elle?" He turned down the volume on the TV.

"She told me today why she's here." I made a sad face. "It's

not a happy story, but at least it explains everything." I noticed that since finding out about the pregnancy, I took bad
news with new buoyancy. Not that I didn't feel for Elle; she'd
come through a terrible ordeal. But I stood outside of her
suffering, as though looking in a window. For the first time in
my life, I discovered the meaning of the word *smug*.

"She's lost her job, hasn't she?" he asked.

"Much worse than that." I began to relay all the sordid
details, re-creating, as best I could, Elle's take on the matter.
"A year ago, Elle started sleeping with her agent, also her
manager, also the head of the media company—"

"All three at once?" Alfie, intrigued and impressed, raised
his eyebrows.

I laughed. "No, her agent is the same person as her manager and the head of the media conglomerate. He's also the
father of three sons and a married man; his wife is CFO of the
company."

"Big mistake," Alfie said, now muting the television and
giving me his full attention. Clearly, Elle's story had more de-
ception than his football game.

"Before the wife found out about the affair, Elle got pregnant." Alfie took on an appropriately appalled face. "When
she went to him with the news, he told her he'd fire her if she
kept the baby."

"Wow."

"It gets worse. She had an abortion. After that, he let her
go anyway. He claimed some infraction in her contract, but
I'd venture to guess he simply couldn't bear to look at her,
knowing what he'd done. He said she could keep the column.
'Only if I can write the truth,' she told him. She wrote one

column telling a loosely fictionalized version of her story. Bethany, the wife, read it, and that was the end of her career."

"When did she start drinking?"

"You've noticed?"

"Nora." Alfie squeezed me in tightly. "A blind man would notice. She smells like a bar at eight a.m."

"I don't know when that started. I feel so sorry for her."

"Why did she come here instead of to her mother's?"

"I didn't ask. I didn't want to press her. I assume she feels the same way about her mother that I do about mine. As awful as it is, I'm relieved to know at last. It makes sense of so much of her behavior."

"I don't think the worst is behind her, though," Alfie said. "If she keeps on drinking like that, she'll kill herself, one way or another."

"I can't ask her to leave now."

"No way. She needs you. You're her family." Oh, for Alfie's optimism in regard to all things family! Because his own family possesses all the good sense mine lacks, although no more fashion sense, he can't understand my irritation over my continually interfering relatives. He and his twin brother, Artie (Alfred and Arthur), were raised by an indulgent mother, Happy—her real name, and boy does it suit her— and a gregarious, involved father, Alan. Happy insists that I call her "Mom," treats me like royalty, and occasionally sends me packages full of home-baked brownies and cookies and these special oaty things she makes with Tabasco sauce that not even Fruity will touch. If you put the Galusha family on an elevator, they would exceed the recommended weight limit, but you can overlook such imperfections in the face of their respectful distance from our life, which they maintain with an equal amount of intelligent loving care. They neither speak of Satan nor of private body parts during family meals. And they have never once called to inform me of the best way to conceive a child.

"My family," I sighed, spreading out on the sofa with my head in his lap. I did love them, I only wished them to act less eccentric. "Soon I will have a family that belongs to *me*."

An hour later when Fruity whimpered by the door, I begrudgingly got up to take her out, not wanting an accident of any kind. After running her down to the woods, I raced her back up the path, at first mistaking the approaching figure for a shadow until I looked down to see boot tips covered in snow. The man had on a dark cap and a heavy green jacket. It was too dark even to guess at his identity.

As I got closer, I recognized not his face, but his gait, a strong, looping stride. It was David. Coming back from somewhere? Going to somewhere? It would have been nothing, and nothing unusual, to pass him on my way to the dorm, to stop and say hello. He'd been woven into my days for years. I had learned how to live with him and the ghost of our love affair. Or my love and his affair, as it now seemed.

I almost turned and walked the other way. I had no idea what he knew of the holiday party debacle with Elle, or if Cynthia had relayed any of it. It felt foolish to keep walking, ensuring our bumping into one another on the path. It also felt immature to run in the other direction. A tiny desire rose inside of me, one I immediately squelched by squeezing my eyes closed tight and picturing Alfie. I reprimanded myself as I kept walking. I was no longer in love with David. Whatever yearning bubbled in me to see his face must have another origin; perhaps I simply craved closure? I'd been done with him completely, without a single regret, hadn't I, before Cynthia came along and with her pregnancy changed my view of everything?

As we got closer to each other, I tried to think metaphysically. Could I need something from him, something I didn't know how to articulate, before I could heal and move on to the next step of my journey?

He stopped when he saw me, close enough to touch. He patted Fruity on the head. I couldn't see his eyes in the heavy winter darkness. I wanted to scurry back inside like a little mouse who knew she shouldn't be out in the cold. But I didn't. Oh, for all my simpleton ways, why did I need to be so complicated?

24

Annie

January

The first Save Our School meeting occurred on January 3. Having been asked by a number of girls in my dorm as well as being enlisted by the entire YFC, I took my role as emissary seriously, though I didn't take this Dixbie political stunt seriously. Still, I am only human, and even I can't ignore the glamorous appeal of such high drama. Once upon a time, a long, long time ago, in a land far, far away, I would have abstained, would have found the whole situation a waste of time and energy. However, having lost some of my scruples through motherhood, I looked forward to being a bit of a voyeur at the meetings. I could at last understand the connection between stay-at-home mothers and poorly acted, wildly unrealistic television dramas. Escape is a lovely thing.

As an example, while I dressed for this trendy meeting (everyone would be there), I dealt with the topic of snot, which, though common, is clearly not trendy.

"Please don't wipe your nose on your hand," I said to Hannah while attempting to attire myself in something worthy of Dixbie financial intrigue. Hannah picked up the edge of her T-shirt and used it instead. "Try this." I passed her a tissue.

"No, you, Mommy."

"Okay," I said, holding the tissue up to Hannah's red, crusty little nose. "Now blow."

"NO blowing!"

"Fine." I wiped her nose and threw the tissue across the room, just missing the garbage. I pulled on some black pants and a black sweater before noticing Hannah's little tongue reaching up toward her nose. I passed her another tissue.

"NO!" Hannah wailed.

"Don't shout. You'll wake the baby."

"NO!" Hannah said more loudly.

"Fine," I said. "Find your own methods of snot removal. You're your own person."

"Read this, Mommy," Hannah said, pressing a book into my tummy.

"What's going on in here?" Ted asked, peeking his head around the door.

"Just offering Hannah instruction in how to play with her snot."

"Play with my snot!" Hannah giggled. She then, very delightedly, stuck her finger up her nose to excavate.

"Fantastic!" Ted rolled his eyes. "When do we leave?" Both of us, of course, were destined for the meeting. Suze's babysitter, Cathy, would come and watch the girls.

I checked my watch. "Nine minutes and counting."

"Good. I'll read to Hannah by the Christmas tree."

"Sounds nice." Amazingly, Christmas had come and gone, in the way it does, in a rush of ribbons and hysteria and egg-

nog and a zillion telephone calls from Ted's family and a singular one from my mother, who hasn't left Chicago in nearly
twenty years. She told me once she'd rather eat Spam every
night for dinner than get on a plane. I've always wondered if
they're too phallic for her . . . a joke she would appreciate if
she had any sense of humor about her feminism. We also
received our annual-to-semiannual phone call from my father, who, busy with his fourth wife and an obscure sales job
that requires extensive travel to unpopular destinations like
Detroit, called from his second home in Tucson.

I turned to catch Hannah in the act again. "Hannah, for
God's sake, use a tissue!" Hannah started to wail in protest as
I forcefully held her little body down and glopped up what I
could.

"Psyched for this meeting?" he asked.

"I consider it a night out. A date." I winked at him. "Other
than that, I find it all rather tacky. Can't the school do its own
fund-raising without forcing the staff to create a committee?"

"Your cynicism has reached new heights. I gather from
Friedman that this is no joke."

"We'll see. How about we make a bet?" I said, an idea suddenly hitting me. "If I'm right that this is all noise and the
school is fine, we get married in the courthouse. If you're
right, and they really are financially destitute, we get married
in the chapel."

"A woman with strong convictions. I like that." He came
over and kissed me on the cheek. "I see you coming down the
aisle right now!"

"Ted." I shook my head.

"I accept the bet, seeing as I am certain of its outcome."
We shook on it like poker buddies.

Before leaving, I snuck into Lily's room and gave her a quiet kiss. Ted took Hannah into the living room, where I found them happily cuddling on the couch reading her new *Fancy Nancy* book; I kissed Hannie.

After Cathy arrived, we layered on piles of coats, scarves, and hats in hopes of staying warm on the walk to Lyle Hall. As we approached the building, I saw Cynthia, with David by her side, walking up the steps. She wore a fur coat.

"Who died to keep her warm?" I asked Ted.

"It isn't real."

"It looks real to me."

"If it's that upsetting, you should be a vegetarian."

"Remember, I tried once. I nearly starved."

"If that woman were wearing *your* clothes you'd find something to criticize."

"If *I* wear my clothes I find something to criticize. At any rate, she makes herself easy to find fault with." I dropped my voice to a whisper and slowed down so they wouldn't overhear. "Miss Stealing the Excellence in Teaching Award herself. Do you know that I tried to tell Nora the truth about the prize? She doesn't believe me. She is blinded by her love."

"To be fair, Cynthia didn't *steal* it, Annie. A committee voted for her."

"Based on what?! Three months' experience. She *paid* them. I'm convinced of it now."

"Why would anyone pay a committee to win an award?" Ted shook his head and held a gloved finger to his lips as we climbed the steps to the hall. We walked into the meeting side by side.

Dean Friedman stood at the front of the classroom, looking down at a large stack of papers. I could feel the anxiety pouring off him.

My heart dropped into my feet, or farther maybe, to the floor. I got that sick feeling that makes my hands tingle and sweat. Something about the top of Friedman's half-bald head looked exactly like my father's had when I was younger— before he lost his hair completely. All of a sudden, unbidden, I found myself remembering the day he left, the last hug he gave me in our family home, the way he looked waving to me from his tiny sedan, packed with boxes and trash bags full of clothes. When my mother came back from wherever she'd gone to hide during his leave-taking, she found me at the window and said, "Don't stay there all day." To hear it from my mother, my father caused all the trouble, yet that day I found it hard to believe. He looked so forlorn driving off alone. I was thirteen.

Holy shit, I thought to myself as Friedman looked up and the memory fell off me like a cape. *I'm becoming sensitive.*

The perfect antidote to such unprecedented feelings materialized before me: Friedman somberly passing out the Dixbie financial statement. It was hieroglyphics to me, but most of the present faculty read it quickly. A low murmur moved around the room as the numbers were scanned.

I checked out the usual victims of Dixbie neediness, the same faces that volunteer over and over again when the school needs something. Nora, oddly enough, sat not next to Cynthia but beside Melanie Jones, the physics teacher, known among the students primarily for her pervasive halitosis and unusual homework experiments. Melanie called out, "Where's Harry?"

Harry Stone, our head of school, makes a rule of absenteeism. Occasionally a rumor circulates concerning his death, although to date none of them have been founded. Meanwhile, he hasn't been found.

"Dr. Stone will lead the next trustee meeting. He didn't feel it necessary to attend today."

I nudged Ted with my elbow, certain that Stone's absence was a sign of the relative insignificance of the financial problem.

The meeting went on interminably with a general atmosphere of shock and awe. From what I gathered when I wasn't busy thinking about other things, someone had severely mismanaged the school funds. Moreover, the economic decline had affected our enrollment numbers, with that missing revenue creating a substantial shortage. Suggestions flew up from the crowd: laying off teachers, selling off buildings, fund-raising from our most famous alums. Friedman called for volunteers to head up different subcommittees to explore all these options. When Beverly Slater turned to ask me to chair a committee, I told her I would volunteer as soon as pigs ice-skate.

"Oh, Annie," she said scoldingly. "Can't you step out of character for once?"

The main SOS committee needed a leader. When Cynthia volunteered for the position, I restrained myself from laughing and rolling my eyes. Later Ted and I would talk about her contribution to the matter.

"She has enough money to save the school herself," I told him.

"No one has that much money," he answered. "The school

is in the red three million with a three-million-dollar operating budget."

"Sell Meadow House," I said, feeling as flip as I sounded. I had bigger fish to fry.

I left the meeting distracted, disregarding Friedman's entreating gaze. I knew he wanted an answer from me about Tabitha's classes; I didn't have one and I wasn't going to stay and chat. In addition, I had no tolerance for watching Nora cling to Cynthia like a koala on a tree. I'd been dutifully waiting for her apology for weeks by then. Nora, if nothing else, made excellent apologies, having received good training from her mother in selflessness. I knew she stood in the wrong; I didn't even have anything to be sorry for. Had I forgotten *her* birthday? Had I stopped visiting her, calling her, meeting her for lunch? Had I *replaced* her? Had I done anything? Anything at all? I hadn't. I had done nothing but continue to be myself, and if she didn't like that, she ought never to have bothered with me in the first place. I left with a glance over my shoulder at her, dismayed to find that she stood beside Cynthia looking forlorn. For someone so smart, she acted so stupid.

That Wednesday, I dared myself to take the children to the BFC knowing Suze wouldn't make an appearance. "I must proceed with my new friendless life," I said as I dressed myself that morning, the children hanging on my ankles, giggling like hyenas, preventing me from moving.

When I arrived, I settled down near the musical instruments. Lily enjoys chewing on them, and Hannah has a real gift for drumming loudly.

"I'm an orch-stra, Mama! Listen!" She alternately

pounded on a drum and blew into a harmonica. No, spit into a harmonica.

As I watched Lily power-crawl over to one of the shelves loaded with instruments, I felt a squeeze on my shoulder.

Startled, I turned around. Julia Tucker looked down at me with a troubled expression, which I quickly realized belonged permanently to her Botoxed face.

"I'm so glad you're here," she said without changing her expression, though to be charitable, it occurred to me that she might not have been able to. Really, what's not to love about the woman? She personally hand-bakes the snacks that get served in the snack room, dubbing them "health cookies." They have sweet potato in them. Her "health crackers" contain spinach. And if that were not reason enough to hate a person, she has four children and publically proclaims to employ no nanny, although word has it she's got a "cleaning lady" working outside the specifics of her job description. On top of all this, she is ambitiously cheerful, has the figure of a tongue depressor, and has never once complained about anything. She either has a strong relationship with Prozac or a strong relationship with Jesus. Her banker trust-fund husband may also play a contributing role in her paradise-life and general well-being.

"Why would that be?" I asked.

"We need to discuss the class you'll be teaching. The parent board is thrilled to have a real artist offering the children their education."

"Did you mean real artist or *starving* artist?"

Julia looked flustered, and I can't say I didn't enjoy it. She doesn't often look flustered. She knelt down beside me and spoke to me as though being at eye level, the way one talks to toddlers, could improve our communication. "Suze informed us you are a painter with teaching experience at the college level. She mentioned your many gallery showings."

"*Group* shows," I corrected. "And I haven't taught art since I was a size twelve."

"I see." She took on a variation of her troubled expression, something I wouldn't have noticed if we weren't practically nose to nose. With such high hopes for the local four-year-olds, I almost felt bad disappointing her with my résumé.

"I do trust Suze. I'm sure your experience is fine for our kids." She paused. "Don't sell yourself short." Was Julia Tucker being nice to me? I looked at her lips, shimmery pink, still frosted with the morning's lipstick, and while doing so noticed a black spot on her teeth—food from breakfast? This touch of humanity struck me; Julia was a *person,* not a robo-woman.

"Most days, I don't have the time to shower, let alone paint a masterpiece."

"That's the way of motherhood." She looked around for her daughter, Plum. "Did Suze mention the stipend to you? The center got a grant from Brownston National Bank. We'll be able to pay you somewhere around three hundred dollars for the eight-week session. Now I do need to let you know that we've moved the starting date back. The course won't begin until the summer."

"I'll do it," I said, which is not at all what I'd planned to say. In fact, once I said it, I took on a troubled expression of my own.

"Just the confirmation I needed!" Julia stood up and brushed her heavily pressed khaki pants. "I'll send you an email with the details." She walked away briskly in Plum's direction, leaving in her wake a faint hint of a perfume that cost me a year's worth of groceries. Lily crawled to me and made the nurse sign. I'd begun teaching her baby sign language and she learned rapidly, only confirming my suspicions of her genius nature.

"Julia's a person," I whispered to Lily as I picked her up and cradled her in my arms. "Julia's a person who gets food in her teeth and I'm a bride committed to teaching art classes for the children of my enemies." I made a mental note to report all of these incredible changes to Meg, who I decided had to be at the bottom of the slow melting of my glacial heart.

25

Nora

My mother called late one early January evening to check on my health. I decided not to share the news of Dixbie's demise in case she suggested I come back to Iowa in the summer. Aunt Bertie came on the line and entertained me with tales of how close she'd come, recently, to getting every question on *Jeopardy!* correct. She did this by actually replaying the complete show while I listened on the phone. She has an entire library of VHS tapes with *Jeopardy!* shows on them. They've been organized in her bedroom closet according to the number of questions she answers right. Grandma Lucy took the phone after Aunt Bertie. When I mentioned the morning sickness, she recommended French toast, first thing in the morning, with a heavy sprinkle of cinnamon.

I could tell what they really wanted to talk about: Elle. Though none of them said much, the duration of the phone call signified their keen concern. When at last my mother came back on the line, she coughed into the phone, then said,

"Please inform Elle that her mother would appreciate a phone call."

"She's right here. Do you want to talk to her yourself?"

"I would never thrust myself upon someone," my mother inexplicably replied. She makes a regular habit of thrusting herself upon me, after all. "She should talk to her mother," my mother said with all the warmth of a polar bear.

I wished I could relay this bit of the conversation to Elle, that we both could laugh together over our family's idiosyncratic ways, bond over them, but I doubted the family interest in her situation would warrant any humor. Not only had Elle been a particularly grim visitor the past month and a half, but I had a hard time rallying a whole lot of love for her those days. Her David drivel at the holiday party was a perfect example of how my family's quirks ruin my life, or, in this case, my friendship. On the other hand, I felt for her. I went out of my way not to say anything hurtful. Luckily, I have a lot of practice in that area.

"It's no wonder you've never had an orgasm," Elle said when I got off the phone. Thankfully, Alfie had already retired for the night. "Your mother is sexually wounded."

"What?" I started to get nervous. Was there something I didn't know about my mother? Another deeper level of dysfunction in my family? I didn't want to hear about a long-lost history of sexual abuse. As quirky as my family acted, at least our problems tended toward the comical, not the tragic.

"Repression can be very damaging. My mother isn't much better, but at least *I* found an outlet for my pent-up sexual frustration." I wasn't sure if she meant her work or her ex-boss.

"They mean well," I said, sounding exactly like Alfie.

"Do they? I'm not so sure. Do they know why I'm here?"

I shook my head. "I would never tell them." I wanted to add *even though I'm* mad *at you for losing me my Cynthia*. But who can yell at a case like Elle?

"Nora, did it ever cross your mind why I came to you instead of my own mother?" This, of course, had crossed my mind any number of times.

"Why?" I simply asked, taking quick note of the amount of wine left in her glass, as it foretold how long she would talk. She could really hold forth about midway through her drinking spree. I saw she had half a glass left; she was on her fourth drink.

"Can you imagine what my mother would have said if I ever told her about the abortion? First, she would have cried indefinitely for her lost grandchild. Then, she would have cried feverishly for my soul, now damned to hell. Then, she would have guilted me into living with her for the rest of my life and insisted upon a curfew and wholesome encounters with men she'd personally chosen from her church choir." I tried for a laugh. Elle froze it with a grimace. "And that's *after* a lecture on unforgivable sins that would have driven the nail into the coffin of my heart. You, on the other hand, have not spoken a single word of judgment, on me or my soul. Now I know why you were always the favorite child in the family; you are the kindest, the most forgiving member of our entire clan."

Selfishly, I ignored everything she said save the last part. "I'm not the favorite! I don't even belong to the family. I'm the black sheep, the odd one out. I'm *adopted*."

Elle picked up her wineglass and looked down it to the empty bottom as she drank. When she came up for air, she nearly slammed it onto the coffee table for emphasis, turning to stare me down. "You were *chosen*," she declared. "Chosen is very different. What was I? A mistake of the rhythm method? You were hand-selected. And it is very true you're the favorite. Gram has always doted on you, making a special thing of everything you accomplish. Even my mother makes a regular habit of pointing out your virtues, how infinitely good you've been your whole life."

"No, Elle, you've got it wrong. No one in the family has ever connected with me; they sense my difference." I didn't mention the other part of the equation, that infinite good-ness has some distinct downsides, chief among them a kind of claustrophobia. "You're just upset."

"And you're obtuse!" she practically screamed at me. "Close down your pity party! It's time to go home. Some of us *really* have hard lives, instead of your made-up troubles. How about having your baby vacuumed out of you? Want that on your wish list? And while they're going about routine busi-ness, you're crying like a dying woman, asking them to stop because you realize that HE isn't worth it, with all his money and power and connections, he isn't worth the sound of that machine and the numb tug in your uterus, and the knowl-edge that you wanted that baby, stupid woman that you are, you wanted that baby and when you say, 'Stop,' they look down at you without emotion and say, 'It's too late. It's half done,' so you have to imagine half a fetus left inside, little waving arms and nothing else. You know what people say? They say, ask to bring it home. Plant it under a tree. Plant it!

Under a tree!" By this point, Elle's face was saturated with brutal tears and my own was wet, though I hadn't realized I was crying.

"Don't feel bad for me," she said, standing up, wobbling, scuffing her feet on the ground as she made her way into the kitchen for another glass of wine. "I don't want to ruin your perspective. It must be so hard to have everything you want." I could hear the wine splashing carelessly into her glass.

When she returned and sat down, she seemed much calmer, more like herself. I almost expected another comment on orgasms, but she didn't say anything.

"Do you really think I have everything I want?" I finally asked, embarrassed by my own self-focus but unable to let go of the opportunity to find out.

"Help me," she said in reply, and she put her head in my lap and sobbed.

I took it as a sign of my progress away from uniform niceness that I spent the remainder of the evening not thinking about Elle and how I could help her, but trying to solve my own problems. I found my selfishness vaguely uncomfortable. Given Elle's more tragic problems, my own issues hardly compared. But my mind did what it wanted to, and while it seemed wrong, while I even knew it *was* wrong, I kept going back over and over again to my conversation with David and my friendship with Cynthia. Ugh. I sat down on the bed, careful not to disturb Alfie. Could I be more lame? I'd been hoping my lame days were over. I'd imagined shedding the Helpsom-Fulch requisite kindness would feel good, as though casual disregard for other people generated hipness.

Sitting on the bed pondering my own challenges, I still felt remarkably like my uncool self.

It struck me as an aberration that Elle fancied me the favored one. She clearly had no idea about my childhood. And to think that I had everything I wanted! True, I was pregnant and I had Alfie, but weren't those the most ordinary undertakings? She also had no idea of the mess she created at the holiday party. Easy enough to be a verbose drunk who wakes in the morning blessed to have forgotten all her embarrassing moments; there really is a bright side to blackouts. I, on the other hand, recollected all the details in full color, not just the events of the party but my conversation with David that dark night in December when we stood face-to-face on the Dixbie path.

"I came by today to see Cynthia," I said to him, watching the cloud of my breath break between us. "I wanted to talk to her before you two left for vacation."

"She's been packing and running errands," he said, though his heavy tone said something more ominous. The musical theme to *Poltergeist* began to play in my head.

"Will you ask her to call?"

"I'll ask her." He knew. He knew that she knew. He knew that she knew what we knew.

"Is she mad at me?"

"Did you really find it necessary to talk to her about our," and here he stumbled on the word, "history?"

"I didn't! My cousin, Elle, she had too much to drink." A hundred apologies came to mind; my conciliatory words tripped on one another trying to get out of my mouth in such a hurry. Then I put a hand on my lower belly where some future person, probably resembling Alfie, was taking shape. I swallowed my pretty words and said, "Did you really find it necessary to keep our history a secret?"

"I didn't keep it a secret. I told her we dated. I just didn't include the intimate details that your cousin chose to pass on." He looked at me stonily. "She's worried that you're still in love with me. She *thinks* you're still in love with me."

I choke-laughed. It was awkward, sounded awkward and felt awkward, and I realized as soon as I finished that it would have been more convincing to stay silent. "That would be ridiculous," I said at last.

"I suppose none of it will matter after June, anyhow."

"Why do you say that?"

"The school won't be here."

"You don't really think it will come to that, do you?" I had asked, melancholy digging into me at the mere thought of Dixbie closing.

"We'll find out soon enough." He moved around me to keep walking down the path toward Meadow House.

"Have a nice vacation," I called after him.

"If my wife speaks to me, I will," he shouted back.

After Cynthia returned from the Caribbean, our pattern of weekly teas and lunches in the cafeteria and trips together to the spa did not resume. The few times we did meet up, she never discussed that evening. It dawned on me that Cynthia and I held something other than adoption in common; we kept our feelings to ourselves. Not knowing her thoughts about the situation only made things worse, an odd revelation to come to since I'd always imagined the tight-lipped ways of the Helpsom-Fulchs to be the virtue my mother claimed them to be. Instead, the silence separated us. It wasn't a virtue; it was a mistake. Maybe, had I mustered the courage to bring it up myself, had I possessed Annie's bold confidence rather than my family's own reticence, things would have unfolded differently. Instead, Cynthia withdrew her friendship, and with it all the party favors of her charm. I had come to rely on her luck. We shared an optimistic friendship. By Annie's standards, it was a shallow one, if you consider how much we didn't discuss. But we had so much fun talking about our pregnancies. She would have stacks of baby magazines when I came over. She'd helped me plan the baby's nursery.

I felt obscenely grateful, given her withdrawal, when in January, she helped me schedule my first prenatal visit with Dr. Mercy on the same day she had an appointment. We ran into one another in the mailroom. She wanted to talk about her baby kicking. I mentioned my first appointment.

"We could drive together," she planned. She called Dr. Mercy's office while we stood by the mailboxes.

"I'll slip you in," the bubble-gum-chewing receptionist said conspiratorially as she gave me the same date in February.

But despite this random act of kindness, I mostly talked to the ghost of Cynthia. I had elaborate conversations with her in my head during which I brought up the topic of my relationship with David. Our imaginary talks always ended quite well. I would explain everything in helpful detail. At the end, she would laugh. Then we would go shopping for strollers.

One Wednesday toward the end of January, I saw her in the lunch line. "Cynthia!" I called. She gave me a cheery wave. Whatever she may have thought internally, she never stopped acting outwardly friendly.

"Look at you," she said as she made room for me next to her in line. "Did you sleep at all last night?"

"The nausea wakes me up. At least I'm not throwing up anymore."

"Let's get some healthy tummy food," she said, as we grabbed trays and walked down toward the hot food selections. "My afternoon class is having a field trip, so we're eating lunch early. You can join us to eat, if you'd like." I accepted eagerly. I did feel, for a brief moment, like a dog catching a crumb from a table full of feasting food. I scrubbed the idea out of my head. Not that I don't like dogs. I love dogs. Dogs may even be better than people—except in this one case.

She picked out a bagel and cream cheese, a cup of fruit, an apple, a large glass of milk, and when the woman behind the hot food station asked, she requested a large helping of macaroni and cheese.

"What about you?" said the woman, Evelyn, whom I often chatted with.

"I'll take what she has," I said, hoping Cynthia's diet would cure my morning sickness; Cynthia hadn't suffered a single symptom so far in her pregnancy. Almost six months in, she radiated good health. I found my own ability to forgive her this level of perfection a testimony to my affection for her. I did not envy her as Annie had said; here was proof. In fact, I realized as I loaded up my tray with Cynthia food, Annie had pegged my relationship with Cynthia dead wrong. She wasn't getting anything from *me*, I was getting things from her. Cynthia had more generosity in her little finger than Annie could gather on a good day. Just see how kind she was to me, inviting me to lunch, in spite of the fact that for all she knew, I actively pined away for the bedroom prowess of her husband.

My cell phone buzzed in my pocket, jarring me back to the moment. I took it out and looked at the number.

"I'll join you in one minute," I told Cynthia. "It's my mother."

It frustrated me that my mom would call during the ten minutes I actually had time with Cynthia. It did not surprise me, though; couldn't they let me have anything special? I answered quickly, hoping to make it short.

"Nora." My mother emitted her most grave sigh, which never ceases to set my heart to racing.

"What's the matter?"

"It's your grandma," she choked. She started to cry.

I put a hand to my heart. "What is it? Did she . . ." I couldn't bring myself to say the word.

"Nora," my father's voice came over the line. "Your mother's too upset to talk right now."

"What's going on, Dad?"

"Now, I don't want to alarm you."

"I'm already alarmed! Just tell me."

"It seems, well, it's hard to explain exactly."

"You mean Gram's still alive?"

"We're not sure."

"How can you not be sure!" I'd walked far enough away from Cynthia to be out of earshot, but I doubt she missed my shouting. "Dad, what are you talking about?"

"See, here's the thing: we can't find her."

"You can't *find* her? How is that possible? Where could she go? She's ninety-three."

"She's pretty spry," my dad said, pausing to swallow, the anxiety stuck in his throat.

"Did you look for her?"

"Of course we looked for her, Nora. She's not in the house. Or in the yard."

"What about Aunt Lucy or Aunt Shelley? Maybe they came to get her for an appointment." I could practically hear my father shaking his head.

"Everyone is here together," he told me. "Nobody knows where she is. Some of her clothes are missing too. And her suitcase."

"Oh my God." An awful idea hit me. "Do you think she was kidnapped?" I barely had a chance to get the words out before my mother came back on the line.

"She's the most stubborn person I've ever known. Intolerably stubborn," my mother said, recovered now from her crying jag. "We had a fight last night about Elle. And you too."

"Me? What have *I* done?"

"This is no time to think of yourself! My mother is a missing person."

"But she can't have gone far. Doesn't she have friends there? Anyone's house she could have gone to that isn't family?"

"We've already thought of that," my mother said sharply. "We've thought of everything. We simply wanted to inform you."

"I can't believe you lost her."

"We didn't lose her," my mother said indignantly. "She *ran away.*"

I got off the phone, appalled. Who loses an old lady? A *slow* old lady. It's not as if they couldn't have run after her, taking her down, if necessary, with a pinkie finger. I found it totally irresponsible, and so unlike my parents, to lose a person. They prided themselves on their mutual fastidiousness. And what did she mean they had argued over Elle? Did they know about her abortion? And what about arguing over me? What had I done wrong? Did they fault me for harboring Elle? As far as I knew, they had no idea what Elle had gone through, and I hadn't done a single thing wrong since seventh grade when I lied to my mother about homework.

I walked back to Cynthia, who sat amiable amidst her sophomore history class. I did not want to tell her about my grandmother. Naturally, as with most things relating to my family, it embarrassed me. I felt confident Cynthia did not have grandmothers go missing.

"Everything okay?" She smiled brightly as I sat down in a free seat across the table. In the past, before Elle's glib tell-all, Cynthia would have saved me the seat beside her. I tried not to notice.

"Bit of a family emergency."

"Oh, dear." And then the question I hoped she wouldn't ask. "What happened?"

"Well, my parents have misplaced my grandmother." Given my family's superstitious ways, had it not been winter I might have entertained the possibility that they buried her in the backyard under the geraniums, had anyone not liked her, that is. "My grandmother's a fireball," I quickly added, taking note of the many worried faces around the table. "For all we know, she took a vacation."

"Hopefully to the Caribbean," Cynthia said, looking out at the heavy gray clouds. "It was exquisite there."

God, I hoped not. What would we do with Grandma

Lucy in the Caribbean? What would Grandma Lucy do with Grandma Lucy in the Caribbean? Put on a bikini and order a mai tai? (Scarily, I could actually see this; I did not want the image of her stuffed into a tiny polka-dotted two-piece bathing suit stuck in my head.) "I think I'd better head home," I told Cynthia, getting up again from the table. "I don't feel much like eating, and I know my family will need me soon."

"Of course," Cynthia said sympathetically. As I got up, she stood and came over to me. She pressed me into a hug, the firm crescent of her belly nudging mine. "It will be okay," she whispered into my ear, her warm breath a tickle, so that for a moment she felt like a lover.

26

Annie

February

By February my young feminists, still fat and rested from the extended three-week December/January vacation, wanted to meet weekly to discuss dovetailing their educational event with an SOS fund-raiser and asked if I could personally invite Gloria Steinem to come speak. I found the request outlandish, outrageous, unlikely, and touching in its hopefulness, so of course I agreed. Cynthia missed this meeting due to a prenatal doctor's appointment. I pondered how I could arrange every YFC meeting to fall on her doctor's visits. I enjoyed her absence immensely.

The next morning, with Ted watching the girls during one of his free periods, I headed out to Meg's office. I spent a great deal of time catching her up with all the details of my life, including what I considered a major breakthrough—agreeing to teach at the BFC. I assumed she would take this as a deep bow to my ambivalence, an acceptance on my part of my own internal conflict between working and staying at home. I was, as a matter of fact, excited to bring her this news, as it beautifully illustrated my growth as a person and the positive outcome of all my therapy.

"Would you go back to the story you told me about your father?" she asked, when I finished speaking.

"My father?" In the middle of my recap of the weeks' events, I'd told her about the memory that came to me during the SOS meeting on account of Friedman's bald spot. "Don't you want to talk about how I'm going to teach again? How I'm returning to my pre-mother passion? How I will soon no longer be a soulless, unrealized SAHM?"

"I think that class will be fun," she said noncommittally. "You don't often speak about your dad or your parents' divorce. I'd like to know more."

Why, I wondered, did she always linger on topics that were so clearly *off* the topic? "I told you everything. I simply remembered that moment in time. Not that I ever thought Friedman looked like my father before—"

She stopped me. "And how did it feel to remember your father driving away?"

"Awful, of course. But that's obvious, isn't it?"

"Have you thought any more about your inner child?" she asked.

"Not really. I've been too busy looking at tuxedo websites with my obsessed husband, caring for the monkey-children who live with me, and dealing with my school-slash-home and its fictional death."

"Annie, what was life like when you were Hannah's age?"

The question caught me off guard—even given the fact that I was in therapy and knew this kind of emotional excavation was required for graduation from my bimonthly sessions, I didn't want to play the memory game, and so I said, "I can't remember."

"Try to remember."

"This is not what I came to talk about."

"I promise you we're going somewhere with this."

"Fine." I stared up at the white ceiling. I tried to remember being almost three. I thought about Hannah, her sweet, funny, immature take on the world around her, her deep, thick innocence, her enraged protests against unfairness.

"What was it like for a little girl to grow up with angry parents fighting all the time? To have her father leave and her mother harbor such hatred against her daddy? Can you imagine Hannah going through all that?"

"Meg," I said, because it felt as though she was manipulating me, forcing me back to an unhappy place I no longer needed to inhabit. As a matter of fact, it felt as though she wanted me to cry. I sat up taller. "I do not enjoy being sad. Why are you so keen on making me sad? On making my inner child sad?" I said without shedding a single tear.

"My dear," she said lovingly. "If you really want to know my intention, I'll tell you. I hope for you to embrace your inner child for what she is: lonely, frightened and, yes, sad."

"Why? I'm the least lonely, scared, depressed person I know. Most women my age are on medication for lonely/sad/scared. Not me! Sure, divorce sucks for children; we all learned that from Jerry Springer and Lifetime specials. I came to see you in order to get *happier*, and yet since I've been coming, I've gotten sadder. The therapy isn't working."

She smiled a small smile. "Have you noticed," she asked, "that as you've grown sadder, you have grown less angry?"

I didn't want to give her the satisfaction of an answer, for I knew, as soon as she spoke the words, that they were true. Why else my agreement to teach at the BFC, and my ability to, for once, see Julia as a person like me? Or the relative new ease with Hannah? Anger is a blinding presence; it was starting to fall from my eyes like scales. "I prefer anger," I replied.

"The sadness will not last as long as the anger. It is a much quicker way back to happiness," she said, but I wasn't sure I believed her. "Let's try an experiment, okay? For a month, I want you to do the *opposite* of your instinct."

"What's the point of that?" I asked, feeling my native rage rising.

"It's time for you to unlearn your habituated responses to life. Those are the responses of the young girl at the window watching her family fall apart." I grimaced. Maybe I didn't like Meg after all. "You won't do it, will you?" I shook my head. "I'll tell you what, my dear Annie: if you take this experiment on for one month, only one month, I will *pay you* for your visits to come see me during that time."

I couldn't help laughing. "I'm beginning to question your methods."

She cackled rather impishly. "Accept or decline?" She held out her hands, palms up, every finger banded by a ring.

I am not one to refuse a dare. I consider bravery a hallmark of my irritating personality, maybe even a saving grace of my temperament. I have never been able to refuse a challenge. "Accept."

A week later, I stood in front of the mirror fulfilling Meg's challenge while I attempted to get dressed. Despite my low fashion expectations, it took almost an hour to get ready and out of the house. I was standing in a bra and underwear, Lily crying at my feet to be picked up, and Hannah rifling through my drawers pulling out random clothes for me to wear, when Ted looked in to see if I needed help.

"Oh, no, I'm fine. I'll just go teach dressed like this," I said, and giving up, I sat down to nurse Lily.

"Me too," Hannah pleaded.

"Fine." She climbed onto my lap.

"Put my head on mommy's nipples," she said to herself. This, she had somehow gathered, was what Lily did when nursing; she wanted to do it too. She'd forgotten the many months I'd breastfed her as well as the exact method, which was fine by me. In a week she would turn three. I hardly needed her to take up breastfeeding for her birthday.

"You're a picture," Ted said from the doorway. "They just adore you."

"I adore them," I said, kissing their heads. "So why am I leaving them?"

"You are not leaving them. You are going to teach for two hours, then I'll meet you at the awards ceremony. Then you'll come home and spend the rest of the day with them. That hardly counts as child abandonment."

"I may be making a big mistake."

"You won't know unless you try."

"What if I don't want to try?"

"What are you afraid of?" Ted asked. "That you won't be any good? Or that you've forgotten how to teach? It may take some time to get back into a rhythm. And the girls will be fine. Are you afraid they'll miss you?"

I looked down at the two cherubs in my arms. Hannah was idly twirling a lock of hair. Lily sucked lazily, no longer hungry. My vision blurred with tears; damn that Meg. She'd opened something up inside me. I pressed my eyes closed and held my breath until I no longer felt like crying. "Up now, girls. Mama has to get ready for her big day." I gently pried them off my lap.

I managed to pull on some dark jeans and an oversized cream sweater before getting accosted again by little hands.

"Well?" Ted said as he watched me pull on some socks. "I can't help you if you don't tell me."

I went right up to him so I could say it into his ear without the girls hearing. "I'm afraid I'll like it more than staying at home, like it more than being with the girls, and then I will become Suze and your mom and your sister and everybody else. We will have more money, but I will be gone. Gone for good. No one will be here to bake them cookies. I will become my mother."

"Love, you have drunk the melodrama coffee this morning."

"You asked, I answered."

"I hope you do enjoy it," he said pulling me into a hug. I bit my lip so I wouldn't cry; it felt like crossing an invisible line. No, more like an invisible Grand Canyon.

I did mightily well, too busy even to consider myself or the girls as I rushed through the two classes, one art history and one a basic painting course. It took all of my brain power to focus on the lesson and the twenty kids in the room. At the end of the second class, I had to tidy the room, which left me no time to make it to the awards ceremony, and as I jogged there, something I only do when chased by large animals, I reflected on how anticlimactic the whole morning seemed in light of my dread.

I got to the chapel out of breath and self-satisfied. I *could* have it all. I could teach a few hours and spend the rest of my time with the girls. How foolish my early ideas seemed as I tucked myself into the back row, giving a cursory glance around at all the students and faculty gathered for the big event.

There were many awards to sit through, first for the students. As a rule, freshmen are excluded in the same way first-year teachers cannot be considered for a prize. I scanned the crowd for Nora's head while anxiously awaiting the Sylvia Sternberg Excellence in Teaching Award announcement. When Tabitha Hunter won it the prior year, for the fourth time in her Dixbie career, Nora took it well, with the same equanimity with which she takes everything. I swear I've prayed during our friendship for her to be moody. Now I wasn't sure what to hope for. I wanted to be right, for one thing, and I'd told her in no uncertain terms that Cynthia would receive the award. On the other hand, I hoped Nora would get the award she deserved.

So I sat there torn by my own motives, playing out the imaginary scenarios in my mind. If Cynthia won the award, Nora would come to me after the ceremony, apologizing profusely and begging to have our friendship reinstated. She would shake her head and wonder what she ever saw in Cynthia, who clearly bought her way into whatever she wanted. If Nora won the award, Cynthia would pout. For once she would be denied something. I found this idea awfully gratifying. I found her blond tiara of a head in the sea of heads, unmistakable in its sheen. I bored a hole in the back of her head with my gaze, willing her to turn and look around. She sat motionless like a storefront mannequin, and not for the first time did I question her humanity.

Ted turned and waved at me, mouthing, "How'd it go?" I nodded and smiled like a cat post–milk dish. He gave me a thumbs-up.

When they called Cynthia's name, I felt prepared. After all, I'd known for a few months that she was the award committee's chosen recipient. What I wasn't prepared for was the wild applause from the student body as she took the small elevated platform at the front of the building, waving like royalty at the peons below her. Disgusted, I did not clap. Ted sent me a knowing look with a hooked eyebrow. When we were dismissed, I stood at the back of the room waiting for Nora to come by, and when I'd been waiting forever and didn't want to pay another cent for the babysitter, Cathy, to watch the girls, I looked up to the front of the chapel to see Nora talking to Cynthia, *congratulating* her.

That Nora. Her kindness makes me think of Buddhists. I sighed and walked out, heading home to my beautiful children, disappointed that Nora would choose Cynthia over me *again*.

But then that made sense, didn't it? Cynthia bewitched the vulnerable, easily impressed Nora. What about Cynthia? I thought as I walked home. Forget why she liked Nora, why did Cynthia get the award? *How* did she get the award? My own theory on her buying her way into it didn't truly hold up under scrutiny. Not even I thought it held much water. If Cynthia was up to something, I would have heard about it from someone, probably from Beverly. I knew some of the faculty on the award committee and doubted they could be bought off. And this was Dixbie after all, stodgy and formal and rule-abiding. All the reasons in the world, however, as to how she *didn't* buy her way into the hearts of the Dixbie School didn't produce a single answer as to how she managed to get what she had. I needed a new theory, a more plausible one. My walk home didn't last long enough to generate anything good. Without knowing motives and reasons, I still knew one thing: something fishy was going on.

"I smell a tuna," I said, coming into the house where the girls, one running, one speed-crawling, came and threw themselves on me.

"I don't know why," Cathy remarked, bewildered. "Hannah had grilled cheese for lunch and Lily ate mashed peaches."

"Wait until you get out on the campus. It smells like a fishery."

27

Nora

Grandma Lucy did not go to the Caribbean.

I'd been standing in the living room looking out the large window onto the parking lot behind my dorm, mourning the future of the school and trying to think of a single thing I could do to help, when I saw an elderly woman being hoisted out of a taxi cab. She had on a red beret, a natty gray down coat, black orthopedic sneakers and carried a shiny gold handbag roughly the size of Maryland.

I'd like to say that I instantly knew. I actually stood there for a long while, watching the cabbie take her walker out of the trunk, as well as two small bags, before I realized that the senior citizen with the horrendous fashion sense belonged to me. It was so out of place, my grandmother at Dixbie, that even after I made this realization, I stood motionless at the window, looking down. Then wouldn't you know, Grandma Lucy, being herself, lifted her head and looked up, as if she'd known I'd been watching her the whole time. She waved enthusiastically.

It took her twenty minutes to get up the stairs to my apartment, during which she asked me in the neighborhood of eight zillion times whether we had an elevator. Finally, in frustration, I said, "If we did, don't you think I would have put you on it?"

Speaking of putting Grandma Lucy somewhere, we had only one spare room, and Elle was in it. I guess I should say Elle was *still* in it. As I shuttled Elle's stuff out of the guest room and into the office, I realized even a depressed person can outstay her welcome. Once Gram settled in, she immediately took a three-hour nap.

"Travel wears out the body," she proclaimed as she took the pins that held her fragile white bun in place.

As soon as I heard her snoring, I called my mother.

"Send her back!" she shouted into the phone.

"She just traveled across the country by herself. She needs a rest."

"I'll come and get her," my mom said. "I'll fly out and drive her back. That way she won't have to endure another flight."

"Driving across the country sounds worse. She'll be uncomfortable in the car for so many hours."

"Then I'll fly back with her," my mother went on. "Harold," she yelled at my father. "Gram's at Nora's. NORA'S."

"I thought you'd be relieved to know she's safe."

My mother let out one of her classic sighs of exasperation. A total indictment of my ignorance and incompetence. "I will not be relieved until she is home with me."

"But I promise you she's fine! She looks good. She clearly came here on her own volition. You can't keep her locked up in the house like a child."

"If she's going to act like a child and run away without telling anyone where she's going, then I certainly *will* treat her like a child."

"Mom."

"Has she told you why she's there?"

She hadn't given me a reason for her mysterious appearance any more than Elle had when she arrived three months before. I could only hope that Grandma Lucy did not have anything like Elle's tale to confess. I'd had more than enough of my family's drama. At last, with the pregnancy, I'd finally begun to feel like a normal person. Then what happens? All the maniacs in my family steal the spotlight. There is no feeling normal with your alcoholic cousin and unconventional grandmother using your home like a bed-and-breakfast.

That night when we all sat down to eat dinner, I still had no idea why Gram had come.

"He's a wonderful man," she said about Alfie as he put his finishing touches on the lasagna. "Neither of my husbands ever lifted a hand in the kitchen."

"Yes, thanks, Grandma. I agree."

"I hope you appreciate how lucky you are."

"Of course I do!"

"She doesn't," Elle chipped in. "She has no idea."

"You've always seen the glass half-empty," Gram went on, much to my surprise.

"I'm an optimist."

"You're like your mother. You fixate on the negative."

"What?!" I cried. Alfie sat down with us and began to serve up the food. "I am nothing like my mother."

"Actually," Elle said, "now that you mention it, Gram, I totally see it."

"Do you have any butter?" Grandma Lucy asked, picking up a chunk of bread. After she slathered on a veritable Great Lake of butter, she put the dish in front of me and nudged me. "Butter for you too. Keep that baby growing smart."

After eating for a few minutes in hungry silence, Elle took a long sip of her wine and looked over at Grandma Lucy. "What brings you here, Gram?"

"Funny you should bring that up," she said, smiling knowingly. "I was just going to ask *you* the very same question."

Life has this way of going on regardless of the madness one's family may contribute to the mix. I still had a job, and I still had to get up every morning and teach, leaving Elle and Gram in a foolish face-off. Gram wouldn't say why she'd come to visit until Elle said why she'd come to visit. "I will die before I tell that Bible-thumper what I'm doing here," Elle said to me late that first night.

"That's not fair. Gram is reasonable and loving."

"She's old-fashioned and conservative."

"I'm sure she came here for you. To help you."

"I don't want her help. She'll help me right back to church every Sunday and ankle-length skirts. No, thank you."

I'd debated inviting both of them to the awards ceremony, hopeful that this year I would come home with the Sylvia Sternberg Award. Just as well that I didn't. I don't suppose they needed to be there to watch Cynthia Cypress, in a red polka-dotted high-waisted maternity dress with a white satin sash and shiny red knee-high boots, accept the award. I congratulated her afterward, hugging her and trying with all my might to be happy for her. It was selfish to want the prize for myself. All the students adored Cynthia; she deserved to win it. If anyone was worth bending rules for, Cynthia was.

"I had to change my appointment with Dr. Mercy," she told me then, as I heroically maintained a smiley face. "We won't be able to drive together after all."

"Oh, okay!" I said with a forced cheerfulness.

"You'll have to tell me how it goes," she said, turning away from me already to talk to Jennifer, the dance teacher. I'd been seeing the two of them in the cafeteria more and more often. *She can have more than one friend*, I told myself as I walked away, although it was becoming increasingly clear that I wasn't a friend, or wasn't much of one. I had to breathe deeply so that I would not cry. Hormones, I thought, which made me smile. At least I had the ultrasound to look forward to.

And that's how I came to miss Annie. I no longer had Cynthia to talk to. It was like getting kicked out of your fairy godmother's castle. As a replacement, it so cosmically seemed, my apartment served as the Helpsom-Fulch Zoo. At least Annie knew my family, almost as well as I did. The actual act of going to talk to her, however, felt insurmountable. What could I say? She'd been so rude, so impossibly cranky and mean. I wanted *her* to come to *me*.

As a middle ground, I took to walking past the room where she taught. I learned from some of my students that she'd taken over Tabitha's classes. I decided an accidental meeting might work best. Annie's big voice booming out of the classroom made her hard to ignore. I couldn't resist the urge to eavesdrop. I would stand at the door listening. Once, I peeked around the door frame and saw her sitting on one of the desks, her hands covered in paint. She'd rearranged the chairs into a circle. One student sat on the floor.

"I don't want you to paint what you see," she said. "I want you to paint what you *don't* see. Anyone could paint a chair, a pear, a bowl, a sunset. But the paintings that catch us capture the invisible—the emotion of the viewer watching the sunset, the familiarity of that wooden bowl on the table, the sense of expectation in the chair waiting for someone—for whom? Every still life has context. You paint what's outside the frame by putting it in the frame, in the shade and shadow and color. You want every piece of art to tell a story *without an ending*. The viewer adds the end; that's what makes art successful, the collaboration between the artist and the witness. Make sense?"

Her eloquence hit me. It had been a long time since I heard Annie talk about anything other than her children or her gripes about the Brownies. Actually, it had been a long time since I heard Annie talk about anything that didn't constitute a complaint, not that I minded hearing about her problems. That's what friends do, listen to one another. I kept standing by the door, listening, fascinated by this part of Annie. Had I forgotten over the years that she was smart? Had I forgotten that she was interesting? Had I forgotten that our friendship covered more ground than a shared painful past of exclusion, or was it possible that it simply never *had* covered more ground?

When the kids came charging out, I held my breath, ready to walk into the room, but Anthony Pullman came up to me and wanted to discuss that night's SOS meeting. His father, a famous screenwriter, had offered to come speak at a fundraiser. I'd volunteered for the fundraising committee. I took out a notepad and wrote down the details as Anthony proudly relayed them. "He'll draw a huge crowd, you know?" Anthony said.

It was heartwarming, all the work for the Save Our School mission. I doubted anyone loved Dixbie as much as I did, having found in the school a place where I could be at home for the first time in my life, yet the similar sentiments from the students and the other teachers encouraged me in my fondness for the place. I didn't think I'd ever loved it more than during those months when we all banded together to try and save it. It always seemed possible to rescue the school. Despite Friedman's grave financial documents, none of us believed it would close. We had too many alums, too many satisfied parents, too many students. True, if you added up the decreased enrollment and the years of minimal advertising and a not completely unearned reputation as a prep school for kids who couldn't get in anywhere else . . . Well, no point dwelling on the negative. It was only a matter of time before something good happened, or so my optimistic self told me.

I walked with Anthony toward the campus green as he continued to talk, and when I went back to find Annie, she had gone already. I decided I'd talk to her after the meeting that night.

"I need to leave right after dinner," I told Alfie, Gram, and Elle. "There's an important school meeting."

"Dixbie has suffered a huge financial collapse," Alfie supplied.

"We're busy trying to fundraise as well as acquire some major investors."

"Why don't you invite me to speak?" Elle asked. "I'm famous."

"What you talk about isn't appropriate for teenagers," said Gram.

"You're kidding, aren't you? Nothing could be *more* appropriate for teenagers. When are they supposed to learn about sex if not when they are busy thinking about it twenty-four hours a day? Sex education during the teenage years is absolutely critical for our social and public health. You do have free condom distribution on campus, don't you?" she asked, turning to me.

"Maybe at the nurse's office?"

"Life is about more than sex," Gram said. "You of all people ought to know that, Ellie Mae."

Hearing Elle's full name threw me back in time. I could see Elle didn't appreciate a reminder of her granddaughterly status.

"And without sex, there is no life," Elle replied with a steady gaze and a flourish of a hand.

The meeting exhausted me. As it turned out, things were more complicated than they first appeared. Many years of mismanagement had convoluted the whole system. The meeting room filled with tension and annoyance and a barrage of questions aimed in Friedman's direction that he could not answer.

The enrollment for the upcoming year stood at 50 percent of what it had been the year prior. A situation that could only be partly blamed on the "hardship economy," as Friedman kept calling it.

"Even an infusion of cash from fund-raising won't improve our admissions numbers," Friedman dolefully told us. "And then there is the matter of the property."

"Someone needs to talk to Tabitha," Beverly commanded.

"Tabitha, well," Friedman began to clear his throat. "She is gravely ill. This is certainly not the time."

"What about Tabitha?" Melanie Jones asked, voicing my own question.

"As some of you know, Tabitha's parents helped to found the school." I nodded. I knew this. Everyone knew this. "As part of their gift to the school, they gave the majority of our land and six of the dorm houses as part of an agreement. The school purchased the remainder of what makes up the campus. The conditions of the land use were to last ninety years, at which time the school was to purchase the land and buildings at market value, paying into the Hunter Family Trust. The Hunters didn't plan for the other contingency. The agreement states that if the school is unable to buy the property, it will revert back to family ownership."

I'd always suspected that Tabitha Hunter's prestige and power at the school had a family origin, but the intricacies of this story were new to me. I snuck a glance at Cynthia. Had she known all this? As Tabitha's niece, would she be able to support the school's cause? Or did she stand to inherit the hundreds of millions in land and property?

She looked regal in her student desk, her back as straight as a pin. "Surely you can talk to her?" Beverly said directly to Cynthia. For once I felt grateful for Beverly's obnoxious forthrightness. "Convince her to extend the agreement for a few more years?"

"She comes and goes from consciousness," Cynthia replied, not hiding her sniff or shaky voice.

"There must be someone else to speak with in your family," Beverly retorted with no compassion. It occurred to me that she might not like Cynthia, though I had no idea why.

"I am only family by adoption," Cynthia pointed out. "My mother was Tabitha's sister-*in-law*," she stressed. "I am afraid I don't have any say in the matter."

"Now, we've got to consider many different factors," Friedman said, looking more fretful than before. I noticed a small sheen of sweat on his nose. My heart went out to him. I didn't want his job. All things considered, he held up admirably, especially in the absence of any other administrative presence at the meeting. "This, uh, situation with the property is only one piece of a very complicated problem. Before we ever made the announcement in December, the administration looked at all the options. I can assure you we have done everything in our power. Why don't we all go home and sleep on it, shall we?" He aimed for a smile and grimaced instead.

I got up intending to catch Annie before she walked out with Ted. As I walked toward them, I heard him saying something incongruous about a "white wedding," to which Annie let out a groan. Just as I drew closer, Elle ploughed through the door and strutted up to me.

"What are you doing here?"

"I had to get away from Gram. She won't stop grilling me."

"Elle," I pulled her away from the crowd of teachers. She smelled like the victim of an all-night keg party. "Why don't you tell her the truth?"

"No way. I will not subject myself to her punishment. If I wanted to be tortured, I would have gone home to my mother."

"Okay, okay," I said, eager now to get her out of the room before anyone caught a whiff of her. As I pushed her out the door, Friedman came up to us.

"Long day," I said. "Just heading home."

"Thanks for your support," he said, though I hadn't spoken a word during the meeting.

"This is my cousin, Elle," I said as we were all standing in the doorway and I could see him giving her a discerning look.

"We met at the holiday party," Elle said, reaching out a hand to shake his.

"You are still as lovely," Friedman replied, causing my jaw to bruise as it smacked the floor. Elle tittered. I am neither sophisticated nor sexually aware, but, as improbable as it seemed, Elle and Friedman were flirting. If Annie and I had been talking, I would have taken it for a practical joke. Elle maybe, considering her past, flirted indiscriminately and didn't mind batting her eyelashes at a man who resembles a reptile. But I have never seen Friedman look at anyone the way he gazed at Elle.

"I am heading to the cafeteria for a decaf," he announced, speaking more to her than me. "Would you two care to join me?"

"I have to—"

"I'll come." Elle and I spoke at the same time.

"You go ahead," I encouraged her. "I'll see you back at the apartment. I'm exhausted." They were off before I had time to finish my sentence. I hoped Elle, being so clearly not sober, would not engage in another regrettable act, although I gave myself a laugh imagining a Friedman baby with big fish eyes and a bald head.

Forgetting about wanting to talk with Annie for the second time that day, I rushed home with the shocking/appalling and potentially exciting news that Elle and Friedman fancied each other. Naturally, I was also eager to share with Alfie the latest on the state of Dixbie, although I knew it wouldn't affect him the way it did me. He's wonderfully adaptable. Whereas I may not have a job or a home-sweet-home in a few months.

I made up my mind on the way home. Dixbie couldn't close. It simply couldn't. It was where I belonged. I needed to think of some significant way to help.

28

Annie

"That woman is like the devil," I told Ted as we walked back from the SOS meeting. "I might have assumed she would be behind Dixbie's demise. '*I'm adopted*,' like we ought to feel sorry for her. What a pathetic line of crap! She *has* to be connected. It explains her wealth—no one that young has that much money—how she got Meadow House, and how she 'won' the award. I haven't figured it all out, but I am on to something bad, and frankly, I'm disgusted."

"She could be telling the truth about her family," Ted said, not angry enough as far as I was concerned. "At any rate, Dixbie's woes far exceed our capacity to problem-solve. I need to look for a new position."

"How can you give up so easily? This is our *home*. You love it here. I love it here. The kids love it here."

"Because I run toward the practical and if I don't look for a position now, when the school closes in June, all the teaching positions will be taken."

"Oh, what a disaster! It's like the Republican National Convention. There must be something that can be done."

"Annie, you can't single-handedly untangle the mess."

"Don't underestimate me."

Ted raised his eyebrows and grinned. "You're sexy when you're passionate."

"No way, King of Virility, are you getting anywhere near me, or we'll be cheaper by the half-dozen in no time. I've got more important things to do. Like scheme a way to keep this place alive."

"You have more important things to do like plan a wedding. Did you see I got my suit pressed?" After much emphatic lecturing, Ted had seen the error of his tuxedo-loving ways and opted to use one of his suits for our big day—whenever it would happen—saving us cash better spent on a new pair of shoes for Hannah.

"I'm not talking wedding plans yet, honey. The school closing isn't a done deal."

"Even if I don't win the bet, we'll get married."

"In the courthouse."

"In the courthouse or in the chapel. Either way, I will at last have you for life." He stopped me walking and pulled me in for a delicious hug and kiss.

"I'm scared of marriage," I said.

"But you don't lack courage. Think how you took on Tabitha's classes, and you were afraid of that."

"I suppose." I did enjoy the teaching. I had fun with the students. I looked forward to going to class and I looked forward to coming home. If anything, it felt anticlimactic. The mountains hadn't fallen into the sea, after all, at the surrendering of my stay-at-home values.

As for the wedding, given Meg's dare, I felt inclined to capitulate to Ted's chapel request. After all, my first instinct was to go for the courthouse. And if that meant some sad, sorry little part of me was making such a decision, why not go for the white wedding? I wanted something to shift. Deep in my heart, I knew I wanted change or I never would have put up with Meg and all the sentimental personal growth that she required. Way down in my cracked and Grinchy heart, I wanted to have a happy inner child. I did not want to have the dejected fat kid from the broken family toted around with me for the rest of my life. I knew that. But I didn't feel ready to give her up. Yet.

When we got home, I paid Cathy for babysitting and went to check first on Lily, who slept crossways in her crib on her belly. When I looked in on Hannah, her eyes were open. She reminded me of a raccoon caught in the headlights.

"What are you doing awake?"

"I need to see your face last thing at night or the sleep won't come."

"Oh, I see." I walked over and sat on the side of her big-girl bed that we'd given her for her third birthday. "Here I am." I looked down at her tenderly, washed with the kind of love that catches your throat and tightens your chest.

She reached up and stroked my cheek with her baby-soft hand. She traced the outline of my face like a blind person might have, and for all I knew, in that dark room with only a shaft of light coming in through the crack in the doorway, she couldn't see me. I closed my eyes at her touch.

"You're my best mommy, Mama," she said to me, then finished with her caresses. She took her hand back to cuddle her top blanket. "I'm all done now. You can go."

"You are an infuriating, endearing child," I told her as I got up.

"What's en-furating?"

"I'll tell you when you're six."

"When will I be six?"

"In three years."

"How long is three years?"

"As long as you've been alive."

"What's alive?"

"Breathing."

"Am I breathing?"

"Yes. Now, good night."

"Are you breathing?"

"Yes, Hannah. Please go to bed now. We can talk more in the morning. It is very late."

"Is my bed breathing?"

"No, not your bed."

"My bed isn't alive!" She began an open-mouthed Hitchcock-type scream. "My bed isn't alive!"

Ted ran in. "Are you okay? Is she okay?"

I sighed, smiled, and shrugged. "You can talk to her about it. I've just broken the news that her bed isn't alive and breathing. As you can see, she didn't take it too well." Then I walked to our bedroom, put on my pajamas, and curled up in bed, welcoming in a new, strange friend who felt rather like contentment.

Suze called the next morning.

"I can't talk now. I'm running out the door to teach."

"Ha! You took the position. I *knew* you would." She sounded both exultant and proud. Still, I took it the wrong way.

"What does that mean, that you 'knew' I would?"

"Just that. I knew it was too good an opportunity to miss and no one loves staying home with their kids *that* much. Anyhow, it seems like the perfect position, only a few hours a day and you can walk to work."

"You *knew* I would?" I said again, stuck on her assumption. "What would you think if I told you I'm only doing it as a dare?"

"Well, that probably wouldn't surprise me either." She paused, maybe to sip some coffee. "Who dared you?"

"My therapist."

"Huh." She considered this for a minute. "How's it going, the therapy?"

"Hard. I'm in touch with my sad inner child now. I can't say I'm enjoying it, but I think it may be improving things."

"Good for you. Self-scrutiny is not for the faint of heart. I'm too much of a coward; I admire you. I always have."

"Right," I said, laughing, as I slipped on my shoes. "You wish you lived on a tight budget in a small apartment with two spirited children bossing you around all day? No nanny, no four-thousand-square-foot house, no obstetrician husband?"

"Money's not everything, sister," she said. "I'd better let you go. I'll be late too if I don't. But I wanted to tell you I'll be at the BFC this Wednesday if you want to come play."

"I think I can. Then I can fill you in on all the Dixbie dirt. You probably don't even know about how Cynthia won Nora's award. Did I mention that? And that she's connected to the Hunter fortune that established the school?"

"That's what I wanted to tell you! I took Finnegan over to St. Anne's for an interview the other day." St. Anne's is the private elementary school in Brownston. The only thing that exceeds its reputation is its endowment; no danger of closing for them. "Of course we're nearly assured of a spot for kindergarten. I stopped to chat with my friend Annette, who teaches fifth-grade science. You remember her? She's not all that memorable to look at, sort of frumpy and blue-stocking, only she's the most excellent teacher. She's always winning state awards. My point is," Suze unnecessarily whispered, "she told me Cynthia Cypress has already interviewed for an open position on the sixth-grade faculty."

"Really?" My brain began to work overtime, a rare occurrence in those days. "She's the head of the Save Our School committee. Why would she be working so hard for that committee if she had another job lined up?"

"Maybe she's not working so hard for that committee. Maybe she's practical, thinks the school will close, and wants to work somewhere. You must not tell, but Annette let me know they already hired her."

"And has Cynthia accepted yet?"

"Apparently, they're drawing up the contract now."

"You're kidding!"

"Annette's Catholic," Suze said in all seriousness. "She never lies."

"Incredible," I said before Suze hurriedly wished me good-bye. It was the first conversation I'd had with her since she started working that didn't leave me with a lump of resentment sitting in my belly, but then there was so much else to think about, who had time to hold a grudge?

Ted kissed me at the door. I hugged the girls good-bye and walked outside, the breezy spring air foreplay for the ap-

proaching season. As I headed over to the academic buildings, I felt like skipping. I would have, if the girls were with
me; without them I worried about looking slightly deranged.

When I stood up in front of my twelve pupils, they listened. They did as they were told. They seemed interested.
They laughed at a few of my jokes. Who knew art theory
could be so funny? At the end, Amber Crossman said, "That
was the funniest art history class ever," which had me consider (ever so briefly) the possibility of a career in stand-up.
Until I remembered it would require me standing up in front
of large groups of people who aren't half my age and will not
be receiving a grade from me at the end of the night.

"What did you like about it?" I asked Amber.

"You know, you make it so it's not all, like, *dusty*," she said,
picking up her backpack.

I thought about this on the way home, how dusty old art
can seem, how irrelevant to our modern lives. Yet one of the
best things about art is its longevity, the way it can capture a
place in time long forgotten. The beauty of historical art is
that it, unlike most things in our current lives, does not demand your immediate attention. You don't have to quickly
respond, send a speed-typed text, answer it instantly, make a
lightning-quick decision about it. Art can sit on the walls of
museums for decades, centuries, waiting. And when you see
the image, it's not less than it was before. Its value and interest
does not diminish over time, but gains. How many things in
our modern culture, save perhaps wine, can claim to grow
better through the passing of time?

I heard the children before I got to the house. Ted had
them out playing in the soggy, half-snowy grass. The sun had
melted much of the snow, though great piles were left around

the edges of the driveway and walkway. I watched Hannah
digging in the ground next to the dorm porch. I hung back to
observe, listening to Hannah's ongoing chatter, the occasional reply from Ted, and the coos of Lily, who Ted pushed
about in a small red plastic car.

Hannah's third birthday had come and gone so quickly. In
April, Lily would celebrate her first. They had both changed
so much in such a small amount of time. It seemed possible
that they'd grown even since I'd left them that morning. By all
means you may call me cliché now, yet it is true that in children, particularly in our own children, we can see the pas-
sage of time acutely. They are life clocks marking the days in
stages and skills and height and words. In them, time stands
like a relief, an etching in smooth glass. They show time differently, wear it, flaunt it, present it to the rest of us so we can
be aghast and stunned and reminded. The sound of the three
voices, so curious and jubilant and alive, punctured the bubble of self-satisfaction that I'd walked home with. My children were the anti-art. The one thing they did *not* do was
remain, in any way, the same. Unlike the paintings of the
great Masters I could show my students slides of, my children, their beauty and preciousness, could never hang in a
museum, and they did not wait for nor depend on a viewer
or a witness to acknowledge it.

Because I wanted to run to them, I stayed for the longest
time simply viewing, taking Meg's dare to heart. Hannah
began to explore a pile of stones. Ted took Lily out of the car
and held her hands so she could stand on the driveway and
squawk like a parrot. Then a funny thing happened, unexpected and curious. A pierce of jealousy rose in me, a kind of
envy, even homesickness. Can you envy someone for doing

the thing that you do most of the time? I didn't know I could. I wanted to be among them, listening to Hannah's inane and ceaseless banter about the size and shape of her stone. I wanted my upper back to break leaning over Lily's small body.

Just as I had these deep thoughts, Hannah caught sight of me and ran over at breakneck speed. She threw herself into my arms.

"Mama, darling," she crooned at me. She'd begun to use my terms of endearment on all and sundry. She called her favorite Panda Bear "angel-love." The other day she put her hand on Ted's cheek and called him "cutie."

"Good, you're here," Ted said. "I've got to run." He grabbed his bag, which sat leaned up against a pole on the porch. "Love you girls," he shouted back as he galloped away. They waved, or maybe they didn't even wave. They took his leaving for granted. It meant nothing special to them that Daddy would race away into the important world of adult adventures. They turned to me. They welcomed me home as one of their own. Their world was my world. I picked up Lily. Hannah took my hand.

"Come on, girls," I said. "Let's skip."

29

Nora

"I'm not in the mood to talk about it," Elle said for the millionth time.

"I've known you since the day you were born. You can't pull the wool over my eyes. You're miserable and angry and you drink like a World War II veteran. You've escaped into Nora's house like it could save you. Nothing will save you from yourself, my friend. Let me testify to that." Grandma Lucy had called a family meeting. She forced Elle and me to sit opposite her in the living room. "Go to the movies," she told Alfie, and he obliged. As he put on his coat to leave, my heart warmed for him. Not once had he complained about Elle or Gram. When I asked, he always said, "They are your family. Of course they can be here."

"I didn't come halfway around the world to suffer the silent treatment," Gram went on. Neither of us corrected her geography.

Elle shrugged noncommitally. "You can't make someone talk."

"Child!" Gram shouted, and I thought for a moment she might reach out and shake Elle's shoulders. "If you don't talk, you are going to kill yourself. Booze isn't going to fix your problem."

"Are *you?*" Elle asked, sending Gram a sharp look.

"As a matter of fact, yes. I can personally guarantee you that I can fix your problem, whatever it may be."

"Grandma, you have no idea."

"Just because I'm old does not make me stupid! I've lived a lot longer than you."

"All you care about is who's going to hell and who's going through the pearly gates."

"Ridiculous," she said, not even bothering to defend the accusation. "I love Jesus, and if you had any sense, you would too. But that doesn't make me a fool or a simpleton or an idiot. In fact, if I've been doing anything right these ninety-three years, it ought to make me more compassionate. So what do you have to say that's so bad you're going to drink yourself dead over it?" Something in Gram's speech must have affected Elle. She dropped her gaze. Nobody spoke. Nobody moved. A tiny whimper broke the silence.

By the time Alfie returned, Elle's full confession lay at Gram's feet like a tangled ball of yarn. My very small role consisted in answering Gram whenever she said, "Is this true? Is this what she told you?" and nodding my head.

"I'm ashamed," Elle said at the end.

Gram didn't speak. She sat regally in the armchair like the Queen of England, an inscrutable expression on her face. I tiptoed out of the room in search of Alfie. When I woke up the next morning and went to the kitchen to fix everyone breakfast, I noticed every bottle of alcohol had been emptied and carefully rinsed out. They overflowed our recycling bin.

"You're next," Gram said, startling me as she huffed into the kitchen. "So don't be thinking it's all about Elle."

"What did I do?"

"We'll talk later." She turned and made slow progress toward the bathroom, where she generally spent the first two hours of the morning. Alfie set his alarm for an hour earlier than usual just to get a few minutes in the bathroom before work.

No one had set the dishwasher to run the night before, so I started it up. Then I began making oatmeal for Gram. When the phone rang, I answered it while the kettle hummed. I could barely hear the voice on the other end.

"Sorry, can you say that again?" I said, wishing I could turn off the swishing dishwasher.

"This is Hendrix Peterson," a man practically shouted at me. "From Holfer and Newton."

"Oh." It took me a moment. "Cynthia's brother?" I took the kettle off the stove so I could hear him.

"We're not really siblings," he said, with a dark, hearty laugh, which struck me as more frightening than funny. "That's for another time. Over lunch, perhaps. Can you come to the city?"

"Excuse me?" I said, my voice beginning to shake.

"Put that kettle back on," Gram shouted insistently from the bathroom. "I'm almost done." I put the kettle on and left the room. Elle was sitting in front of the television watching the morning news. I walked past her and into the bedroom. Alfie had already left for the day.

"I could meet you on Thursday," he said. "Eleven o'clock."

"Oh, but I'm outside of Boston," I said, thinking it might explain everything.

"Look," Hendrix said firmly, "I'm going to sign you. You won't find anyone better, so don't bother looking. In fact, I've already talked to one of our closest connections at Pierson House. She wants it."

What I really wanted to say was *excuse me* again, because honestly, I couldn't follow. He spoke like an auctioneer with ADD.

"I'm sorry," I decided to say instead. "I'm not following."

"I'll represent you. I can have the contract Fed Ex'd. Of course, if you have a lawyer he can look it over with you—"

"My husband's a lawyer."

"Well, that's handy. Anyway, do it on the double. Jillian Felix wants this thing in her hands. Ogres are in *now*. Pierson doesn't have a kid adoption book. They're ready to niche it."

"Okay." What had I just agreed to?

"I'll let you know what they're offering. Sign first, then we'll work out the details."

"Right. Of course."

"Felix is pure business. She won't stroke your ego, but she'll make you a mint."

"Excuse me?" I heard myself say, caught on the words. "Did you just say 'make me a mint'?"

Nobody actually *heard* me fall on the floor. Between the usual commotion around the place and Elle's blaring television, they wouldn't have heard me if I'd screamed. But since Elle had to get up to take the kettle off the stove (Gram can walk but not lift heavy items), she'd decided (given how delinquent I'd been leaving Gram with the job of making her own oatmeal while still in the bathroom soaping herself with a cloth) to come find me. That's how I got discovered, phone still in my hand, passed out on the floor.

"You would have come to eventually," Elle said. "It's not as though you hit your head. That would have been truly dangerous. I once had a friend who fainted and hit his head on the sharp edge of a table, or maybe it was a counter. Actually, I think he might have hit it against the high heel of a shoe." She arched her eyebrows. "Shoe fetish. At any rate, he almost died."

"Reassuring, I think," I said, not at all comforted. I'd *only* fainted, she pointed out, which was true. I wasn't ill or hurt, merely overwhelmed. Who wouldn't be, given the situation?

And you're thinking—what situation? Why not break open a bottle of bubbly and have a party? One of my greatest dreams was about to come true—if I could believe Hendrix. He certainly seemed believable. He had that New York City way of talking that made it nearly impossible to disbelieve a word he said. In Iowa, it's called high-handedness. In my family, it's a cardinal sin. But, then, really, what isn't a sin in my family? Walking in the mud, of course.

First, though, I had to get up off the floor, where Elle had deposited three wet washcloths on my head, and then I had to go make Gram's oatmeal, and then I had to go and teach my classes. Which meant I didn't have a chance to think about my possible future of great riches, not to mention Gram's threat to talk to me, until later, at nine p.m. to be exact, when she called me into her room for a chat.

Gram sat propped up on a dozen pillows. Her flannel nightie, with enough eyelets around the neck to rival Mary,

Queen of Scots, fanned out around her round, wrinkled face. She held a trashy novel in her hand.

She patted the mattress beside her. I felt like a small child.

"Have I done something wrong?"

"Not exactly, kitten. You've done right by me; I'm proud of you. I couldn't ask for a better granddaughter. You're the only one who treats me like a person, did you know that? When you get old, people stop treating you normal. They start acting like you're a dog or a rabbit or something that just poops in its cage and needs fresh water in a bowl. It's not good getting old like that, is it?" I smiled at her in agreement.

"Are you mad with Elle?"

"How could anyone get mad at a girl like Ellie Mae?" I tried to look understanding, though I wasn't sure what she meant. Elle, with her sexual antics, chin-wagging habits, and disastrous love affairs, seemed fairly easy to get upset with. "But we aren't going to talk about her. I want to tell you about Lois Green."

"Oh." My birth mother, the woman of mystery, my mother's nemesis. "I don't know if now is the right time." I wanted to say, twenty years ago would have been the right time. That day, I didn't care so much about Lois Green. In fact, I felt almost *lucky* to have been adopted, considering that Olive the Ogre might, at some point in the future, "make me a mint."

"She's a redhead, Lois," Gram said. "Orange-y red."

"You're kidding!" I reached up reflexively and touched my own drab, brown hair.

"Who knows? Maybe she dyed it, but I doubt it, being such a young girl and from such a religious family. It was thick and red and unruly. She grew up down the street from us, Mrs. Pallentine's only girl. She had six boys. I don't know why Lois turned out so troublesome. She got pregnant at fifteen."

"Wait. I thought I came through an adoption agency."

"You did. For the most part. It just happens we knew her, that's all. Fifteen! And coming from a Catholic family, you can imagine. If she hadn't been pregnant, I'm sure Leo Pallentine would have whipped her."

"Gram," I said, not sure I wanted to hear more.

"Don't worry, it doesn't get any worse. She had you, and her parents moved her out of state, to a boarding school, nothing as fancy as this place. For a while, they kept their house on our street, and Mrs. Pallentine, why can't I remember her first name? She looked away every time your mother took you out in the carriage. We never knew if she was ashamed or full of grief, her own grandchild a few houses down."

"This is awful."

"Is it? Is it any worse than the scenarios your imagination cooked up all these years?" She had a point. "Kitten, this sort of thing is life! It happens all the time. Your mother never got so blessed as when Lois got in trouble."

"But wait a second. Why is she Lois Green? Didn't she have her parents' last name?"

"Soon as she got pregnant, they changed it. They didn't want their good name on the adoption certificate."

"Wow." I really was speechless.

"After the Pallentines moved to Ohio, we never heard from them, not even once."

"They didn't care," I said.

"To the contrary. I imagine they cared too much. It would have broken their hearts to know even the slightest thing about you. And you can't blame Lois, now can you? She was just a girl."

"Right," I said, looking off into the distance above Gram's head. "But she's not anymore."

"She's not?" Gram gave me an inquiring look. "Let me tell you one thing, dear heart, none of us really grows up. I get the surprise of my life every morning when I look in the mirror. I can't believe there's this old lady looking back at me! I expect to see *myself*, the person I am here." She tapped her chest. "Who knows what Lois Green thinks or dreams of now. But she was a blameless girl back then, as innocent as you when you came to us. I imagine, at least in some places, she's still that same girl. Can't have a thing like that happen to you without staying stuck in that time and place a little bit. I ought to know. I've got pieces of me left all over the past." Grandma Lucy smiled at me. "Don't look so worried, Nora. Nothing I tell you now can change your history. The only thing you can change at this point is how you see the matter, and that's why I wanted to tell you the real story."

"So I could move on?"

"So that you could deal in facts and not fantasies. All your life, you've pretended you were better than us—"

"Better?! That's not true at all." She shushed me.

"Let me finish. When you were eight, you came and told me your real mother was a princess who lived in a castle in Ireland. At fourteen, you told me your real mother was a Hollywood actress."

"I don't remember any of that!"

"When your mother first told you, at five, for a week all you did was ask if your *real* mother was beautiful, or a fairy, or a queen or a mermaid." She chuckled at the memory. "Your *real* mother was just a real person, a young girl, no more special than your adoptive mother. Or, perhaps, less special." She paused to take me in. "Because she didn't get the chance to raise you."

"Gram." I felt myself tearing up.

"I said the same thing to Elle, kitten. *Let the dead bury the dead.* You need to drop the old, dead weight holding you down. Elle's crying over that dead baby. She can't get her back, and you won't ever be anyone else but Nora Harriet Helpsom-Fulch, the adopted daughter of Janet Helpsom-Fulch. You can't get something back that you never had. Understand? You've nursed that wound for long enough. I'm going to die soon myself—"

"Don't talk like that."

"Ha! I'm a ninety-three-year-old realist. If I expect another decade, I'm an optimist beating the odds. Either way, I don't fear death. I fear leaving behind two granddaughters so mired in their sorrow over things they cannot change that they don't live fully. You can't take circumstances so personally!" She patted the back of my hand. "Inequality, sadness, injustice—it's all really quite democratic; it visits all of us in one way or another. Why, consider my life." She launched into an account of her ten pregnancies and four miscarriages.

"I have my first prenatal appointment tomorrow," I told her when she finished recounting the tale I'd heard a hundred times.

"Will Alfie join you?"

"I didn't think to ask."

She eyed me suspiciously. "He is a good man, Nora. Go invite him into your life." She stopped speaking and waited. "Go on! I need my beauty sleep."

. . .

When I crawled into bed next to Alfie after cleaning up the kitchen and brushing my teeth, the whole while listening to Elle's echoing snore, he shifted beside me and let out a low, sleeping grunt.

"Alfie, you asleep?"

"Mmm," he replied. He rolled over in bed to face me, reflexively reaching out a hand to touch me.

"I go to the doctor tomorrow. I was going to go with Cynthia, only she canceled on me." A little pang of loss hit me in the gut. "It's my first visit for the baby. I know you're working. Would you like to come?"

For a minute, his eyes stayed closed. I couldn't tell if he had heard me. Finally, in a scratchy, tired voice, he said, "Do you want me to come?"

"Of course!"

"Why didn't you ask me before?"

I didn't know the answer to that question. I'd planned the appointment with Cynthia. While finally getting pregnant created closeness between Alfie and me, it was Cynthia I'd shared the pregnancy with. She and I held it in common. It united us. I knew Alfie was happy to have a baby, but I didn't assume he wanted to be a part of every nuance, every uterine twinge, every fantasy of state-of-the-art buggies.

I wouldn't recommend it, but because I didn't know why I'd done what I'd done, I didn't answer. It wasn't an uncomfortable silence, either. Alfie rarely makes a big deal of anything. He doesn't get rattled or worked up. In a way, he reminded me of Fruity, with his easygoing disposition and tendency toward large meals and frequent naps.

"It's okay," he said in the sweet, widening silence. "I for-give you."

"Oh. For what? For not thinking to invite you?"

"For wanting me a little less than you want this baby." His eyes popped open, cloudy-dark in the black room. I felt sick at his words, embarrassed and exposed. When he kissed me, pressed into me with a purpose, it caught me off guard, and I found that feeling in my belly turn into desire. Of all the things that happened that day, the news of my book, the news of Lois Green, nothing surprised me as much as the intensity of emotion that Alfie drew out of me that night. It took thirty-three years for me to have an orgasm like that one. I felt con-fident it had been worth the wait.

With the dawn, I tumbled out of bed with a Cheshire-cat grin and an elation I thought belonged only to small children in candy shops. I wanted the scarlet O for my shirt. I flitted about the house, humming and remembering, savoring and anticipating; it felt distinctly like falling in love. When the doorbell rang, I didn't bother brushing my hair or changing my clothes to open the door. Students often show up in the morning with a question or a request and they have seen me in all sorts of disrepair.

But this was no student.

"You look awful."

"Mom?" You can picture me, open, innocent blank stare spread across my face, in complete bewilderment.

"What did you think I would do? Sit around in Iowa wait-ing for you to send Gram back?" She stood solidly in a pair of ugly black utility sneakers. Her gray hair, which she refused to dye, vanity being another sin, hung, much as mine did, limply by her ears. She held the handle of a simple black suitcase in one hand, a cloth L.L. Bean tote slung over a shoulder.

"Where are your glasses?" I asked, astonished.

"I wear contacts now. Do you plan on inviting me in?"

"Oh, I'm sorry! I'm just amazed." I moved out of the doorway so she could walk in. Once inside, she placed her tote carefully next to the door and released her grip on her suitcase. She held me at arms' length for a moment and then pulled me into a perfunctory hug. "You're as thin as a rail."

"Dad didn't come?"

"You know how he feels about planes." My father harbors a not-so-secret morbid fear of flying. She took her hands to my cheeks and scrutinized my face. Her own expression, the usual deep gash of worry in her forehead, the thin lips pressed strongly together as though something smelled, softened. "I *am* happy to see you, Nora."

"I'm happy to see you too," I said, not at all sure that I was. For one thing, I didn't have anywhere to put her. For another, Elle would take her arrival as a sign of contention. Whether my aunt Rose had sent her along to check on Elle or not, Elle would perceive my mother's presence as a fight. Lastly, I don't particularly like my mother, although this point must be abundantly clear by now. I certainly didn't want her hanging around. As broken and annoying, as sex-positive and verbose as Elle could be, we got along. And Gram, though bossy, forthright, and a bathroom-hog, held a special place in my heart. I felt closer to her than to any other relative. But my mother. My cold fish of a mother. No wonder I asked if I had a beautiful mermaid for a *real* mother. She's like an Edward Gorey character come to life.

"Right, enough of this," she said, clapping her hands briskly together. "Where is your runaway grandmother?"

I showed her to Gram's room. Gram, startled awake, woke with a scream of humorous terror. "How did she get here?!" she cried. Her hysterical cry brought Elle running. Naturally, Elle, not one to be upstaged, gave a short, spiky scream herself, one of total disbelief. "Janet?!" Alfie lumbered in last, looking sleepy and satisfied and smelling warmly of bed. "I thought there was a hostage situation," he said dryly. I was the only one to laugh.

30

Annie

March

I bumped into homesick Ginger on my way back to the dorm. She wanted to know if I would be teaching the Intro Art History course next fall, provided she still had a school to attend.

"Everyone says you're the best. Tod Bracken told me he slept through all of Tabitha's classes and now, even when he tries, he can't fall asleep while you're talking."

"No one can sleep while I'm talking; I'm far too loud. And no, even if there is a school, I doubt I will teach. In fact, I just taught my last class. Buttle will take over for me."

"Oh, no, Buttle!" Fred Buttle, another aging Dixbie veteran, whom the students call "Butt," has a love for ditto sheets and stale coffee. While he usually teaches photography, he agreed to take over my two art classes as well.

"At least we have the Feminists' Day to look forward to. Honestly, without that, I don't know how I could go on. I totally, like, love this place so much. You're like family to me."

"Thanks, Ginger. I love Dixbie too."

"Do you think it will really happen?"

"I'm afraid so. The trustees are preparing to take a vote."

"You'll vote yes, won't you?"

"I'm not a trustee, Ginger. I'm only a housemother."

"Sorry. I don't know anything about how schools run. Cynthia already told me how she's voting, so I assumed you must be a trustee too."

"I'm not." I decided not to make a big deal out of the shocking little treasure of information she'd passed to me. Instead, I said good-bye and went in pursuit of Beverly Slater. I doubted that Cynthia could have become a trustee without my knowing, yet it seemed entirely plausible given her financial ties to the school and her familial ties to Tabitha. Buying herself a seat on the board wouldn't surprise me. I counted on Beverly to provide some semblance of the truth.

When I arrived at Beverly's, she opened the door a crack and allowed me to slip into her apartment. "I have a new kitty who can't escape," she told me. Her house smelled like mothballs, lavender, and popcorn, the remains of which I could see in an enormous plastic bowl sitting on her coffee table.

I quickly conveyed my concerns to her.

"Annie." She shook her head. "*Where* have you been? Everyone knows Cynthia took a trustee position this past summer right after her hire. Sylvester McDougall died rather unexpectedly. Don't you remember hearing about that? He fell off a merry-go-round at the Brownston fair?"

"I would remember hearing *that*."

"Sure you would, dear, though you *have* got your hands full with those two little girls. No time for bothering about school politics, whereas I don't have anybody. I'm lucky to have found Felix the other day, nearly starving on the dorm front steps." She bent down and picked up the smallest kitten I have ever seen. Felix came dangerously close to suffocating in her cleavage. She propped him up with a hand. "I always did hope for children," she said wistfully. "Female problems."

"I didn't know you were married."

"For three years. I only married in order to have children. I certainly wasn't going to spend the rest of my life doing someone else's laundry *without* the benefit of procreation."

"Perfectly understandable," I told her. "But back to Cynthia. If she's a trustee, she'll have a vote in the school-closing decision."

"Well, naturally."

"I assume she'll want to help keep it open." Then I remembered my talk with Suze. "Although I did have a friend mention to me that she'd been over to St. Anne's for an interview."

"Fickle woman, that one," Beverly said, gently stroking Felix's head. "I wouldn't doubt that she'd close the place down. She stands to gain a great deal of money."

"She said she wasn't a recipient of the trust," I pointed out.

"I don't believe her. Do you?"

I wasn't sure. And as much as I appreciated Beverly for her faithful cranking of the rumor mill, I hardly believed everything she said. "What will you do if the school closes?" I asked.

"Here." She passed me a brochure. I did a triple take. "I have *always* wanted to retire to a nudist colony."

"I owe you some money," Meg said, aglow with a silly smile of delight.

"I don't want your money. Besides, I don't feel I earned it. I only taught for a month. I quit, so it doesn't count."

"Let's go back. Tell me again how you felt seeing your girls playing with Ted while you were meant to be at work?"

"Jealous." I laughed. "Isn't that weird? I felt like *I* wanted to be looking at rocks with them and playing with them. All along you've made it out that this ambivalence ought to lead me somewhere, help me to change my life or change my work."

"Not at all," she replied. "I never once intimated that your ambivalence required changing."

"You didn't? I don't understand."

"Tell me more about your decision to stop teaching."

"Like I said, I want to be the person with my children. As I've been telling you all along, that's the thing I want to do, even when it doesn't make me happy or satisfied or completely fulfilled."

"You *are* ambivalent about staying at home with your girls."

"See, you're doing it again, trying to get me to *do* something."

She smiled patiently. "Not at all," she said again.

"Are you acting confusing on purpose?"

"I never said there was anything wrong with ambivalence. You assumed ambivalence was a bad thing."

"Of course! If you're ambivalent, you ought to find a way to fix the situation, or fix yourself."

"Living in contradiction is the hallmark of adulthood," Meg offered sweetly. "*All* of us, even the old fogies like me, feel ambivalence over our choices, at least some of them. The trouble isn't feeling ambivalence, it's *fighting* ambivalence. Just like the trouble isn't feeling motherly guilt when you get angry at your kids, it's judging yourself for that emotion."

"I suppose," I said.

"I admire you."

"Why?"

"For your decision to give up teaching."

"Do you?"

"Yes. You made a decision not based on anger, resentment, personal criticism, or personal politics. Your *adult* made a choice, not your wounded child." She looked at me with such hope and approval, I wished she were my mother. Or, at the very least, that my mother had looked at me a few times in just such a way.

"All the 'famous women of the past,' posters are up," Ginger said.

"Melanie Jones even taught on female physicists in class today," Sarah added. "So people are taking it seriously." She stood beneath a huge banner that read: Young Feminists of Dixbie School: The Who and the Do.

"How's it going with the feminist food?" I asked Hattie Martin. The culinary brainstorm had been her contribution, and I personally could not wait to see her pull it off.

"Go see!" she shouted gleefully. I walked with the group of girls over to the food tables, where a dozen large plates were filled to the brim. In front of each stood a little plaque indicating the type of food and the famous feminist who favored it. I was duly impressed by her research, until I came across five large dishes of ice cream. *Annie Fuller's Favorite Food*, it said on the paper in front of mounds of ice cream.

"Hey," I said to Hattie. "I'm not famous."

"You are locally," she answered with a grin.

I hung around for the duration of our Feminists' Day feeling mighty pleased with myself and the new results of my maturity. For one thing, everyone seemed more attractive; even the sweet, gangly, pimpled girls looked better, and not simply because they gave me a prominent place on the chow table. Indulgent though I may be, ice cream alone cannot sway me. No, it had simply never occurred to me before that my anger colored my view of the world; until Meg, I thought I perceived the world accurately.

A few minutes after we opened the doors to allow students and faculty to mill about in the dining room, where a number of exhibits, posters, books, and papers were set up, Cynthia flitted in as though she were the belle of the ball. She wore a gorgeous long, red-and-black maternity dress with a plunging neckline and a bouncy hem. Earlier, she had arrived with several boxes and set up her collection of African women's clay pottery on one of the dining room tables. "Feminist identity is global," I overheard her saying as she held up a piece for Jennifer to look at.

It would be extreme, bordering on schizophrenic, to say that without my angry glasses Cynthia appeared wonderful. Not every one of my opinions was wrong. In fact, without the lens of my old resentments, I saw Cynthia more clearly than ever. She was truly beautiful, but shallow, superficial, and, for someone who spoke so little about herself, profoundly self-absorbed. She was also immensely self-possessed, carried by the good fortune of her wealth, and so accustomed to privilege that she did not know to expect anything else. For once, I could understand what Nora saw in her. The way Cynthia could float across a room with a ballerina's grace symbolized the whole attraction. Nora had never been graceful. What remained a mystery was Cynthia's pull to Nora.

When Nora entered the dining room where we were holding the event, she and Cynthia chatted briefly before Nora wandered off to look at some of our Feminist History posters. I assumed the reason I rarely saw the two of them together anymore was because I rarely saw Nora anymore. That day, I noticed how they separated quickly.

Nora approached me, a tentative smile on her face. That new sensation of sadness Meg so kindly introduced me to visited me in that moment; I realized how much I had missed her over the past several months. I had done awfully well with my loneliness, using it productively and constructively. I suppose the loss of friends had its advantages, freeing one up, as it does, for time with yourself. It was with no small amount of satisfaction that I'd come to realize, as a direct result of all this time with myself, that I wasn't nearly as impossible to get along with as I'd first imagined.

"You did a lot of work," Nora said. "This is great!"

"The girls did most of it. And Cynthia, of course. She has tremendous energy."

"She does," Nora affirmed.

I tried to recollect the last time we shared a conversation that wasn't an argument. Before I had time to think about my words, I said, "Look, Nora, I owe you an apology."

"You do?" Something akin to alarm flew across her plain features. Considering how rarely I make apologies, I'm not surprised my words scared her. Although I could remember one time, at ten years old, when I made a big deal of apologizing for stealing her My Little Ponies for an entire week and lying about their whereabouts. I claimed they had been taken by robbers; Nora said she didn't sleep well that week. "I thought *I* owed *you* an apology," she said.

"No. I owe you one."

"But I forgot your birthday!"

"Come around here," I said, gesturing to the alcove behind the lunch line. As compelled toward tender honesty as I felt in that moment, I still didn't want my gaggle of feminists to overhear whatever it was I had to say, which I still had not planned.

"Has something happened?" She looked worried now.

"Lots of things have happened in the past few months."

"I'm sorry—" she began again, interrupting.

"Nora, quit with the apologies and let me speak. I'm trying to say something important, okay?" She nodded. "I want to apologize for being such a bitch." Her small brown eyes widened, I'd like to say in confusion, but I do believe it was recognition. "I *have* been jealous of your friendship with Cynthia." Boy, was it hard to say, but then going against my instincts, as Meg instructed, had hopes of being a good thing. I wanted more of it, more satisfaction, more, dare I say, *peace.*

"You have?"

"Shocking, isn't it? I didn't even know myself until two seconds ago when I said it." I paused to take a breath, then I gathered my courage, one of my few strengths, after all, and said, "I always felt we had an irreplaceable, unique friendship. It hurt to be replaced, not that I can't see how much more *cheerful* life must be with Cynthia by your side. You know I've always been a bit of an Eeyore."

She laughed, a slightly hysterical variety. "I find this very funny."

"What? That I'm apologizing?"

"No! That you felt threatened by Cynthia."

"Well, before you start making fun of me, let's consider the facts. You spend all your time with her and none of your time with me. You missed my birthday, my daughter's birthday, and you haven't seen the inside of our apartment for months, when—pre-Cynthia—you showed up nearly every day. Thankfully you wrote that Ogre story down for me, so at least I didn't have to listen to endless crying from Hannah, who has missed you terribly."

"I'm not laughing *at you*, Annie. I'm laughing because you've got it all wrong. I mean," she stumbled over her words, "you have those facts wrong. I really did spend a lot of time with her, at least until the holiday party. Elle pretty much ruined our friendship when she carried on in front of Cynthia about how much I loved having sex with David."

"Please, tell me it isn't true!"

"I don't think David ever told Cynthia the whole story about us," she whispered, leaning in to me. "Because after that night, our friendship was never the same."

"She feels threatened by you."

"Threatened by me!" Nora laughed again, as though this were the most uproariously funny thing anyone had ever said. "I don't think so, Annie. I think she felt offended. Maybe I ought to have said something earlier."

"Why you? David ought to have said something. I don't know why he'd turn it into a big mystery anyway. Unless, of course," now my mind took off flying. "Unless he's still got a thing for you."

"Annie, you are not in touch with reality."

"Nora, you are not in touch with yourself."

She faux bristled. "I could say the same about you."

"You *could* have, a long time ago. No longer. I have found my inner child. She's a bit of a disaster, but I'm working on her. I have a good therapist if you want a recommendation. Anyway, back to the issue at hand. At any moment, a young empowered woman will need my assistance in selling one of our 'Was Your Mother a Feminist?' handmade board games."

"I saw those. So cool!"

"Yes, these girls are industrious. But what I want to talk about is Cynthia, now that I've finally got you to myself for a few minutes. I did wonder how you could go on as her friend after she weaseled her way into that award, not to mention complications with her work for the SOS Committee and her role as a trustee."

"Like I said, Annie, I haven't seen much of her since December. Everyone adores her, so there's no surprise about the prize."

"I think she'll vote to close the school." The SOS Committee had another week of fund-raising before the final vote would be taken.

"Why would she do that?" Nora seemed genuinely bewildered. I realized in that moment that Nora still held Cynthia in high esteem, despite their fractured friendship. How Nora could maintain such naïveté continually amazed me.

"Tell me about your life," I said, rather than pointing out Cynthia's glaring character defects. I didn't want to have my first conversation with Nora in months turn into another battle.

"My mother, my grandmother, and Elle have lived with me for the past three weeks. Did you know that?"

"I always liked your mother," I said, recalling a few times

when Janet baked brownies for us from scratch. I had not known, until then, that brownies did not come in a box.

"I have so much to tell you," Nora said warmly.

"So we're on speaking terms now?"

"Did we ever stop?" she asked, then looked as though she wished for a rewind button—it really would have been a good idea in the design of the world, I think.

"I have a lot to tell you, too" I offered, as a way to smooth over the tiny bubble of conflict still floating in the air between us. But then at least *that* felt familiar.

31

Nora

Standing in the dining room chatting with Annie seemed as good a time as any to deliver my news. Keeping it in was beginning to give me heartburn, or maybe it was the pregnancy. Either way, I had to tell her.

"I have some big news."

"I already know about the pregnancy," Annie said. "If you forgot, Cynthia informed me of that exciting development."

"Oh, right, I'm sorry about that," I said, not up for discussing my mistake at the moment, too afraid it would lead to a rehashing and a fight.

"Anyway, tell me."

"I went for my first ultrasound." I could feel the smile stretching out my face. I'd begun to get jaw aches with all my joyfulness. I had no idea beaming could have negative side effects, and now I imagined it in one of those TV commercials for medication that lists a novel's worth of possible disastrous consequences. "Happiness: side effects include jaw pain, facial tenderness, and unexpected laughter."

I stood still, watching Annie's face. I wanted to know if she could guess. In a way, I wanted to test our friendship. Annie prided herself on knowing everything about me before I knew it myself, yet in the past months I'd proven I didn't need her to live a decent life. Not that I can't see the upsides to having a bossy, dominating best friend. It's always made decisions much easier.

She looked back at me, scrunching up her eyes as though it would help her to see me better. "No way!" she shouted, loud enough to attract the attention of some of the girls around the corner.

"We aren't ready to tell anyone else yet," I whispered back, hoping no one would come around the corner to see what the noise was all about.

"Twins?" she asked. And then she hugged me, a girdle of an embrace, knocking the air out of me.

"Go easy. I want to keep those babies in."

"If I ever say that people don't get what they deserve," she said, "remind me of this moment."

In a few days, the circus of my apartment would return to normal. My mother and Gram had tickets back to Iowa for the middle of March. Elle kept mysteriously dropping hints about moving out to somewhere special without informing any of us of the details. On the bright side, her sailoresque drinking had somewhat abated, thanks in no small part to Gram's many lectures on the dangers of alcohol. She never once made a comment about drinking as sinful, immoral, or wrong. Instead, she kept ripping articles out of newspapers and magazines on the negative health effects of abundant drink.

"Think of your ovaries," she once said, taking a beer out of

Elle's hand and dumping it ceremoniously into the kitchen sink. Another time it was, "Think of the mental health of your future children." And later, "Too much wine will make you fat."

I discovered in early March that Elle's progress toward sobriety, which I attributed to Gram's efforts, had a much different source.

We were sitting around the kitchen table, knee to knee and elbow to elbow as we had to be, given our number and my table's size, when Elle took up her wee glass of wine for a toast.

"To love," she toasted, clinking glasses all around. The rest of us waited expectantly for the follow-up to this dramatic salute.

"I have found the one," she said.

"Congratulations," Alfie, slightly oblivious and kindly disinterested, offered.

"It's amazing. I'm going to lose my virginity at last."

"Very funny," Gram said.

"What a thing to say!" my ever-humorless mother said.

We all waited encouragingly for her to say something else.

"You're not going back to that wretched man, are you?" Gram asked, appalled at the mere thought.

"I've found the love of my life." She looked shyly in my direction. Given that Elle is the antithesis of shy, this raised my suspicions. "You must promise not to tell anybody." She was looking directly at me.

"I've always been good at keeping secrets."

"That's true. I know that about you. That's why I'm here and not with my mother." She said "mother" as though she'd taken a bite of moldy fruit.

"Enough with the wibble-wobbling," Gram commanded. "This isn't twenty questions."

"Dick and I are in love."

Dean Friedman? I felt my eyebrows traveling ceiling-ward. It didn't seem polite to act dumbfounded. I quickly coughed into my napkin to cover my expression.

"Who's this?" my mother asked.

"Really?" Alfie asked. "Dick Friedman? Well, he's a nice man. A nice man." Alfie's approval touched me. I reached down under the table and squeezed his hand. He smiled at me.

"He's the dean of faculty," I told my mother.

"The man who looks like a troll?" Gram asked.

"Gram!" we all said at once.

"Love is blind," Elle announced to the table, unruffled by our astonishment.

"He *is* a truly kind man," I said.

"Is he religious?" my mother asked.

"He's given me a religious experience in bed, if that's what you mean," Elle replied, smiling brightly at my mother and registering, with sweet delight, the look of despair that crossed her face. I felt grateful she didn't look over at me. The thought of Dean Friedman having relations with Elle made me woozy; at least, had I lost my dinner, I could have blamed it on the pregnancy.

The next morning, Hendrix Peterson called. Alfie, not aware of the significance of the call (or the voice of the man behind it), passed the phone over to me while I had one hand in the sink pulling soggy oatmeal out of the drain.

"Are you going to send those papers back in this millennium?" he asked.

"Oh, Mr. Peterson, I don't think—"

"I don't see how you could pass this opportunity by. Unless you're considering working with a different agent?"

"No. No, that's not it." When I received the agency papers sometime in February, I'd pushed them into an office drawer without looking at them. There was too much going on to even contemplate my book. With my mother and grandmother and Elle around, nothing was private. Meanwhile, the book felt very private to me. I wanted to think about it, to make sure I was doing the right thing allowing Cynthia's brother to *favor* my book all the way to publication.

"Glad to hear it," he was saying. "So, listen, sign them, send them back. Let your lawyer look at them if you don't understand anything. Bonny Chiver at Cappywon Press wants it on her desk yesterday."

"Who? Isn't that a different editor than last time?" I searched my memory for the name of the editor he'd mentioned before.

"I've changed my mind. Cappywon is a better fit. They do well with author rights, and lately they've been fantastic at branding new authors, especially with merchandise-friendly characters like Olive."

"You mean dolls?" I asked. "Toys?"

"Let's not get ahead of ourselves," he said, while I pictured a stuffed Olive the Ogre in an impossible-to-open plastic package at the local Barnes & Noble. "One step at a time. Sign your name. FedEx the papers. Got it? And say hi to Cynthia for me, won't you?"

"Of course. Did you say you *aren't* her brother?"

"Nah! Not a blood brother, an honorary brother. We grew up in the same neighborhood, until her mother died, poor thing, when Cynthia was only five years old. As you know, her father didn't want her, and you can't really bring a kid along in the cocaine trade, now can you?" He laughed. I didn't. "But she always watched out for me. She gave me money for college, got me my first job. You know what she's like, trying to help people, figure out what they need, do whatever she can to fix things up for them. I guess she felt like she needed to do something with all the millions she inherited from her father when he died; nice way to make up for ignoring someone, I suppose. Anyway, I don't have time for Dr. Phil. Get me the papers and then we'll talk!"

He hung up without saying good-bye, leaving me standing there, the phone cradled against my shoulder, speechless. Never mind about small, stuffed orphan Ogres, what about Cynthia?

"You okay?" Alfie asked. "Is it about the babies?"

"Oh, no! I'm fine. They're fine." I wasn't sure what to do first. "I need to call Annie," I said, replaying Hendrix's words in my head. I *didn't* know what Cynthia was like. Cocaine trade? Mother dying at five? I was baffled. Of course, she'd said she was adopted, and ever since then I'd felt kindred to her. In fact, it had occurred to me, upon finding out about her adoption, that I didn't need to feel so *ugly* because of mine. In fact, during my ultrasound, when Dr. Mercy pointed out the two swimming starter-people in my uterus, he'd asked, "Do twins run in the family?"

"I have no idea," I'd answered. "I'm adopted." It flowed off my tongue as though I said it all the time, which wasn't in any way true. I *never* liked telling people about my adoption, too afraid that they would see what I saw, someone unwanted and unlucky.

But who could be luckier than Cynthia Cypress?

I dialed up Annie, and when she wasn't home, I left a message. After that, I got an idea, piecing together the small crooks of the puzzle. Hadn't Hendrix said she inherited millions and millions? Hadn't he implied that she loved helping people? Why, it was perfect! I even smiled lovingly at my mother as she scowled her way into the kitchen with Gram at her heels. Cynthia could save the school. All I needed to do was convince her.

I planned my conversation with Cynthia as I puttered around the kitchen, dodging questions from my mom. (How had I slept? Could I feel any kicking? Was my back bothering me? Who got up in the night to pee? When was anyone going to tell her about Elle?)

"Janet! It's not even eight in the morning." My mother shot her mother a scowl.

"Fine," my mother answered. "I'll go do my morning *Bible study*." Somehow my mother managed to make *Bible study* sound like a direct insult against Gram. Gram, however, remained unmoved, sipping a cup of coffee and reading a women's magazine.

I showered and dressed quickly, hoping to catch Cynthia before the first class of the day. The sooner I got to her, the more time we would have to organize. I knew she was the head of the SOS Committee. Whatever Annie thought, I didn't doubt Cynthia's intentions. It was hard for me to imagine anyone couldn't love the school as much as I did.

Of course, the little issue of our not-so-close friendship

might get in the way. Still, she always smiled when she saw me, always greeted me warmly, always asked about the pregnancy. When I told her about the twins—a fact Alfie and I wanted to keep to ourselves, but I simply could not withhold it from Cynthia given how much of our pregnancies we had shared—she'd jumped up and down like a little girl. Her enthusiasm meant something. Maybe working together for the school would reconnect us. I certainly didn't see why I couldn't have both Cynthia and Annie as friends.

Frankly, anything seemed possible. I had *two* babies growing inside me, a book deal with a major publisher in the works, and a husband I liked; I'd experienced an orgasm in the current calendar year; and luck, at last, felt like something that grew, like a plant or a flower, not like something you either have or don't have.

I made it to the door before being accosted by another relative. This time Elle had something to say.

"Before you go, I wanted to let you know I'll be moving in with Dick next week. I'm sure you're eager to have your home back. I'll never be able to repay you for all you have done for me."

"You don't need to repay me! You're family. This is what family does," I said, repeating the quote Alfie so frequently thrust upon me, except I actually meant it. In fact, I would miss Elle. "Please don't leave on my account. Don't you think it's a little soon to move in with him?"

"When you've been waiting your whole life, yesterday isn't too soon."

"But you two have only been dating for a few weeks."

"He knows my situation. He offered. He wants to help me.

He even knows," she lowered her voice, "about the *abortion*.
Do you know he wants children?"

I had no idea. In my years at Dixbie, it hadn't occurred to
me to think of Dean Friedman as a man. He figured more
like a congenial authority in my mind.

"I'm happy for you, for both of you. I just don't want you
to rush into anything on my account. You could stay a little
longer, until you two know each other better."

"Really?"

What was I saying? What was I thinking? "Really." I
smiled. I loved her. She was strange and awful and she'd destroyed my friendship with Cynthia. And I loved her.

"Maybe just for a few more weeks," Elle said. She hugged
me. "Thank you, Nora. You are the world's kindest human
being, did you know that?"

"Oh," I said, "I hope not."

"What's going on?" Gram asked, freed from her morning
bathroom ritual.

"Why is everyone standing at the door?" My mother
joined us.

"I'm leaving for work," I told them.

"Nora's going to let me stay a little longer!" Elle announced.

My mother and grandmother looked at me, then at each
other.

By the time I came home late that evening from a Creative Writing Club meeting, I discovered Elle wasn't the only
one with a new plan. Gram and Mom intended to stay also.
Much to my horror, my mother had called and exchanged
her tickets.

"We want to stay and help you," she said, though I had no sense of what she meant. Help with Elle? Help with the pregnancy? Or help with me? For once, I didn't feel I needed any help at all, except, perhaps, with extracting family members from my house.

My conversation with Cynthia didn't go quite as planned. I recounted the details over the phone to Annie, replaying also my conversation with Hendrix.

"The ogre book? You have an agent? You're getting published?" she kept saying, over and over.

"Can we talk about that later? We have to do something about the school *now*."

"Why is Cynthia the head of SOS if she doesn't think the school can be saved?" Annie asked, a question I didn't know how to answer. When I'd spoken with Cynthia that morning, I inquired about her strategies to save Dixbie.

"Any new ideas?"

"Sadly, no," she said.

"What about major donors? There must be an angel somewhere who wants to invest in the program? Some kind person who likes helping out, who has some money to spare?"

"We would have found them by now," she said simply. "We contacted every important graduate. The problems keep multiplying, issues of enrollment and endowment and the property buy-back and some legal troubles too with the town over land use. Money is only one of the problems. Even if it could be fixed, how would we repair everything else, including our reputation?"

"Maybe you and I could do something," I suggested gently.

"I *am* doing something," she answered, vaguely taken aback. "Running this committee has taken a great deal of time and effort."

"Of course. I'm sorry to press. I love this place so much. It feels more like home to me than anywhere in the world."

She smiled beatifically, placing her hands on the round hill of her belly. She carried her seven-months-pregnant body with unusual ease; I envied her that. "Me too, Norie. I feel the same way."

32

Annie

A spookily happy Dean Friedman called me into his office to interrogate me kindly as to my decision to stop teaching.

"The students complain about Buttle," he told me. "You have been personally requested dozens of times."

"I'm flattered, but I'm also certain. I want to take care of my girls. You can ask me to come back and teach in ten years when they're older."

"I don't mean to be rude," Friedman said, scratching his left ear energetically like a rabbit. "But isn't this the sort of situation most mothers want? A part-time job that uses their talents and allows them to spend the majority of time at home? Not that I've ever been a mother," he hurried to add. "Or a father, unfortunately." He looked misty and hopeful all at once. "My mother used to teach preschool part-time; she always said it was a perfect fit for someone who wanted to stay home."

"You know, Dick," I told him, "I think I've discovered something. Back before I had Hannah, when I first got pregnant, Ted and I decided he would work and I would take full-time care of the baby. I was under the mistaken impression that as adults, we make the big decisions of our life *once* and permanently. I am currently acquiring some new knowledge." He looked curious. "Every day I wake up, I get to decide all over again to be a stay-at-home mother, the same way that I decide again to stay with Ted. Did you ever think of that? When I was a child, I imagined you made a few choices at twenty-five and your life flowed out from there, like dominoes tripping down the line. I had no idea being grown up would be so much like being a kid."

Friedman laughed, something like a guffaw, only unaffected and contagious. I laughed with him, all the while trying to recount seeing him laugh like that before.

If I didn't know better, I would have taken him for a man in love. No, it couldn't be that. Maybe he'd found therapy.

"While we're both feeling so jovial, can you explain to me how I missed Cynthia Cypress becoming a trustee?"

"She took the position in the summer."

"I gathered that from Beverly." I decided, given the school's imminent demise, that I had nothing to lose by being forthright. "Dick, why did Cynthia win the Sylvia Steinberg Award?"

"Yes, well, she *was* voted on by a committee."

"And Sally Whetstone gave her Meadow House, wrote the housing into her contract."

"I did know that too."

"She's a relative of Tabitha Hunter," I pointed out, trying to get him to reveal something I didn't already know.

"Only by marriage," he said.

"Does that matter anymore?"

He looked surprised. "Of course!"

"Dick, level with me here. How much money did Cynthia give to the school when she came on as a trustee?"

He shook his head. "None. Not a penny."

"I don't understand!"

He coughed and cleared his throat. "Just between me and you," he began.

On Wednesday, I loaded my girls and all their accoutrements into the minivan and drove to the BFC.

I didn't see Suze's car in the parking lot when I pulled up. I dragged the kids and bags in with a heavy heart. She'd promised she would be there, but her promises that spring were as flimsy as streamers. Something kept coming up, some work commitment, some project that *had* to get done. I tried not to care. I tried not to take it personally. I tried to pretend she and I could pick up where we had left off, but our friendship wasn't bearing up well under the strain of infrequent visits and rare phone calls and different lives in separate worlds. As I lugged Lily into the building, Hannah valiantly attempting to open the door for me, I worried for the first time about Nora's future life of motherhood. Would she keep teaching once the twins came? And would that further strain our friendship?

Julia and Plum were playing in the mini ambulance when we arrived. Julia waved at me, sending her pursed-lip smile my way. I took the girls' coats off, and my own, and hung them up in the hall. To my great dismay, Hannah, running, and Lily, walking and falling over and walking and falling over, headed directly for the ambulance.

"Hi, Annie," Julia said.

"Hi, Julia."

"I haven't seen Suze yet."

"She said she'd be here."

"Well, I'm glad to have a minute alone with you."

"Oh?"

"Thanks for being so patient with the preschool art class. There's so much red tape with the grant, and we had a dozen committee meetings. Suze mentioned you took a teaching position at Dixbie. You must be unusually busy. Hopefully you can keep your commitment to the center," she said, as though she expected me to back out. "Can you draw up a curriculum?"

Draw up a curriculum? For the three-year-olds! Maybe Julia drew up curriculums for savages who drop more food on the floor than they eat and think biting is a good means to solving disputes, but I did not possess the ambitions or the worldview of this supermom.

"Actually," I said, "I gave up the Dixbie position. I'd rather stay with my girls full-time. Impossible as they may be."

"Oh." Julia almost smiled, undoubtedly enjoying my failure. "Then you'll be able to devote yourself to the children's class."

"Something like that."

"That's great!" Julia clapped her hands together. "All the moms are excited. I told them about your education. They're so impressed."

I couldn't tell if she was serious or mocking me. Most of the Brownies had educations; they just didn't use them. I guess in that way, I'm like them.

Plum charged out of the ambulance and ran into the arts-and-crafts room.

"Off I go," Julia said, standing up. She'd been kneeling on the floor. "Can you send me your plans for the class by email?"

"Sure."

"Wonderful. This is going to be excellent."

"Great." Any more adjectives to add? Boy, if I had penny for every banal conversation I'd had at the BFC, even Ted wouldn't need to work.

"I'm sure you did the right thing," she said, as an afterthought, while she walked away. "It must have been a tough decision. Most women prefer the public accolades. It's hard to make do with the unrecognized victories of motherhood. I've always admired women who stay home with their children—*especially* when they can do something else."

Minutes later, Suze found me in a state of stunned suspension. Had I just shared a bonding moment with Julia Tucker? Had she, in fact, *complimented* me?

I recounted the entire conversation, word for word, to Suze, while the kids played with musical instruments. Julia had gone to the snack room to lay out her squash cookies.

"Doesn't surprise me," Suze said. "You and Julia have more in common than you'd believe."

"I hope not!" I wracked my brain trying to remember if there had been a single other occasion when Julia Tucker had been nice to me, or nice at all. Countless rebuffs came to mind, countless cold shoulders. Meanwhile, Suze kept talking. I could barely hear her over the racket the children were making. "What did you say?"

"I *said*, it's just like I've been telling you all along. They're much nicer to you when you get involved. All they want is for people to be engaged with the center."

"That doesn't make any sense. All the women here have been rude to me, and no one has ever asked me to join any kind of committee or teach anything. Until now."

"No one asks," Suze said. "They want you to volunteer. I wouldn't doubt that Julia thought *you'd* been the standoffish one all this time."

"Suze!" Now that was going too far. I was willing to believe that maybe, maybe Julia Tucker and all her Brownie cohorts weren't quite as conniving as I'd once imagined. But to say that it was me who had created the rift? I couldn't buy it. Or could I? I thought of Meg's dare. "You have to at least admit that the money is an issue. The Brownies only socialize with other moms in their income bracket."

"I don't agree. Or maybe some of them, but not all of them. Think about it, Annie. In three years you've never come to a single meeting. You've never volunteered for any of the field trips or organizational committees—"

"Oh, stop it! One moment of kindness from Julia shouldn't warrant all of this. I feel as though you're blaming me for the unkindness I've lived with all these years."

"Not at all." Suze put a hand on my shoulder. "I'm simply pointing out that you may have been wrong."

I may have been wrong.

Ted and I rolled around in the bed in fits of laughter that night imagining my new life of friendship with the ice queen Julia.

"Will I have a Brownie for a wife?" he asked. "Wow! That's still weird to say. 'A wife.' Did you reserve the chapel for May first?"

"Begrudgingly."

"Honestly, I'm as upset as you are about Dixbie. I'd much rather have the school around next year and lose the bet."

"I have one smidgen of hope left," I told him. "The trustee decision is next week. Maybe they'll vote to keep the school going but sell off a number of buildings, maintain a smaller campus. But after what Friedman told me about Cynthia, I know she won't help make it happen."

"I don't want to leave Dixbie," he said. For a few minutes, we didn't speak. "About the wedding . . ."

"Oh, no, don't tell me."

"My family wants to come. They thought of coming for Lily's first birthday on the sixteenth. This would be so much more practical for them; they could celebrate her special day and be at the wedding."

"Ted, we decided no family, remember?"

"Maybe things will be different now."

"What do you mean? They won't descend upon us with gifts of medical tape and woeful tales of the latest shingles outbreak elaborated upon during the reception toast?"

"Unfortunately, you can trust that they will. No, I have bigger news. Lindy left her medical practice to stay home with the twins."

"What?" I nearly fell off the bed. "Is it April Fool's Day?"

"I kid you not. My mother is beside herself. She called to yell at me; she says Lindy claims you inspired her decision."

We talked about this impossible occurrence for some time. Ted dubbed me the the new Rosie the Riveter for SAHMs.

"I don't remember saying anything particularly powerful that night," I said, trying to recall the better parts of the Thanksgiving meal.

"I think it may be that it never *dawned* on Lindy that she had a choice. As you know, my family isn't big on freedom of choice. Maybe you holding your own opened up a new possibility for her."

"I am speechless."

"You always inspire me," he said sweetly with a nuzzle.

"You want to distract me! Let's go back to the original topic at hand. Your family showing up uninvited to our wedding."

"I *did* invite them," he said guiltily.

"Ted! Now I'm going to have to invite my mother."

"What's the harm in that? She won't come. When's the last time she left Chicago?" He had a point. My mother wouldn't come. Maybe that was part of the problem.

I dutifully phoned her the next day, dreading it so much it felt like I had spiders crawling all over my body. I speak with my mother twice a year, in between her All Women's Choir rehearsals and organizational meetings for Women Rule Chicago, the feminist think tank she founded. On purpose, I called when the girls were at their most ill-behaved. I couldn't wait to use them as an excuse to get off the phone.

"Annie, what a surprise!" she said. "I was just talking about you to Bethany."

"Who's Bethany?"

"My lover."

"Mom, you're not a lesbian."

"Well, we don't have *sex*," she said, as though that ought to clarify the matter. "I mentioned to her how you did those paintings of the vagina in college."

"Oh, God, Mom."

"They are so lovely! I don't know why I let them stay in a

box all these years. We've put them up in the hallway. You have such a gift. What a shame to let it waste away! The world really needs radical feminist representations of the female body."

"Right. And my children need a mother. Anyhow, I'm not calling about that."

"Why are you calling?"

"Ted and I are having a wedding."

"Aren't you already married?"

"No." I sighed. "We had to wait for his divorce from his first wife to get finalized."

"Oh, yes," she said, then whispered something to someone, I assumed Bethany. "I keep forgetting you're a *second* wife."

Lily, who now loved to walk, though did it imperfectly, nose-dived in front on me, hitting her head on my knee. She began to wail. Hannah came over. "I'll fix it," she said, then she rushed out of the room to get a Band-Aid. When she returned a few minutes later, she held a fistful of Band-Aids. She slowly took them out of their wrappings, one at a time, and began to minister to Lily's little head. This effectively ended Lily's screams. Lily, enthralled by the wrappings, began eating some of the backings from the Band-Aids. I reached down and fished the paper out of her mouth a number of times.

"Mom, the girls need me. I'm going to need to go, but I wanted to call quickly to let you know the date; May first, here in Brownston at the Dixbie Chapel."

"I couldn't possibly," she said. "On such short notice."

"I completely understand." I felt instantly relieved. I didn't want her at the wedding, certain she would ruin it. But then that sad little mini-me raised a hand with a question: What did it mean that she didn't even pause to consider my invitation?

"Why don't you let your father know? Maybe he can come."

"Oh." I hadn't thought of that. I spoke with my father about as often as I spoke with my mother. He was remarried to a Swedish woman named Inge who taught rock-climbing.

"I'll email him, how does that sound?" she said.

"You'll *email* him? What does that mean?"

"You know, when you send a letter over the computer from your in-box."

"No! I know what email is." I wished one of the girls would start crying again. Unfortunately, the Band-Aids were a fantastic babysitter. I would have to remember that for another time. "I didn't know you two were in touch."

"He friended me," she said. "On Facebook."

"I thought you hated him." I was in a state of shock. My lips felt numb. No two people disliked each other more than my parents.

"I hated being *married* to him; that's an altogether different situation. As you know, Annie, marriage is enslavement, the fiercest tool of the patriarchy." I could hear Bethany saying something in the background. "Anyhow, your father can't help being a man."

"Oh-kay," I said, now doubly dumbfounded.

"I do hope for your sake that it's a lovely day, good weather and all that."

"Thanks." My heart sank.

"I'll post it on Facebook! How's that? But please, for women's sake, leave out the 'obey' from your vows."

When I hung up the phone, the girls climbed up from the floor onto my lap. Lily, old enough to get what she wanted, lifted my shirt to nurse. I could see in her tired eyes that it was nap time. Hannah reached up and pressed her fingers onto my eyebrows.

"Mama," she said. "Where do you think *my* eyebrows are?"

"Right above your eyes," I told her.

"Really?" Delighted, she scrambled away. I heard her using the step stool in the bathroom to check herself out. When she returned, she came back up onto my lap, pushing Lily to the side and complaining about how she was using up "two" laps instead of her allowed one. When she got properly configured to snuggle into my side, she said, "Mama, I didn't know. I thought only *you* had eyebrows." And then, deliciously and ridiculously, she followed this up with, "We are twins."

The girls' antics kept my emotions well at bay. I began to wonder how I had made the time for teaching, given their ceaseless demands on my time. I was grateful for their petty, foolish distractions as I worked with Ted on the wedding plans. They kept me grounded in the real world of soggy diapers and trauma over ripped pieces of paper. ("It will never be the same!" Hannah cried, after Lily tore apart her latest drawing.)

I called my father and left a message, satisfied that I had fulfilled all my familial obligations. I thought of Nora's ever-present family. I couldn't count the times growing up when I'd wished her parents were my parents, but I finally knew the upside of my neglectful mother and father. Sometimes, it can be very nice to be left alone. Planning a wedding is surely one of those times.

When, later in the week, as I stirred the batter for Lily's birthday cake, Suze phoned. I jumped at the chance to talk to her.

"I only have a minute," she told me. "Finnegan was accepted at St. Anne's."

"Wonderful."

"I'm so proud! They only accept seven percent of all applicants."

"Wow." I began beating the batter again. "I'm glad for him."

"I'm not calling to brag, however. And I have to get back to work."

"Of course," I said, irritated that she would call me, then act as though I was keeping her on the line. "I'll talk to you another time."

"Well, I haven't said why I called yet. Annette told me something in absolute confidence. You must not breathe a word until it goes public, but I had to tell you."

"Go on."

"St. Anne's offered Cynthia an administrative position. A *senior* administrative position."

"Oh. I see."

"I asked Annette, 'Whatever happened to the teaching position?' She *is* a teacher, after all. Annette said they want her in a more powerful position. You don't need a Ph.D. to read between the lines—"

"They want her money. They want her to invest in the school."

"How did you know?"

"I had a long talk with our dean of faculty the other day. I finally cleared up all my Cynthia confusion. I'm sure St. Anne's is doing the same thing Dixbie did, courting her for money."

"She's a bit of a ladder-climber, isn't she?"

"I don't think it's entirely her fault. According to Friedman, they interviewed her for a position knowing about her connection to Tabitha, but Tabitha, after they hired her, came in and made a point about their loose family ties, disclosing that Cynthia had inherited an enormous sum of money from her birth father after he died. Apparently, giving her Meadow House and the teaching award, as well as putting her on the board of trustees, were all meant to woo her. The school knew when they hired her that its future looked bleak; here was a young *billionaire* interested in teaching, with a husband connected to the school and an aunt who built her life and devoted all her days to it. Dixbie thinks: make her happy and she'll invest."

"And she didn't invest?"

"Not a dime. And really, how do you sway a woman who has everything she wants and no personal love for the school?"

"St. Anne's seems more like her. They're much wealthier, more socially conscious, at the cutting edge of prep education."

"What are you saying?" I asked as I formed the batter into the cake pan.

"You know I love your school, Annie. But we can both agree it's a little outdated and conservative. St. Anne's is much more progressive. Why would Cynthia invest in something that isn't her style?"

"That's a little crude, don't you think? She ought to invest in the school because it's a wonderful place that really educates teenagers."

Suze laughed. "Annie, she's not a philanthropist. She's a hip, self-aware heiress."

"To a drug fortune."

"No one cares how people get their money."

"Well, I don't like her. I still don't like her. I never liked her. Besides, with all that money and a baby due any day, I can't understand why she's taking on a new position."

"Some women," Suze said brightly, efficiently. "Some women just *have* to work."

Later that day, when the trustees took their vote to close Dixbie after eighty years, I would be blowing out a candle over the towhead of my youngest child, Ted taking pictures, Nora, Elle, and Hannah singing painfully out of tune.

When Elle and Nora first arrived, I took Nora aside in the kitchen to ask what Elle was doing at my daughter's first birthday party.

"She's family," Nora said, with an apologetic shrug of her shoulders. "She did bring a gift!" She handed me a small bag. Inside lay a children's book entitled *My Amazing Body*.

"I'll go thank her," I said, feeling largely uncharitable.

"Be grateful my mom and Gram didn't come," Nora said, stopping me with a hand on my shoulder. "Because they wanted to." I gave a rueful laugh. "What's so funny?"

"Your mom and grandmother want to come to Lily's

birthday party and I can't get my own mother to come to my wedding!"

"That's sad," Nora said.

"I guess it is."

"Can I come?"

"Actually, I've been meaning to talk to you about the ceremony. Would you serve as my matron of honor?" Nora's eyes welled up and overflowed. She embraced me, her ever-enlarging belly keeping us a distance apart. "Is that a yes?" She didn't speak, only nodded.

"Bring in that cake cutter!" Ted shouted from the other room. "They keep sticking their faces in it and licking off the icing."

"Come on," I said, taking Nora by the hand. "Let's go eat some cake."

33

Nora

April

I slipped on my mini-heeled Mary Janes with the small flower strap, the ones Mom picked up for me at a sidewalk sale in town. "These are so cute," I'd said when she passed them to me. "It's rude to look astonished by my good taste," she answered. Now she said, "Do you really want to take a walk in those? Don't you have sneakers?"

"They'll do for now." Truthfully, she'd bought them in a size too large, but with the pregnancy weight, none of my other shoes fit me well. What joy it gave me to find myself finally the sufferer of the pregnancy symptoms I'd read about for twelve months straight. I hooked Fruity up to her leash and we headed out.

Lately, every time I walked on the campus, I cried. I couldn't stand the thought of Dixbie closing. I wished my book had sold sooner, that I had a fortune and could save the irreplaceable grounds, my irreplaceable home.

I saw Cynthia in the distance pushing an enormous imported retro buggy she had shipped from London. I debated walking toward her. Her vote, the deciding vote in the trustee meeting to shut down the school, appalled me. Hadn't she said how much she loved the school? Hadn't she agreed with me that it was special? I still found it hard to see her without saying something.

When I asked her once, the first time I saw her after the campus received the news, she said, "It was the only practical decision. You can't run a school without money." She spoke without emotion. A word flashed into my mind: *treachery*. I didn't want to think badly of Cynthia, but hadn't she told me she loved the school like I did? Wasn't she the one who ran the SOS Committee? Didn't she have the ability to make a difference?

"I had hoped for another alternative," I said. "Or a special donor."

She made a sad little face. "Dixbie, you have to admit, is over. It had its day in 1950. Look at the buildings—everything needs to be repainted and repaired. The faculty hasn't received any ongoing training. The school doesn't even have an updated computer lab! Norie, not everything can be saved."

"I guess," I said, though I disagreed. Everything *could* be saved. That's how I lived; that's what I'd learned. I thought of Elle and all her loss. I thought of Elle and Friedman and the hope of their future. I thought of Grandma Lucy. I thought of Lois Green. I thought of myself and my mother and our relationship and the way she'd taken to making me tea every morning and leaving out a cup of juice and my prenatal vitamin on the counter. I thought of Alfie forgiving me for something I could never forgive myself for. Everything could be saved. What was the point of all Cynthia's money and luck and fortune and blessedness if it didn't help her to believe such a thing?

"What will you do?" I asked politely, some part of me still hungry for her friendship again. "Where will you go?" After July, when the dorms would close, my connection with Cynthia would end. I didn't know that I would ever see her again.

"I've accepted a position at St. Anne's. Dean of Community Relations," she said merrily. "Unlike Dixbie, St. Anne's has a strong base, a solid endowment, and a unique niche as the only private elementary in the county. They were just featured on *ABC News* for their innovative, new realization curriculum."

"Oh." I swallowed stiffly, a wave of nausea overwhelming me. The thought that Cynthia had already acquired a new position hit me as another act of treason. How could she be so disloyal? And what in the world was a "realization curriculum"?

"What about you? Where will you go?"

"I plan to stay home and take care of the twins," I said proudly, happy to think of something positive.

"I'm so excited. I have just found the best nanny. The last family she worked for had infant triplets! She's an RN. It couldn't be more perfect."

In my own unconscious act of loyalty, Annie came quickly to mind, her devotion as a mother, not without sacrifice and suffering, and so I nodded at Cynthia, and said, "Could it be more perfect than taking care of them yourself?"

Now, Nora-pants, where have you gone? It came out so rudely, Cynthia took a step back. Despite her reaction, it felt infinitely good to say. I was angry at her; I felt immensely let

down by her betrayal of Dixbie. It felt personal. It meant she
had not truly done all she could for my school, my *home*, for
me. It meant she wasn't my fairy godmother all those times
she did something nice and helped me out. Why *had* she
helped me out, anyway? I could see now it had more to do
with her than with me. It wasn't personal.

That late April day, walking side by side with my mother,
or waddling, as I seemed to be doing already with the two
babies gaining weight every day, I wasn't sure I wanted to talk
to Cynthia again. She approached *us*.

"What a beautiful day!"

"Hello," I said. "And hello, baby." I bent down to look at
Elizabeth. She smelled, not surprisingly, overwhelmingly of
baby, not that I could describe that sort of smell, only that it
got me in wild expectation, like a torrent of butterflies in my
belly. "Have you met my mother, Janet?" My mother reached
out and perfunctorily shook her hand, incredibly enough
immune to Cynthia's charms.

"I have seen you around campus," Cynthia said. "Did you
come to help during the pregnancy?"

"You could say that," my mother replied.

Cynthia set her eyes on Elizabeth's sweet newborn face.
Without looking at us, she said, "She looks just like my
mother."

"How nice for your mother," my mother said.

"Yes," Cynthia said, now looking up, her eyes bright. "She
would have loved having a grandchild. She died many years
ago. My birth mother would have also loved her. She passed
when I was a child. It's funny, isn't it, that I see my adopted
mother in Elizabeth's features?" She laughed lightly, harmo-
niously, and a little sorrowfully. "Doesn't make any sense, but

it's still the truth." And then, as if she regretted sharing anything with the two of us, she put her hands on the buggy, finished with the conversation. "How lucky, you two," she said, before she walked away, her elaborately jeweled thongs flapping against her heels. "To have each other."

In that moment, as she elegantly pranced her ballerina-poised self away from us two dowdy, nerdy, fashion-challenged women, I had my first moment of holding and having something that she lacked. I let myself imagine having my twins without my mother in the picture. What *would* I do without her annoying, interfering, peculiar love?

"Poor girl," my mother said as she walked away, a statement that struck me as so impossibly inaccurate. How amazing that my mother could look at the glamorous, lovely Cynthia and see anything "poor"!

"She's a friend," I pointed out.

"Is she? She's not very friendly."

"I've always found her very warm," I said truthfully. Cynthia had always been kind to me. I thought of Hendrix. I'd yet to tell my mother about my book.

As if she could read my mind, my mother said, "Looks aren't everything, Nora. In the grand scheme of life, they are almost nothing."

I considered again Cynthia's vibrant figure in the distance. I shook my head.

"What? Are you okay?" my mother asked.

"I just had a thought, a lightbulb moment."

"Ah-hum," she said. She did not ask for more details.

"You don't want to know, but I'll tell you anyway. Until this exact moment, I thought I wanted to be friends with Cynthia. It isn't true. I wanted to *be* her." I felt giddy with the insight of this revelation, as if a series of interlocking puzzle pieces were clicking into place, including one great piece with a picture of David on it. And it was true. I hadn't really wanted to befriend her; we hadn't ever been truly close. I didn't want her, I wanted what she had.

My mother *tsk*ed and kept walking. "What a waste of time," is all that she said.

The emptiness of the apartment hit me. Normally, after teaching a full day, I arrived home to find Gram on the couch, my mother in the kitchen making supper, and Elle on the computer engaged in her new job search. "Someone will want me," she mumbled to herself. "I'm a *good* sex therapist."

Not even Fruity met me at the door, quite unusual given how eagerly she looked forward to our late-afternoon walks.

"Hello!" I called out. I walked into the vacant kitchen. Since my mother's arrival, the appliances shone brighter than the sun. When I asked her once what my dad thought of her prolonged absence, she pursed her lips and said: "He may learn, at sixty, how to pair socks and clean counters."

"Fruity!" I listened for her long-toed scratching footsteps in vain.

I put my hands on my swollen belly and sat down gratefully in one of the kitchen chairs. Whatever carrying one baby was like, carrying two gave new meaning to my understanding of hard work. More and more I found myself utterly exhausted. I had assumed, wrongly, that it was for this reason that my mother didn't return to Iowa. But when I asked her, she and Gram made furtive faces at one another.

"You have to tell me. It's not normal to stay for so long. At least I know Elle's motivation."

"Your mother came to get me," Gram pointed out, "and bring me back."

"Right, but now you both have stayed much longer than you expected."

"We worried about you when you couldn't get pregnant," Gram offered.

"That makes no sense. You knew I'd conceived when you arrived." I directed this to my mother, who released one of her put-upon sighs.

"Your mother has a tendency to fear the worst."

"What does that mean?" I asked Gram.

"She wanted to be here if you miscarried."

"What? Really?"

My mother put on an offended face. "Mother," she said to Grandma Lucy, "I see no reason to elaborate."

"Well, I do, Janet. The girl needs some context." Gram rapped the table with her knuckles. "Go on." She rapped them again. "Tell her."

I looked to my mother, curious. "I had six miscarriages," she said, as though she were describing the weather.

"Oh, Mom! I didn't know that."

"She worried you might also," Gram explained. "She didn't want you to be alone. It's a terrible thing to go through, something only a mother, someone who has been through the experience, can understand. Once you discovered it was twins, we worried even more. Twins can bring all kinds of complications. No one should have to endure troubles like that without family at their side."

I stared at my mother, her thin, pale skin wrinkling around the corners of her mouth. "That's a lot of miscarriages. Why didn't you ever tell me?"

"You never asked. And what's to tell? Goodness knows there is no reason to relive *that*."

"You stayed to make sure I wouldn't miscarry?"

"I stayed because Elle and Gram wanted to stay," she answered.

"She stayed because pregnancy is a fragile time," Gram said loudly over my mother's voice.

"Mom?" I looked at her. I wanted *her* to say it, not Gram. "Is that true?"

"The thought of you," she started to choke up, and her words crumbled in her mouth as she held back a sob. "The thought of my little girl having to go through what I went through without me there—I couldn't bear it." She took a deep breath. "Now, please, the two of you. Enough."

As I recalled this conversation, I let my eyes close and felt safe in the near-suffocating love of my family. The fatigue crept up on me. Sometimes, those days, I fell asleep at eight o'clock. Just as I started to doze off, I heard a sound. When the door didn't open, I pushed myself up and walked into the living room to search for Fruity. She had to be hiding somewhere.

As soon as my big, pregnant body stepped into the living room, a dozen voices screamed "Surprise!" and out from behind every piece of furniture and every door off the room, a person appeared.

"Happy birthday," Annie said, coming over and giving me a quick squeeze. "Did we surprise you?"

"Completely."

"You should have seen the look on your face!" Elle squealed, coming over to us. "Total astonishment." She was pulling Dean Friedman along by the hand behind her. "Isn't this so fun? I love parties." I smiled at the both of them. "It was your mother's idea," she told me. "And wait until you see the cake. I tried to get her to make it in the shape of a pregnant woman. Of course your mother thought I meant a naked pregnant woman and she refused to add extra mounds for the breasts, which doesn't make sense—if a cake is a person it ought to be anatomically correct. It's not as though I requested licorice for pubic hair or anything." Annie and I both chuckled. Elle gave me a short hug. "Isn't our family the best?" she said as we pulled apart.

I nodded my head in the affirmative. "What would we do without them?"

34

Annie

May

On the morning of my wedding day, Nora called to tell me the Olive the Ogre story she wrote out on account of Hannah had been sold to Cappywon Press for one hundred thousand dollars.

"I am agape," I told her.

"I hope only your mouth is."

"You. Go. Girl."

"I can't believe it! I'm going to be published. I know you're so busy getting ready for your big day, but I wanted to tell you first, after Alfie, my mother, my grandmother, and Elle, of course."

"Of course." She seemed to have collected family members over the course of the year the way Tabitha Hunter used to collect cats.

"Cynthia hooked me up with her brother, my literary agent."

"I'm glad to hear she wasn't too busy voting our school out of existence to do a good deed."

"That's not my point, Annie," she said impatiently.

"Aren't you going to be here in a few hours to help me get ready?"

"*Yes*, but I had to tell you right away. I want to give some of the money to Hannah."

"Nora, have you gone mad? If you give her money, she'll write on it with markers, turn it into an envelope with an excess of Scotch tape, then accidentally flush it down the toilet."

"I know. That's why I'll give it to you for safekeeping. Rightfully, she deserves some of the profit. She helped me come up with the story and she insisted I write it down. I want to give her a commission, so to speak."

"I don't want your money," I said. "I continue to find all of life's supplies at the Salvation Army."

"I'm not giving it to you. I'm giving it to Hannah. You will merely hold it for her. Also, you can't say no."

"Fine. Congratulations." It was certainly one way to start the first day of the rest of my life as a married woman. I used the good news as a touchstone for my sanity as the day progressed. Every time I felt overwhelmed by the idiotic stress of wedding preparations, say while inserting my children into tights as they flayed and attempted to kick me, or while Ted hovered anxiously about me reading aloud from his wedding checklist ("Send invitations," he said at one point. "We get married in two hours. I sure hope you already took care of that one," I replied), I thought of that small sum of cash beginning a college account for Hannah, and it made me happy.

Undoubtedly, inquiring minds want to know if I carried on Meg's dare and instead of attiring myself in black, decked myself out in proper wedding garb, with oceans of lacey marshmallow frills. I am sorry and proud to say I did, in fact, look goth at my own wedding, with a black skirt, black shirt, black hose, black shoes, and a pair of long black gloves that I found in Hannah's dress-up clothes chest. However, I allowed the girls to make up for my lack of festive girlyness. Each of them wore a princess gown with a ballerina tulle underskirt. Nora wove baby's breath into our hair.

"Marriage is slavery," I told her as she threaded some of the flowers through my wild mane.

"Maybe a hundred years ago."

"It's so quiet in here."

"Ted took the girls out to visit my grandmother so you could finish getting dressed in peace."

"Peace? I'm beginning to be familiar with that word." Nora laughed softly.

When she finished with me, I looked like a proper bride from the neck up.

Suze came into my bedroom with a lush bouquet of reds and purples. "I asked the florist to make something that would look good with black."

"See you down there!" Ted shouted to us from the living room.

"Is it time already?" I asked.

"You're beautiful," Suze said, hugging me strongly. "I'm proud of you." Then she walked to the door. "Don't forget to enjoy every minute," she said as she left for the chapel.

"I don't want to be at a wedding," I told Nora as we stood waiting by the enormous chapel doors.

"Annie, it's *your* wedding."

"All the more reason to go somewhere else. Do you think they'd notice if we never walked in?"

"It's just nerves," Nora said. She took my hand and held it for a moment.

"I wish I smoked. I would smoke right now." I could hear the music playing inside.

"Smoking is so bad for your health! Anyway, I can't be near smokers. I don't want any secondhand to affect the twins."

"Right. I would never smoke in front of you." I began to restlessly tap my foot, searching for something to think about other than the eternal vows I would soon speak. "It's so sweet that your mother and grandmother came."

"Since they basically live here now, they wouldn't miss it for the world. My mother has always thought of you as an almost-daughter."

Instead of sticking with the usual bridal topics of flowers, appetizers, and danceable songs, I said, "I'm sure you can understand how hard it's been for me to have you for a friend."

"Come again?"

"I had the broken family; you had the perfect family."

She broke into flabbergasted laughter. "Am I on *Candid Camera*? Or have you lost your mind? My *perfect* family consists of a recovering-alcoholic sex maven, an aging Jesus freak, my mother with an Addams Family temperament, an aunt with a *Jeopardy!* obsession, and various other relatives all of whom conspire to make my life difficult to live."

"Don't sidetrack me. You've always been so placid, so undisturbed by things. Don't you think it's hard to be a raging lunatic with a Buddha for a best friend? You assimilate and adapt and flow. I fight, protest, and get unhappily entangled. I always wished to be more like you."

"You're kidding, right?"

"Believe me, I wish I was."

She paused, tilted her head to the side, which made her look distinctly like Fruity, then smiled a curious smile. "Annie," she said. "Have you finally taken pharmaceuticals?"

"Very funny!"

"Partial lobotomy?"

"That occurred after Hannah's birth."

"So you aren't on antidepressants?"

"No! And I'm offended you need to ask. Can't I have a heartfelt, sincere pre-wedding now-my-life-is-changing-forever chat with my oldest friend without being accused of drinking the purple Kool-Aid?"

"In that case, *I* have always envied you."

"Yes, yes, I know. We went through this one before. You wish you could have your sleep cycle and wardrobe destroyed by small, sticky fingers. My friend, your wish will be granted *times two* in three months."

"Not just that! I envied you long before you ever had children. For one thing, I always wished Alfie and I could be like you and Ted."

This was new. This she had never said out loud before. I forgot about my terrifying nuptials and gave Nora my full attention.

"I wanted to be in love with someone and have someone love me the way you and Ted love each other. You once said to me that more than you loved Ted, you loved yourself when you were with him. You two have a closeness I've never mastered with a man. Not even with David," she said in a whisper. "I always loved him more than he loved me."

"David can't love anyone more than he loves himself," I

pointed out. "That's why he and Cynthia are perfect for one another. Two narcissists."

"Do you really think that? I never thought that."

The doors to the chapel pressed open and Hannah spilled out, hopping imperfectly on one foot. Suze, holding Lily, tried to shush them. "It's time," she said.

We walked in all together.

While the judge spoke, Hannah fluttered about our feet, periodically screaming for cake. I let Suze hold Lily, as Nora's ponderous belly left little room for wriggling one-year-olds. Lily herself held forth with remarkable endurance and stamina; Suze attempted fearlessly to hush her. After about ten minutes, Lily gave up and fell exhaustedly asleep in Suze's arms, much to the relief of Judge Watson, who'd been forced to say every word three times so we could hear him.

For a judge officiating a secular wedding, he certainly had a lot to say. There was a great deal of preamble, *love, contracts, eyes of the law,* and so forth, which I kindly refrained from rolling my eyes about. Before our vows, Watson asked us to join both hands, which forced us to face each other; not that I don't like Ted, but I wasn't up for a sentimental moment. Yes, I realize it was a *wedding* and that "wedding" and "sentimental" are essentially synonymous, but "Annie" and "sentimental" are not. More to the point, when I held Ted's hands, my inner child decided to make her presence known.

I had to stand there holding his hands while Watson asked us the traditional question, the richer-and-poorer-for-better-for-worse-till-death-do-you-part question I had not imagined got included in a civil ceremony. Why hadn't I asked to look at the ceremony before the fact? I wanted something short, quick, and dry. And here, a wizened old man all of five feet tall with a Pinocchio nose and watery eyes was demanding I answer the world's hardest question. And not merely *answer*, but *vow*.

Yikes.

I looked into Ted's eyes, gathering the courage to speak, but when he met my gaze, I found I didn't need courage. I wasn't afraid of my best friend. I wasn't afraid of giving him the best of myself.

As the judge declared us husband and wife, Ted beamed. I decided Suze and Nora ought to have brought *him* the bouquet. He was more suited for it. He smooched me with wild abandon, forcing Judge Watson to cough into his tiny, wrinkled hand.

We processed out and meandered over to the terrace attached to the dining hall for the reception. I excused myself quickly to hit the bathroom, hoping to pee in privacy for once in my life, absent my children, only to find Suze standing by the sink when I came out of the stall.

"Annie, are you okay?"

"Fine, why? And aren't you supposed to be watching my children?"

"Nora is watching your children. And I am your friend, and I am watching you and you look like a woman who could cry." She put her arm around my shoulders.

I wanted to say something smart and barbed and, well, Annie, only I couldn't think of anything. Suze smiled encouragingly at me. *My heart feels like an old, broken mug that someone has at last found the time to glue back together,* I thought as I felt the tears threaten.

"Let's talk about something else," I said.

"Okay, ice queen, although you are allowed to cry at your own wedding." She tried to force some mascara on me. I had flatly refused to wear makeup for my special occasion. I wanted my girls to see that natural complexions did, in fact, belong to people lucky enough to get married. What would they think otherwise? That princesses must wear ball gowns and only the pretty girls get happily ever after?

"Did I see Julia Tucker out there?" she asked.

"She's my new friend."

"Wow. Pigs are flying. And who's that guy?" Suze asked, as she attempted to tidy up my hair.

"What guy?" I'd invited the entire school, all my YFC girls and fellow faculty, deciding at the last minute that it would be more fun that way. We'd received a number of regrets, David and Cynthia among them; they were spending the weekend with David's family so they could meet baby Elizabeth.

"The old dude in the fancy suit."

"I don't know. A trustee?"

"Annie." She paused as though she had dreadful news. "He looks like you."

"He looks like me," I heard myself say, only I didn't feel my lips move.

"I'll show you." Together we left the bathroom and headed out onto the terrace, where already the large group gathered and drank. "There." She pointed across the length of the patio to the bar table the kitchen staff had set up.

I left her side and walked over to him, conscious of my kneecaps trembling.

"Dad?"

"I came in at the last minute, Annie dear," he said. "I

would have arrived early but my GPS sent me to Brownston, Vermont." His amber eyes crinkled into a smile. "I wasn't sure I could make it, but I had business in New York City and decided to give it a try. Now, why are you crying? I always called you my tough nut. Boy, the way you used to head-butt me."

"You came," I managed between my crying-binge hiccups. Boy, if Meg could have seen me, would she ever have been honored at the progress my adult self had made integrating that dejected inner child. It's as though twenty years of tears flooded out of me.

"I did get your invitation. Like I said, I didn't want to make any promises I couldn't keep. I'm on the road so much these days."

He reached over and wiped the tears off my cheeks, which only made me cry more, and then I got the stomach-heaving sort of sobbing, which brought Ted to my side, and then Hannah and Lily, neither of whom my father had ever met, then Nora showed up, and she instantly hugged my dad and went to get her mother and grandmother so that they could enjoy a great Iowan-roots reunion. Suze brought me a glass of champagne, saying, "Don't wait for the toast. Drink it now."

When Elle came over with Dick Friedman, followed in short order by Beverly Slater, my tears finally abated as, in the company of so many weirdos, I no longer felt like crying. Amazing how odd company can instantly cheer you up.

"Aren't you Elle Blenderhorn? Don't you have that radio program?" my father asked.

"Did, I *did*." She blinked her eyes rapidly. "I needed to move on. Sex is so yesterday. The only people who talk about it are those who aren't getting any," and then she laughed, and so did Dick and it made his cheeks rosy, and so I thought probably he wasn't that unattractive after all.

Ted came and stood beside me. He shook my father's hand. "Holy shit," he whispered in my ear.

Then Betty and Lindy strolled over, wanting to know if we could have the toast yet. Betty wanted to know if we had read the latest article in the *Journal of the American Medical Association* about the long-term health benefits of wine.

At some point, I sat down. Lily wanted to be nursed, and she wrangled stealthily with my black top in an attempt to uncover a breast. After someone passed me a plate of hors d'oeuvres, Beverly floated over to me, carried like a hot-air balloon with the wind behind her flowing caftan. She bent over and whispered loudly into my ear for a long time.

"What? Are you sure?" I asked her. "You have to be sure, Beverly."

"I heard it from Friedman," she said haughtily. "I never spread a rumor that isn't true."

"I'll be right back," I told her, getting up, Lily still clinging to me like a joey, in search of Nora. I found her standing with Alfie, looking out over the athletic fields. They were holding hands and looking romantic. Normally, I would have left them to their bonding, but this news required immediate release.

"Nora," I said. She turned around. "I just heard. Tabitha Hunter died yesterday."

"Oh, no!" Her hand flew to cover her mouth. Why do people do that when bad news comes, I wondered. As though something unusual might come flying out of their mouths at that very minute.

"It's awesome!"

"Annie! That's terrible. Just because you didn't like her isn't any reason to be happy she's dead."

"No, you fool," I told her. "She died and she left all. Her. Money. To Dixbie! She left all her property. She rewrote the property trust before she died. She gave the entirety of the land and buildings to the school forevermore."

"Really?"

"Really."

We stood, dizzily happy, staring at one another.

"I've never been so glad to hear that someone died," she said.

"My point exactly."

"Cynthia won't be happy. If she stood to inherit from that trust. Do you think she'll stay and teach?"

"Oh, she wasn't going to get any of that money." Nora looked curious. "I'll tell you sometime. Anyway, her position at St. Anne's is so much"—I searched for the right word—"better suited to her temperament," I finally said.

"I guess." Nora looked wistful.

"Come on," I encouraged. "We have to celebrate! I'm married, you're pregnant, and Dixbie will go on forever. How could it get better? It's just what we wanted."

Hannah ran up to me. She knocked me into Alfie, who kindly propped me back up.

"Mama, Mama! Ice cream! Quick, quick! Hurry! Let's go! Ice cream!" I smiled down at her. In lieu of a wedding cake, I'd ordered a table's worth of ice cream in thirty different flavors. "Come see it! Quick! Hurry before it melts!" I took her hand and laughed.

"All that ice cream won't melt for days," I told her as she

pulled me over to the table. She started jumping up and down and panting. The woman behind the table looked at her adoringly. Lily slithered down beside me and began yanking on the tablecloth.

"What flavor would you like, sweetie?" the server asked.

Hannah looked at the table, amazed by the quantity of choices. She looked up at me, then back to the incredible array of goodies spread before her. "I'd like one of each," she said in her very best big-girl voice. "Please."

"I have one of my own," the server said with a wink in my direction, as though we both knew Hannah's cute, childish, and silly request would never be granted, though she was prepared to indulge her for a moment before one of us would insist maturely that she could have *one* flavor, and, maybe, if she was well-behaved, another flavor later on. That's the way adults are, after all. We've been trained out of our foolish, spontaneous, awake, moment-to-moment youth. We know how things go, the right decisions, the right way to be, and we have decided the course of our life.

"Mine's a *spirited* little thing just like her," the woman added. And then she picked up her scooper and asked, "What about for the bride?"

"I'll take what she has," I said. And I looked down at Hannah, with whom I shared so much, and winked.

PHOTO: NEIL FORBES

SAMANTHA WILDE, the mother of three young children born in just over four years, openly admits to eating far, far too much chocolate, usually to keep her awake during nap time so that she can write some books. Before she took on mothering as a full-time endeavor, she taught more than a dozen yoga classes a week (now she teaches one). She's a graduate of Concord Academy, Smith College, Yale Divinity School, the New Seminary, as well as the Kripalu School of Yoga. She's been an ordained minister for more than a decade. Her first novel, *This Little Mommy Stayed Home*, helped a lot of new mothers get through the night. The daughter of novelist Nancy Thayer, she lives in western Massachusetts with her husband, a professor of chemical engineering.

samanthawilde.com